FROM THE CHRYSALIS

A NOVEL

Karen E. Black

Viceroy *Power* Press
2012

ISBN: 978-0-9879866-1-0

If you enjoy this book, please write a review on Amazon or Goodreads! Or email the author at: karen.black@sympatico.ca

Viceroy Power titles by Karen E. Black

From the Chrysalis
Feeling for the Air
Take to the Sky

Praise for *From the Chrysalis*

2012 Readers Favorite Award! Dace...reminded me of James Dean, handsome, tempting and sure to cause suffering. Karen Black...has provided a very descriptive account of (the) prison. She brings the scenes in her book to life and they march off the pages.
—Anne B. for *Readers Favorite*

I'd like to congratulate Karen Black on her new page-turner, *From the Chrysalis*. It tells the twisted and winding tale of Liza and her dashing and dangerous older cousin Dace (D'Arcy Devereux is his full, resplendent name). Set in Canada (where Toronto's Christie subway station makes an appearance), it's the tale of a relationship blighted by uncomprehending relatives, social conventions, a harrowing stint in Maitland Penitentiary (complete with riots and semi-totalitarian 'people's committees'), the well-intentioned galumph Mel, and a conundrum Liza has to bear calling for an ever more inevitable decision. You'll just have to read it if you want to know what I mean by that. I found the prison scenes, with their occasionally stark violence but underlying ethical probity, especially fascinating, but there's also lots of romantic tension, a kind of yearning whose fulfillment seems always out of reach, even when its physical manifestation is realized. What a potent novel! I spent the rest of the day shooting mysterious dark looks at people.
—Julian Fauth, *2009 JUNO Award Winner* for Blues Album of the Year

Drugs, bikers, prison breaks and incest provide surprising plot twists in this rough-and-tumble romance novel...set in '60s and '70s Ontario... Black has a flair for historical novels...and she shows remarkable storytelling depth.
—*Kirkus Reviews*

For B.B. and the people who still love him

I have been struck by two facts; the extraordinary sympathy or similarity between the pair. He is her cousin, which perhaps accounts for some of it. They seem to be one person split in two.
—Hardy, Thomas, *Jude the Obscure*

Chapter One

Monarchs

Devereux Farm, Eden, Ontario, July 10, 1966

Who hurt you so, My dear?
Who, long ago
When you were very young,
Did, said, became, was... something that you did not know
Beauty could ever do, say, be, become?-
So that your brown eyes filled
With tears they never, not to this day, have shed...
Not because one more boy stood hurt by life,
No: because something deathless had dropped dead-
An ugly, an indecent thing to do-
So that you stood and stared, with open mouth in which the tongue
Froze slowly backward toward its root,
As if it would not speak again, too badly stung
By memories thick as wasps about a nest invaded
To know if or if not you suffered pain.
—Millay, Edna St. Vincent, *Mine the Harvest: A Collection of New Poems*, #7

A shadow fell across her path as she rounded the veranda. A long shadow this late in the day. Her eyes followed the shape as it stretched across the worn boards, then stopped when she recognized the source, still as a statue in their Aunt Sadie's garden.

She resisted the urge to touch him, to convince herself he was real. People said she could write a little, but words never said enough. If only she could take pictures or draw. Something that would freeze her cousin, D'Arcy 'Dace' James Devereux, at eighteen. There was just something about him.

A bottle of beer dangled from his fingers, so maybe he had slipped out the back porch door of the farmhouse, through a phalanx of his elders. When he cracked a smile she was so startled she stepped backwards, disturbing a pair of butterflies which hovered by her head. He spoke, though she didn't see his lips move, and she was so busy listening to the sound of his voice she almost didn't hear what he said. The words were low and sounded a little rough, like his voice was almost never used.

"Little Liza," was all he said. He held out his brown bottle to her, an unfathomable expression in his eyes.

She recognized a little bit of their Granny Debo in him, as well as some of his father, but there was also something that was just him. She ignored his offering. He hadn't said a word to her all day. Besides, she had a monarch on her right shoulder which was far more interesting than a bottle of beer.

"Are you sure?" he asked.

The butterfly explored, lured by false promises in her yellow shift, and Dace and Liza watched the insect probe the shoulder seam of her dress. Aunt Sadie's garden was full of massive yellow sunflowers and wild lupine. Besides Liza's monarch suitor, butterflies flitted everywhere: Black Swallowtails, Clouded Sulphurs, Painted Ladys and Red Admirals. The last two were sometimes mistaken for monarchs, but Liza could distinguish the orange and black markings of all three species by now. When she was twelve, she had brought a book called *Field Guide to Butterflies* to the farm, much to the amusement of her relatives. Despite their teasing, she had taught herself to recognize the more common species.

Liza was afraid to move and even more afraid to speak. What if she disturbed her guest?

"I'll bet he thinks you're a flower," said Dace. She watched him tip the beer to his lips and knock it back in two swallows. In a flash, she realized he had become a new man. His almost black eyes lit with amusement, his full mouth softened, and he relaxed. "You kind of look like one, you know? All that hair, your long legs, your little dress ..."

"Yeah, right," she whispered. She stood frozen, her head bent on her shoulder, hair spilling down the left side of her chest. "He just thinks I'm food. Are you old enough to be drinking that?"

"It's okay. Uncle Eddie pried the cap off with his teeth and gave it to me the moment I moved. For some reason he looked mighty glad to see me go. Probably wanted to talk about me. Hey, little girl, don't look so scared."

"Why? What's there to talk about?" she asked softly, but even this was too much for the monarch. It fluttered away, joining the others.

"Man stuff," he said, his eyes still on the butterfly.

"Is it something bad? Aunt Debby said —"

He waved a hand, dismissing what she'd said. "The aunts are good people, but they don't know crap. I'm not supposed to talk to anyone. The lawyer said— Ah, never mind. I don't care what that goofball says."

Liza's brow tightened. Nothing was going right. She had waited all afternoon to talk to him and now he wasn't making any sense. "A lawyer? You have a lawyer? Why?"

Dace shook his head. "You ask way too many questions. Like I said, I'm not supposed to talk to anyone. Especially little girls. What are you, thirteen, fourteen now? Besides, it's not just me. There's a bunch of other people involved. Rick, my friend, all we wanted was some beer and suddenly all hell broke loose. Oh, heck. I can't—" He stopped mid-sentence, an anxious, black look almost ruining his face.

"Says who?"

"Everybody in Maitland. And my father. He wanted me to come here today as a show of faith, but he can't stand the sight of me. He really can't. Not that I blame him. Nobody could."

"Uncle Norm? Why would he— why would anybody blame you for anything?" She thought a moment. "What— what did you do? Peddle drugs? You didn't sell drugs, did you?"

"Liza, for God's sake, of course I didn't peddle drugs! I want to play pro football someday." He chuckled, but it didn't really sound like laughter. "*Wanted* to. Fat chance now. What Dad actually said was: 'Watch out for that strange little girl who's always following you around'."

He let the empty beer bottle slide to the ground, then lifted her hair away from her face so that the backs of his fingers brushed her jaw.

Something funny exploded in her chest and for a moment she couldn't breathe. She felt like she had climbed too many stairs. She wanted him to touch her again, but she also wanted to argue with him, to fight, to set him right. Don't you dare throw your beer bottle in Aunt Sadie's garden, you big oaf, she nearly said.

"What do you mean?" she asked instead, rising on her tiptoes until her eyes were almost level with his. "When was the last time I saw you?" When? At his own mother's funeral? She knew he'd been there for sure. "You weren't even at Granny Debo's funeral last March. Both your father and Rosie were. I looked for you all over the place. Even if you weren't at the rest of our stupid family dos, you should have been there."

Dace shrugged. "Well, that's what he said." One of his shiny black shoes booted the beer bottle into a bed of double pink Impatiens and silver Dusty Miller.

Liza's face went hot. "He did not!" she shouted and left the garden, running off in the direction of the pond. That was another place she liked to visit by herself. If the pond were anything like last year, the water wasn't much, but there would be bulrushes. Maybe even a great Blue Heron. Besides, she had to get away from Dace. Had to. Or…what? It didn't matter. Getting away was the right thing to do.

She spied a big, black motorcycle ahead of her, propped against the fence. Motorcycles all looked the same to her. It must have been his; nobody else at the farm had one. They had a tractor maybe. A bike was way too impractical. They were more like toys. Had Uncle Norm followed Dace all the way from Maitland to the farm in his Ford? If Liza had known how to ride a bike, she would have taken it. The hell with him, the way he looked, the story in his eyes, the touch of his hand … He was such a phony. And the sun was too bright. It hurt her eyes. No wonder she couldn't think straight.

The shortcut to the pond veered off through a patch of tall grass. Liza was full grown at five and a half feet tall, but the grass was so high at this time of year she had to part it with both hands. Panting, she slowed to a walk, self-conscious enough to fear observation from the farmhouse by both the living and the dead. Of course her people were watching. They always were.

Although she pretended not to notice, he caught up with her in a couple of strides, walking in her grassy tread. Clouds of dragonflies and iridescent green grasshoppers rose in the air. He'd taken off his tie and looked less immaculate in his open-necked shirt. More like the boy he used to be.

Against her will, she liked him even better this way, with sweat trickling down the smooth planes of his face. She especially liked his determination to follow her anyplace. He smelled of starch and deodorant and something else, something not unpleasant at all. For the first time in her life, she wished it would rain. He reached for her hand, but she pushed him away. *You're too used to getting your own way*, she thought.

Butterflies were following them. Common as monarchs were, they were her favourites. Some people called them Wanderers because they migrated to Mexico every year against all odds, although it was a mystery how they found their wintering grounds. She knew from an old *National Geographic* article that it wasn't from memory. Somehow they just knew what to do. There was no record of a monarch living long enough to return to its wintering place the following year.

Did monarchs rely on their own instincts and built-in biochemical forces? Or were they led by the moon and the stars?

And why? It was 1966, but nobody knew. Did they even have a choice? The returnees might be the grandchildren of the generation who had flown south, their forebears having made the ultimate sacrifice for their descendants, but nobody knew for sure.

Whoever said butterflies were free? she wondered, watching the boldly coloured insects navigate through the tall grass.

Liza watched her cousin clear a path for her through overhanging branches.

Dace seemed mesmerized by the monarchs, too. He tried catching several in his cupped hands, but they escaped him. "I don't want to hurt them," he explained when she laughed. "They're so free."

"No, they're not," she contradicted him, although she had a feeling that wasn't exactly what he'd meant to say. "They look free, but they just do what they're told, what they know. They fly all the way to Mexico just because."

She broke off, hating the way she sounded like a show off. She wasn't actually convinced he was interested in anything she had to say.

"Really?" Dace asked, reaching out and briefly touching her arm. "All that way?"

Liza glanced sharply at him, walking innocently at her side. Was he mocking her? She didn't think so, but...

"Yes," she said, deciding to continue. He snapped a blade of grass in half with his teeth. "They make their great migration against all odds, blessed with only one advantage: they are partly protected by their body chemistry. As a caterpillar, each monarch feeds on milkweed leaves. The chemicals in the plant make both the caterpillar and the butterfly distasteful to birds. The black and orange markings tell predators about this defence, so the birds don't even try. The smaller ones, the Viceroys, mimic the monarchs, so they share the same protection." She stopped again, afraid of boring him. *Never mind about the Viceroys,* she thought.

He stopped and stared at a brown bump on a low-hanging

branch. "Look," he said. "I almost didn't see him."

Liza hesitated, wondering if she should continue sharing what she knew. "That's a stick insect," she finally said. What's your protection? she wanted to ask. By now she knew almost every living creature had evolved a protective camouflage, all except humans. They were far more complicated and varied in their defences. This implied humans had some choice. Was Dace's secretiveness a protective device, or was he just being bad? He was more complex than a monarch or a stick insect, though. They both were. His behaviour had been learned.

So had hers, she thought, her throat aching with unshed tears. She didn't know for what, except back in the farmhouse kitchen he had looked so sad. It came to her then how much she'd wanted to see him again. What had gone wrong since the last time she'd seen him? Was there no way she could help him? Was there nothing she could do?

Besides burst out of her own skin, that is.

Minutes later they emerged from the tall grass onto a rutted dirt road where pioneer wagons had once rolled. Before that it had been walked by Ojibwa natives. In lieu of pummelling Dace — she didn't dare — she aimed several vicious kicks at a border ditch of yellow snapdragons, pink phlox, Queen Anne's Lace and milkweed, watching in satisfaction when silken strands from the milk pods exploded in mid-air.

"Whoa, girl," Dace said, prompting her to move farther away. She hated the stupid smile on his face. A part of her was still angry at him for ignoring her all afternoon, no matter what his reason.

"Why don't you get lost on your bike?" she asked, glad she couldn't see the expression on her own face.

"Well, sure, if you come too. It's exciting, you know, the wind in your face. You don't look like the kind of girl who would be worried about mussing up her hair. A little free spirit like you..."

Maybe he wasn't the one with the problem, maybe she was, she thought, refusing him the satisfaction of an answer. First she'd wanted him to talk to her, and now she didn't. She would have ridden with him on his bike earlier, but now she was too scared. When, oh when, were her parents and brothers leaving? she wondered, smacking a black fly as it buzzed in circles around her head. Dace caught the bug in his large hands and crushed it. She hated being stuck here, being at the mercy of her parents' decisions. At home there were books to read, dreams to dream and, somewhere in the future, a man to love.

Clearly she had been mistaken, entertaining fantasies about this boy. It was sad, but it looked like she had nothing in common with her cousin D'Arcy Devereux anymore. Just like she had nothing in common with anybody else here.

She'd asked many times if she were adopted, but her mother had bemoaned her first pregnancy and labour far too many times for her to belong to anyone else. Trapped. Liza was trapped with these people, and there were a hundred or more here today. Why on earth had her grandmother had so many children? She slapped at another insect, a bloodsucking female mosquito this time.

Liza just about boiled over with pent-up frustration. She was crammed into the hull of a sailing boat which had pulled to a shore she had never seen. She was sandbagged in a wagon and crossing rough terrain. She was pulled to places no sane girl would visit on her own. Well, the Devereuxes had immigrated before. All the way from County Wexford, Ireland in 1818. No wonder. If she got the chance, she'd leave her homeland, too. There were lots of other places besides Canada and loads of other people.

"That's it. We can't go any farther," Dace said, motioning at an electrified fence strung on the horizon, just above the small pond. They stopped and stared at the slime-free water and shared the same thought: Uncle Tom had been through here with a back hoe and cleaned up the place. Yellow flowered lily pads floated on the surface, bluish purple pickerel weed poked through bulrushes near the shore, and a Great Blue Heron glided in for a landing on the opposite shore.

"Maybe it's as far as you can go," she said, kicking off her shoes. They fell just short of the spongy earth at the pond's edge. Briefly she considered pushing him into the bulrushes, but she was afraid of his reaction. He would do something worse to her for sure. She sensed there was something in him waiting to be unleashed. The same thing was in her.

A cicada sang in the trees. It was usually a rather pleasant sound, but she found it annoying now. It was too soon, wasn't it? The bullfrogs sounded even worse. Guttural, almost obscene. Mating, she supposed. As she eased a foot into the cool water, he unbuttoned his wrinkled shirt, damp now under the arms.

"What are you doing that for?" she snapped, though she was enchanted by the subtle movements of his chest muscles in the sunlight. She blinked, determined to keep her eyes above his waist. Her twin brothers were only twelve. She had never seen a grown man naked. She didn't want to now. Not even Dace.

"Don't," she said, anticipating he would remove his shoes and the rest of his clothes. She squeezed her eyes shut when he did. That thing. It was somehow incongruous. And much bigger than she had expected. Almost another entity, in fact. And why was it so red?

He laughed, a changed person, stretching his arms towards the sky, unfettered, free. Like he owned the world, no matter what had happened, no matter what he couldn't quite confess. He grinned at her, raising an eyebrow.

"Let's go swimming," he said.

She couldn't look him in the face. "My parents would kill me. I didn't bring a bathing suit," she demurred, realizing her continued presence had already implied consent. It was too late to run.

"Uncle Eddie and Auntie Maeve are busy. Eddie's with his brothers and Maeve's in the kitchen."

"My mother's always in the kitchen."

"Go behind those old rosebushes and take your clothes off. Everything, little Liza. I promise not to look."

Hearing the strength in his voice, she almost obeyed. She

wanted to, but she couldn't. Because it was wrong. "Oh, c'mon. I read books," she said, folding her thin arms across her chest and watching the Great Blue Heron.

"Really?"

"Yes, and that's what all the boys say. Besides, the farm is an aunt-hill of relatives today. Somebody might see us. It's broad daylight, you fool."

"An aunt-hill. Hey, that's good."

"Well, it's not mine. It's from Louisa May Alcott's *Eight Cousins*."

"Another book, eh? Don't you want to live life instead of reading? Look, we can't wait for cover of dark, little darling," he countered. She couldn't help but notice his organ, that thing, was still doing a salute. "If we come back tonight, the mosquitoes will eat us alive. Besides, what does a girl like you care what other people think?"

Glancing at him sideways, she smiled. He had her there. She didn't care what other people thought about her. She never had. If she had, she would have been in one of those Italian or Ukrainian cliques at school.

Besides, the water looked inviting, and he had used an endearment even after she'd called him a fool. He didn't care what other people thought either. Come to think of it, the two of them had always done what they wanted to do when they were small. And although she had been younger, it wasn't always clear who was following whom. *Liza,* Dace's Mom had threatened on more than one occasion, *you need a smack.*

"I don't know. I don't like other people knowing my business, that's all," she protested. A part of her wanted to oblige him, but she was reluctant to remove her clothes in front of him and lose face. And what if he didn't like what he saw?

"Me either, although in my case, it might be a little late for that," he said, staring across the pond, where the Blue Heron had taken up residence on one foot.

Liza folded her arms across her chest and groaned. "Oh, here we go again, all cloak and dagger. You're like the mystery guest on *Front Page Challenge*. I'm sure it's all right, whatever you've done."

"Well, I'm going someplace next week," Dace said, moving closer to her as he talked. "Don't believe what you read in the *Maitland Spectator* or the *Toronto Star* if it goes that far. My father's convinced everybody already knows. But I don't know. Why would they? They don't want to know stuff like that about me, about one of their own. Still, he's madder than a hatter. Worse than that, he's just so low. Not that I blame him. Never mind, Liza. But the thing is, I'm not sure when I'll see a girl again."

Ignoring his nakedness, she stared him in the face. "But why?"

"You have breasts now. Show me you're not a little girl," he whispered, slipping behind her. He unzipped the back of her dress so fast she didn't know what had happened until she felt cooler air kiss her back. Shrugging a little, she stepped out of the dress and plunged into the water in her bra and panties, just to cover up.

"I told you to take everything off," he said, following. He caught her around the waist and gave her a look that almost scared her. His eyes had narrowed and his mouth looked tighter.

The tepid water was only about five feet deep and their feet were almost immediately anchored by weeds. *No use swimming,* she thought. They weren't going anyplace. She sank underneath with him for more coverage, then felt his cool hands gloss over her breasts and slip between her legs. Although she had never touched herself down there, she let him.

Briefly, her mind shut down. She had never felt this way before, so alive in her own skin. He broke the surface first, gasping and pulling her up with him. If he hadn't, she might not have bothered to come up for air. She was ready to die right there, with him, in Uncle Tom's pond. It would be all right. He lifted her high in the air, almost letting her fall. Her hair streamed over her shoulders. *More,* she thought, looking down into his laughing face, more.

When she slid back down into his arms, she knew he

would catch her. "Wrap your legs around my waist," he urged her, then pressed his mouth against her throat. How did he know that what's she had always wanted, somebody to kiss her neck? *Dace,* she thought, opening her mouth and laughing right out loud. *What was I thinking? I can't leave here. This is where I belong.*

The straps were still on her shoulders, but he pulled the cups of her plain white bra down, freeing her breasts. He could see them now, but she no longer cared. He bent his head and touched their tips with his tongue. "I guess you're not a little girl," he said, catching drops of water as they dripped from her little pink nipples into his mouth.

Their hands were on each other's shoulders when they heard Dace's father. The sound of his voice started her heart thudding so hard it felt like a fish jumping in her chest.

"What the hell are you two doing?" Uncle Norm stormed towards the shore, the late afternoon sun hiding his face. "Outta there now! You're cousins, for God's sake. Jumping, jumping Jesus Christ!"

She was so scared she didn't remember getting out of the water, much less letting go of him, but she must have, for she was scrambling into her dress and trying to slide into her shoes when he said:

"I'll write, Liza, I'll write," and left her alone on the shore.

Chapter Two
Biting Off More than She Could Chew
Christie Pits, Toronto, August 27, 1966

Dace didn't write her, and she knew it was her own fault. She must have heard or read him wrong. The sun had been in their eyes. What must her uncle have thought? For several nights afterwards, she hardly slept. Why in the world had she thought Dace might want to write to her? She was just a little girl, his cousin, and not even in high school yet. At least Uncle Norm hadn't said anything to his brother. Her father would have killed her on the spot.

Despite her doubts, she waited weeks for some word from him. Then one Saturday afternoon, when her father started yelling again, she set off for the big Central Reference Library. She always walked the streets when her father got mad, strolling past the shops on Bloor Street or Harbord, even heading all the way downtown. Sometimes she went into the Woolworth's west of Christie and poked around the crowded aisles, but the stores were closed when she went out at night.

Several dogs fenced in their backyards barked at her as she hurried down the dirt lane, but by the time she'd reached the main sidewalk they had gone back to drooling in the shade. The man in the house across the lane who was always rubbing his groin had more endurance.

"Madonna," he called. He whistled through stained and broken teeth. "Very nice. You like some nice wine? Very nice, very sweet." She hurried past him, eyes on the ground.

It was the dog days of summer. School was about to start and this year she'd start high school, heading into the dauntingly huge building called Harbord Collegiate. She doubted she'd have much time to spare after September. She wanted to find out more about Dace and had put off this expedition for too long. After the family reunion at the farm, she had tried pumping her overworked mother for information, but to no avail. She didn't know anything, except it had been difficult for his father to raise two kids alone. There might be something in the local newspaper though. Especially if it involved a lawyer and the courts.

Liza was a little nervous about what her research might reveal, but anything was better than sitting on a kitchen chair in the shady alley beside her house, staring at her neighbour's brick wall and trying to catch a breeze.

Her hair hung halfway down to her waist, damp and cool, almost straight when it was wet. She wore white canvas sneakers, pedal pushers, and a green shirt, and carried a two dollar bill in her pocket so she could buy subway tickets. That was her allowance.

Christie station, on the Bloor-Danforth line and one block north of her house, had been open for six months. The opening of the subway had been a big event. She loved the underground, the rush of adrenalin when the red rocket disappeared into the dark and the wind from the tunnel whooshed through her hair. Standing tall and waiting for the first sight of lights, she felt like the figurehead on the prow of a ship.

The electrified rails scared her though, so she always stood well back on the platform, allowing twenty seconds to get into the subway car before the doors cut her in half. When the subway had opened on February 26 she had stayed on it for two hours straight, riding late at night in an almost empty car, Christie to

Woodbine in the east, Woodbine to Keele in the west, then Keele back to Christie again.

She'd had lots of time to walk and ride lately. Her parents were arguing more than usual, or at least her father was. Her mother never said much, not even when he shouted she had no control over the boys and she had damn well better get control of them soon, or he would have to knock some sense into them. Then they'd see. Liza had escaped the house just before he shifted his attention to her. His problems with his daughter were more specific: her face had started breaking out and he couldn't stand the way she looked.

One of her school assignments the year before had been to research the educational system in the Australian outback. Her local library hadn't had any information, so she'd gone to the Central Reference Library. After taking the subway from Christie to St. George, she walked the rest of the way. It was hot and humid in the city and the red-bricked buildings lining the street looked closed and unused. It looked like everybody else had stayed home.

Upon reaching the biggest Carnegie library in Ontario, she climbed the grand stairway on the corner. She liked the building's classical lines, the lavish medallions over the windows and the dentil moulding. As she entered the spacious hallway, which led to several well-proportioned rooms, she noticed the shades had been pulled down in all the long windows. The darkness meant it was a little cooler inside, but the compacted dust and ink of so many books made it difficult to breathe. Still, she felt at home here, protected from the blinding glare of the street.

She took her time, almost afraid of what she might find now that she was finally here. She wondered if they even had copies of Dace's hometown newspaper, the *Maitland Spectator.* Eventually she located the newspaper section on the first floor and walked around a couple of moments to give her eyes time to adjust. She stopped under a sign that said Index Table and practically crowed with delight when she discovered what was in

17

one little box. From there she went to the microfilm for the *Maitland Spectator*, stored in filing cabinets along the farthest wall. The microfilms were filed by date, so it wasn't difficult to find the one she wanted: July 1966. It was the newest film in the drawer. The last four weeks of the *Maitland Spectator* would be on newspaper shelves in the periodicals section, mauled over and incomplete.

A sign warned her she was going to need a take-up reel, and she looked around again. Against the far wall stood an Information Desk, or at least that's what the sign on the long, shiny surface said. Liza approached grudgingly. She hated asking for anything.

"I'd like to borrow a reel, please, so I can use this," she said.

The young woman behind the desk glanced up from the document she was studying, brow creased with annoyance. "And do you have the right microfilm?"

"Well, yes. There's an index in that little blue box for the *Maitland Spectator*." Smiling, Liza pointed to the Index Table on her left. That was a lucky find, for only major Canadian newspapers had been indexed in the *Canadian Periodical Index*.

"Would you mind lowering your voice?"

"Sure. I didn't realize I was raising it," she shot back, eyebrows raised.

The clerk, wearing brown horn-rimmed glasses, her glossy brown hair in a perfect shoulder flip, handed her a plastic reel without another word.

Liza stared at it, then quietly asked, "Excuse me, could you please show me how to set this up?"

The woman waved her hand at other people milling around her desk. Why did everybody always come at the same time? Her phone had started to ring, too. She ignored it and glanced around, looking slightly confused about what to do next.

She blinked up at a man by her desk. "Would you please form a line? No, we don't do that here," she said, turning back to Liza, but never looking her in the face. "Just follow the diagram on the reader. And mind the thirty minute time limit. Other people are waiting. Have you written your page numbers down?"

"Yes," Liza lied.

The rest of the Newspaper Reading Room was busy. She found a free microfilm reader in the back of the room, but the moment she plunked down her cardboard box of microfilm beside the machine, the plastic spool burst from its container and reeled out onto the floor. Old people occupying the reader stations on either side of her glanced up in irritation, cross-eyed from perusing narrow columns of journalese.

"Sorry," she whispered. Retrieving the *Maitland Spectator* from under her chair, Liza spent the next six minutes trying to coax the plastic film from the left spindle onto the right. Her fingers sweated and slipped. Beginning to feel little frantic, she wiped them on her pants.

Much to her relief, a disembodied voice to her right volunteered, "It's supposed to go between those two plates of glass."

"Thanks," she whispered back, reloading the film and turning the advance knob right.

Ah, there. The whole newspaper page. Great! Her attention was snagged by a photo of a luckless blonde who had been charged with speeding, rather big news in Maitland it seemed. What if she'd had to go through months of an unindexed newspaper looking for a small reference to Dace, perhaps in the Courts column, only to read a Maitland boy had spent a night or two in jail and was then released? She speed read the dates across the top of the pages for the first half of 1966, checking them against her mental list of dates. The index references she had found must be about Dace. Surely no other Devereux could have made the news. Especially in Maitland.

Small town life played out before her eyes until suddenly the news from July 14, 1966 was highlighted. Two-inch-tall letters on the front page screamed: *Eight Nurses Strangled in Chicago*. Oh God. That had been and was still such terrible news. It had happened the week after she saw Dace at the Farm. Thank God they had arrested Richard Speck.

Of course Dace wasn't on this page. What would he be doing there? What would he be doing anywhere in the company of a murderer? Still …

Her hand stopped on the reel and she glanced at the big round clock on the wall. 4:30. Almost time to leave. Her scalp prickled. *Don't be a coward*, she admonished herself. *It's probably nothing, nothing at all.* She scrolled to page three. The newsprint was hard to make out. Then she saw both Dace and a headline, centre page: *Maitland Man Found Guilty Of Manslaughter In Neighbour's Death.* The photo was wallet-sized, but it was him all right. She fumbled with the focus below the screen, almost lost her place, and had to start over. Her heart hammered so loudly she could barely concentrate.

> Two Maitland residents, D'Arcy James Devereux, 17, and Richard Robert Lowery, 16, have been charged in the shooting death of Alan Aubrey Turbot, 38 on May 10, 1966. Turbot died from a single gunshot to his shoulder, which stopped his heart. Although Devereux and Lowery maintain they shot the victim self-defence…

No, she thought, squeezing her eyes shut. *No.* She tried and failed to reconcile this newspaper report with the memory of water sluicing off Dace's perfect body as he shallow dove after her into the pond. She took so many deep breaths the man to her left glanced over with some alarm, but she reassured him with a flicker of a smile.

She drew closer, studying the grainy picture of her cousin accompanying the article. His grin tipped up the left side of his face so he looked like he was sneering, but it still felt so good to see his face. There were actually two small photos, plucked from a school yearbook. One was of Dace and the other was of his friend, Rick Lowery. They looked so young. Apparently Rick had provided Dace with an alibi after he'd fled the scene, and he might face charges of aiding and abetting a crime.

Her face flushed, she reversed the microfilm, forcing herself to read some earlier articles, items the indexer must have missed.

> Accused testifies victim joked, "It feels good"
> … Pathologist says death caused by unattended bullet wound …

The dead man had assaulted somebody — Rick perhaps — but the testimony of the witness was unreliable. Even the Judge had said so.

Liza's head swam, but she couldn't stop reading. If nothing else, she had to find out why. The victim was a bootlegger and a drug pusher, a man in his thirties. Somehow Dace had ended up with his friend's gun. Oh, brother. What did that matter anyway? The boys shouldn't have been there at all.

She shouldn't be here, either. She felt sick to her stomach and figured this was what she got for being so nosy. She had to go to the bathroom.

Except it was too late. She knew now. None of this could be undone. She glanced furtively around, wondering if anyone else could sense it, the feeling in the pit of her stomach which she realized was shame.

Her cousin had... Maybe. Well, who knew? Even though she had read something terrible about him, she felt sorry for him. If she hadn't known him it might have been different, but she did. Besides, he was her kin. Her skin crawled with pity. He must never know that she knew. That she knew something she wasn't supposed to know. Something he'd hoped to hide.

She was a private person herself and would have been horrified to be so exposed. In the newspaper. And what was worse, Liza had gone looking. She glanced over her right shoulder, half expecting some relation to rebuke her. Dace's dead mother perhaps. This was none of Liza's damn business. What on earth was wrong with her? Why was she reading such trash? Even if the man had died, it didn't mean Dace had killed him. It didn't mean everything in the paper was true.

She could almost hear her mother saying: *you've bitten off more than you can chew*. For once she was powerless to refute her. Her mind stopped processing what she read while her heart raced on. Was it possible to have a heart attack at fourteen?

Now what? If she photocopied —

No, she'd never manage such a complicated task today. Besides, she didn't have any change. *Stupid, stupid*. She couldn't ask the snooty clerk for any, either. She just couldn't. But wait. Her brain leapt briefly to life. She turned the crank at the side of the microfilm reader and scrolled forward, checking for an appeal.

There was none, but another headline on the Editorial Page a few days later caught her eye: *Tougher Jail Term Called For Teenager*. She closed her eyes and considered not reading the article, but in the end she had to know what the fool had said.

> D'Arcy Devereux, who is now 18, got off lucky, some will say. Too lucky. How can a man's life be worth only seven years?
> According to unconfirmed reports, Devereux, whose juvenile records have been sealed, is rumoured to have first gotten into trouble with the law when he assaulted a priest. Devereux, a vicious young punk who was only ten years old at the time, was eventually released to his father under what is now termed a conspiracy of silence. Then, as now, rather than having the decency to own up to his crime, he claimed that a man of the cloth had indecently assaulted his sister ...

Liza stared at the words. Golden-haired Rosie, a little girl who could pass for a boy. Liza got to her feet and passed the Information Desk, ignoring a posted request to re-file her microfilm. *Bad girl*, she thought. She hadn't turned off the reader, either. This time as she walked by, the desk clerk was openly puzzling over her document, a rather complicated looking recipe for veal cordon bleu. She was also getting more irate in response to demands made on her time.

"No, you can't borrow a staple. How are you going to pay it back?" she snarled at a library patron. Catching sight of Liza fleeing by her desk, she said, "Excuse me, Miss, did you put—"

But Liza was on automatic. Somehow she located the front doors and walked down the wide staircase, digging her fingers into her crossed arms until she was outside on the busy street where rain dripped onto an unloved lawn. The sidewalk shook as a red and yellow streetcar lumbered by.

She felt like bawling. Now that she'd read it, the *Maitland Spectator* had raised more questions than it had answered. Who was Rick? Not that she cared. Dace was the only one who mattered. He, that beautiful boy, was a puzzle for her and the only one she wanted to solve. His face loomed large in her mind and she could still see him, the water dripping from his body, the pond... At least now she knew why he hadn't written her. He had gone to court and lost. No doubt he was too embarrassed, not to mention angry and afraid. What else was a convicted felon supposed to feel? Guilt? She supposed so, but really she had no idea.

Maybe it was better if he didn't write. What could she say? He might be guilty. *I shot a man in Reno just to watch him die*, she heard Johnny Cash singing in her mind. Was it possible to be attracted to a killer? How far was love supposed to go?

But it had been an accident, she reminded herself. Not premeditated. Maybe that's what manslaughter meant. Accidental killing. Even so, he had killed a man and was in jail. Him and Rick Lowery. Self-defence. Could a competent lawyer have gotten them off? At the farm, Dace had obviously hated his lawyer. He hadn't thought much of the media, either. *Don't believe what you read in the papers*, he'd said.

No wonder. Those articles had obviously exaggerated the exploits of their hometown boys for the sake of news. They'd almost spoiled Dace even in her eyes. Even if some of the stories were true, was she supposed to give up on Dace just because of what some stupid newspaper had said?

"Yes!" her father roared later that week. He licked his thumb and paged through her journal, which he'd found at the bottom of her closet. "Yes!"

Curiously enough, he seemed more upset by what she had written about *him* in some of her earlier journal entries than her rather complicated feelings about his nephew. Standing by his easy chair in the living room, she prayed he hadn't read everything, that she hadn't been completely exposed. Thank God she had felt too conflicted to write about what had happened at the pond. Watching his eyes as they scoured the pages, she thought she had never felt so naked, not even when she'd stepped out of her dress for Dace. She wanted to leave the room, but the habit of obedience was so engrained she didn't quite dare.

"And what does this mean?" her father shouted, reading from her journal here and there. "*I have my books/And my poetry to protect me/I am shielded in my armour?* What the hell are you trying to protect yourself from? I haven't laid a finger on you—yet!"

Her heart thumping, Liza backed away from her father, more frightened by the look in his eyes than anything he'd said so far. Her life was so easy compared to his. He wished she didn't exist. He did not exactly say this, but it was implied. Similar scenes continued over the next several weeks, whenever her mother went out. Even sometimes when she was there.

Although her mother had a lot on her mind that year, the only thing she talked about was packing Liza away. First she consulted the next door neighbours who'd overheard her husband roaring, then Liza's Sunday school teacher and a social worker recommended by a friend. It was easier than talking about the real problem: her husband's moodiness. That was exacerbated by his drinking, which was episodic but had become rather frequent by 1966. He was in his forties and acted like he'd been gypped in life, like he should have had more. As in: is this all there is? But if Liza left, her mother hoped he might settle down.

Besides, the girl was crying in her sleep. Liza's mother told everybody, much to Liza's dismay. A foster home was one option. Anything to remove her from the path of her father's rage. It flared intermittently and unpredictably, like a wildfire never quite put out. And if sending her away also took her out of range of her cousin Dace Devereux, so much the better. That boy was nothing but trouble. He always had been, no matter what his people thought. This last bit, at least, she saved for her daughter's ears alone.

By Thanksgiving, October 10, Liza had found out they were sending her to Dublin, to live with her Granny Magill. Both mother and daughter were numb, and Liza was more than ready to go. It was supposed to be just for the school year. She could go to Mount Temple Secondary School there.

Her mother would keep the boys. Her father, well, it didn't matter, because he would do what he wanted anyway. Men are like that, aren't they? her mother said. He might stay, but only if Liza went away. He couldn't stand having her in his house. That wasn't exactly what her Sunday school teacher, the person elected to help tell Liza, had said, but she saw it in Miss Comeau's teary eyes. It had been cool in the church, but her cheeks felt hot. Liza was embarrassed for herself, for all of them. She had fled through the darkened vestry, running out into the street without even waiting for the woman to finish. She never went back to church as long as Miss Comeau volunteered there. The only saving grace was that at least Miss Comeau had listened to Liza's mother's stories, so she was on her side. For there were many sides and many secrets.

Coincidentally, a real divorce—a separation—was taking place in Liza's friend Linda's family. Linda lived just down the street. Strange, because nobody else was getting divorced. Everybody else lived with both a mother and a father, unless the father were dead.

Liza didn't think about what was happening to her most of the time, maybe because of the look in her mother's soft hazel eyes. And because she couldn't think about it, she stopped thinking about her mother too and her memory of wanting to rescue her mother began to dim.

She thought of Dace instead and wondered what he was doing in jail. She had no idea about his routines, so she concentrated on his feelings. In a bad situation, she figured he would retreat to somewhere in his head. Like she did.

Chapter Three
Wayward Cousins
Granny Magill's, Dublin, Ireland, 1966-1971

My cocoon tightens, colors tease,
I'm feeling for the air,
A dim capacity for wings,
Degrades the dress I wear.
—Dickinson, Emily, "From the Chrysalis"

Liza had always half-wished they would send her back home to Ireland, so she could grow up quickly and move away. And get away from her father, even if he were going to pay her grandmother for room and board. A win-win situation, he'd said. The old girl's always griping she doesn't have enough money and now she will. And if Liza went to Dublin and lived in another world, maybe she could stop thinking about Dace. She could stop thinking: even if there is a reason, is any reason good enough?

Aside from her mother's unexpected reluctance to let her go, the worst part about leaving Toronto was the flight. She had never flown before and was more scared than she let on. The stranger in the aisle seat beside her, a Country and Western guitarist in his twenties, held her hand and slept on her shoulder for most of the flight.

She'd expected Dublin to be different from Toronto, but once she'd arrived on the north side, near Findlater's, it felt like she'd never left home. Bricks and mortar. Cars racing in the street. A school filled with girls in little cliques, and teachers too tired to teach. Except it rained in Dublin instead of snowed. And the food was different. Chips and beans for tea, cheaper cuts of meat—when they had any—overcooked peas, lots of potatoes and maybe tinned fruit for a treat.

"Maeve," her grandmother said the first time she saw her. "You don't look anything like our Maeve. You're a Devereux, aren't you?"

Observing the older woman, who was now less than five feet tall, Liza tried to reconcile her fading blue eyes and orthopaedic shoes with the only photo she had ever seen: a black and white studio portrait of the newlywed Mrs Brigit Magill at eighteen. Now she was a brisk, bustling woman with a copious amount of white hair bundled up at the nape of her neck who still looked strong.

Liza had no idea what to say to her. She had never even written to her before. Her mother did all that. She was shown to her own little room at the rear of the four room house. *Thank God,* she thought. *My own room.* Her mother had said she might have to share her grandmother's bed if she had a lodger, but she didn't have one right now. Maybe she wouldn't get one as long as Liza's father paid. Still, the ceiling sloped so low over her flat pillow she was bound to feel buried alive. She would have to focus on the unfamiliar tree close to the tall window, still green in October. And ignore the overflowing garbage pails. *Oh, brother,* she thought as she gazed out the window. *Was that a rat running down the street or just a skinny cat?*

"Do you miss my mother?" she asked.

Her grandmother stood in the doorway, the jamb of it just above her head. Liza had never seen a doorway so small except in an illustrated book of children's fairy tales. The two rooms downstairs had high ceilings, but the upstairs was more like an attic. Where had her mother and all her brothers and sisters slept?

"I don't miss her any more than the rest of them," the older woman had replied, restless hands reaching out and smoothing a worn chenille cover on the small bed. It had once been pink or perhaps white. Liza soon discovered her grandmother was like her mother in that she never stopped working. Liza gazed back out the window. "At least your Ma's brothers and sisters write regularly. Maeve, now, she only writes when there's trouble. Speaking of trouble, a letter arrived for you, from your Da's nephew. A Devereux."

Liza swung her head around so sharply she almost hurt her neck. "Dace! Did you read it?"

"Mother o' God. That's the first spark of life I've seen since you arrived. Such a skinny, dark little thing you are. Why don't you take off that poufy-looking coat and stay a while, Missy?" She shook her head, then extracted the letter from her apron pocket with the air of somebody yanking out a bad tooth. "Someone should have told you that boy's a convicted felon. The envelope was postmarked from the jail. Why's he writing here? The cheek of him!"

Liza stuffed the letter into the pocket of her coat without looking at it. At home it was 7:00 a.m. She was exhausted, almost comatose, from the long, sleepless night on the plane. *Knackered,* she'd heard the Irish say. But the minute she was alone, she sat on a wooden chair in front of a tiny table overlooking the crammed and cobbled alley, and savoured what Dace had to say.

> By now, you probably heard that I'm in Maitland Penitentiary. It's not so bad. I would have written sooner, but I had to earn the privilege (sic). I just wanted to let you know there's a wayward cousin thinking of you in this godforsaken place. If you don't want to write me, it's okay. What are you doing in Dublin? I had a devil of a time getting your address.

She wrote him back the next day, borrowing an Irish stamp from her grandmother for the first and last time, in spite of the disapproval in the old woman's eyes. Liza had to know Dace's side. Even if it were a bad side, she no longer cared. At the end of a ten page letter, handwritten in her small, neat script, she tucked in, *What happened?* then set off for her new school and began another long vigil, awaiting his reply.

But she must have scared him, for the long nights ticked by without so much as a note or a postcard arriving. Probably because she'd asked why. Had he really shot that man? If so, why? What was happening to him now? Was he scared of everything the way she was all the time? At least she hadn't asked if he thought he'd get out of there unscarred. If he didn't hate her, he must at least think her a fool. You don't ask questions like that of somebody in prison, you just don't, no matter how much you wanted to know. She saw that now.

Christmas came and passed, with letters and cards from her far flung aunts and uncles in Canada and Australia, but she still didn't hear from him, even after sending him a greeting card with a short, *I-don't-care-what-you-did* note inside. She wrote longer letters as well, but somehow they never made it into the post. *If you don't answer me, I'm going to die.* If he didn't answer her by New Years, he probably never would, she despaired.

Dear D.D., she scribbled in ink on the inside covers of her notebooks, *do you remember me?*

Sometimes she wondered if her grandmother were hiding his letters, but she doubted it. For one thing, although she'd always been a late riser, now she sprinted down the skinny linoleum hallway to intercept the postman long before the older woman had even lit the gas for their morning tea. For another, her grandmother was too tired. Too tired to have custody of a young girl, she said. Especially a girl like Liza who ate every speck of sugar in the house and forgot to shut off lights. No matter that both these things, forgetting to turn off the hall light and eating the last sugar cube, had happened only once. Did Liza think money grew on trees?

It got worse after Liza met Tony Harper, because now her grandmother could say: And let's not forget the way 'she showed her skin to a man who wouldn't cover it' — at sixteen! And after all she had done for her, too. Liza did her best not to think about Tony. Now she bit her knuckles so she wouldn't cry. *Well,* she thought, *she has me there.*

Many evenings the older woman fell asleep before 8:00 while Liza reread C. S. Lewis's *Tales of Narnia* and daydreamed through William Butler Yeats. Narnia seemed even more magical knowing Lewis had woven Ireland into his work. Although she would have loved to visit the Mourne Mountains and Dunluce Castle more often, places that had given birth to Lewis's dreams, she almost never left Dublin over the next five years. Her grandmother, careful as she was, couldn't afford it. The money Liza's father sent, when he remembered, wasn't enough. On the rare occasions she went on a school trip to Dunluce Castle, the Giant's Causeway, or Newgrange, she was thrilled. It was always a hassle crossing the border, though.

Ireland, she thought, her fingers tracing an ancient Celtic swirl on one of the stones. *I've come back to the land of my ancestors' dreams.* But the school trip she treasured most was going to see the *Book of Kells*. For an hour or so she escaped her classmates and walked the streets where some of her favourite authors had once walked. From the moment she saw Trinity, that's where she wanted to go to university. Oscar Wilde, the author of *The Ballad of Reading Goal,* had gone to school there.

"None of the Magills have ever gone to university," her grandmother said. Her lips were pursed around a clothes peg as she stripped sheets from a clothesline slung over her stove. She was also canning jelly, so a big pot of roiling water sat on the stove.

"Maybe my father would pay the tuition."

"I doubt that, girl. And do you really mean to keep living here?"

Listening to her, Liza's heart sank. *You don't want me,* she thought, although it was silly to feel hurt. Her grandmother had already raised eight children. On impulse, she stepped forward and almost flung her arms around the older woman's neck but stopped herself just in time. Her grandmother hated public displays of affection. Not that Liza blamed her. She was a little like that herself. It was her family's style.

Still, she thought her grandmother had gotten used to having her around, that she was company at least. On Saturdays they always talked late into the night. Granny Magill, much as she held her emotions in check, was a born raconteur. Liza knew all the Magill family secrets now, but knowing them wasn't enough. She was lonelier than she had ever thought possible. Lonely for her old neighbourhood, her sad mother, even her brothers. And as it turned out, lonely, achingly lonely for a man.

Within a short time Liza had wanted to go back to Toronto as well as the more familiar tensions and rhythms of her own house, but she couldn't. She hadn't been gone six months when the worst happened, at least from her mother's point of view. Her father left for good, leaving her with nothing except the twins. They'd sold the house, so there was no place for Liza in Toronto. Not in her mother's little place, anyway.

Then one day, just when she needed him most, Dace wrote her another letter. His parole was coming up for review and he needed to contact the outside world.

I'm sorry I didn't write before. I was afraid of what you might think of me.

As if that mattered. Life wasn't black and white, like a newspaper, and love wasn't either. She knew that now. And who was she to judge, based on the decisions she'd made while living here? At least she'd had a second chance. Everybody said so, her grandmother and the infirmary staff. And as long as she was real careful, nobody would ever know what she'd done in Dublin to survive. It wasn't all over the news like Dace's life story had been, even if it felt that way sometimes. With any luck, she'd even forget herself, no matter what Granny Magill said. *A girl is always marked by something like this. Even when she knows it's the only way.*

> Also, I spent a lot of time in solitary, so it was hard to get letters out. Oh, yeah. Then there was a sit-down and I got involved in that. But I'm okay now. I'm taking some correspondence classes and the librarian and I are in cahoots. You'll like this part. I read all the time. I live in books, just like you do.

It bothered her, though, all those lost years. What had he been doing? Look what she had done! And his family, how had they coped? Her own family was settling down a bit. They'd lowered their hopes, she supposed. They mustn't know about her either, and Gran had promised she wouldn't tell.

Okay, she wrote back, determined to focus on him. *But what about Uncle Norm and Rosie? How are they?*

Of course he was sorry for what had happened, for what he'd put his family through, he persevered, his energy sparking from his letter to her. And even though there were mitigating circumstances — the man was going to hurt Rick — Dace knew he was responsible. He said he had to accept responsibility for what had happened or he would never be free. And if deep down in her heart Liza felt it might be just what the parole board was waiting to hear, she didn't say.

A man died, Liza, he wrote. His words echoed, reminding her of how she had felt when she'd first read about the crime. Somewhere she had also read it took about two or three years to get over a bereavement. If somebody died at your hands, it was more or less the same. *Do you still think about him? A man you hardly knew? Not if I can help it*, he answered. *I'd go crazy if I did. I'd really rather think about you.* And at the close of every letter for the two years, he also added:

> So now you know there's a wayward cousin thinking about you in some godforsaken place.

He didn't mention that he was also writing to everybody else he knew, anybody smart enough to toss him a rope. And he didn't mention the pond, either. Why? Because she had been fourteen? Or because of the prison censors, those prurient men who got off on reading other people's thoughts. What a job. She knew he hadn't forgotten though. Because she hadn't. And somewhere inside they were the same.

She ended up staying in Dublin almost five years, and during that time he wrote her eighty-three letters.

> Tell me, Cousin, just how do you feel about me?
> I'd like to see you open a bit yourself. Or am I
> blind?
> P.S. Take care of yourself. I don't know what
> happened to you there in Dublin, but it seems to
> me you haven't valued your heart.

She counted and re-counted his letters the same way some girls do their friends, poring over them like the poems she loved. She agonized over droughts, for there were still periods when he either couldn't or wasn't allowed to write.

> ... because some nut stabbed me in the back. We
> both had to go to the hospital. The blade broke off
> in my back. So the Director charged us both with
> fighting. He put us in lockup and took thirty days
> good time off us. Can you believe that? Can you?

Her grandmother was usually scouring pots or hand washing clothes in the background, a sour expression on her face, though Liza helped with the housework now. Gran had turned sixty-six in 1971, but she seemed older. She'd been almost used up by the time she was forty-five, and if she'd ever had any use for a man it was hard to remember it now. *Strong hands, strong backs, but most of them don't use them,* she said. *And dear Jaysus, they wore out so soon!* Just look at her. Her boys sent what they could, but she'd been on her own for almost fifteen years.

"You're a right lunatic, girl," she'd say, scrubbing the cutting board until the thin skin on her knuckles glowed. "What do they call it in the States? Boy crazy? I've never seen a girl so bewitched by men. First that would-be actor and now a jailbird. Never seen nothing like it. Unless it was your mother Maeve."

I just want one man, Liza yearned, reluctantly letting go of her dream of Trinity and scouting out the closest university to Maitland Penitentiary instead. She also wrote more and more letters to Dace, to everybody except her estranged parents, the closer she came to going back. It had been a long time coming, but she and Dace were both grown up now. They could do what they wanted.

When she got home everything was going to be all right.

She just had to get back to Canada, that's all.

Chapter Four
Yard-Out
Recreational Yard, Maitland Penitentiary, July 1971

> Maitland Penitentiary is about to explode.
> We are doing everything to prevent it, but so
> much is outside our jurisdiction. First, we are
> understaffed. Roughly one third of our inmates
> require psychiatric care, but our hospital is too
> small and our staff too overworked to process the
> necessary paperwork. Second, there is still
> widespread anxiety about the scheduled transfer
> of inmates to Maitland Supermax.
> —Warden's unanswered letter from to the Regional
> Director, June 17, 1971

> I am not of that feather to shake off my friend
> when he must need me.
> —Shakespeare, "Timon of Athens"

Sun sprayed through the barbed wire and sparkled on the mica in the dirt. For a super-sized dog kennel the Big Yard looked pretty good.

Dace Devereux, a.k.a. #2909, was soaking up the sun. It took a lot of heat these days to reach the chill in his bones. B Block had just gotten out, so they had almost an hour in the Yard unless some stupid fucker jerked the screw's chain. His eyes cut to the black scaffolding in the corner. Fat Frank stared down the barrel of his gun, aimed directly at Dace.

So let him. The last thing he needed was to get some institutional charges written up, like Rick had the other day. Dace had got all that fuck you stuff out of his system the first year, thank you. Prison had its charms all right, giving losers a lifelong sense of belonging, but it was high time he left.

Although he was taking a bit of a chance and he knew it, he leaned back against a brick wall and closed his eyes. The bricks felt hot. What the hell was keeping Rick anyway? Maybe he had gotten slammed down again. Or maybe... His mind leaped ahead, anticipating a variety of calamities. The sun was a two-faced bitch sometimes, but an hour in her rays sure as hell beat eighteen hours in a cell.

It was too good to last though. He had just about dozed off when he heard somebody say, "Hey, Iron Horse!" A friend, since he'd used a nickname. It sounded like Eugene, a guy up his tier. Dace cocked an eye open just in case. Yeah, it was Eugene.

"Hey, man," he said without moving his lips.

"Hey, man," a different, unexpected voice said. "Stay alive."

His eyes popped open, but there was nobody there.

Maybe he was going crazy, this close to parole. Guys did. Straightening up, he panned the yard, something even the dumbest fish did if he valued his life—and he sure did. People were waiting for him outside. His father, his sister Rosie, and little Liza. Every time he thought about Liza, he grinned.

A flash of light distracted him, but it was just the sun glinting off the Iron Pile at the bottom of the yard. A crying shame. Not that he expected much from the stupid bastards who ran this place when they'd cut athletics, school and work programs. *Boohoo*, he thought, mocking himself and wiping sweat from his brow. The sight of all that rusty metal still bothered him, though. It cost nothing to maintain a set of weights.

His shoelace had come undone. *Damn,* he thought, as he

bent down to retie it. A pale blue letter dislodged from inside his shirt and began a slow, tantalizing descent to the ground. Lunging forward, he swiped the letter in mid-air, almost crushing it in his hand.

The next thing he knew, a couple of greeners were staring him in the face. *Stand a little out of my sun*, the library con always said.

"Hey," the smaller, bespectacled man said.

The second suckhole must have thought Dace was deaf. "Fuck," he said, "Look at his sneer! What's he mad at us for?"

Undeterred by their poor reception, the smaller goon held out a smoke. Dace really wanted a cigarette, but he declined. The Pen was a small society with a three-tiered hierarchy of men and laws governing where everybody belonged. People were always better off with their own kind.

"Hit it," he said just as Rick showed up.

"Yeah, get the fuck out of here," Rick added, kicking at their rears.

Both guys jumped. "Okay, okay, we're going," they said, bowing away. "Looks like you don't need no more friends anyway."

"A real sharp pair of jerks, eh?" Dace said, high-fiving his friend.

"Brilliant," Rick said and looked both ways before he opened his shirt. Dace caught sight of cigarettes and something else that was white.

Rick had done hard time, but after five years in — with a bit of a break — everything was cool. "Where the hell you been?" Dace asked, as if he didn't know. The guy loved to talk. And bum cigarettes. *Hallelujah*, he thought, taking the tailor-made Rick was waving under his nose. Some of the T.M.s weren't bad.

He could have happily stayed right where he was for the next forty minutes or so, but Rick wanted to go walking. Peeling his body off the wall, Dace checked his sweaty outline on the bricks. *Dace was here*, it said. Where the hell did Rick get his energy? The guy was practically skipping while Dace's own legs felt numb. At the door back into the Big House they got a couple of lights from a droopy little joint man, the prison trusty posted there.

Rick inhaled half his cigarette in one drag, the way he always did. "Jesus," he complained as he expelled the smoke. "Nothing ever happens in this stupid place."

Dace shrugged. Shit happened, but it was the same old, same old. What the hell did he care? He was getting out soon. Still smoking, they strolled around the high-walled gravel yard while Dace mulled over Liza's letter again.

Dear Dace,
I got accepted into Maitland University! I'm coming home. Well, not to my mother's flat on Clinton. And as for my father's house in Scarborough—yes, I'm a wonderful girl, but when are you going to understand he really doesn't want to see me? It's okay, I don't mind. He's not the only man in my life. You're my family, too. I'm going to stay in a new student residence, in a fresh, modern room overlooking a stream. I'm so glad I'll still be near water. I got a scholarship and Granny Magill is helping. I feel guilty taking her money, but I don't know what else to do. Besides, she has good reason for wanting to see me gone. She thinks it will be better for me, too. I just hope I can pay her back someday.
Dublin is so beautiful. If only you could have visited. But everything here is so tired and old. The Troubles are a hundred miles north, but people are still afraid. And a woman's life, well, it's not good. No birth control, and Women's Liberation has been slow, probably because most of Ireland still feels enslaved.

He smiled a little to himself, noting that she had struck out "Goddamn the English."

Even so, I've walked the streets so much, Dublin's in my soul.

When I get to university I want to major in
English or maybe Psychology. Anybody can read
books, so I was tempted by Biology, but I don't
have enough Math. More than anything, I want
to see you. I'm coming straight there. How do I
get in? Please, please, make sure I'm on your
visitors list. Are you behaving yourself? Dear
Cousin, you've just got to make parole.

Although he didn't understand all the things she said, he
liked the way she said them. She worried him, though. She was
hiding something, but he had no idea what. Take that stuff about
her grandmother, her other grandmother. What was all that?

He stuffed the letter back in his shirt and looked around. A
small crowd had gathered near the dismantled weightlifting
equipment.

Rick didn't notice the crowd. "What's the problem?" he
asked when Dace steered him in the opposite direction.

"It's just Sandy McAllister preaching again. He's NG,
absolutely no fucking good."

"I mean your cousin, you lucky bastard. What did she
say?"

Dace looked away. If it had been anybody else, he would
have ignored him. But a friend could take liberties. He took a
couple of drags on his cigarette, hoping to make the smoke last,
but they both knew he was stalling. "She's coming home soon,"
he finally said.

Rick's face lit up and he actually did a little jig. "Really?
When?" His words tumbled over one another. "Why didn't you
say something before?"

"Jeez, I dunno. I guess she's coming when school starts."

"So when the hell's that? Do kids still start school in
September? Hey, can I read it? I like the stuff she writes about the
IRA and her dear old Granny. Let me over there and I'd bomb the
hell out of those bastards too. She's cute, right?" Rick asked,
shaping an hour glass with his hands.

Dace groaned. God, maybe the prison authorities—make

that "Authorities" with a capital A — were right. Cons didn't learn fast. Talking about a girl around here? How stupid was that?

"Yeah, I guess," he said. He had to say something. Rick hardly ever got any mail. Jesus, could the guy even write? He'd had a lot of trouble in their parochial school and the nuns hadn't helped. "At least she was. But you'd look cute too if you were the last set of tits I saw before coming to the Joint." He stopped, a bit uncomfortable. "Ah, scratch that, she was just a kid."

At this, Rick looked even more interested. "Well, if she's eighteen or nineteen now, she's probably done it."

Done it? Done it? What the hell did that mean?

"You hear the stuff that's going on out there," Rick waxed on. "Everybody's getting it on. No more of this wait-until-we're-married shit. And if something does happen, you don't even have to marry the broad. They've all been living together in little free-love communes since about 1967, man."

Dace tried butting Rick on the shoulder, but he danced out of the way. Little Liza with somebody else? Crazy. She wouldn't, would she? Not that she belonged to him. Or ever would. What the hell did he have to offer a girl like her? The way he was, the place he was in. Not to mention she was his cousin. Sure she flirted a little in her letters. To pass the time. For years, she had been a young girl far from home, far from everybody who loved her.

Somewhere a door slammed shut. "I don't think so," he said. "Anyway, who cares? You know me. It's her mind I love."

"The hell you do. Give me that," Rick said, making a grab.

Dace feigned an upper cut, but Rick ducked out of the way. "Not here," he said, nodding at Sandy McAllister, whose head and shoulders had just popped up above the crowd, straight across the yard.

"Ah, he's just a lunatic," Rick said, grinding his cigarette butt into the dirt. "The silly bugger never knows when to stop."

Maybe, Dace thought.

Sandy was about their age, but he wasn't getting out anytime soon. Nobody knew exactly what he had done, but he was a lifer, so it probably had something to do with a cop. With nothing to lose, Sandy usually had something up his sleeve. A born storyteller and a natural agitator, he was responsible for most of the rumours circulating the Joint. The proposed move to the new Supermax had really got him going, and he'd let everybody know it. He said he wasn't putting up with that electronic surveillance shit. As if he had a choice.

Sandy's solution was a takeover. Every so often he buttonholed a couple of strong guys like Dace and Rick to make them see things his way. Somebody had squealed to the Authorities, but they didn't care. For once, they were relying on their shrink. The shrink speculated that Sandy had a "conspiracy mentality."

Sandy McAllister altered his looks from time to time, depending on his target, but it was always something showy: a sports figure, a circus ring master, a Bible salesman. Right now he was aping Jesus with disciples at his feet, but Dace thought he looked more like Rasputin, with his long, stringy hair slicked back from his forehead and his mad monk eyes. He had quite an audience, though. A bunch of dumb cons.

Dace glanced back at Fat Frank in the tower. He was cradling his assault rifle like it was his firstborn child. The jerk even kissed it from time to time.

"C'mon. Give me the effing letter." Rick spat on the ground. "What do you think I'm gonna do with it, use it like the Bible and light up a smoke?"

"Not on your fucking life," Dace said. "The rest of these goons will just want to read it, too."

Nobody got the mail Dace did. Like a good book, Liza's letters transported him right out of jail. He kept them in his mattress, removing just enough stuffing to make room. The screws were supposed to check the bedding, but they never did.

Rick looked so agitated that Dace almost relented. The poor guy probably just wanted a diversion. Maybe he'd read him a chunk. He wasn't fast enough, though.

"Keep your kite," Rick said, then took off to talk to a man

from another range. A short termer who was due to be paroled in a few days. Most of those men, short termers, were future oriented. Almost nobody talked about their pasts and only a real goof asked. B Block had their hour in the exercise yard every morning between 7:30 and 8:30. This was their only opportunity to talk to people on other ranges without bringing down the heat. Whatever happened in the Yard, the guard in the gun cage turned a blind eye as long as he could. There was supposed to be a guard walking along the inner wall, but he was usually busy someplace else.

Dace wanted to talk to a couple of guys too, but he got distracted. A hawk soared over the barbed wire and he thought about the farm. He walked the perimeter of the yard, checking for a nest.

Minutes later, Rick caught up with him again. He waved a hardball he'd found someplace in Dace's face. An older con and a few companions were hunkered down in a corner of the yard shooting craps, but nothing else was going on. Even broom ball, an easy game to equip, had been nixed. Too many people getting hurt. Ha! He'd never met a screw who gave a good goddamn about cuts and bruises.

Dace glanced at the ball in Rick's hand. It was perfectly round, the soft curve of a woman's breast. Christ, he wished he was still dead down there. It had been easier that way.

"Nah," he said, nodding towards the crowd at the bottom of the yard. "You give me that ball and I might—"

"—ram it up Rasputin's ass."

"Yeah, well, look at him. Thinks he's a Prophet or something. And the screws let him. Sure he's harmless, but there's no way he should be here."

Rick rolled his eyes. What the hell did he care? Cons like Sandy came and went. With any luck, somebody would ice him in the shower. "Absolutely nuts," he agreed, tossing the ball from one hardened palm to the other as he scanned the yard for another partner.

"He's up to something. Maybe I'll go have a listen."

"Yeah, you do that, buddy. You're shit for company today."

Dace hadn't gone more than ten steps when he heard somebody say, "Hey! That's mine."

By the time he'd spun around, a well-built farm boy was staring Rick down. Where the hell had he come from? Dace had never seen him before, but he knew his kind. The guy didn't want a friend, he wanted a name. Dace started back. Somebody behind him caught the half-smoked cigarette he flicked to the ground.

Sandy McAllister heard the farm boy, too. "Vengeance is mine, saith the Lord!" he shouted, trying to divert attention from the new kid on the block.

Every eye had shifted to Rick and the kid, though. "Nobody owns anything here," Rick said softly, his voice cool, his eyes hard and flat, his reputation on the line.

Christ, Dace thought. Why the hell had he left him?

Many of the spectators were already drooling with anticipation. "It's a fight!" *they* crowed. It shouldn't have been, except the fish was too stupid to know it. To cross a solid like Rick or Dace, you had to be pretty damn new.

The kid had time to say, "Well, I do," before Rick clocked him in the mouth.

In the commotion that followed, Dace lost sight of them both, but the kid was awfully confident for a fish in a fight. Then he saw it: a little spark of light. Aw Jeez, another stupid punk. They were hatching in the dirt today.

"Watch it," he yelled at Rick. The kid pretended to fall to the ground, but pulled a thin-bladed knife from the seam of his pants instead. "He has a shiv. Or did," he said, coming up behind him. He kneed the kid in the kidneys, grabbed something and twisted hard. Luckily, it was just the boy's arm. The shiv clattered to the ground. A loud snap elicited a single scream and the next thing Dace knew, the boy was sliding like water down his legs.

His heart beating fast, he sidestepped the mess. The boy, who looked about eighteen, was twisting in the packed dirt.

Dace's eyes raked the ground, but the weapon, a homemade stiletto probably made from a sharpened spoon, was gone. Maybe it was under the boy, but Dace didn't dare touch him again. If he did he'd kill the little bugger for sure. The boy rolled on the ground, clutching his wrist. Dace could see the kid's fat tonsils when he screamed. By this time, everybody had taken a giant step back.

Fat Frank was still in the gun cage. "Shut the fuck up," he shouted, before radioing for more help. Not supposed to be by myself, not with all these bloody cons, they heard him say. Why the hell are we always so short staffed? What's the point of sending everybody to the new place? What am I supposed to do with this crazy lot? My gun? Of course I have my gun, asshole. Dropping the radio, sweating hard, he bolted downstairs in his heavy duty boots. Dace half-expected him to keep on going, but he didn't.

The boy's screams had downgraded to moans, but he was still writhing around. Two or three more minutes passed. The guard's eyes darted over the scene, rabbit-like. Nobody moved while he made up his mind what to do.

"Everybody up against the wall," he finally bellowed. Pointing his gun straight at them, he spat out some stale gum. He was shaking a little, but trying not to show it. He sighed and smiled, displaying a set of stumpy teeth. Oh, Christ, he must have an idea. "Well," he said, "Let's have some fun here. Everybody strip! You guys were fighting over something. I want that shiv or whatever it was. And somebody'd better tell me who started this, or you're all in the Hole."

When they didn't move straight away, he hollered again. And waited some more. It was the boy on the ground who finally broke the silence. "Nobody started anything," he gasped, his face wet with tears. "But I think I broke my goddamn wrist playing ball."

"You ain't supposed to have no ball," the guard said, kicking the boy in his left side and getting another piercing scream.

Everybody started to undress, almost welcoming the hot air on their sweat-soaked skin. The wounded boy was exempt.

"Hey," Rick whispered to Dace as they shrugged off their pants, "For a punk, he sure learns fast."

Chapter Five
The Convict's Cousin
Maitland, Ontario, August 26, 1971

> There will be time, there will be time
> To prepare a face to meet the faces that you meet;
> There will be time to murder and create,
> And time for all the works and days of hands
> That lift and drop a question on your plate;
> Time for you and time for me,
> And time yet for a hundred indecisions,
> And for a hundred visions and revisions,
> Before the taking of a toast and tea.
> —Eliot, "The Love Song of J. Alfred Prufock"

Liza folded Dace's most recent letter, already a month old, and put it inside a suede shoulder bag with her wallet, her passport, some bits of Kleenex, a lipstick tube and her new keys. She had a couple of paperbacks, too. The downtown Maitland bus was here, its doors gaping open. She climbed the steps behind a couple of older ladies, thinking someday she'd be old too, but it was hard to imagine. The steps shook under her feet. What if she hadn't tightened the ankle straps on her wedged sandals enough?

Her mind bounced to and fro, a butterfly trapped in a jar. A good thing that boy had dummied up or Dace would have ended up in the Hole, no visitors allowed. He'd been caught before. Helping out a friend? What kind of friends did he have in there? He never mentioned names. He couldn't.

The bus fare was clenched so tightly in her hand she had to force her fingers to relax. When she dropped the change into his box, the driver looked her up and down like she was put on earth for his pleasure. She hesitated, realizing she had almost forgotten how to count Canadian coins. More women came up behind her, some with children yapping at their heels. Instinctively, she backed away from the sticky little hands. The bus driver looked at the young mothers in the same proprietary way, his bright blue jay eyes almost dangling out of his capped head.

"Make up yer mind, honey, I haven't got all day," he rumbled in his old man's voice, motioning her to the back of the bus with a nicotine-stained thumb. "The sc—" If he were saying scum, she couldn't believe her ears, so she revised what she was hearing to: *the guy waiting for you might have all day, but I don't,* and bowed her head to hide her blush, embarrassed other people could hear.

Damn, she thought, easing down the aisle, hiding her anger behind her waist-length hair. Styles were a little behind in Ireland, so back in Dublin she had let her hair grow and grow. The floor of the bus slanted slightly, tilting up to meet her face and she grabbed hold of a seat for balance. What was wrong with her? Why hadn't she told that old coot off? She had to speak up. If she didn't ... well, who cared.

She was going to see Dace. Nothing else mattered. Searching for a window seat, a single line of poetry flitted through her head: *There will be time, there will be time, to prepare a face for the faces that you meet ...*

Time. Yes, she reminded herself, she still had time, no matter what had happened in Dublin, no matter what she'd gone and done. Because the world belonged to the young and privileged in America in 1971, or so the older folks said, people like her grandmother who'd struggled through the Great Depression and World War II so a girl like her could reap the benefits: a university education.

And she would, she would. It was her chance to make good, to do something with her life. Everybody said so. Get an education. Fall in love, write books, have children, do anything she wanted. *Hurry, hurry,* she thought. She was the same age as the rest of the first years at Maitland University, but an accelerated sense of time made her feel older than she was. Used up. That and knowing what she had done.

Several uncensorious Irish people had told her she still had time to make a new life, but she wasn't sure. Life had a way of plummeting forward. *Hurry up, hurry up, let's be forty. Let's have some peace.* Not that she expected to make forty. Forty was old. Her parents were still in their forties, and their forties looked like a mountain peak with a landslide down the other side, rushing past the sites of all their old regrets. *As if they had exhausted all their possibilities,* she thought, irritated with herself for having anything on her mind today except her cousin Dace.

Sitting on the edge of the last vacant window seat, her purse on the aisle seat, she looked out at some battered brick walls. Why were bus stops located in such dismal places? She might as well be back in Dublin gazing at warehouses on the north side instead of in Maitland by the lake.

My God, was the bumpy-faced driver on a coffee break or what? What on earth was taking him so long?

At last the bus jolted forward, dislodging a tattered copy of *The Great Gatsby* from her bag. It was the kind of story she'd always favoured, one with a dark Byronic male character. She looked around, hoping nobody else had noticed. Not that most people cared about books. Still, she hated people knowing what she was doing, even what she was reading. Maybe because she'd been keeping secrets for so long: the divorce of her parents, her cousin's incarceration, and dear God, her relationship with an older man in Dublin. Jesus, she wished she'd waited and that she'd had another choice. But she hadn't. Her lover had taken what wasn't his and she'd let him.

Tucking *Gatsby* out of sight, she stifled a sigh, too keyed up to read, but a magnet for any fool who wanted to talk. Something about her had always invited confidences from strangers. Or maybe it was just that any sort of sounding board would do. Much as she enjoyed listening to other people's stories, finding out what made them tick, she wasn't in the mood today.

So much had happened since she'd disembarked from her Aer Lingus flight at Toronto International Airport three days before. She'd stopped overnight in the Ford Hotel across from the downtown bus station, then headed straight to her assigned university residence in Maitland, a city she'd never even visited before.

Liza had left for Ireland five years earlier. Then the twins had gone to their father's house in Scarborough last year because dear Dad had gotten a new wife. He hadn't wanted the boys, but he'd had no choice after they were picked up for drinking underage and his ex-wife got hysterical.

Liza chewed her lip and looked as if she were focusing on the bustle outside her window, but the street scene had vanished.

Dad had tried to knock some sense into her hard-drinking, truant brothers, with predictable results. The twins, as they would always be known, were almost seventeen and keen to avoid finishing high school. They spent their days sleeping until noon and their nights drinking bootleg beer and smoking grass. Dad had a grade eight education. He wanted his sons to get their grade twelve diplomas at least, but Liza, well... *She's a girl*, he'd said when her grandmother wrote to ask if there were any money for her university tuition. Just wait. Someday she'll get married and all that education would be wasted.

He was her father. Sooner or later she would have to visit both her parents and make amends. That's what an adult would do, Gran said so, and of course she was right. Even if it were a colossal waste of time. By now she'd read enough of the great American authors: Dreiser, Faulkner, Hemingway, Williams, and

Thomas Wolfe, to know she could never go home again, except in the physical sense. She was grown up now. Somehow, somewhere, she'd make a new home for herself. But she couldn't just forget her parents, no matter what. And she couldn't expect them to visit her. Too expensive. Too... Well, lots of reasons really.

Her mom, especially her mom. Maybe when she felt stronger she could visit her. After she settled into residence. Her classes in Sociology, English, Psychology, Philosophy and Journalism were beginning next week though, and she was already so nervous she could barely eat.

Squirming on her seat, she thought about getting into university. How on earth had she pulled off such a stunt? Where had she even come up with such an idea? Sometimes she didn't understand herself. Maybe it had something to do with walking through Trinity all the time, where so many writers had studied. She'd loved that place.

A small smile crossed her face. It was exhilarating to be back in Ontario on her own. Nobody knew she was back from Dublin, never mind that she was going to Maitland University. Well, almost nobody. Dace knew, except he was in no place to share his knowledge. Maybe he'd told his father, but Uncle Norm was a silent, solemn man, a slow leak like herself when it came to sharing tales. In her secret heart, she was thrilled with her own daring, and at night when she imagined her father finding out and getting absolutely stiff with rage—because he really did think education was wasted on women—adrenalin flooded her body from her head to her toes. As long as she wasn't living with him he didn't worry her at all.

A nicer girl might have felt sorrier for Dad. He'd been angry for as long as she could remember. And Mom, well, she didn't get mad much. She tended to be a talker, more prone to migraines than rages. Mom was always wrong when she opened her mouth. *Don't be so stupid!* her husband had been apt to splutter, inciting spectators to nervous laughter. Over the years, although her mother's conversational skills had been honed to chatter, her listening skills had remained undeveloped. In the end, even her usually failsafe intuition about her husband's moods had eluded her.

So Liza knew better than to plan a tête-à-tête with her mother, although she would have liked another confidante besides Dace. The part of herself that she recognized as unkind might even have enjoyed upsetting her, though she didn't want to hurt her. There was no reason to hurt her, since her father already had. Why had she let him? He wasn't worth it. No man was. Granny Magill was right. She was always right.

The woman in front of Liza had a strident voice. Liza had hesitated to use that word ever since she'd noticed it was only applied to women, but this one definitely qualified. And she also had, as Liza had noticed before she'd even sat down, bleached blonde hair and a blubbery body too old for her face.

Her voice took over the entire bus. "So this is the last time, I told him. Get straight, or me and the kids is outta here. I been visiting guys in prison for twenty years. First my Dad, now him. Whatsamatter with me? I goes to Jonesy: Why do I get only garbage? I ain't garbage."

"You never said he was garbage! You never!" her younger companion shrieked. Liza, who was used to much softer spoken Irish women, surreptitiously covered her ears.

"Well, no, but I thought it. I am too sick of gettin' garbage," the blonde repeated.

"Well, sure you are," her friend murmured. Liza detected the burr of a Scottish brogue in her speech. "And sure it's a hard life, but you'll feel better when you lay off the sauce. AA saved my life."

"Oh, Christ. Irma, you sound like you got religion or something since you went with that there AA. Bunch of Jesus freaks is what they are."

Liza cleared her throat, hoping the women would take a hint.

Irma turned around and glared. "Yeah? What can I do you for, college girl?"

Liza gazed back out the window and resisted the urge to stick out her tongue. She pretended she hadn't heard, but in truth she was puzzled why some people enjoyed airing their problems in public. Liza was always able to put on a face. At least Irma had recognized her as a college girl, she thought, smoothing her long, flared denim skirt across her lap. Liza had made the skirt back in Dublin on her grandmother's sewing machine.

A younger girl across the aisle turned up the static on her radio, trying to get a clear transmission of *Hey, Jude. ... Take a sad song and make it better. Remember to let him under your skin ...*

Liza wrapped her heavy, waist-length hair around her and daydreamed. It had been a little shorter then, but Dace had loved her hair at the farm, he'd written. This was one of those moments where she imagined him, one of those unused, in-between places of her life. Like those no-man's moments that happened just before sleeping or waking. Or queuing up. Or spinning through a revolving door. Whenever she was waiting for something to happen, he snuck up behind her and made her feel alive.

Even if he were just a phantom lover, he was the one she'd courted since she was nine or ten. He had been everything to her, every day except for those urgent weeks she'd spent with an Englishman named Tony Harper in Dublin, who was so much larger than life. *How romantic,* she thought sarcastically, scooping her hair off her shoulders and letting it fall again. *Romantic and ridiculous.*

So much had happened since the last time she'd seen Dace at the farm. To both of them. In hindsight, she knew now he had ignored everybody because he was headed for jail. Like a leper with open sores under his clothes, he had feared exposure in front of his relatives, especially in front of a little girl. She might have loathed him — or worse, been afraid. The rest of the family might settle for secrets, rumours and innuendo, but not her. She'd ferret out the truth.

Damn, Liza. You had the most beautiful, the most knowing eyes. And those monarch butterflies were so thick in the air. It looked like you were leading them somewhere. I wanted to tell you everything, but you were only fourteen.

So tell me now, she'd written back.

And he had, or almost, the way he remembered the whole story now, anyway.

Although they had both sought common reference points in those introductory letters, she had always been more curious about him than he'd seemed to be about her. Maybe he thought she was too young to have a life story filled with drama. After all, she was living with her other grandmother in Dublin. How thrilling could that possibly be? Ireland was ancient history, as far as he was concerned. Even the Troubles meant little to him, although surely he would have been drawn to the IRA and cared about what was happening in Londonderry if he'd been there. For all she knew, he didn't even read the news.

In time his correspondence with the rest of his friends and family had faltered. They had little interest in the written word and even less skill. And a part of him was afraid they despised him. But the teenaged Liza was different. She knew he'd written to her to revive his own hope, but by doing that he'd given her hope, too. Hope she'd survive her exile and hope she'd come home soon. And all the time he was in real danger, even though he said,

I'm getting out. I'm going to get my life back.
And when I do, I'll live to be a hundred and
you're going to, too.

From her bus window, she saw an old woman trundling her whole life down the sidewalk in a shopping cart. Gran loved to poor-mouth, tell stories about how Ireland had suffered such horrible wartime shortages. How lucky her children were to be in Canada, how much they owed her. How she was a mother who had loved them enough to let them go, to let them think she was glad to see them go. How she'd known they would never come back again because they would look like dismal failures if they did.

Oh God. Why was Liza wasting time thinking about the Magills?

She had been exchanging letters with Dace for almost three years now. Would she recognize his voice? And what would he think of hers when they finally met face-to-face, after all these years? It was almost like she was living in a song. He was living for her letters, he told her over and over. For her, his little cousin Liza. And, of course, for his father and his sister.

What would they talk about? None of that jail stuff, if she could help it. All she wanted to know was when he was coming home. For years the Devereux, especially Uncle Norm, the chief gatekeeper, had tried to keep Dace's location a secret. Dace was just "away". When Liza had confided the truth to a few people, they'd asked, *Why? What did he do?* No matter what she'd volunteered, their eyes shifted and they changed the subject. To spare her? No, to spare themselves, she felt sure. Although, if they had no insight into their own characters, they were sometimes pushy enough to imply: Why do you do what you do? Why do you care what happens to somebody like that, anyway? And her personal favourite: Is there something wrong with you, too?

The bus stopped a couple of times to pick up more passengers. Many of the people on this route were on their way to visit an imprisoned loved one. Dace had even written about a special little community of female pen pals who had relocated in Maitland just to be near their loved ones.

A recent newspaper article alleged some of the women belonged to a cult; their Messiah was fathering children they bore Outside. Exactly how he accomplished such miracles without conjugal visits was both a scandal and a mystery, but somebody was either lying or on the take. The Messiah was in prison for murdering one of the sister wives, something his women condoned for reasons nobody could fathom. Some crimes were apparently more forgivable than others, but which ones, and why? The sister wives had set up housekeeping above the ceiling of a local convenience store. They shared twenty-six children with two more on the way.

Several of the other ladies-in-waiting on the bus also had children in tow. Not that the authorities cared. Especially not guards paid a measly wage to do a dangerous job. No, guards didn't care why people did things, and they didn't expect anything from the men they guarded, either. Why should they? Why should anyone? People in prison were damaged goods.

Like me, Liza sometimes thought, but only when she was feeling low. And if Dace hadn't already told her, she would have figured it out from the non-fiction she sometimes read: library books about the theory of criminology and paperbacks of true crimes. They never explained why.

She was different though. She expected something from him. His father did, too. Uncle Norm had always expected something from his son, if not when he was sent away, then shortly after.

Oh, Christ, she didn't have time for snivelling, sad songs today. *Just get me to the prison on time!* Thankfully she was in the back of the bus, she thought, scrubbing in controlled fury at a single tear. The bus hurtled along, sticking to its schedule, while the driver ogled the female passengers in his overhead mirror. A ride that felt like forever took about fifteen minutes.

Everyone clammed up when they saw the fences: high stone walls with double rows of razor-barbed wire on top. Her stomach felt suddenly as if it were full of lead. Almost reluctant to get off the bus now that she was there, she forced herself to follow the rest of the passengers into a parking lot and then proceeded towards the arched, double-gated entrance.

"Visiting, visiting, visiting," the ladies said to two armed guards.

Liza shivered. She couldn't help it. The penitentiary looked so dark inside.

She hesitated for just a brief moment, took a deep breath and then plunged headfirst into the rest of her life.

Chapter Six

Connecting

Maitland Penitentiary, August 26, 1971

He looked at her as a lover can;
She looked at him, as one who awakes:
The past was asleep and her life began.
—Browning, "The Statute and the Bust"

L iza studied the other women at the second checkpoint inside the Great Hall, hoping to emulate acceptable behaviour, but she was still afraid. Having got this far she knew she would do anything to get inside. Besides, the first part had been relatively easy, so the rest might be too.

An armed guard waved them through like it was no concern of his how such ratty-looking women chose to waste their lives. He was a small man with a crossed eye, and he carried a large revolver strapped to his right side. Mute evidence of the weaponry used to guard men in a federal jail.

She shuffled in a queue behind everyone else. It looked like the federal penitentiary, but who knew? There were so many prisons in and around Maitland. Dace was in the worst one, though. For months there had been rumblings about discontent—more than usual—from the Pen. Dace made it sound like he was living in a volcano rather than a prison, and he ought to know.

The line picked up speed. She followed the other women until they were intercepted by two uniformed guards standing behind a formidable wooden counter. A sign stated visiting privileges could be suspended at the penitentiary's discretion, but they were open for business today.

Neither penal representative asked, "How are you?" Neither guard nor prospective visitor said, "Good day".

Everybody opened their bags. Most of the female crowd, who she assumed were repeat visitors, were allowed behind the counter to pass through a metal detector.

The first guard ran his stubby finger down his clipboard and mumbled, "Roberto Bellissimo? He's in the Hole today." Bellissimo's visitor went as limp as a greasy french fry. Turning, and nearly flattening the woman behind her, she stumbled away.

When it was Liza's turn, she squeaked, "I'm here to see my cousin, D'Arcy Devereux. He's arranged to put me on his visitors list." Shut up, she told herself. Less was usually best. It was that way with the Gardai in Dublin, anyway.

The younger guard stuck his face in hers. "Who?"

"D'Arcy Devereux," she said, keeping her voice as steady as she could.

He had been listening, though. He was only playing with her. Cat and mouse. "So how do we know you're that one's cousin?" he said with a smirk. That one's? Fumbling in the bag he had just pawed through, she slid her newly minted student ID across the counter and waited. The guard's eyes travelled from the scalloped edge of her embroidered peasant blouse to her flared denim skirt and up to her chest again. A razor cut on his chin caught her eye. He couldn't have been shaving long. What was he going to say?

"You look like one of them hippies to me."

Them hippies all bought the farm, she nearly snapped, her cheeks reddening. This was 1971, for Chrissakes. A whole new decade. A fact apparently lost on this backwater jerk.

"I'm on his visitor's list," she repeated, hoping her almost Irish accent would sound superior to her regular Canadian pronunciation. She wanted him to feel resentful, but suitably impressed.

The young guard might have been impressed, but he was stubborn, too. "Well now, I don't know." He peered at his clipboard an eternity longer, fishing around in his snout-like nose with a rubber-tipped pencil. When he lifted his eyes, she stared him down. She had to, or he would play with her all day. He was so transparent she knew when he had made up his mind, she just didn't know which way. As the walls of her stomach cleaved together, a thought surfaced out of nowhere, like a gas bubble. *How I despise being under your dirty thumb, you …*

"Let her go," the other guard said. "The little cock-teaser." He turned back to his work. "Betcha five bucks it's a complete lockdown by next Wednesday anyway," he added in a stage whisper.

… filthy pigs, Liza almost blurted, but she forced herself to remember they were under educated, poorly paid and barely smart enough to be afraid.

Dace, she thought, drifting through metal detectors into another world. *Where are you?*

The smell reminded her of damp locker rooms at public swimming pools. Sweating, chlorine, fear came to mind as she tried to keep her footing, although all she had to do was walk a straight line. There was no turning back. She had stumbled headfirst into one of those in-between places in her mind and she had to stay. She'd stopped breathing, and her heart almost stopped pumping, but she was kept in motion by other women nudging up against her. If she stretched out her left hand, she'd touch a wall of slimy green concrete blocks. If she stretched out her right, she'd brush the first in a line of door less stalls, each equipped with glass wire mesh dividers, stools and black telephone receivers.

She stopped, adrenalin surging through her. It had to be him in the first carrel. She hadn't seen him in years, but the rest of the men in the room looked too much like convicts to be him. They ranged from one unfashionable extreme to another. Either their gleaming pates were shaved bald or they wore their long hair slicked back from lean, hungry, wolfish faces.

But he … Dace was sitting on a stool with his hands folded in front of him and his neck craned to watch the entry door, every shining wave of his chin-length hair combed in place. In the past, they had sheared off everybody's hair, but it was the seventies now. Wearing a pressed khaki shirt, matching pants and an expression of eager expectation, he looked like he'd been waiting for her all his life. Well, maybe he had.

You're the only one, he'd written her. And when he stood to greet her, she felt like she'd been awarded a prize.

May's kids always had such good manners, she heard her mother say as she took her place onstage. Every eye in the visiting room drew their way—or rather, his way. Just the sight of him was enough to draw her onto the stool facing him. She forced a nervous smile and when she did, she remembered to breathe.

D'Arcy Devereux smiled too, the left side of his mouth pulling higher than the right. When he sat back down, the other prisoners and visitors pulled their eyes away to give him more space.

A small, careful smile blotted out the darkness in his eyes, but he had aged ten years in the last five. Little wrinkles radiated from the corners of his eyes like spokes in a wheel, although he wasn't yet twenty-five. Almost as if he were shy, he kept smiling. Suddenly she was fourteen again. All she wanted him to do was, well, speak to her. She thought briefly of the pond and a veil dropped. It always did. What else could a pubescent girl have wanted in 1966? With her own cousin, yet?

She opened her mouth then closed it. It didn't matter. He couldn't hear what she said. The glass divider was in the way. But for the first time since she'd gotten off the plane at Toronto International, her arrival unheralded, she felt a powerful sense of homecoming. Here she was in this strange place, this prison, and she never wanted to leave. Forget her dual citizenship, forget school. She belonged here. She belonged with him. And she'd die to keep this feeling. No matter what happened, no matter what people said.

When Dace motioned her to pick up the telephone receiver and said into his, "You're so beautiful. I can't believe my eyes," joy flooded her veins, but the words didn't matter. All she cared about was his voice.

She shook her head, blushing. "I am not beautiful," she said, shifting under his intense stare. Of course he was staring at her, she thought, stiffening on the stool like a butterfly impaled on a pin. Where else was he supposed to look? She was backed by a green wall with a round-faced clock ticking the seconds off, and already she was praying their hour would never end. Her own view was more compelling. A scowling, fat-faced guard was scrutinizing her and Dace more closely than he was watching anybody else.

"You really don't know?" he asked, a puzzled expression on his face.

She shook her head again, her throat almost swelling shut with unshed tears. There was a steady hum of chatter in the visiting room, then the bus blonde in the next stall erupted, yelling at the shrunken little Dustin Hoffman creature she was visiting. "I can't take anymore! You've got to stop!"

Stop what? Stop stealing? Stop drinking? Stop killing? Stop hurting me? Anxious to write her own script, Liza shut the woman out. "But," she demurred, "at least I'm not getting acne anymore."

"You?" He shook his head, trying to look serious. "Acne? You're imagining things. You never had acne. Although I do remember a certain yellow polka dot dress." He grinned when she reddened again at this distressing evidence of his memory. "And the way you drank tea. The old aunties wanted to get rid of us, but you wouldn't leave."

"Old? I'm not sure. Everybody had their children so young in those days."

"That was the last farm-do I ever went to." He paused, staring off into space. "I think that's why I remember it so well.

That … and you," he added. "And the butterflies. It was my final outing before I came here. All those rednecks, well, most of the cousins turned out okay. Except for Randy."

"What do you mean? I thought he was a police detective in Hamilton."

"Yeah, he's a copper all right," Dace agreed, his hand tightening on his telephone receiver. "Remind me. What was happening at the farm that day, an anniversary?"

"Aunt Sadie's and Uncle Tom's thirtieth or fortieth or something. Who knows? We have so many aunts and uncles I don't know how anybody keeps track."

"Jeez, forty years is a long time. My father was so mad that summer he used to slam me into a wall every time he looked at me. And my mother — "

He suddenly stopped talking and stared down at his hands.

Wait! Liza almost shouted. Come back to me! "Oh, she'd understand," she said. Planting her hand against their glass partition, she appealed to him with her eyes. "She would! She'd come to see you every visitors' day."

Their fat overseer materialized so fast she almost fell off her stool. He gestured at the reinforced glass divider and Liza dropped her hand without taking her eyes off Dace's taut expression. There was no time to spare.

"What's his problem? Is he worried about me smudging the glass?"

Dace's face relaxed. "Maybe," he said. "You know, I've been away so long, Liza. I've done my best to pay, well, as much as anyone can. When I get Out, it's going to be for good. I meant what I wrote you last time."

She nodded because she had memorized everything he wrote: I'm going to be a son my father can be proud of. You'll be proud of me, too. Of course he couldn't be expected to say a thing like that out loud. Not here in this place, where it would be met by a chorus of jeers.

She searched her mind for the right thing to say. Every word was so precious today. "In your last letter, you said you were getting out real soon."

"Well, maybe." He shifted. When he jerked his eyes in the guard's direction, she felt such a fool. She should have known. Of course the guards could lip-read. Locking her hands between her knees, she leaned in even closer until their reflections collided in the streaky glass.

"My parole review's coming up in November," he volunteered.

"That's good, right?"

"If I get paroled. But that's a big If. I can't say I'm looking forward to my parole review."

"Things will go better this time. They will. It's not like you're a shit disturber anymore. You're what, one of those 'solids'?"

"Sure, it's just like I told you, I'm a good boy. But that's when hard time begins. When you're just about out."

A chill passed through her.

"If you're a quick change artist, it's okay. Except sometimes it comes back to you, how fucking stupid you've been. You want everything right now, and you don't care how you get it."

"Hey, are we talking about you or some other guys?"

He shrugged. "Other guys, I guess."

Almost sagging in relief, Liza smiled again. "Do you miss things as much as you did when you first came in?"

"Not as much. You can't or you'll go crazy."

"What things do you miss most?" she stammered, surreptitiously glancing at her watch. Oh God, visitation was almost over. And here she was behaving like a stranger at some stupid social tea. What's your horoscope? Are you anything like me? She'd already asked about that stuff in her letters anyway. That was when they had all the time in the world and everything was going to be all right.

I'm a Gemini like you, he'd written back. He was good at chitchat when he wanted to be. A quick-minded, dual personality, easily bored. Of course a girl like you craves excitement. I do, too.

Although she was careful not to touch it, she leaned even closer to the glass divider, hoping to recapture their initial intimacy. And it worked. Extracting a loose Export `A' from his shirt pocket, his smile widened and he let her in.

"What do I miss most? Well, talking to a normal person like you, little darling. Although sometimes when you get a visitor, you feel like such a goddamn jerk. Because there's no way you deserve such ... kindness. There's gotta be a reason you're doing time with a bunch of losers, right? And you get scared when somebody comes to visit that you won't even remember how to talk. Hey, don't look like that. You know I don't feel that way with you. Look, just stop me if it sounds like I'm feeling sorry for myself. I'm on a real roll today. Because you ... But that's why I liked writing letters to you, I had lots of time to think about what I wanted to say. In a letter you have a world of time to make things right."

A world of time. That's what we need, she thought, wanting to be the smoke he sucked into his lungs. "Well, you're talking today. But what makes you think I'm normal?" she teased.

"You gotta be, darling. You're on the right side of this glass." Dace was doing nothing more than pointing at the divider, but his overseer still looked alarmed. "Okay, now. That's enough about me. Now you. You're a bird in flight all the way from Dublin. A clever little college girl."

"Oh, well. You know." Liza sat up straighter and smiled brightly, although her unsupported lower back had already started to ache. "I was allowed back to go to university after being in exile just like you. It was actually a toss-up between Dublin and you."

"Really?"

"I got ... I wasn't going to, but somehow I got attached to the place. Did you know there are no monarch butterflies in Ireland? And Trinity, I wanted to go to Trinity but I wanted to come back to my home, too. Besides, I was never going to belong in Dublin unless I had goddamn children or something." Yes, a baby. Right. She stopped, reluctant to go on. What would he think of her, if he knew?

He mimed astonishment, his eyebrows riding right up into his hair. "Ah now, little Liza, you were always such a lady in your letters. I had no idea you ever swore! What else don't I know about you?" he teased. "And there I was, always in such a sweat to clean my letters up for you. I can't tell you how good you've just made me feel. So you got back Tuesday last? Who met you?"

"Well, nobody. I didn't tell anybody I was coming home except you. I don't know. Um, Gran, I had sort of made a bargain with the old dear. Oh, don't look at me like that. Trust me, she was glad to get rid of me. She's getting old, you know. She's like sixty-five or something. So I went ahead, making one plan at a time, like applying to Maitland University. I didn't expect to be accepted. Boohoo, it looked like nothing was ever going to work for me. But then boom! I was on my way home. Gran paid my way back and I had nothing left to lose, sort of. Then there was you."

Dace was starting to look puzzled. *Oh God,* she thought, almost halting. *Keep talking. Don't stop now.* She chattered some more, feeling like a complete fool.

"You should have told everyone that you were accepted at the U!" he interrupted. "You've got to tell your parents, Liza. Don't you want to see them? I know they've had their troubles, but, well, your Mom was in the hospital for a while, wasn't she? And go see my Dad, too. They'll be so happy to have you back. A grown girl. They'll be so proud of you, little darling. The first person in our family to go to university."

"Oh, our family doesn't dream so big." She snorted. "As long as we're all respectable. The Devereuxes used to be such big shots in Wexford, don't you know." Tapping her memory for the family history, she recapped some of their story, her mouth pulled into a grimace, although the Devereux story was common enough. Like Steinbeck's family in *East of Eden* and half the Irish, they had been almost kings in Wexford, Ireland at one point, but then ...

"Ah, c'mon. You're respectable enough for both of us." Dace laughed, not caring how far the Devereuxes had fallen or even if he'd helped them in their downward spiral. "Your accent. I could listen to it all day. All you have to do is talk and you sound so educated, so respectable."

"But I'm not ..."

...respectable, she almost confessed. She couldn't help it, she was definitely jet-lagged, because her eyes filled with tears for the second time that day. Except now she had an audience. Dace glanced to either side of him then back at her. She nearly laughed in spite of herself. Here he was, a prisoner, and like most of the men she'd encountered, he was attracted to a soft-hearted woman but embarrassed by emotional displays.

"Educated or respectable. Maybe I can still be both," she confided.

He stared into her eyes, a quizzical smile on his face, oblivious that his cigarette had burnt down to his brown, calloused fingertips. "C'mon, Liza," he urged. "You've danced around some problem in your letters for two years now. Open up and let me in. There's nothing you can say that would upset me. Hey, look at me. Look where I am. There's nothing so terrible you could have done. What's wrong, darling?"

Open up and let me in. She was almost undone hearing him say what he had only been able to write for the past couple of years. She couldn't open up here, though. Liza, people had told her for years, don't tell. Stupid, stupid to tell him, or anybody else, about Tony. What would he think? She'd had a choice, hadn't she? Well, sort of.

"I'm sorry. I can't believe I'm doing this, upsetting you in prison," she blurted. She blinked her eyes dry and lowered her gaze, unable to look at him again.

She couldn't unload her problems on somebody incarcerated in a federal penitentiary, no matter how much she ached to feel cherished and protected and uncensored. He couldn't help her where he was. He couldn't even help himself. Not now, anyway. But he would. He'd take care of it all when his fate, like hers, was no longer in somebody else's hands.

Are you the captain of your fate? he used to ask if she so much as hinted how much her life had spiralled out of control. As if he were. As if anybody were. For the love of God, even butterflies weren't free to do as they pleased.

A dirge had started playing in her head and no wonder. For the umpteenth time, Liza wished her feelings of dread would evaporate like Dace's apparently had. Strange what a few years in prison could do. Surely he still felt guilty, though, about a man dying, no matter what kind of bastard the victim had been. And about his own family. The trouble he'd caused. She would have. She did. What had he said about his father? Oh Christ, what if she forgot something he'd said? She should have smuggled in a tape recorder. Yeah, well, fat chance. They were too big for a pocket. She couldn't afford one anyway.

"Someone's always crying here. It's okay," Dace lied.

"You've got your own problems," she insisted. In one crazy moment she imagined hiring a helicopter and spiriting him away. Way to go, Liza, she chided herself as she snapped back to reality under his stare. It was a good thing men tended to be so focussed.

She took a deep breath, hoping she sounded more informed and confident than she felt. "Your big problem is getting out of prison," she coached. "Any way you can. For good. Your letters, oh, you write such beautiful letters, Dace. You don't belong here, you know. These other guys here, aren't they all supposed to come from bad homes? Poor homes? Nothing like you. And I want to help you stay out, too. Recid ... recidivism? Recidivism is supposed to be about 70%. I've already started reading my Sociology text so I can get ahead. I can be your outside contact, you know. Well, one of your contacts, anyway."

He laughed, apparently relieved she had regained her self-control. Well, of course he was. He didn't want people thinking he'd made a little girl cry. He took a drag on another cigarette.

"Well, sure, darling. You're right. After all, look at me. I'm no position to rescue a little damsel in distress."

"Just don't get used to living here. Isn't that what happens when people get institutionalized?" she asked and promptly shrivelled inside. What if he told her to mind her own business and stalked off ... to what? What was behind those locked doors? What didn't they want outsiders to see?

And Dace *was* annoyed. One short visit and she could already read his masked face. If he'd stood up and shouted, I've heard all this shit before, she wouldn't have been surprised.

"I'm doing hard time," he said. "I'm not getting used to anything. At night I wake up busting to shed my own skin."

"Oh, I know what that feels like, too! You can't breathe, you think you're dying and there's no one," she chattered on, trying to appease him until —

"Time's up, Devereux," announced the fat guard who had snuck up behind him.

Liza blinked at Dace. He was prepared, but for her the reinforced glass divider had almost melted away. Then she noticed the black stick the officer carried, in addition to his revolver, and jumped off her stool so fast she had to steady herself by grabbing its swivelling base. The guard's "Get movin'," was superfluous. There was no time to say for her to say anything else to Dace.

"Goodbye, Cousin," he said and smiled. He rose in a single fluid motion and walked away.

Caught off guard, Liza stayed put, watching his back. How could he? she wondered.

She was a frightened girl watching her lover head off to war. But Dace was no soldier. He was more like an actor exiting his private stage, an Academy winning virtuoso, or maybe just a man a little too expert at hiding his emotions. For his own protection, any regrets he had about leaving her were well concealed, his face its usual mask. She might as well go. He would never look back, no matter how much she hoped and prayed for one last glimpse.

She had ceased to exist. Her bit part was over. When she turned to leave she noticed the visiting room clock was not quite on the hour. The fat old guard, who Dace later told her was named Savage, had cheated them of precious time.

Don't leave me! she nearly screamed, but to what purpose? She was much too old, too experienced, too wise, to make a fool of herself over a man again. If there were a reason for everything, that was the reason for Tony Harper, the lesson he had been. He made a fool of you! Gran had wailed. Among other things.

So here she was, controlling herself so Dace could walk away scot-free. Scot-free. What did that even mean? She almost hated Dace in that instant, then it was gone. He was like nobody else she'd ever known. How could he be like any other man when he'd written her eighty-three beautiful letters? She let him under her skin. *Hey Jude* … She wasn't going to be able to lose him. It was too late. It had always been too late. She couldn't shed him even if she tried.

Chapter Seven

Terrible Lies
Maitland University, August 26, 1971

My love came up from Barnegat,
The sea was in his eyes;
He trod as softly as a cat
And told me terrible lies.
—Wylie, Elinor, "The Puritan's Ballad"

Exalted and elated, she floated in a bubble back to her new home on campus. Her fellow bus passengers looked beat up, washed out, down, as if they had just returned from a long trip. They stared at her, envious of the glow in her eyes. Maybe they were numbed by the intense emotions they'd experienced in the prison visiting room. For Liza, it had been her first visit, her first opportunity to talk to Dace in five years, and she throbbed with joy.

Everything was going to be all right. My darling, my life, a little voice inside her sang. Any fool could see he was in a bad place: the Big House, the can, the clink, the cooler, the coop, the hoosegow, the joint, the jug, the pokey, the slammer, the stir. But when he got out, their lives would unfold again, like a clandestine script she'd written. She was author cum protagonist cum minor character in her own story, a person determined to chart her own life. Maybe she could yank him back from his private hell too.

What does anybody know about either one of us? He's gone to jail and I've gone to university, both anomalous events in our working-class families, she wrote in her journal, the one she made sure nobody ever found.

For that matter, what did she know? Maybe the family had been right to insist he was just 'away.' Maybe it didn't matter what had happened or why it happened as long as he got back on track. They both had to get back on track while they were still young, while they still had a chance. While time was on their side. Because in a perfect world nobody should be limited by stupid choices they made when they were less than eighteen.

Her euphoria was as short-lived as her bus ride. For Liza it was always like this: a dazzling high, a precipitous low. She deflated at the entrance to the university as the sun began to set over the gates. *I've been home three days and I'm not even sure how I got here*, she thought as she squeezed through the rear accordion doors of the bus. She was relieved to feel her feet touching solid ground. She followed the long winding road, past the closed limestone buildings, to the newer residences at the back where the campus was dark and green. The air was pungent with freshly cut grass and carried just the slightest whiff of decaying leaves. Almost too tired to walk, she fought an overwhelming urge to throw herself face down onto the lawn and inhale the cool grass. Somewhere in the back of her mind came the thought of dying, of oblivion, of the big sleep.

A solitary monarch butterfly drifted by her, caught on a southern breeze.

When she reached the ninth floor of her student residence, she looked back out the panoramic windows in the elevator lobby, seeing the green ravine below. In the dusk, the ravine was spread out like an invitation, like a pair of girl's legs. A gully begging, Come to me!

Dusk. Dregs. She always did this when she got tired. Fell into one of those in-between places. Trouble, getting in trouble.

Words evoked pictures in her mind and the word 'trouble' bothered her. She and Dace had both been in trouble. What did that say about them? At least she could escape, as long as she stuffed the cracks where memory seeped in. She had all the imagination she needed, plus she was in a good place. It would be even easier when the residence was full, crammed with other lives. With her life. Especially if her courses were compelling, if her professors were charismatic, if her social life were distracting, if she made just one good friend.

If, if, if. Right now she would have settled for a female confidante, but she had about as much chance of meeting one as she did of eating a home-cooked meal. By special permission, she was marooned in an almost empty residence with the capacity for six hundred students. Frosh Week didn't start for three days, if it started at all. Somebody had plastered the campus with posters, warning young women not to walk alone or they'd get what they were asking for, what they deserved. The posters hinted about a rapist or rapists stalking the green ravine, driven to desperate deeds by co-eds anxious to throw their lives away.

Damn, she thought, entering the bedroom wing to her right. Somebody had been there. A single letter with New York postage was propped on a side table, so she couldn't miss her name: *Miss Elizabeth Lavinia Devereux.* The envelope hadn't been there this morning. She took a step closer, puzzled by an atavistic wave of fear. Then she recognized the cultivated Gothic script, the self-important loops and swirls and broke out in a cold sweat.

Goddamn it! she exploded, almost dropping her bag. Tony Harper. Dear God. How had he gotten her address? From Granny Magill? Oh, surely not. She'd begged Liza not to correspond with him. For God's sake, have some self-respect! Granny had told the young girl who had squandered her favours.

Ah Gran, she thought, close to tears yet again. Sometimes she felt even more upset by the grief she'd caused the older woman than for what they'd had to do. Even if in the end she'd done what she was told, the only thing she could. Now she must never tell anybody what had happened. Especially not Dace. The fact that she had conceived a child with an irresponsible man.

Tell me you love me, he used to say, the first time after he just took what he wanted. What was wrong with her? Why did she stay? Why had it taken her so long to finally walk away?

Empty as the residence was, she looked over both her shoulders before picking up the air mail envelope and trying to guess its disturbing and perhaps salacious contents. Worse, she felt an unexpected flurry of hope in her chest. *Baby, I'll stay with you,* she remembered wishing he would say. Could she have made another choice? What could she have offered an infant? A faint but impossible whiff of scent issued from the thin, airmail paper. That Brut stuff he used to wear. Suddenly it was too late to retreat to a safe place in her mind. Too late. She'd been late. Another word she hated.

Standing in the hallway, she abandoned all caution, tore open the dirty envelope with her teeth and almost ate his note. Not his letter, but his note. Because that's all it was.

> Your grandmother said you didn't have the baby. Those old ladies usually know what to do. When were you planning to tell me? A pity. Our baby would have been lovely, especially with my blue eyes and maybe your hair. Of course it was your mistake and your choice, but I hope the experience didn't turn you bitter against all men. Especially me. You never did tell me you loved me, but it seemed like you did in the end. But you understood that I had to go to New York. 'Hair!' was a hoot and lots of other good parts have come my way since then. It was by far the best decision for me. It's safer for me here, too. New York girls know how to take care of themselves, if you know what I mean.
> Good-bye, Love. Good-bye for now.

She stared at the letter, disbelieving, then read it over again. *If you know what I mean.* Thank God no one else was around, or she just might have spilled her guts like the stupid blonde on the bus had. Tossing her bag and the letter onto the nearest bed inside her room, reality hit her like a slap. Her cousin wasn't safe in an ancient prison. She wasn't safe in a brand new student residence. But Tony was safe. Safe from entrapment and safe enough to send her a self-serving missive. Why had he even bothered to write? Did he have a few days between auditions and a stamp to spare?

She went over the note in her mind, searching in vain for some illumination between the lines, some way she could rewrite what had happened. *I just hope you haven't turned bitter against all men. Especially me.* Ah, Tony. Handsome, handsome Tony with his laughing blue eyes and endearing Manchester accent. As if being disillusioned by him was the worst thing. Who did he think he was? Did he have any idea what it was like for her to feel so ashamed of her own acquiescence in her predicament and so betrayed by her own body? Those feelings implied choices she'd never had, for she had been doomed from the moment he'd found her at sixteen. Any fool could have predicted what would happen to an isolated young girl primed to fall in love.

How powerful he must have felt. Well, he'd always had an inflated opinion of himself, blessed as he was with the conventional good looks of an American soap opera star, but then again, actors need a lot of confidence. And she'd loved that self-confidence, the knowing little twinkle in his eyes and his sardonic smile. Everyone was drawn to him: a beautiful blond man with blue eyes, although he had helped the blond along a bit. The only mystery was why he'd wanted her. She was just a dark little thing, far from beautiful.

Eventually she laid down and tried to sleep, to forget this unwelcome intrusion from the past, but she couldn't. Rising from the bed, she glanced around the room, her face shrouded by her heavy hair. She went over to her window but there was nobody outside, not even a stray dog by the stream. She imagined her hair floating on the water, a flower in her hand. *Call me mad Ophelia*, she thought.

Forget, everybody had said. Everybody who had known, that is. *Forget. It's for the best.*

But how? She resolutely pulled a metal wastepaper basket out from under her built-in desk, lit a match and deposited Tony's flaming missive inside. Not that he would write again if she failed to reply. Proud. He'd been so proud. But what if her own resolve crumbled and she wrote to him? Loneliness did strange things to people. Look at what it had done to her in Ireland. By now she was so furious with herself she couldn't even cry. The onion skin paper crackled into flames and settled into a gratifying ash, but Tony was still there, still laughing, a little ruefully perhaps, his own life not destroyed. Christ, it made her mad.

Suddenly she remembered the black and white studio portrait she had pressed flat under her new student mattress. Tony had given it to her just before he'd left. Why in God's name had she held onto his headshot for so long? She rescued it from oblivion and stared at it for a second, then tossed it into her impromptu fire.

The orange and blue flames licked his smug face as she watched, and she wondered if he were performing on Broadway yet. Probably not. He would have said. He'd wanted to be an actor since he was a kid, but his family had been too poor to pave the way. They'd had that much in common: their families never could have wasted money on dreams. *I'm going to be somebody,* she heard him say as his blue eyes played to an invisible audience. But he was almost too old even then, especially for film.

Why am I always drawn to the exciting and the unusual? she mused. She tugged back a thin beige spread on her bed and slipped, fully dressed, between the sheets. Because if Tony, or somebody like him, walked into the residence right now, she would be powerless to resist him, give or take an hour or two. Maybe even less. Sure, she was older and wiser now, but somewhere inside her the dreamy girl she'd always been still lurked.

Damn. The waste paper basket was still smoking. Getting up again, she poured stale water from her toothbrush glass onto the stinking remnants before curling into a ball with both hands tucked under her pillow. The room was tight, crowded already. It was bound to feel even smaller when her roommate arrived — a farm girl, she'd heard. An orange padded desk chair was so close to her face she could touch it.

Liza sunk into the mattress, feeling utterly drained. Thoughts of the prison, of Dace, then of Tony and his carefree life and the choice she and her grandmother had to make, mingled in her mind. Exhausted, she gave in and cried for the man who had left her and the one she had left today.

So good-looking. Why did they both have to be so good-looking? It made everything so much harder. Her mother used to say looks were wasted on men. Liza had to agree. This when her twin brothers were still rather cute and she, well… It wasn't fair. And both the men haunting her were so goddamn hungry for their misspent youths: Tony because he feared growing old, Dace because he'd never been young.

Dace. He must be crashing. Worse than she was. What was he thinking about right now? Liza felt almost guilty, knowing that whatever she'd done, she was the lucky one. She still had everything to look forward to, but his life was awful. He'd looked so sad. Prisoners were supposed to feel sad, though. If they didn't, they'd just keep going back to prison, to what they already knew. Maybe he was thinking about what had happened to land him there.

Yes, prisoners had to suffer, but not just because they had committed unspeakable crimes. They had to suffer because they were stupid enough to get caught in the first place.

Tony had said the same thing to her. *I don't care what I told you. You were stupid to get caught.*

Chapter Eight

A Rock Feels No Pain
Maitland Penitentiary, August 26, 1971

More and more teenagers, especially males, are
committing violent acts. Various studies indicate
that being a victim of violence is the strongest
predictor of violent behaviour in male teenagers.
The question surrounding these findings is whether
the correlation between victimization and violence
stems from lifestyles or whether exposure to violence
makes teenagers respond to certain situations in a
violent manner.
—J. McCall, F.S. Turner & T.D. Smits, "Early Risk Factors for
Violent Behaviour in Adolescent Males," *Journal of Adolescent
Behaviour*

A rock feels no pain.
Liza had really gotten to him. What a jackass he was to
have let her come. She didn't belong in a place like this.

And now that he'd seen her, it was too late. He had to
see her again. She was like him. She was trying to forget
something too.

Memories are useless, he'd felt like telling her. Especially in
here.

He'd seen it before, people who went crazy because they
couldn't move on. So why had he gotten trapped at seventeen? *A*

rock feels no pain. What kind of garbage was that? Folk music was all right, but not Simon and Garfunkel. Give him the Rolling Stones or even that skinny little guitarist, Bob Dylan. Somebody with more bite.

Diving face down onto his cot, he tried thinking about something else, but it didn't work. It never did, not on the Sundays they spent in their cells. Everybody else on his tier would be napping except for the old bastard in Cellblock C, who cleared phlegm in his throat all day, every day. Dace turned his head to the side and stared at an ant picking its way across the wall. Just one. Where were the rest his busy little friends?

Sure, Dace knew he'd killed somebody. He understood that was how he'd ended up here. But what he didn't understand was how everything else: the fear and self-loathing, the horror he felt about the dead, the look on his father's face, all of it had been lost to him for years. Then Liza had appeared. She made him think about these things again. She thought she knew everything — she'd read the newspaper, she said. But she didn't. No one did. And for as long he could help it, no one would.

He'd heard worse stories in here, but on days like this, on days when he saw nothing but ants and heard nothing but a pig clearing his throat, his own story came back to him. His and Rick's.

...they were sixteen and seventeen then, old enough to drink, they thought, but underage by anybody else's standards, so they had gone to the bootlegger's to buy beer. *As if I didn't give you enough,* his old man yelled at him later. His father, who had always wanted to make up for having a dead wife.

The boys had a couple of Harley Sportsters earned from working in his father's shop. They liked to dress up in crisp shirts and chinos and party down by the lake. That's what all the townies did in Maitland in the spring, the moment the university kids left and they could call the place their own. People said Rick and Dace were lucky, lucky to be young and good-looking, and for Dace to have the hardworking Daddy he did. As if they had never been young and lucky themselves.

Alan Turbot, the bootlegger, was a man in his late thirties with a thatch of prematurely greying hair growing around the bald spot on his head. He had a one bedroom apartment, a place with high, ornate plaster ceilings and water-stained walls. The front room, where he conducted his business, was outfitted with a badly cracked, brown vinyl couch, an assortment of mysterious boxes serving as end tables, battered doors leading to a galley kitchen, a bathroom, a boxy bedroom and not much else. The apartment was located in a three storey building in a commercial area on the port side of town.

Turbot had only lived in Maitland a year or two. One day he'd just been there. He'd come out of nowhere, a man with no legitimate employment who was willing to supply kids with beer for their parties. Sometimes he had other goodies, too: cheap cigarettes from the Akwesasne Indian reservation east of Maitland, home-grown marijuana, and stuff on little squares of blotter paper he swore was really good LSD. What a trip, he'd say, twirling his necklace until one day the string broke and wooden beads the size of marbles rolled on the floor.

Alan also had a young boy, Paul, who he treated like a wife. Paul did all the cooking and housekeeping in the apartment, if opening up canned food and picking up stray beer bottle caps counted as housekeeping. To be fair, it was probably hard for him to cook and clean much when he was always strumming his guitar, singing the same mournful lyric over and over...*a rock feels no pain*. Sometimes the bootlegger threw something at him, like a piece of paper or a shoe, anything that was handy.

Or sometimes he went nose to nose with him when he was feeling mean. "Don't you know any Stompin' Tom Connors, kid?" Paul would get busy with the bootlegger's merchandise then, sorting and bagging, presumably for his room and board and all the beer he could drink.

It was hard to imagine Alan and Paul having sex. Dace didn't want to envision that. What did a couple of guys do anyway? Turbot was ugly with a pock-marked face and a beer belly peeking out from under a dirty white Nehru shirt. Paul was a slim, rather good-looking kid of nineteen or twenty, who did what he was told. Maybe drinking helped. God, he hoped so.

Judging by the unfocused looks in both Alan's and Paul's eyes, they were both out of it by 10:00 a.m. on May 10. Or maybe they were just hung over from the night before.

May 10. That date was burned forever in Dace's head.

Alan held out his hand, palm up. "Try some," he coaxed, letting bits of the drug-soaked blotter paper join the beads on the floor.

"Hey," Paul protested, fetching a splayed broom from the corner. "You're wasting good stuff and you're making a mess."

"Don't tell me what to do, you lazy little bitch."

Aw, Jeez. The boys shuffled their feet, uncomfortable at witnessing the domestic scene. It was worse than watching somebody's parents fight. Rick blushed to the roots of his rust red hair. "Look, Ozzie and Harriet, we don't want any," he said. "Just give us the fucking beer."

Alan Turbot pursed his lips and raised his eyebrows like he was thinking. "Don't want to," he slurred, then collapsed onto his couch. Paul tried to help him up, but he slipped on the beads.

For a moment, Dace and Rick just stared, confused. "Why? What's wrong with our money? Ain't it good enough for you?" Rick asked. A wiry, ex-hockey player in the junior league, Rick had no trouble sidestepping the beads.

Alan waved them both away with the back of his hand. "Listen, you little pissers," he said, "I heard what you did to my friend the other night at the bar. Yeah, that's right. Stan's a good friend of mine. One of you busted him good in the chopper. He lost a couple of teeth."

"That old guy?" Rick asked, his hands tightening into fists. "He was bothering a sixteen-year-old girl who was just walking down the street, minding her own business. So Dace and me—"

"Yeah, Jennie from high school. She couldn't talk for crying," Dace added.

Alan laughed and started to heave himself onto his feet again. "Well, the way I hear it, she was asking for it, the cheap little tramp, all dressed up in a mini skirt with her tits hanging out to here."

Dace was pretty sure Jennie had been Rick's first kiss. His stomach heaved, imagining her with such an old geezer, so Rick was probably feeling a helluva lot worse. "That's a fucking lie!" Dace shouted, the full weight of his shoulder knocking Alan back onto the couch. "She wasn't doing nothing."

"Look," Paul said, fiddling with the buttons on his shirt, "why don't you guys just leave? I never should have opened the door."

What the hell, Dace thought. Nobody told him what to do. For one thing, he'd spent too much time with the priests as a boy. For another, he was almost eighteen. Plus, stupid Alan had a job to do and he wasn't doing it. It bugged him when people didn't do what they were supposed to. Pissed him off, actually.

"We want some beer first," he said, sotto voiced.

"Well, you ain't getting any!" Alan roared, rearing up from the couch. His eyes narrowed and he gave Rick a carnal grin. "But maybe if Ricky boy here is real nice to me … I've always fancied a redhead, you know. Oh, sure, you've got reddish hair too, D'Arcy Devereux, but it's a little dark for me. Besides, you're a bit too old. And you're a real big boy. What are you, eighteen, nineteen?" He pulled a face. "Oh, shit, Paulie, I was just fooling. Don't be such a silly little Sheila. Put your toy gun away."

"It's not a toy," Paul said, pouting. He removed the safety on what looked like a little black cap gun. A bb gun maybe. He had probably dressed up as a cowboy last Halloween. Tears quivered on his long lashes. "Look, I t-t-told you guys to g-g-get out," he stammered, unable to steady the gun he waved in the air.

Everybody looked at the gun. Everybody except Alan that is, who kneed Rick in the groin and laughed his head off when Rick doubled over. Oh, he'd got him a good one all right.

"C'mon, Paulie," he grunted. "Don't you want to see if this boy is red all over?"

Dace flew forward, trying to kick Alan in the face, but Rick was in the way, clutching his genitals and making a hideous noise: a cross between a stuck pig and a muzzled woman.

"C'mon. Lemme see," Alan persisted, reaching behind Rick's back and fondling him between his bent legs. "Let go of my arm, Paul. Ah look, stupid. You've gone and dropped the gun. Cool Ass Luke's got it now."

"It's not loaded," Paul bawled, tears streaming down his cheeks, his face in his hands, crying the way only a drunken man can do. "For Christ's sake, Alan, why can't I be enough for you?"

Dace raised the gun and pointed it at the wall behind Alan's head. He couldn't remember the last time he'd played cowboys and Indians and he didn't want to now. He didn't put the gun down, though. He stuck his forefinger through the trigger instead. For a toy, it was a nice fit.

"Are you sure it's not loaded?" he asked, playing for time. With his free hand, he grabbed the back of Rick's shirt, trying to pull him towards the apartment door. One thing for sure, he was passing on the beer.

Rick couldn't move. Or maybe he just wouldn't. His throat pulsed and there was a dangerous gleam in his pale green eyes. If looks could kill, Dace thought.

"C'mon, Rick, let's go," he insisted, but Alan made a second drunken lunge and something popped.

"What the fuck?" Dace exclaimed, staring at the gun in his hand.

"It fired!" Rick crowed.

At first, everything was okay. Alan laughed, holding his left hand over his chest. Even when he slid to the floor in slow motion it looked like he was acting, and doing a pretty poor job at that. Dace stepped back, reluctant to dirty his new clothes.

"Get up," he spat at Alan, his voice choked with contempt. The gun clattered to the floor.

"Blood!" Paul screamed as he ran around the small, cluttered room, his hands fluttering in the air.

Dace forced his eyes down to the floor. Something red was seeping out of Alan's shoulder, but other than that he looked no worse than usual. The genial grin of a drunkard was still plastered on his face. Dace's stomach lurched the same way it had when he'd seen a little tiger cat get flattened by a car.

Jesus, they couldn't just stand around here all day. "Let's go, man!" he shouted. He had never given any thought to neighbours before, but he did now. My God, what if somebody had heard the gun? "Let them take care of this. We gotta get out of this place."

In his haste to unlatch the door behind him, he stumbled over the short landing and fell downstairs into an assortment of rubber boots and galoshes in the entrance.

He had to get some air or he'd puke. A cool breeze blew through the open front door and up the stairs. They should have been carrying a case of beer out right now, but all he could think about was getting away. Why the hell had they come here anyway? Racing down some cement steps two at a time, he looked back over his shoulder. What the hell was Rick doing? Giving Turbot an extra lick or two? Although he might lack the older man's size, at least Rick was sober.

As he ran, he thought he heard Alan say, "It feels good," so maybe it was all right. But then Paul really started keening and a valve shut off in Dace's ears. Oh God. He had to get the hell out of there before somebody heard.

Panicking as he burst onto the busy street, he almost forgot where he'd parked his bike. Then he spotted it in the laneway between the old brewery buildings, its chrome parts shining in the weak spring sun. Rick's bike was beside his, looking like it always did, like nothing could possibly have gone wrong. Goddamn it. What was keeping Rick? He stared hard at the building, then back at his bike. Nothing—not even a girl with her clothes off—had ever looked so good as that bike did just now.

"Rick!" he screamed at the apartment building, no longer caring who the fuck heard. A woman passing by glanced at him curiously. Where the hell was Rick? This was no time to take a leak. They had to get out of here, they had to! Wait. Was that a siren? An ambulance might beat the police if Paul had called, but he couldn't take the chance.

"Rick!" he yelled again before he jumped on his bike and kicked the stand free. He turned the key he'd left in the ignition because they hadn't planned to be gone long, and coaxed his darling, his baby to life. The roar of the bike cut out Rick's and Paul's screams.

It was a couple of weeks before he found out Rick had tried to staunch the open wound in the dirty fucker's shoulder with his bare hands, promising him, "You die and get us into trouble and I'll kill you all over."

Although Turbot didn't die from the bullet, his heart, already damaged by alcohol, was shocked into slowing down. When he realized what was going on, Rick had wanted to get help, but Paul, silly little Paul, kept sobbing into his hands, "It's all right! It's all right! It's all right!" Alan didn't want to call an ambulance either, probably because too many drugs were stashed in his rooms. He must have known something was up though, for he sent his boy lover for a glass of water just before he died on the floor. A week later he was identified as a drifter who had drowned his past in a river of booze.

"He would have survived if we'd called an ambulance," Rick said when they met up in court. The police had located Dace in Timmins. Although Rick had spent the past two weeks in local custody and Dace had been on the run, they were both dirty and dishevelled, their eyes blank, their hands cuffed behind their backs. The courtroom was filling with friends and relatives, neighbours and schoolmates, Rick's blank-faced mother, Dace's stone-faced Dad.

They had fifteen seconds, maybe ten.

"The lawyer says to act like I care that he's dead," Rick said, adding with a sidelong glance, "But I don't. He should be dead. He ..."

"I know, I know. But I'm the one..."

"Ah, c'mon. Don't wimp out on me! You did a public service, you know you did! Guys like him don't deserve to live."

Dace's throat tightened. Maybe. But what did he really know about Turbot except that he got into a blind rage one day and that he liked young boys? Strange, he thought, how everybody's a good guy when they're dead. "My father said you tried to help him, stop the bleeding ..."

Rick shuddered and looked down at his hands. "The only reason I tried to help him was because I was scared. I was scared we'd end up here and people would find out. He didn't touch me there, you know. I know it looked like that, but it's not like it seemed. You know guys in the locker room. Stuff like that happens all the time. Aw, Jesus, here's Jennie and my Mom. Don't tell, don't tell, Dace."

Their cuffs were unlocked and their keepers stepped back. "I won't," Dace whispered out of the side of his mouth. Rick was right. There was no point in telling what the bootlegger had done. All their friends were in the courtroom. Besides, what good would it do? Dead was dead.

Both Dace's and Rick's families came to court, but nobody showed up for the victim. Somebody said Paul, a young man from Cape Breton, had gone light in the head. Rick's mother thought that was really sad. The Judge more or less added that the victim was a worthless son-of-a-bitch, but a man just the same.

The jury called it manslaughter and Dace was paying the price, the one exacted by the legal system anyway. And life in prison was okay as long as he got some peace and quiet and didn't think too much. *As in*, he had to stop asking himself *what if?*

What if he had stayed at home in his room, listening to records. *Hiding in my room, safe within my womb/I touch no one and no one touches me.*

What if he hadn't taken Rick to the bootlegger's? It had been his idea, his fault.

Or what if they hadn't liked beer? Oh, sure. Everybody liked a good buzz. Everybody in Maitland, anyway.

What if the gun had been a toy? Or not loaded? Or not there at all?

And for the love of Christ, what if Dace had gone for help instead of running away? One thing was certain: a real man wouldn't have left his friend behind.

If he could just make it up to Rick.

Chapter Nine
Love the One You're With
Maitland University, September 1, 1971

There were never any pictures of Liza on campus, of the girl she was or the woman she hoped to become. But even then she knew how memories ended up layered under fresher ones or got buried in the avalanche of the past.

There were no photos of D'Arcy Devereux with his prison eyes, either. He never once set foot on campus.

But everything was young and green in September as the class of '75 blended into an exquisite cauldron of anxiety and hope.

Frosh Week was underway. First Years climbed sloping lawns to grey stone buildings draped in English ivy, while older students met in the cafeterias, smoked cigarettes, ate chips or dallied over coffee. Some Second Years were in the midst of bitter break-ups or were even more uncertain about their future plans than they had been the previous year, but they flaunted the self-confidence of people who knew their way around campus.

Liza had been billeted in a brand new high rise, girls on the right side of building, boys on the left, a state of affairs that would prevail for one more year, before the housemothers and the university authorities bowed to the liberalism of the seventies. Elevators provided a natural split between the sexes in

1971. Most of the whitewashed, cinder block rooms were doubles, equipped with beige covered single beds, built-in desks with bookshelves and goose necked lamps, two orange padded chairs, a large shared dresser and a walk-in closet with more space than Liza or most girls could fill. Smoking was permitted. The ashtrays and the trash were emptied twice a week by non-English speaking maids who scorned the privileged inmates, especially the careless girls. The maids also cleaned the rooms once a week and changed the linen, reporting any damage or suspicious behaviour to the housemother, a graduate student with her own room at the entrance to the main hall.

Liza's shared room overlooked the courtyard and the student parking lot. The rooms on the other side backed onto a married student residence, and two single rooms at one end of the hall faced a stream. Each floor had two communal bathrooms, a small study room, a kitchenette, a laundry and a public phone. There was also a student lounge on every third floor, but not on hers.

She had learned about Frosh Week from novels, and judging by the behaviour of the Second Years at Maitland University, she hadn't been too badly informed. The organizers had good intentions and would have oriented the First Year students to college life if they hadn't dissolved into a drunken, giddy rabble within a matter of hours. After sacrificing half their summers to get back to university for the social event of the year, they couldn't afford to waste any time. Most of the organizers were blonde girls with long, slim legs who wanted an engagement ring on their left hand before they graduated, or else they were well-fed, handsome boys who had played on the football team last year and won. Supremely self-confident, they didn't mind wearing homemade hats with coloured streamers, flogging monstrous paper clubs and screaming orders through cardboard cones.

The whole event might have collapsed if the new students had announced in unison: We don't want to play. But of course they didn't. Pressed to explain their complicity, they would have shrugged, acknowledged that they wanted to be accepted, they wanted to belong and besides ... this was fun, wasn't it?

The whole thing made Liza feel a little gypped, not to mention old and silly. University was supposed to be more academic. Never had she expected to feel nervous of students just slightly older than herself.

Didn't anybody here read? Surely people had heard about the landmark Stanford University experiment where twenty-four students were randomly assigned to be either prison guards or prisoners for two weeks. The experiment had come to a screeching halt when the pretend guards turned swaggering and sadistic. Even Liza, an expatriate in Dublin, had come across references to the American study.

The study had focussed on the behaviour of students assigned to be guards, but what about the victims? Maybe it was an experiment, but the study showed the victims had willingly co-operated with the bullies. And here she was in Maitland, watching the experiment in action. She saw one student, a heavier girl with greenish-blonde, seaweed hair and granny glasses, get down on the floor of the common room and actually lick an older resident's shoes.

Liza squirmed but didn't say anything. She knew from previous school experiences that the girl wouldn't be grateful for her interference. So she headed back to her room, relieved to walk away, to remain on the periphery. Did Dace do this too? Was this how he survived? It was okay for her. She was an outsider, not that she minded. She was used to it. They had called her the American when she lived in Dublin, no matter how many times she said she was Canadian.

She couldn't stay in her room a moment longer. It felt close and fetid, although there was a fresh coat of paint on the walls and the furniture was almost brand new. There had to be something she could do outside, but what? Drifting over to the aluminium framed window, she stared into the courtyard for inspiration and inhaled the humid evening air. A couple of disc jockeys were setting up audio equipment for a heavily promoted street dance, snaking thick black cables behind a wooden platform. She might have resisted the temptation except the outside air felt so soft on her skin and she could hear music. Just a few bars from a loudspeaker and her body wanted to dance. Before she knew it she was downstairs, dressed in the same blue jeans as everybody else.

Love the one you're with! was blasting from the loudspeakers when she came into the courtyard. Confronted by the ruddy and triumphant faces of the Frosh Social Committee, she almost turned on her heels and ran. Good grief. Betrayed by a song. Everybody had to go to a rally before the dance started, the older students announced through their toy megaphones, their eyes sly. The First Years, all shapes and sizes, gave a collective groan, but merged into alphabetical surname order without any more protest, decked out with their name tags. Everybody except her. Oh, she was such a renegade, she thought. Her tag was upstairs on her bed. She considered leaving, pretending to fetch her badge and never coming back, but there was nothing else to do. Scanning a couple of names near the beginning of the line, she slid in between two girls, a Campbell and an Ensley.

A rally for what? she wondered as she was swept along in the crowd to Alumni Hall, running to keep up. She was afraid of being crushed. The Hall was only a few blocks away, but she was crossing unfamiliar terrain. The plaintive notes of Crosby, Stills and Nash faded.

Coaching their unruly marching band to sing the school song, the Committee appeared to be taking their job as seriously as they could.

Meds we're tops! The words didn't make any sense, though. Written in the nineteen thirties by a drunken student, the song had never been edited by anyone in either the English or the Music Faculty.

When they reached Alumni Hall, the Committee flogged everyone onstage with their mock clubs. The co-eds squealed as strong-armed young men reached down and pulled them up, and the upper class men applauded.

The First Years were no longer in alphabetical order, but nobody cared as long as they sang. *We're tops! Rah! Rah! Our colours green and orange...* Ireland's colours, but what the hell did the lyrics mean? Liza was diverted by the stranger beside her, the boy who had given her a hand up onto the stage. Stuart Melville, Trenton, Ontario, she read on his chest.

"I'm Mel," he said.

He *was* cute. He had shoulder length hair, granny glasses and a tie-dyed shirt, probably purchased for the occasion, but that was the extent of his co-operation. She pegged him as a clownish middle child or perhaps the much loved baby of his family — whatever she was not. He had no qualms about altering the words to a beloved school song in an effort to entertain the girls standing on either side of him. Oblivious to Liza's reluctance to sing for fear her Irish accent would single her out, he sang loudly enough to satisfy even the most zealous Committee member. He still held her hand as she pulled farther back into the crowd, praying for the whole ordeal to be over. She had never liked standing and she enjoyed making a public spectacle of herself even less.

Finally, to her immense relief, the Committee threw up their hands. "What a bunch of dorks," she overheard the blondest girl complain as her makeshift choir jumped offstage and bolted through a series of double auditorium doors. "Look at 'em. No fucking school spirit at all."

Trooping out of Alumni Hall, she felt quite content to have ended up with Mel. The girl on his right had been snagged by her hometown friends and walked off with barely a wave. Music was playing again when they got back to the residence, so they danced in the darkening street.

It wasn't long before he said, "Let's go upstairs."

Maybe she looked alarmed, because he hastened to assure her that he just wanted to sleep, although he still held her hand. He hadn't slept for a couple of days, he said. It turned out they were both on the ninth floor. As they touched hands and parted at the elevator, he promised to call the next morning. Good, because she couldn't call him. She had never called a boy in her life and she wasn't about to start now. He looked like he wanted to kiss her, but he didn't. *Thank God, she thought, a little unnerved.*

You've got a friend, she hummed to herself, retrieving a bar of white Camay soap and a red towel from her room. She entered the multi-stalled washroom and was surprised to find it empty, but most of the girls were still down at the dance. Too bad. She felt like talking to somebody about the boy she had just met.

Not Dace. She couldn't talk about Dace.

Where the hell was her roommate, anyway? Janice Hughes was so late in arriving that Liza wondered if she even existed, although the housemother had shown her a wallet-sized picture of a sandy-haired girl. Anxious about leaving the farm, Liza supposed.

The shower water was already getting cold. She lunged out of the stall, reaching for her towel. Water ran off her sharp, angled hips to the tiled floor, and she wondered what Janice was like. What if she didn't like the hours she kept? Liza wanted a confidante, but what were the odds of having anything in common with a girl who was most likely a virgin?

Liza had made several friends in Dublin; however, they were the friends born of circumstances rather than the meeting of souls, and those friendships had faded. Her last good girlfriend had been in sixth grade at Alexander Muir Public School in Toronto. She had grown up with Linda Jones, and their relationship had solidified when both sets of parents threatened to divorce.

Stranded on the opposite side of the Atlantic Ocean, Liza had soon lost track of all her friends, even Linda. She still dreamed of her, though. She had to, for it didn't look like she would ever find anybody like her again: a girl with the physical courage to jump off the high tower at the swimming pool and the imagination to transport them both right out of Christie Pits. It had been too long.

She fell asleep rereading *Wuthering Heights*, having remembered to double-lock her door before she lay down. An hour into a good night's sleep, she found herself safe and warm on a tropical island with Mel and Linda and Dace. A balmy breeze blew as they strolled along a sunny beach, but the voices were all wrong. Women's voices—drunken, excited and high-pitched.

Liza's eyes flew open. Clutching the bedding to her throat, she stared at the locked door with her heart pounding in her chest. It was the Committee. They were here, in the dorm, rallying in the narrow hall leading to her room. They were raising their fists to pound on her door. They were busting in.

"Come out, come out!" they carolled, as if on cue. *Oh, sure, and me in my baby dolls,* she thought, holding her breath and doing her best not to move. Stupid! Why on earth had she fallen asleep with her reading lamp on? Gran would have been appalled at her wastefulness. Her father would have roared.

Glancing at the quilted robe lying across the foot of her narrow bed, she considered her options. Maybe she could. No, she couldn't. Not for anyone. She wasn't about to traipse all over the cool green campus dressed in her night clothes. Who did they think she was, wee Willie Winkie? The trip to Alumni Hall and the unaccustomed dance had almost worn her out. She opened her mouth to say something pithy and dismissive, but nothing came out. Better to play dead. She was going to have to write off her dorm mates anyway, especially after today's dinnertime conversation about their daddies' jobs. Besides, she was supposed to be making a fresh start.

Her old friend Linda would have known better. She had been good at reading people and infiltrating the little Italian and Ukrainian cliques in their concrete school yard. She would have figured out that saying, "Oh, my father's a garbage collector," was apt to embarrass people. Embarrass them for her. People didn't enjoy being embarrassed. She should have considered their feelings at least. Better to have announced that her father was an undertaker, a pimp, a postal worker or a minister to these cool, private school educated blondes.

She would have to be more careful when she met her new roommate. The housemother said Janice was from a farm near Guelph, but what did that mean? She probably hailed from a five hundred acre tobacco farm with a huge swimming pool and a crew of swarthy migrant workers who lusted after the farmer's bikini clad daughter in the summertime.

The Committee in the hallway was undeterred. Confident of their prey, they continued hammering on her door. She had to be in there. C'mon. Where else would she go? Liza's lungs ached from holding her breath, but she was committed to silence now. Maybe they'd forget her if she kept real still. Yeah, better a sound sleeper than a poor sport.

"C'mon, Liza," one girl coaxed, trying the personal approach. She remembers my name, Liza thought as her doorknob rattled. Her fists clenched and her toes curled, but her body sagged with relief when she realized they didn't have a key. If they had, they would have been through the door by now, pulling the covers from her cowering body and tossing a robe into her face. She just had to keep the mad dogs at bay for a few minutes longer. But what if the housemother were trussed and gagged in some broom closet? She quite liked the housemother, a plain-faced grad student who could recognize all the residents from the wallet-sized photos they'd submitted with their applications. No. On second thought, she was probably a co-conspirator who had handed over skeleton hall keys to her rebel charges. *You can do as you please, girls. Enjoy your good clean fun.*

Her lungs started to ache, but eventually the girlish voices of the Committee faded down the hall. It was some time before she dared take a good, deep breath. The intruders pounded on another recruit's door down the hall and went through the same routine, this time with more success. Surprised out of sleep or just eager to please, the new target opened her door almost immediately. *What a bunch of silly cows!*

Liza collapsed back on her foam pillow, too excited to go back to sleep. But she had to sleep. How would she survive here if she didn't? What if she didn't understand her courses? Her worries ran on and on, a stream of concerns washing away yet more precious sleep. What if she lost her scholarship and wasted all the blood money Gran had promised to pay until she was back in Ontario long enough to qualify for a student loan?

Stealthily, although stealth was no longer required, she got out of bed, went to a tall dresser and unlocked her assigned drawer. *Genie in a bottle*, she thought, enjoying the scent of the new wood. Everything about Liza lived inside: her Canadian birth certificate, Social Insurance number, and an Irish passport, but there was also a small cardboard child's jewellery box. When she unlocked the box with a minuscule key, a plastic ballerina twirled in time to Edelweiss.

Reassured at seeing an amber prescription bottle of pearly pills and Dace's letters inside the pink, satin-lined box, she locked both the music box and the drawer and lay back down in bed. After angling the gooseneck lamp properly, she continued reading *Wuthering Heights*, a considerable feat now that Dace loomed larger than Heathcliff in her thoughts. For years she had read almost nothing except Byronic literature. The tragic, doomed heroes and heroines practically leapt off the pages at her. She read the same books over and over, always hoping the characters' lives would somehow be made right. In theory, anything was possible in their fictional lives. People lived forever.

"Cathy!" Heathcliff hollered, and Cathy rose from the grave.

"Dace!" Liza hollered, and Dace walked out of jail.

Liza read so much she had even started to write her own novel, in the same vein. The manuscript, a single chapter, was stored safely under her mattress, right beside where Tony's picture had been.

It was just before 1:00 a.m. She read until her eyes ached, then she daydreamed, thinking of the good things in her life. She was back home in Canada, she was in university, and she had made a friend: Mel. Plus he was cute. And Dace was getting out soon, repentant, redeemed and magnificently reformed. When the book slipped from her hands at about 3:00 a.m., it was because the residence was finally quiet and she believed in a wonderful tomorrow.

Dace was getting out. In her fantasy, the Parole Board was very impressed.

Chapter Ten
Rumblings
Maitland Penitentiary, September 3, 1971

In the now defunct Maitland Penitentiary, there was no mess hall. Inmates ate meals in their cells. They also spent two hours most evenings in the recreation hall and provision was made for a half hour exercise period for each inmate each day. It was obvious from a review of this schedule (even prior to the lockdown) that inmates had averaged 16 to 18 hours a day locked in cells.
—Commission of Inquiry into Maitland Penitentiary Riot, April, 1972

There was nothing unusual about that evening. Nothing at all. The new bull, Robert Saksun, didn't count. The prisoners were let out of the recreation hall in groups of ten and led back to their cells. It was Dace's turn now, but this new guy was too fat to walk beside him. The catwalk, built in the early 1800s, had been made for smaller men. Just as well. Dace hated the nasty familiarity of a 'correctional officer' by his side.

He had been in the first shift tonight. He was missing *Kojak*, but he didn't care. Because he'd had a note from Liza. She was coming tomorrow and she was worth ten dumb ass cop shows. What did she have to do on a Sunday in a student residence anyway? Go to church? Read a book? A smart girl like that, she could read on the bus.

From the recreation hall it was a bit of a hike back to Cellblock B. They went up a flight of stairs, through another passage, then around. The catwalk jiggled under his feet. He had so much energy buzzing through him he felt like jumping. *Humpty Dumpty sat on a wall, Humpty Dumpy had a great fall,* he thought.

Saksun was looking a little rattled. "What the fuck's so funny, Dev? Or Deb, is it?" he demanded.

Dace didn't answer right away. The tiers were filling up, so everybody in a two cellblock radius could hear. The guard tried to read the stencilled numbers on Dace's shirt, but the numbers had faded, so he poked him in the ribs with his shiny new billy stick instead.

"My name's D'Arcy," Dace said.

"Deverecs!" the guard laughed.

"D'Arcy James Devereux," he said, as if it mattered.

Another guard and a prisoner squeezed by them. "Yeah, and that's Robert Saksun," he said.

"I asked you a question," Saksun growled. "What's so funny?"

You, Dace thought. "Sorry," he said, bowing a little and sweeping his hand backwards into his cell. "I think you're mistaken, sir. Look at this place. You see anything funny here?"

"Listen up, and wipe that stupid, shit-eating grin off your face or I will," Saksun blustered, his jowls shaking as he talked.

"You look a little too happy for me. You guys are all the same. Give you an inch and you'll take a mile."

"Sure thing, Boss," Dace said, shadow boxing into his cell.

Saksun wasn't finished yet. His mouth worked for a minute before he said, "Uh, that girl who visited you the other day. Liza? Lisa? This guy, um, he'd like to meet her." When he didn't get an answer straight away he added, "Although I wonder about her. What's a college cutie doing with a jailbird like you?"

Dace stared at him. Go on, something inside him said. Pop the fucker on the nose. Saksun reminded him of a gummy-faced pit bull. Saksun's legs, short, stocky and dangling under his large belly, looked like pit bull legs. Fuck you, he thought.

"She's family," he said. "She's got no choice."

Saksun made a retching sound. "Your sister?" he shrieked to the prison population at large, "Now that ain't right."

"She's his cousin, asshole!" somebody responded from a lower tier.

Saksun's eyes darted from side to side, but he tried to hold his ground. "A cousin, eh? I hear she has quite a rack." He rambled on until somehow he ended up against the railing, looking more surprised than scared.

"Hey, Dace, whatya doing there?" Dace's cell neighbour, Grumpy, called. "You know, you gotta move more careful-like. You don't want Biggie toppling over the side."

Dace shrugged. "I just looked at him and he stumbled," he said.

"Hey, fella, I'll swear to that," Grumpy agreed.

Dace looked at Saksun, who had managed to right his bulk and was shifting away from the railing. Head down, he locked the cell door and growled at Grumpy, "Mind your own business, you old fart," before he fled down the hall.

"Hey, Debo," Grumpy said. "You gotta be more careful if you expect to get out of here in three months. You letting that stupid fuck get on your nerves?"

"The only person getting on my nerves is you," Dace grumbled.

Everybody was getting on his nerves, though. Guys had been talking about Liza all week. He'd ignored it at first. She was a pretty girl, and they were desperate men after all. But then the Padre had gotten in on the act.

The Padre was an old-fashioned man. A girl had her place. That girl could be a lifeline for some of these boys, just like she's been for you, he'd said, which would have been bad enough, but then he'd added:

"Tell me something, are you having carnal thoughts? Because your relationship is consanguineous. And I think you know what that means."

Oh, Dace knew what consanguinity meant. He just didn't care. A good Catholic could always get around a little problem like that. Are you sure? he'd felt like saying, Not even if I get a special dispensation? Or ask my Daddy for a nice, big, fat check?

Liza had been a little girl at the farm. She was his cousin and a young girl, a person he wanted to protect. Now ... Her strong, heart-shaped face came to mind. Somebody had already betrayed her. He could see it in her eyes. He wanted to slam the bastard's face into the wall. A sweet-talking Irishman, no doubt. It didn't matter to Dace what she'd done, but he'd get the guy who hurt her.

The past is the past, he always said, even though his own past had a habit of creeping up whenever it damn well pleased. The less people knew the better, but stuff always got out. Revelations could be as random as a chance encounter with an old acquaintance or as connived as a journalistic exposé in his hometown newspaper, but they were never his choice. Maybe some guys enjoyed their notoriety, but not him.

Pulling off the shirt he'd worn for the last three days, he lay on his bed and stared up at the ceiling. Men were settling in for the night, but he didn't hear them. When the prison bell chimed 9:00, he was deaf to that, too.

What good was the past? People didn't learn from their mistakes. Take the administration. Hell, take the Joint's architecture. Although the Auburn model had been questioned and minor changes made to electricity and plumbing, the grand entryway, with its triumphal arch, a cross-shaped cellblock big enough to hold six hundred men and a huge workshop, had defied renovation. Maybe if they blew it up…

Something clattered, sounding like a metal key dropping on a concrete floor. He sat up and listened, but when nothing more happened, he laid back down again.

Liza had once asked if the workshop, which had been transformed by local businessmen into a series of small factories which manufactured furniture, metal goods, shoes and other leather products on slave labour wages, gave prisoners much incentive to reform. She had read about it in the newspaper. She was always reading something, the little nosy parker. Through all her questions, she'd forced him to start looking at the prison through different eyes.

Well, maybe, he'd hedged.

You sound awfully sceptical, she'd written back. What about psychological counselling or rehabilitative programs then? To help people change.

Oh, c'mon. How would that look? All those undeserved luxuries, my dear.

The administrative facilities and the library were housed in the front wing of the main cruciform, and the prisoners were lodged in the rear wings with a domed rotunda linking the four pavilions. They called the area under the domed rotunda, surprise, surprise, the Dome.

Twice daily, inmates trooped through an uncovered exercise yard, heading to a workshop in the rear. Except for a brief yard-out, they spent the remaining fifteen or sixteen hours in oversized pigeon coops on five tiers. The cells were eight feet by six feet by ten feet. Within the cell was a single bed suspended from a chain on the wall, a small two drawer dresser cum desk, a folding chair and a lidless, rusty toilet, fully exposed. A bit tight.

He had almost dozed off when Grumpy started banging on their shared wall. Jesus Christ, if it wasn't the bell ringing sixteen times a day, it was some con telling him the time. Grumpy wanted him to know that courtesy of Administration, the Joint's nightly curtain call was about to begin. A minute passed, then two.

"Here it comes," Grumpy warned him, but even so, the scream was so gut-wrenching his toes curled. The rest of the Joint got silent. It always did.

They were hurting somebody worse than usual. Christ, he hoped it was over soon. "Hey, Grumpy," he shouted above the noise, "What did they say was wrong with that kid? You know, the one in the Yard?"

"I dunno. Some kind of fracture."

Oh, yeah, a spiral fracture. Not good. Do your own trip. Don't get involved, he repeated to himself.

At last the screaming stopped and Grumpy started to snore. People from all over the prison complained about his night time noise, but it was no use. Dace was too wound up to sleep anyway. The guards wouldn't be making rounds for another hour or so. Maybe he'd do some push-ups on the floor.

Everybody was on edge lately. A couple of the guards were okay, but even they had started acting like jerks. The Joint had been in partial lockdown for the past six months, all in preparation for the big move to the new Supermax, just out of town.

In lieu of counting push-ups, Dace listed the Supermax's deficiencies, from the inmate's point of view. No windows, just lights and a minimal staff. A lot of electronic surveillance, though. It sounded like a battery chicken farm, for Chrissakes.

Parole conditions had also gotten tougher, which probably explained why guys were a little more tense than usual. Exercise usually relaxed him, but even after Dace had been doing push-ups for about five minutes, he still felt like banging his head on the floor. So he did more. Besides having a beef about electronic surveillance and a reduction in parole opportunities, the problem was most prisoners just didn't like change. Even if sheer boredom got them in the end.

Maybe if they'd had some preparation. Except that would have required planning, a time costing measure they couldn't afford. The Deputy Warden's post had been vacant for months; the Warden didn't have the staff. Reducing paroles, collapsing work programmes and curtailing classes had eliminated some of the work, but slashing the inmate athletic program was too much.

Dace hated thinking about this stuff, but he couldn't help it. Even some of the front-line guards had objected when they'd cut out sports. The ones still here, that is, and most of them were new. Experienced guards had already been transferred to the new Supermax. Inadequately trained to deal with anxious and competitive men with a variety of complaints and grievances, the remaining guards were even less equipped to warehouse men who now had both the inclination and the unexpended energy to experience guilt and express regret.

And bitch. And whine. Just last night the men in Dace's shift had complained about missing a boxing match. Then the Warden got on the P.A. system and threatened to dam both prison visits and incoming mail while the custodial staff stood around wondering what the hell would happen next.

Deprived of mentally engaging activities, most convicts slept all the time, with a couple of exceptions. Dace was one, and he suspected Sandy McAllister, resident loudmouth, was another. Which was pretty fucking sad. But while old Loony Tunes did God knows what, Dace was busy writing letters to Liza, his father and, God help him, the *Maitland Spectator*. He couldn't do anything else. He was way too close to getting out.

Sometimes he jotted down notes for a book. Liza thought that was a wonderful idea. Well, she would. She pointed out he could have written a book, all the letters he'd sent. Not to mention he had all sorts of ideas and loads of time. He shook his head, snorting at the thought. Surely she knew he wrote by the light in the hall, in between the floor screw's rounds. Well, of course she did, because in her last postscript she'd told him to get more sleep.

Lots of time to sleep in eternity, he scribbled back. Just that much. The next day he sent her a couple of poems and a little skit. She must have gotten about six letters in one day. Anything to avoid the truth. No use in scaring her. Besides, what could she do?

He wanted to write more letters to the *Spectator's* right-wing editor, knee-jerk fascist that he was, or better still to the *Globe and Mail*, but uncensored kites were expensive to smuggle out. Of all the people he wrote, only Liza could be counted on to reply. On the rare occasion he ran out of subject matter, he read.

If the prison doctor knew, he would have slipped some sleeping pills into his grub. Not just because inmates were more tractable when they were comatose, but because he'd done much worse. Everybody knew that the croaker was in cahoots with the shrink. Both men loved to prescribe drugs, especially experimental ones. Right now they were involved in a double blind experiment involving Lysergic acid diethylamide, otherwise known as acid, or LSD.

Dace tapped the shrink for Valium every chance he got, practicing the one good thing he learned in both the Boy Scouts and in prison: be prepared. Doing that made him think about the suicide bombers in World War II. You never knew. In between push-ups, he inched forward on his stomach to check his stash, taped behind his toilet. *Good*, he thought, counting twenty-six little white pills into his right hand.

His body felt a little stiff. Christ, he wasn't even in his mid-twenties and he felt like an old man. He got up to brush his teeth and left the water on until he thought he heard some scuffling.

It could be rats. The dirty little devils had made quite a ruckus the last time they swarmed. No, he decided, his nerves were just bad. Not enough sleep. Better go to bed.

Looking at the grey army blanket on his cot was enough to make him forget about the noise and think about sex. It had been so long he had almost forgotten how. For a moment, he saw a girl lying there, curled into the wall. She was naked, her feet tangled in his sheet, but a little too still.

His neighbour Grumpy must have been on the same wavelength. He often was. "Hey, man," he whispered, his voice hoarse like a man waking up from a dream. "I've got a stash of real good shit if you give me your little schoolgirl cousin's address. When's she coming again? I'd give my eye teeth to spank her ass."

She's coming tomorrow, Dace thought, *but there's no way she's seeing you.*

Springing from the bed, he took one step and kicked their shared wall. "Jesus, you're such a dickhead. Shut the fuck up or I'll bust through this wall and shut it for you," he spat. Dace was normally a man of few words, but he would have said more, except he heard another scuffling sound. "Wait. Can you hear that? What the hell's going on?"

"Ah, take it easy, it's nothing, man, nothing. I don't hear nothing. Nothing ever happens here."

Grumpy hadn't had a visitor for years. The guys got more visitors when they first came in — old schoolmates, old girlfriends, curiosity seekers — but it got harder and harder to look straight people in the eye. Besides, most visitors didn't come back. They hated the place, all the little indignities even visitors weren't spared. And Grumpy hadn't been good company at first. *Admissions fog*, the goddamn quack had said.

"Oh, shit happens all right," Dace said, not surprised when he didn't get an answer. Grumpy had a habit of conking out the moment he finished talking.

Across the Dome, Cellblock C was still lit. Why? The last shift should have been back from the recreational area twenty minutes before. Maybe the guards were having a hard time corralling everybody. Dace stuck his head between his bars and listened. The noise was more muffled now. Somebody was running. Aw, Jeez, maybe some dumb con was running around to avoid lockup. It happened all the time.

"Grumpy?" he inquired, but all he got was another snore.

More running across an upper tier, or maybe it was the roof.

It's nothing, he told himself, lacing his fingers together and stretching out his arms. His muscles were a little tight. No wonder; his tendons were shrivelling.

He had a feeling he was in for a bad night, but he got back into bed anyway. Bad nights happened when the moon was full, but they also happened when it waned. Inmates jabbered to themselves or screamed until daylight. Or they just hooted and hollered until the guards screamed back. They didn't need a reason. It passed the time.

Bunching up his pillow and putting it over his head helped until the noise percolated through. Although it bothered him, he wasn't concerned. As a teenager in the Big House, as a fish in a huge toxic tank, he'd memorized the sounds of men going crazy, of men dying, and of the penitentiary's howling winds, often misinterpreted by newcomers as ghostly wails. Christ, men could be fools. True, one of the pipes made a weird noise, but it was more like an air raid siren. The only ghosts in the Pen were the ones people brought with them or summoned during their vigils for the dead.

Dace had tried to live by three maxims ever since he'd arrived: do your own time, mind your own business, don't turn a deaf ear to a friend in need.

Strong loyalties to his peer group, he'd read upside down on an officer's report more than once.

A typical con, another wag had penned in a margin.

Well, what did they know? What did anybody know about him? Reaching under the blanket, he found a sure-fire way to get some sleep. If nothing else happened, he'd sleep for a while.

Chapter Eleven
Smashing Bars, Rattling Windows, then Silence

About 600 of the 723 prisoners in Maitland Penitentiary
went on a rampage last night, smashing windows, rattling
bars, breaking furniture. Then there was silence. The revolt
has been termed 'spur of the moment.' It is not known
what the inmates hope to gain, although there have been
several interim demands for food, medication and security.
Six guards have not been heard from since yesterday.
Family members fear the worst.
—**Maitland Spectator**, Sept. 3, 1971

Tap, tap, Dace heard. Somebody was playing taps on the pipes in his tier.

After falling asleep on the floor, his cheek felt cold and, his neck was stiff. He edged closer to the hall light to check his watch. Jesus, it was 3:00 a.m., his least favourite hour.

Metal on metal. Only guards could clang like that. Nobody else had the tools, or at least nobody else should have the tools.

The tapping got louder. Somebody was coming down the hall.

"Let's get Dace. He's a boxer, ain't he?" a familiar voice said. The next thing Dace knew, a host of ghostlike men had materialized outside his cell. He jumped to his feet and grabbed the bars. He wasn't going to let them open his door. If they got in...

It made no sense. True, the goon squad preferred to make their visits at this hour, but Dace had done nothing to precipitate such an action. The fact that these guys were dressed in sheets and wearing balaclavas should have tipped him off, but it didn't. It was late and he was tired. It was only when the lead guy opened his mouth that he realized who his visitors were.

"Are you with us, D'Arcy Devereux?" Sandy McAllister asked.

No, Dace thought.

Sandy held up a flaming torch. "Pull yourself together, man!" he said, prompting the rest of his friends to laugh. "It's a bingo," he added, seeing the look of confusion on Dace's face.

Well, Dace thought, all the more reason not to let you bastards in. "A bingo?" he stalled. "A riot?"

"Sure. We got some mother fuckin' guards and we got some keys!" one of Sandy's friends practically sang. "And if that don't work, look at Charlie! He's got a crowbar, man. He tore the fucking bars off our drums. We're busting the rest of the solids out now. You're one of us, right?"

That's right, Dace thought. *I'm solid. Too solid to get mixed up with the likes of you.* But then Charlie the Crowbar said something and Dace caught a whiff of male heat so strong that the part of him that throve on trouble and excitement was eager as a hard-on.

But he couldn't just take off with Sandy and his boys. He had way too much to lose. Maybe if he only had a couple of years in, but not now. And their eyes... He didn't like their eyes. They had probably dipped into the dispensary on their way here. He took a couple more steps back and almost landed in the toilet.

Sandy giggled. "Ah, c'mon, man," he pleaded.

Bile rose in his throat, though he'd eaten supper and extra bread, too. How long did digestion take? Four, maybe five hours? They'd had Shepherd's Pie yesterday at 5:00 p.m. It had been a little dry around the edges, but not bad, not lead at least. What about breakfast? Who was going to cook that? What had they done with all the pigs? There must have been at least thirty on duty.

Fuck, he thought, slamming his fist into the concrete wall over the toilet. Why was he even thinking about food?

Sandy waited a moment before walking away with all the dignity he could muster. His nose stuck up in the air and he made every step an accusation. The rest of his crew trailed their self-appointed leader down the catwalk, almost elegant in their white robes.

Dace looked into his toilet just as a scream reverberated from a lower tier.

From a distance, he heard Charlie the Crowbar say, "Sounds like a problem. What d'you want to do?"

He could almost hear Sandy brightening. A man on a mission. "Let's shut the fucker up," he suggested.

Great, Dace thought, upchucking into his sweating toilet bowl. *Now what?*

Chapter Twelve
Golden Grove Unleaving
Maitland University, September 4, 1971

MÁRGARÉT, áre you gríeving
Over Goldengrove unleaving?
Leáves, líke the things of man, you
With your fresh thoughts care for, can you?
Áh! ás the heart grows older
It will come to such sights colder
By and by, nor spare a sigh
Though worlds of wanwood leafmeal lie;
And yet you wíll weep and know why.
Now no matter, child, the name:
Sórrow's springs áre the same.
Nor mouth had, no nor mind, expressed
What heart heard of, ghost guessed:
It ís the blight man was born for,
It is Margaret you mourn for.
—Hopkins, Gerard M. "Spring and Fall"

T he monarchs weren't fooled. They headed south in record numbers while summer lapsed into a hazy, golden September, catching the students in residence ill-prepared. Most had left their lighter clothes back in the bedrooms of their parents' homes where they would claim free storage for years to come. Boxes sat in attic rooms on the farms, in basement dens in the suburbs, in the claustrophobic little worlds the students had yearned to escape ever since puberty had blindsided them, some as early as fifth grade. Parents who had thought they could never relinquish their children to adulthood had been desperate to let go in the end. Anything to avoid the stormy recriminations, the sullen end to their secret dream family lives.

September marked the official start of all their New Years. Whole families forfeited the cherished Ontario summer and flung themselves fast forward through fall, into winter.

The students perspired in their calf-length skirts and faded Levis. They strolled across the sprawling green campus lawns, pausing under shady canopies of maple trees and limestone arches. The more ambitious boys mapped the locations of their classes, casting their futures into the new school year. Most just hoped to get laid and remain free and unencumbered. And although people said fewer girls were virgins these days, they at least wanted to make one vital connection, to meet one special person, maybe even fall in love.

Liza Devereux was no exception. She stopped under a maple tree on the swell of a hill, holding Stuart "Mel" Melville's hand, and was temporarily magnetized by the look in his eyes. What if? she wondered.

"Let's catch our breath here," he said. "Although I really could go for a drink."

For a moment she let him pull her closer, feeling a flood of relief as he wrapped around her. Mel was an uncomplicated personality. Nothing like Tony or Dace. *Ah, Dace. My cousin with prison eyes,* she thought, moving from the safety of her new friend's arms.

Mel looked at her, a five o'clock shadow glistening on his face. "Too hot?" he inquired, looking slightly appeased when she nodded.

It was hot, but she didn't care. Dublin had fed her mind, but she had been cold there for too long. She wore a grey tweed skirt and a teal blue, short-sleeved jumper today, made in Ireland. Pullover, she corrected herself, feeling sweat pool between her breasts. Everything she owned was back in her residence room. Don't leave anything here, Gran had said, I don't want any reminders. She didn't have that many clothes, but she didn't mind that.

The sun shone through a lattice of golden maple leaves and Liza smiled. She had missed the sun while she'd lived in Dublin. At night when she'd slept, she'd dreamt of wide open fields surrounded by shady green trees and monarch butterflies on milkweed leaves. In her dreams it was never winter in Ontario.

Now that she was back home she dreamed of Ireland and her endless fields of green; she sped on a motorbike with Tony up the Antrim coast, her arms stretched towards the sky; she traced a Celtic swirl with her eyes.

Mel sprinted ahead of her, his legs picking up speed as he plunged to the bottom of the hill.

Liza was worn out from living in the past. Better to run after Mel and start living in the present. This was her time, she reminded herself. If she couldn't make a new life here at Maitland University, she never would.

She caught up to him at the foot of the hill. "What are you thinking about?"

She reached towards him and noticed that when he took her hand, every muscle in her stomach relaxed. His problems were so simple. All he wanted was to get A's.

"School stuff," he said. "I have a really heavy course load."

He talked about his chemistry and math courses while her mind drifted to Dace, sweltering in the heat wave in his antediluvian little cell. Some said the penitentiary was air conditioned, but she doubted it. Her newly built student residence wasn't even air-conditioned, for Christ's sake. People also said the prisoners had colour television. Lies, all lies. The penitentiary was all about boredom, monotony and sensory deprivation, with no regard for the man it made. She knew that.

Just last winter, Dace had sent her a sample of his daily routine and encouraged her to fill in the blanks:

6:00 am Bell rings 20 times. Wake up, be counted, go to showers twice a week(marching in single file).

7:00 am Breakfast in cells. Typical fare: dry cereal and white toast.

7:30 am Sick Call or Exercise Yard (to pace or use weights under a tin awning).

8:30 am Work (Mon to Fri.) or back to cells.

12:00 pm Bell rings 20 times. Back to cells to be counted(and cop some prison drugs or gamble).

12:30 pm Lunch in cells: bologna or cheese on white bread; canned fruit.

1:00 pm Work(Mon to Fri.) or stay in cells.

4:30 pm Bell rings 20 times. Back to cells to be counted (and write letters and read or score brew/drugs).

5:00 pm Supper in cells: canned beans, stews, spaghetti.

7-8:00pm Recreation: watch television or play games (checkers, chess and cribbage).

9-10:00 pm Back to cells to be counted (and write letters and read or score brew/drugs).

10:30 pm Bell rings 20 times. Lights out.

11:00 pm Absolute quiet.

Weekends were different, of course. No work. Was that good or bad? Dace had the option of visiting one of three chapels—all-purpose Protestant, Roman Catholic or Jewish—if he didn't want to spend all day in his cell, with the remote chance of receiving a visitor on his approved list. Books and magazines were scarce and restricted unless illegally obtained, and inmate mail was censored as well. (The fact that he agreed to a skin search, including a rectal probe before and after every visitor, was something she would learn long after.)

Slipping off her sandals to walk barefoot on the grass, she wondered what he did all day now that he couldn't even work. Did he spend all that time in his cell? In the past he had played on several in-house teams and worked in the prison library, but the Pen was almost shut down now, incubating some kind of botulism like badly canned food.

Well, he could still read. He had been reading *East of Eden* the last time he'd written. The middle-aged prison librarian, an inveterate reader and counterfeiter, had recommended Steinbeck. And of course he wrote wonderful letters — to her alone, she hoped. He had done a correspondence course. And he lifted weights when they let him. Like the rest of them. Except he was better, much better. He had muscles. Too many, she amended, suddenly afraid. Why did he need so many? She looked at Mel's arms, supple, lean and brown in one of the simple, solid-coloured T-shirts he favoured and a wave of tenderness washed over her. She wanted to look after him, too. He was just a boy, a tall, thin boy, and much better off that way. As she watched him, he brought his timetable up to the John Lennon glasses perched on his nose, pondering where to go next.

"Let's go to the student lounge," she suggested. "It might be cooler."

"Where's that?" he asked. "In the Student Hall?"

She looked around with her unaided eyes. "Over there." She pointed at a sign and Mel followed her gaze.

Dace has 20/20 vision like I do, she thought. Yes, he was smart and strong with perfect vision, but he would never fit in here on campus. She knew that. He was much too old, in so many ways. Where was his place? And what about hers? The question was there because she belonged with him. But where? One look from him and his eyes would ignite the hot green grass as her fellow students fled. One look from her, well, nobody would notice.

People here were baby-faced. Just look at Mel's cute little upturned nose. Nothing had ever gone wrong in Mel's life. Last night he had confided the details of his small town childhood to her. He was the local GP's son with a childhood so idyllic she figured he must be repressing. She'd fought the urge to say something sharp and spoil his evening. Now as she studied his unlined face with its full, youthful cheeks, she touched her own. Did she look as old and used up as she often felt?

119

So good to be walking with this new boy through old limestone buildings. The air was heady with the smell of wood, books and decay, like Ireland, where she had left a part of herself behind. Lovely, old lady Ireland. She remembered the wind tearing through her hair at Dunluce Castle, a place she had begged Tony to take her. She thought again about the coast on his motorbike, as they sped from Dublin and talked their way across the border.

But goddamn the puking past. If she didn't focus on the present, she would end up grieving this place, too. A fragment of a poem drifted into her mind: *Grieving over Goldengrove unleaving … it is the blight man was born for …*

Someday she would leave here, too. Except she would leave with Dace. The moment he got out. Well, maybe not too soon. In her mind, she heard her grandmother say: And what about your education? She had wanted to go to university for so long. She would have to finish school first.

Her reverie was interrupted when Mel stopped. They were passing a newspaper box in the entrance to the Student Hall. "Oh, shit," he said.

What now? She followed his gaze and saw the headline of the *Maitland Spectator*, displayed in the yellow metal newspaper box outside the Great Hall. PRISONERS IN REVOLT, she read. Her white timetable fluttered unnoticed onto the grass by her feet.

Mel glanced at her, startled by her expression. "You look like you're going to faint," he said and laughed into her pale face, though not unkindly. Mel was kind and good and wanted to be a doctor, like his Dad. He steadied her shoulders with his smooth, brown hands until the life flowing from him almost revived her. "Don't worry. The army will surround the bad guys and all you little campus girls will be safe."

"But my cousin's in Maitland Penitentiary."

"A guard?"

"No. He's an inmate, for God's sake!"

"Why?" Mel looked nonplussed at first, then aghast. "What … what did he do?"

"I don't know," Liza lied. "But what if they go in shooting? Where will he go? They'll mow them down like grass!"

"Hey now, relax. That's a bit dramatic," he said, shooting an appalled glance at the curious students swirling by them. "Better not make a scene. Look, your cousin will be okay. Christ, do you really have a relative in the Joint? C'mon, what did he do, pass some bad checks?" He seized her shoulders and tried to look into her eyes. "Sell grass? Where you from, girl? I thought you were from across the pond, with the lilt in your voice and your black Irish eyes." He paused, perhaps remembering, if not regretting that she'd asked all the questions and he'd done all the talking last night.

"I don't know what he did." *And I don't care.*

"Oh, c'mon. What did you read in the newspapers?"

"I was in Toronto when it happened. I was fourteen."

"Something bad then, if it's been five years. How old is he? When's he getting out?"

"Soon. He's supposed to get out soon. He's twenty-three now. And it wasn't his fault."

"Uh sure, if you say so." Mel's lips kept moving, so he'd said something else, but she didn't hear. Mutely she pushed her clipboard at him and fled in the direction of their student residence, leaving him looking a little stunned.

Although she was panting and her upper legs were burning, she kept running. She had to think. She had to get Dace out. He wasn't involved, he wasn't. Even if the stupid *Maitland Spectator* was screaming: LAST CHANCE. What did that mean? It was their last chance to do what? Jesus Christ. What if somebody had already died? Well, she knew what their bargaining chip was. An accompanying headline had read:

Six prison guards missing and feared dead.

Chapter Thirteen
Anteroom to Hell

Psychiatrist Predicts Inmate Behaviour—
A prominent local psychiatrist, Dr. Daniel Johnson
was responding to Maitland Penitentiary's Warden's
assertion that only half of 723 inmates are believed to
be actively involved in the now two-day-old riot.
Because they 'run in packs' to survive, few will be able to
resist the pull of the inmate subculture. Tension is
building and there will be a power struggle, Dr. Johnson
said. Also, lack of sleep, lack of food and easier access to
contraband drugs is likely to contribute to aberrant
behaviour. There is an increased risk of sexual assaults,
beatings and even death.
—*Maitland Spectator*, September 3, 1971

Hours passed before he had enough juice in his body to send distress signals to the great beyond. Whatever the hell was going on, they couldn't be in the middle of a riot. They just couldn't be. Not with Sandy, that clown, in charge. When Dace wasn't pacing, he jammed his face between the bars. He could just make out a narrow slice of catwalk encircling the domed amphitheatre and some empty cells on the other side. He didn't hear any voices, any banging, nothing.

A black and white snapshot of his father and sister stared at him from his cell wall. "So what do you think, guys?" he asked them now. "Are they all dead?"

Something startled him—a rustle that might have been Sandy's robe—but it was just a rat, streaking from one tier to the next.

How the hell had he ended up in this cesspool? Bang, bang. A Saturday afternoon, a madman, a toy gun and now this. Christ, nothing was supposed to go wrong! He had been nothing more than a boy who loved riding his bike—the wind in his hair, a girl he picked up along the way, the action, the excitement and the thrill of a chase. He looked down at his rough knuckles. The biggest thrill he got these days was smashing somebody's face.

Enough of this bullshit. He had to concentrate. If this were just a minor insurrection, a protest, a sit-down or a slowdown, it made sense to wait it out. He'd gotten involved in one sit-down, the first year he was Inside. What a fuck-up that had been. Everybody had lost their "privileges", their good time, and most of their personal possessions. Now here they went again.

If he could just get out! His eyes swept from the floor to the ceiling, as if he had a hope of finding a chink in the wall. At least he had his body, he thought, getting down to do more push-ups. He never talked about sparring—for him it was almost like breathing—but he was a prison house boxer of some repute, often approached by other convicts desperate for protection.

"Somebody's trying to kill me," they'd whisper. Poor, colourless schmucks, aging and flaccid. He hoped he never got that way. He felt sorry for some of them, he really did. Some guys just shook, and he knew. "I have a wife and kids and I know I can make good," they swore in the little prison library, whispering behind the stacks.

"Lucky you. B-b-blessed with a body well-nourished in infancy and early childhood," the skinny little library con stuttered, observing these interactions. "My mother always fed me c-c--crap."

"You should have seen the slop the priests fed me."

"Still, you have more than your share of inherent muscle mass. Perhaps from some farmer ancestor."

The prison librarian talked like Liza. He used big words. Dace missed some of his speech, but he could catch his drift, courtesy of the books he'd read. He liked listening to him. They all did.

"What, not a warrior?" he'd asked. Sure, the idea of a flaxen haired little farm wife to warm his bed and cook his meals held some appeal. He just couldn't see himself mucking about in dirt or driving a tractor all day.

The librarian was wrong about his ancestry, though, if he meant blind luck was all men had. A man worked for what he got. Take him. He had strong shoulders, a thick neck and bulging forearms, but he worked out every day. Anybody could have had the same body with a little self-discipline and the right motivation. He had started weightlifting the first time he'd been incarcerated. Anything to keep from smashing his head into the nearest wall when he was a blind, scared, stupid, eighteen.

When the racket started up again, it was almost a relief. Somebody cursed God, Jesus Christ, the Virgin Mary and a lot of other people. They were probably looting the chapels in the West Block. God only knew what they hoped to find. To each his own, but Dace drew the line at throwing hymn books — or any books — in the air.

By now he almost wished that the resident goon squad would round up all the loose felons and toss them back where they belonged: in the slammer, in the clink, in the Hole. Where he belonged. In his darkest moments, he knew he belonged there, too.

If the gutless fucking bulls didn't get control of his goddamn cellblock soon, the army would come in. In his mind soldiers burst in and cut down every single upright cocksucker while Dace dove headfirst under his bed, his thin mattress exploding into a mess of chicken feathers, bone meal, and plasma.

Calm down, he told himself. They'd use tear gas first, wouldn't they? Even the guards weren't total fools. Christ. Was that smoke? Instinctively, he held his breath and crouched down. No use hollering. Even if he got somebody's attention, so what? They'd have a hell of a time prying the lid off his can without the key.

His thighs ached. He raised his head from his knees, took a cautious breath and coughed. Jesus fucking Christ! He exploded, wasting more precious breath. Smoke. The sneaky little bitch was funnelling from the tier below his cell, probably from the same place where he'd heard all that screaming last night. Smoke was wending her way into his cell and invading his air space, hitchhiking on oxygen-carrying red cells, like the alcohol in a drunkard's bloodstream.

He lurched to his feet and yanked on the bars. Where the hell was everybody? He wasn't Superman. In fact, he was seconds away from screaming like a snitch stuck with a shiv. And he fucking well didn't want to start screaming. He didn't want to die without anybody knowing. He wanted to see his family again. To make amends. To show everybody who said he couldn't, he wouldn't, with all the stupid, fucking choices he'd made.

The smoke was getting thicker. He yanked his shirt up over his head and scrunched back down, coughing and sputtering until there was a little pool of spittle on the floor. Christ. He'd had enough. "Open the goddamn door! Get me out of this fucking drum!" he shouted.

Sandy McAllister and his masked banditos appeared so fast he wondered if they'd been right behind the fire door. Dace staggered to his feet. "Who started the fire?" he demanded, suspecting it was one of them.

"Easy guy. My boys knew what they were doing. It's all under control. My control," Sandy said, poking an assortment of keys into the cell door lock.

Charlie the Crowbar got fed up. "Good old Charlie to the rescue," Sandy said, watching the man pull a crowbar from his sleeve.

Dace could see all sorts of uses for this contraband tool. "Where d'you get that?" he asked, though it hurt to speak.

"Smuggled it out of the upholstery workshop a long time ago," Charlie said, wedging the crowbar between a couple of bars and prying with all his might. "It was bound to come in useful someday." He grunted until a small crack in the old plaster above the bars appeared.

Somebody else took over then. They all had a go.

For once, Dace wasn't much use. In an effort to conserve his energy, he had sunk back down to the floor. "Hurry," he slurred, slumping forward.

Fortunately, he didn't have to wait long. Chunks of plaster thudded down as two bars pulled loose. "The bennies help, man," Sandy said with a grin. He slid in behind Dace and lifted him into his arms. Somebody else grabbed his feet.

Dace couldn't remember the last time he felt so wasted. As far as he was concerned, Sandy's boys could do whatever they wanted. Darkness came then, though he could still hear somebody screaming *Fire!*

Live, Dace, he whispered to himself. *I want to go home.*

When he woke on the damp floor of the Dome he was wet, either from dirty water or from his own sweat. He couldn't tell. At first he thought he must have fallen, then some part of him recalled being lugged from his cell, an almost comatose man on a phantom stretcher.

He flexed his limbs, relieved to feel nothing was broken, and looked at the ceiling. It looked dark, but the Joint was always dark, night and day. Hooded faces loomed above him. Judgement Day, he thought. Sandy McAllister and the beefy guy they called Charlie were still there. Who were the other clods?

"Look," somebody said. "I see eyes. He's coming 'round. I thought for sure he was a goner."

"Yeah, I see 'em," said another voice, chuckling. "Except

they keep rolling back up into his head."

"Too fuckin' tough, man."

"He should have come with us last night," somebody else said.

"Yeah, well, who the hell's gonna mess with him?"

"Maybe he'll stick with us now."

"What's happening, man?" Dace managed to ask. Why had he been saved? For what purpose? His eyes burned and his throat was parched. Rubbing his eyes with his numb hands, he tried to make sense of the sheeted figures around him, but it was like waking up in a recovery room with masked doctors all around. Or a clutch of jackrabbits from the Klan. Jesus Christ. Just what he needed!

"Ah, we're just having a little fun, Dace. One little, two little, three little piggies … We've got six little piggies holed up in that big old heating duct on the first floor."

And the wolf is at their door. Pain shot through his chest as he fought for a single, uncomplicated breath. *Breathe, breathe, breathe,* he recited. Christ. What if his lungs imploded? He'd read how people rescued from fires died later, their skin unblemished, their lungs a blackened mess.

Goddammit. I've been reading too much, he thought, momentarily forgetting that for the past six months, he hadn't had anything else to do besides read. He liked books all right, but the library was no place for somebody like him. A man could go crazy knowing too much. His unschooled father had done quite well for himself.

"Are you nuts?" he sputtered.

"The creeps are okay," somebody said with a laugh. "And ain't they just the cutest little mother fuckers, all dolled up in our monkey suits?"

"You've dressed the guards in prison uniforms?" Dace's smile stretched over his chattering teeth. Back off, he felt like snarling. "Real smart, guys," he said instead. "They're safer that way. You want some leverage, right?"

"Nah, we just wanna play with them. That Saksun guy's a lot of fun."

"What about your costumes? Did you raid the laundry or what?"

"Ah, we're just playing dress-up, Dace. C'mon, wake up, you crazy mother fucker! You've already missed one hell of a party. Oh, shit, look at that. Some jackass spilled the hooch. Probably the last. We busted into Doc's place too, but the bennies are gone now, man, they're all gone."

Dace folded his hands across his chest and crossed his feet at the ankles. He still wore his St. Christopher medal around his neck. His mother had given it to him. He recalled when—

Shit. His mind was wandering. He probably looked like a corpse lying there, but he didn't care. Storm clouds scuttled across the skylight, far above him. He used to like being outside on a stormy day. That was when he'd had some sort of control over what happened to him. Or at least he'd had that illusion.

Christ, he couldn't keep coughing. His audience was scattering. The minute he caught his breath, he choked to the diehards at his side, needing more information. "So talk to me. Why should I get up? What's in it for me?"

Sandy McAllister was happy to oblige. Watching his rescuer, Dace briefly considered joining him. Sandy could be very convincing. With piercing blue eyes lighting his sincerity, he spoke for several moments about revolution and change. Then his rhetoric slipped.

"It comes down to this. We need a tough guy, man," he said, reaching down and almost jabbing his long finger up Dace's nose. "And that's you, my fine, stalwart friend! We got crazies on the loose now. Look at Charlie. There's no telling what he'd do with that crowbar if we let him. And the borderline nuts are cracking, too. They won't leave the mother fucking hostages alone. Big Joe and his friends are threatening to take the screws upstairs and toss them over the rail to the sharkies below. You've gotta watch crazies. You know that. Last night they had one of the screws hanging over a railing, screaming like a banshee. Sorta funny, but ..."

Funny, right. Looks like everybody's gone crazy except me, Dace thought, allowing Sandy to yank him into a sitting position.

"Nah, I don't have to do nothing," he said. "What's happening, anyway? Where's the man? Are none of them inside?"

Nobody answered. Two of the younger men, teenagers really, stepped out of the circle and brandished their makeshift weapons at each other instead.

Swell, Dace thought. *A couple of kids.* And the rest of Sandy's followers? No doubt the rescuers were the cons with the biggest balls, the solids or the more aggressive prisoners: various assailants and bank robbers, the heartbeat of his prison world. The ones on paper who were the most like him. He sensed only a solid could have instigated a riot, egged on by the larger circle of thieves and robbers. A chill passed over him as he recalled how he'd almost bragged to Liza about being a solid. He had never expected to end up like this: a reluctant rebel of sorts. What the hell would she think?

At least the solids were predictable. Their sneakier associates were not. The sneaks were probably busting walls or tunnelling through heating ducts right now, trying to sniff out contraband: alcohol, coffee, cigarettes, girly magazines, prescription drugs and maybe even some cash. Whatever was going.

His chest tightened. He was in a corner, all right. A place where a man was apt to chew his leg off if he got caught. For as often as he told himself to be careful, he had always loved excitement. He hated what being careful got him.

He thought about the larger, less integrated circle on the periphery of the prison population, those soft, pasty-fleshed boys and stringy, nervous-looking men still in Segregation. Night creatures. Although the diddlers didn't really count, Dace didn't want to think how these men could spark the murderous fantasies of his more volatile friends. If he thought about it, he might have felt the same. The night creatures were made up of offenders least respected by other prisoners: the arsonists, the child molesters and the incestuous offenders.

"Well, let me guess then. It's you, Sandy, isn't it? Got yourself a key." *More hindsight,* he thought. *A fucking lot of use that is.* Sandy had been talking about a bingo for weeks, but so what? Most blowhards just talked.

In reply, Sandy fluttered his eyelashes and flashed a smile as demure as any girl's.

"Look, man," one of his friends yelped. "He got some help. Except we didn't mean to. Saksun oughtna had his key dangling out of his pocket so obvious-like. It was just hanging there, beggin' take me! take me! so Sandy grabs the mother fucking key and bingo! It's a bingo, get it? And we's all on the front page and we're free. Everybody on our shift got loose. We're not sure about the guys in the other blocks, but we think they did too."

"Free? Is that what you call this? So how come I hear bullhorns outside? And what's that whirring? Maybe the good citizenry of Maitland are organizing our getaway cars? Or getting us some airplanes?"

Everybody stopped and looked up. Nobody had noticed the helicopters until then. One of them volunteered, "Well, sure man. Look out the window. There's lots of little blue jean babies outside, too. They're carrying placards. Co-eds—"

"Co-eds?" Liza is a co-ed, Dace thought. And scared. Well, no wonder. Look at him. He was fucking terrified, and he'd been brought up to speed.

Jesus, he could still hear the German Shepherds patrolling the grounds, a sinister contrast to the carnival atmosphere inside the Joint. The goddamn dogs were barking. He liked dogs, but not German Shepherds. In his mind's eye, he dropped them one by one with his gun, the same kind of gun that had helped him out before. A gun from nowhere.

He closed his eyes, not knowing what else to do. Then he slept and his mind raced clean away. *Liza,* he thought he said, but nobody heard him.

"Christ," Sandy shrieked. "We're fucking losing him again. Give him some air."

"Forget about him. I'll—"

"Fuck you. What the hell are you going to do, you useless bag of shit? Just give me the fucking microphone and go check on our pigs."

Chapter Fourteen
The Do-Gooders

Guard Speaks Up—
The steel doors to Maitland Penitentiary
slammed shut as a guard stopped to light a
cigarette. He had just finished his shift,
after being forced to stand by as 600
prisoners tore up the main cellblock in
Canada's largest penitentiary. Clearly upset,
he reported that his friends were being held
captive in the cellblock, and there was
nothing he could do about it.
—*Maitland Spectator*, September 5, 1971

Braiding her waist-length hair over her shoulder, Liza ran through her residence lobby, straight into a waiting taxi. It was expensive, but she didn't care. She had paced around her room as long as she could.

Mel wanted to review his high school chemistry notes. He'd tried half-heartedly to restrain her, but he couldn't really see any harm in her going. Jesus, he'd said, who could catch the wind? He'd said a lot of other things besides. Like what could possibly go wrong? For one thing, Liza wasn't a girl to make a speech and draw attention to herself. Classes hadn't even started and she was already worried about doing presentations. It wasn't as if she were going to get hurt by any of those cons. They were never going to see the light of day again after pulling a stunt like this.

It nagged him that she knew somebody inside the Joint. Even a cousin. He let her know it. He had to admire her loyalty, though. He doubted his family would stick by anybody damaged and misguided enough to end up in jail. What the hell had her jailbird cousin done? Fuck a duck, he hoped he hadn't killed someone. That would be the living end. He tried not to let on, but it bothered him she hadn't really said. For the first time he wondered if she had a secret, though how many secrets could a nineteen-year-old girl have?

He had wanted to take her home to meet his parents in Trenton on Thanksgiving weekend, especially if he ended up sleeping with her, although they didn't need to know that. He and Liza, well, they were getting ready for that. Well, he was. His balls ached. Liza was holding back and he wasn't sure why. When he'd reached between her legs, she'd said something about it having been a long time, but maybe she just didn't want to seem too easy. Free love or not, lots of girls were like that. *City girls just seem to find out early*, he hummed, so she was probably experienced.

Well, so what? She could still be presented as another little co-ed shopping for a husband, much as they had in his mother's time. His mother had trained as a teacher, but she had quit work the moment she'd gotten her ring. Better his Presbyterian family never finds out about the cousin though, especially his paternal grandmother, who ruled the roost from her own home, right next door to his parents' house.

Grandma was going to find the whole mess rather unsavoury. If the cousin earned a starring role in the riot and their relationship became public, perhaps he could tell her he was just some biker who got into a little bit of trouble with the law. Goddamn it, why did they have to have the same last name? The old woman didn't like bikers any more than she did cons, but they were a familiar sight in Trenton and the romantic dream of many neighbourhood girls and boys. Some of them were even law-abiding citizens who just happened to love bikes.

Liza, just the week before, had felt a slow, unexpected flush of pleasure at the lakeside Frosh dance. Mel had told her he wanted to take her home to meet his parents.

Now she focussed on Dace. She climbed in the back seat of the cab and told the driver where she was going. "Look," the driver volunteered, "if you was my daughter, I wouldn't want you going near that mess. What's a girl like you snooping around the Pen for anyway?"

"I just want to see what's happening," she replied, resisting the urge to smack the back of his shiny bald head. Mel had been irritating enough, his expression so pruny-faced she had been tempted to tell him she was going downtown to striptease. At least he hadn't asked her too many questions. Possibly because he didn't want to know the answers.

Hurry up, hurry up! Her mind raced all the way through Maitland. Staring out at the tidy, spacious brick houses whizzing by, she was thankful none of her inner turmoil showed in her face. She put all her early training to use, keeping her feelings hidden inside. Nobody had ever been interested or had the time to deal with her when her twin brothers had been so close to her in age.

The cab came to a sudden stop. The trip was so quick there was no time for Liza to reflect on the short distance between the ivy-covered stone walls of the university and the scrubbed grey walls of the penitentiary.

"Well, Miss Butter-Wouldn't-Melt-in-Your-Mouth, I'll drop you off here. You're two blocks from the Big House and I'm not getting any closer. I don't want to get my cab rolled. There's a real carnival up on the lawn. Just listen to all that hootin' and hollerin'. You asking for trouble or what?"

Throwing two dollars in the front seat—two days food on a diet of Coke and potato chips—she jumped onto the sidewalk and kicked his cab door shut.

"Yeah, trouble," she muttered. "That's my middle name."

If only she could have used her pent-up energy to storm Inside and get Dace Out. Her imagination raced with a fantasy of finding a helicopter pilot—some intrepid soul willing to land inside the prison gates and set him free.

Grey buildings loomed ahead, a limestone fortress pitched on a rocky outcrop beside an endless expanse of water. The prisoners lived in five-tiered cellblocks arranged in a cruciform, but with any luck visitors only got close enough to notice the grey-stoned columns guarding the entrance, some imposing double doors and a bell tower with a Canadian flag flapping in the lakeside breeze.

Among all her other research, Liza had studied Maitland Penitentiary. It had been built about 1833 by the convicts themselves. They had heaved the buildings out of broken rock from a limestone quarry, creating a legacy of nineteenth century Ontario. In those days there was no pretence that men were imprisoned except to be punished. Boys as young as eight were tossed inside, and the lash was employed through the 1960s.

Some of the boys grew old there. Like most people, they succumbed to natural causes such as heart disease, old age and unspecified cancers, but many of their maladies, like appendicitis, blood poisoning, nephritis, pneumonia and tuberculosis, were now treatable with antibiotics. Some of the men killed each other, some were hanged. Accidents claimed a few lives. Family members—if the dead men had any—rarely came to claim the bodies and most were buried in unmarked paupers' graves in the prison cemetery. Fifty years before, the cemetery had been cemented over by the recreational yard, which was something none of the recent inhabitants knew.

Liza approached the compound, an unwelcome visitor. What am I doing here? What can I do? What's Dace going to do? Her desire to know he was safe was so strong that her mind flitted from one outrageous possibility to another. Maybe he wasn't even inside. Maybe he had been transferred over the weekend to a medium security prison to prepare for his parole. Anything was possible. Why, he could have tunnelled out to

Argentina! Or barricaded himself in a bulletproof closet! Did they even have closets in the cells? Where did the prisoners keep their clothes? How many changes of clothes did they have? Just one?

If only a miracle had taken place. Anything that could keep him whole, unbloodied, safe. She clung to the memory of the way he had looked just a couple of days before.

Oh God. Why did she feel so bad? She had tried so hard to accustom herself to blood and gore. The Hinkley murders had scarred anyone living in Britain. Some people coped by pretending nothing bad had happened, but there had also been a sudden surge in true crime stories being published. Like so many people, the first true crime story Liza had ever read was Truman Capote's *In Cold Blood*. The motives behind the crimes were always insufficient, but she had kept reading those kinds of exposés, longing for explanations, looking for some way to anaesthetize herself, to stop feeling, to convince herself evil would never touch her or her kin.

Closer to the main prison building she noticed that an entrepreneurial convict had slung a white sheet marked with red, hand-painted words in a smashed window. *Under New Management*, she read and laughed, then was forced back onto the grass opposite the compound. Scowling, uniformed policemen strode up and down the sidewalk nearest the prison, flapping outstretched arms and shouting, "Keep your distance! The cons are actin' up in there."

The cops almost outnumbered the crowd they were trying to control, about two hundred or so spectators circling and huddling together. Liza blended right in. Dressed in the same blue jeans and T-shirts people would wear for the next four decades, everybody looked like reporters, desperately hoping news would be made before their covetous eyes, hoping they alone might become privy to the secrets of prisoners living behind impenetrable stone walls.

"Christ. Who really knows what happens in these places anyway? Who the hell wants to?" a reporter clone beside Liza remarked, his eyes riveted on the besieged walls.

"Well, you sure look like you wish you had x-ray vision," she replied to his rhetorical question.

The long-haired man looked at her. Later he told her he'd estimated she was a clever seventeen. Maitland University's logo was visible over her right breast. "Where you from, baby, the school newspaper?"

She must have hesitated just a moment too long. She could write a story for the university paper. And she should. From the prisoners' point of view. How they needed better conditions so they could behave better. She supposed she would have to try to sound less naïve, because some of the men at Maitland Penitentiary were murderous fiends. Who among a conservative student body would sympathize?

The reporter leaned closer to her, eyes squinting in his full face. He had a large head, even for a male. She judged he was in his late twenties, with long brown hair which was already receding. He was quite tall, but a little stooped. He might have once had broad shoulders, but he didn't now. Involuntarily Liza stepped back, repelled by the odour of stale cooking grease emanating from his dark sports jacket and buttoned down shirt.

"Hey, look. My name's Joe—Joseph Armitage," he volunteered. "Now tell me, pretty little lady, have I got a story here? You aren't related to one of the hostages, are you? Could you be one of the guards' girls? One of their daughters?"

Liza smiled and shook her head, her bangs falling into her eyes. Christ, she had to watch herself! Stupid to end up in a stranger's story instead of her own. If she did, she wouldn't do Dace a damn bit of good in this town. Every Maitland resident was bound to be worried about the hostages. If something happened to the guards, it could happen to them, too. Of course she was also concerned about the hostages, she decided. What if they got hurt? Some of the guards might be a little overzealous, but the poor buggers were just doing their jobs. It wasn't their fault. It was the fault of the Warden and the Administration.

"No, Joe, I'm not related to a hostage," she replied. "My name's Liza," she added, deliberately omitting her surname. "I'm at the U. I'm just a first year student with an interest."

"Well, lucky you. Those hostage takers are gonna end up as minced meat," Joe remarked. "Those poor suckers get out alive they'll be missing so many body parts they won't have enough left over to splice together a single human being." He stopped short, which Liza assumed was due to her sudden green skin tone. Then she tracked his gaze across the street.

A Ford pickup had pulled up close to the police parading outside the prison door. As they watched, eight to ten blue-jeaned activists jumped out the rear end. Liza was delighted to see their homemade placards carrying messages like *Power to the Prisoners*! Joe whipped out a notebook so fast she felt a slight breeze. She was also clutching a pen in her pocket, but she couldn't make out what the protesters were saying. For the second time that September, she wished she had a tape recorder. Fortunately the roar of the police was audible enough.

"Get the hell out of here! We told you to go smoke some dope so we could bust you yesterday," one of them shouted and shoved the placard-carrying kids closest to them. Two or three of the activists happened to be girls, but the Maitland police seemed keen to avoid body contact with them. Liza wondered if they perhaps recognized daughters of their Legion Hall friends.

One officer shook his finger in front of an offending female nose instead. "Don't you know youse here in bad taste? We got a hostage situation here. And those hostages got families." The girl, who was half his size, backed up.

"In bad taste," Liza repeated, loudly enough for several bystanders to hear. "What do they suppose is happening here, anyway? A prison riot or a breach of etiquette?"

"The cavalry's happening, girl," Joe cooed as several cumbersome black television cameras moved in. He looked happy, adrenalin wracking his body almost as fast as if he had taken speed.

Although he was scribbling so fast correct spelling was impossible, he never took his eyes off the scene. Behind the protestors' pick-up, two canvas-covered army trucks suddenly converged. The protestors took one look at the vehicles and scrambled back so fast into their dwarfed truck it was almost comical.

"Oh my God. They're not. They're not," Liza said quietly.

Joe shook his head. "No, they're not going to shoot yet. But look what they're packin' for Gawd's sakes! Bayonets! Where's the cameras? It's like something in the movies! I can't believe it. What a scene! It's straight out of the nineteenth century! It's a Dickensian dream!"

"Bayonets?" Liza repeated. In horror she watched the green soldiers marching two by two under the limestone arch which led into the prison courtyard, each marionette carrying a sharpened pole pointed towards the sky.

"They'll surround the Pen, I bet. You know, make doubly sure none of 'em bad guys get out. A show of force, like. Whoa, what's this? The prison guards must be changing shifts. Lookee, lookee, here comes one of the old codgers. I love it!"

A guard in his fifties approached the reporters. He was fat, tired and cranky looking. *It's Savage*, Liza thought, unaccountably relieved to recognize a familiar face.

"You gawkers." His cheek jowls shook in their faces.

Joe responded to his salutation. "You just get off your shift, sir? So what's it like in there?"

Savage waved his hand with disgust, started to walk away, then changed his mind in mid-stride. "Well," he said, deciding to open up. "There's five hundred cons on the loose in there, and maybe a million bucks worth of damage: busted cells, busted furniture blocking the main entrance and I don't know what all. Nobody can get near the bastards. My friends, six of my buddies, nobody knows what's happening to them. There's not a damn thing anybody can do."

"So the riot broke out spontaneously Wednesday, sir?"

The guard laughed mirthlessly. "Hah! Spontaneously? This was a well-planned operation. What d'you think those guys inside are? Girl Scouts? This is a maximum security institution we got here. Murderers, thieves, rapists, child molesters, those are our customers. Probably about two dozen men are responsible: that Sandy McAllister, and Debo. Devereux is the bastard who's got my friends hostage. Oh, what the hell. I'm too tired to jaw with you fellas all day."

Liza staggered when the ground beneath her feet suddenly wobbled. Dace? Hostages?

Joe pressed on. "Well, do you have any idea why they're rioting, sir? What do they want? Steaks? Air conditioning? Colour television? More time off for good behaviour?"

"I thought they already had air conditioning at the taxpayer's expense," somebody quipped.

"Who the fuck knows? All I know is we saw this one coming, only we couldn't tell when."

"But why, sir?"

"I told you I don't know!" Savage exploded, sticking his face in Joe's. "But listen. Youse fellas want somebody to blame? Take a look at yourselves, all you do-gooders, you civil rights people, you bleeding hearts. That's who I blame! What the hell do you guys know about rehabilitation? We're the ones trained to handle them, and we'll rehabilitate them too, but excuse me if we gotta bust a few heads first."

A snicker rippled through the crowd, and Liza flushed. She knew she shouldn't speak her mind, but she couldn't help herself. This ... this bellyacher was blaming everyone but himself for the debacle behind those locked doors. And alleging Dace had taken hostages? He couldn't. He wouldn't. He was reformed. At least he sure as hell sounded reformed in all his letters. Not to mention he was just weeks away from parole. Did this stupid jackass really think her cousin was a fool?

"So"" she spat back at Savage. "If you know so much about rehabilitation, why are they rioting inside? You look after the prisoners every day, not the do-gooders!"

The guard whirled in her direction, his small coal eyes blasting her already hot face. "Who the hell are you, Missy? I seen you somewheres before. You got a lover boy inside this here Joint and he ain't never gonna get out! Don't you come down here telling me how to do my job!"

Liza stumbled backward on the grassy knoll, despising herself for retreating, but far too cowed to hold her ground. Shrinking in the guard's shadow, her arms tightened across her chest. Her eyes appealed to Joe, but he was too preoccupied in copying every word of her exchange with Savage to be any assistance. The guard tugged at the tie constricting his throat before turning his head slightly aside. A clump of spittle landed near her feet.

"Go home, all of youse! Get the fuck out of here!" he bellowed over his shoulder, before lumbering off.

Liza rarely spoke in public, but she knew she might feel embarrassed later. Right now all she felt was drained.

Joe came and stood by her. "My God, you're so pale. Heh, heh. *A whiter shade of pale.* Are you a friend of one of those inmates?" Joe chose that moment to start interrogating her. "What is it? Do you have a relationship with a convicted criminal?"

In response to her silence, he continued. "What do you think is going to happen to him? What will you do if he's killed?"

"I'll die," she said under her breath.

"What's that, honey?"

Liza opened her mouth then closed it. She had to get control of herself and fast. She'd be useless to Dace if she fell apart now. Lowering her head, she clenched her fists and shut her eyes. She had no intention of crying, and no intention of speaking to this ... this insensate clod, either. But she didn't have the strength to resist when he took her by the arm and led her to a coffee shop across the street.

In her daydream she broke past the angry guard, running fast enough to almost gut herself on the barricade. "Let me talk to them!" she pleaded. "D'Arcy Devereux will listen to me."

If only they'd let her negotiate with the rebels inside. Or perhaps with the men who wanted to regain control of them. Hardly noticing him there, she accepted a cup of hot coffee from Joe's cold fingers, although she later picked up the bill. Her mind raced. She'd rescue Dace. All she had to do was get Inside, where she belonged.

Chapter Fifteen
Last Chance

Troops Surround Prison—
A citizens' group, made up of several
lawyers and newspaper men, continued
to hear the grievances of 600 rebel prisoners
at Maitland Penitentiary and to barter for
the release of six guards taken hostage. The
prison picked calm and articulate convicts
to act as spokesmen. "Keep the Army out, get
us some more food and we'll be as good as gold,"
promised one. He insisted the prisoners' decision
to riot was prompted by the proposed move to
the new Supermax. He also claimed that 20 inmates
had committed suicide this past year, a figure
disputed by prison officials.
.—*Maitland Spectator*, September 5, 1971

Dace tossed down his hand. "Fold," he said. The other card players shifted in their chairs, watching him. He didn't give a fuck that he was making them nervous. He hated everybody that morning: the authorities, his cellmates and Sandy McAllister in particular.

Kicking his chair aside, he went out into the corridor. They were on the fourth tier in Cellblock B, right outside his cell. He felt like a zoo animal, waiting for his meat. So far all they'd done was organize some teams. No point in letting Sandy McAllister have all the fun. The deed was done and a man could go crazy just waiting. Dace had gotten stuck heading the inmate security force. Then a negotiating team had been chosen to convey their demands—their concerns, Rick said—to the outside world.

Dace heard Rick whistling as he came back down the hall. He had been at a meeting with some government officials in an enemy building since ten.

The card players waited until he got a little closer. Then, "So what now?" one of them asked. "Mr. Hot-Off-the-Press?"

"The *Star* was there. So was the *Globe and Mail!*" Rick replied, pounding his own chest.

"Give it a rest," somebody muttered. "You're starting to sound more like a groupie than a man with revolution on his mind."

"Yeah," a couple of other men said. "This is a mother fucking revolution, man!"

Oh, yeah, Dace thought. "Or a bunch of rebels without a cause," he said.

Rick looked at him blankly. "We got a cause," he said. "Or causes. Where the hell have you been? There were fifteen suicides last year alone in this place. Now they want to move us to a new Supermax."

"Yeah, so?" Dace said. "I don't see them changing their minds after this."

"But they might!" Rick practically danced around him. "If we make them. If we get the hostages. We need some leverage, like. Something to trade. I dunno."

Dace stared at Rick. What the hell was the matter with him? Had he lost his mind? "Go get 'em, tiger," he said.

"I can't do it by myself," Rick said. "I ..."

"For Christ's sake, let me think!" Dace interrupted. He headed over to the guard rail for another look around.

The place looked quiet enough. The deadlocks were off all the entrances to the cellblocks, except the segregated area in D Block where fourteen baby killers and a bunch of rat finks lived.

Sandy's men had found the keys to unlock most of the individual cells and had busted into the rest, but they had left the men in Segregation alone.

There hadn't been a peep out of them so far. Well, naturally. Guys like that had probably learned to play dead in the cradle. Some of the short timers were quiet too, he noted, sleeping off the effects of alcohol and amphetamines or worse.

Rick was still waiting, his anxiety rolling off him in waves.

"What a fuck-up," Dace muttered under his breath. Christ. What was Sandy hollering about now? He'd been busy all night. First he'd organized the younger, more energetic inmates into work gangs, barricading exits with metal cots and anything else they could find. Then they'd busted through some of the bricks connecting their cells, creating a dormitory where they could hang out.

Their latest project was the penitentiary gong. One of Sandy's cat burglars was scaling the wall in the Dome right now. Dace didn't pay much attention until there was a loud crash. Everybody stampeded to the Dome, so he went too. When they arrived, nobody said anything for a moment. It looked like the bell's cables had been cut with just a couple of swipes, but maybe they had been rotten to begin with. Dace glanced at the perpetrator. He stood by the carnage wearing a huge grin, a knife between his teeth. Somebody volunteered that they had hugged the wall like they were on a centrifuge ride when it came down, then everybody cheered.

"Good work, Peter Pan," Dace said, watching him hide four or five good sized pieces of the bell under some trash. "I thought that baby was cast iron."

When Dace got back upstairs, Rick was already there. "Shouldn't you be in a meeting?" he tried to say, but Rick was busy talking.

The smell of wood smoke hung in the air. Wooden furniture, smashed for container fires, had burned all night. Books had met the same fate, almost causing George the library con to have a seizure. Dace had taken him to the Infirmary, off at the end of the building in a conflict-free zone. As far as the librarian was concerned, nothing worse could happen. Dace hoped he was right, but there were a lot of variables. What if the diddlers or—

Oh, Christ. How likely was that? The army was coming through. That sneaky, scuttling noise on the roof—it had to be them. Or it could be one of Sandy's men, plotting an alternate escape route, but he doubted it. That's it, he decided, going up to Rick and pulling him aside.

"Enough about the press," he said, his lips barely moving. "They write stuff. They don't make it happen. We could, though. Why the hell should Sandy's boys have all the fun?"

Rick's eyes bulged. "You mean you want to take over?"

Dace cocked his head at the ceiling, hearing a sound. "The hostages?" he asked. "Do I look crazy?" What do you think that sound is? he mouthed. "Besides, there's no percentage in taking over, even though we could do a much better job than that asshole Sandy."

"Jesus, your little sister Rosie could do a better job."

"We need to make a list of demands. You can't keep going empty-handed to the press. It's pointless."

"I've haven't been doing that!" Rick protested.

"Let me then," a teenager named Steve, volunteered. Another boxer, he was the youngest recruit on Dace's police team.

People laughed when Rick glared at Steve, but he ignored them. "Forget it, chump, I'll talk to the press," he snapped. "There's no telling what a fish like you might say. Some of us want to get out of here alive. Right, Dace?"

Everybody groaned. They wanted to hear about the press meetings, though. Those were their only hope of a resolution, their last chance.

"Jesus Christ. When are they sending in some food? I'm starving!" Steve ventured.

"Hey, Ricky-man. Tell them we want total amnesty!"

"Flights to Brazil!"

"I'd settle for roast beef on Sunday night."

"More recreational time."

"I want to fuck my old lady."

"Yeah, that's right. What d'you call it? Get some conjugating visits."

"That's conjugal, you dork!"

"Who you calling—"

"Ah, relax, man!"

"And tell them we don't want no physical reprisals."

Dace listened for several minutes, then he grabbed the last speaker by the throat. It happened to be Steve. "Fuck!" he spat into the terrified boy's face. "What a bunch of dreamers! Let's get real here. You know the guards are gonna beat the crap out of us the first chance they get. That's if they don't shoot everybody in the face. Or in the nuts. That's more their style. Give everybody amnesty!" he mimicked, allowing Steve to slump, unharmed, to the floor. "What the hell are you telling them, Rick? These fucking demands for better food and more play time are stupid. What the hell is this, fifth grade?"

"Easy, big guy, easy," Rick replied, patting Dace's shoulder. "You have a point. We want to get across how we've been systematically brutalized by both the employees of Maitland Penitentiary and the penal system in general."

"Yeah, like John Q. Public will care!" Dace interrupted with a derisive snort. "How about modernizing the prison educational system? Or being paid a minimum wage instead of doing slave labour? And why isn't somebody taking notes?"

Rick shoved something at him. "Go to it. Here's a pencil and paper," he said.

"Fucking fancy talk," somebody else muttered, shooting a nervous glance at Dace, but several other men nodded.

Dace snapped the pencil in half, trying to calm down. *We're pulling in way too many directions*, he thought as he jotted down their concerns.

Jesus, everybody had their own agenda, even if it were just to get high. Look at Rick. Every time he got back from one of his goddamn press meetings, he was all fired up with his own frigging self-importance. In prison he was the same person he'd always been: a bit of a show-off. Never mind that Dace had always admired his style, his outgoing personality, his joie de vivre. In another life Rick would have made a fine politician, a character actor or even a circus clown, but he was nothing here.

The men in B Block ran out of demands at just about the same time Dace's pencil broke for good. If he hadn't been used to writing a lot, he would have had a cramp in his hand. Shooting his foot out, he tripped Rick to his knees, bringing him closer. Rick looked a little shaky but he pulled a cigarette from out of his pants and offered Dace a smoke.

"Shit, it's quiet," Dace said quietly as he lit up, although quiet was relative. From what he could tell, a bunch of stupid drunks were arguing in the Dome. "What a difference it makes now that we don't have to listen to that dumb ass bell anymore."

"Maybe we should get some shut eye," Rick said. "I don't know about the rest of the population, but we didn't sleep a wink here last night."

Dace nodded. He hadn't either. Something told him that they were in for a long siege, but he couldn't sleep. Not now. Maybe Rick ... No. Rick looked even more hyper and distracted than usual. Dace's heart sank. What the fuck had Rick gotten into now?

Dace didn't want to say anything. What people did was their own business. But he couldn't help himself. The guy had a responsibility and he was blowing it. "Looks like you visited Sandy on your way to meet the press. I thought you couldn't stand that guy. What did you do—what did you take?"

"Speed," Rick said. "I got a lot on my mind. I need you—"

"You wanted the job!"

"What the hell else was I supposed to do?" Rick gave a helpless shrug.

The shrug set Dace off. "You couldn't pay me to talk to the army, the government or the goddamn press," he shouted. "Goddammit. Nobody has the balls to take charge of this mess!"

On a roll now, he detailed the absurdity of all their demands and the remote chance any of them would ever be met. Pausing for breath, he almost lost his train of thought. He had already lost Rick, who was just standing there, tapping his right shoe. *Jesus Christ!* What was he doing, anyway? He hated talking. He had to think.

They needed a plan. Even if it were just to get more food and water. Fresh water was at a premium and the kitchen was outside the rioters' area of control. The rioters could have guaranteed access to the kitchen if any of this had been planned! Although there was almost no fresh meat and produce in the Joint at any given time, there were gallon cans of pork and beans, peas, corn, peaches, spaghetti and an assortment of Campbell's soups on open shelving in the huge larder. Those staples of prison fare he had scorned the other day now seemed like the number one thing on his wish list.

Stupid, Dace thought, but just because the biggest bingo in Canadian history was underway, it didn't mean anybody gave a fuck if the insurgents got fed. He wasn't sure about the offence's strategy, but starving people into submission was one option. He doubted they'd do that, though. That would mean they'd risk the hostages, too. All six of them. Jesus. Why the hell had they taken so many goddamn hostages?

Rick held out his arm. "What?" Dace asked, but he already knew what his friend wanted. Familiarity. Something to which they both returned when they needed reassurance.

Shit, Dace thought with distaste. The man reeked of sweat and nicotine. But Dace sat on the floor and prepared to arm wrestle him anyway. When they clapped their hands together, part of him was repelled, but Dace also ached for what his friend had so recently enjoyed: more cigarettes and maybe a little something stronger. Ice, speed. Once or twice Dace had cranked up, when a dirty guard had snuck some dope into the Joint, mixed with the white detergent in the laundry truck. That'd be a nice escape right now.

Rick lay almost flat on his back after the first round, his fighting arm bent an awkward angle. He wanted to have another go and at this point it was easier to wrestle than look him in the face. After the second round Dace felt a little better, but Rick re-launched his appeal, like it was the loser's prerogative.

"What's the point of talking to the man?" Dace asked when Rick ran out of breath. "All I want is to get out of here and that's not going to happen."

"I'm not asking you to negotiate, man," Rick insisted.

"No, because you think I'm too fucking hot-headed."

Rick's words raced out. "I've been planning this bingo for ages and I'm on the goddamn Inmate Committee."

"Jesus. You and McAllister?" Dace asked.

"Yeah, well, I know he's crazy, but he couldn't have done it without me. One of my buddies in the kitchen made a working model of the key to the gun cage. Oh man. You weren't there when they busted in, but it felt like we'd all died and gone to heaven."

"Who made the key?"

Rick shook his head. "No names, Dace," he said almost sadly. "You know the code. I didn't expect this to come off. It was just good luck that the new guard was so careless in rec hall the other day. We didn't even need our key. Where was I? Oh, yeah. So Dace, all I'm asking for is a little help."

"Fuck. You sound like the goddamn Beatles. Who the hell's been watching your back?"

"You have! But now you gotta watch the hostages when I'm gone," Rick continued, running his finger through his thinning hair. Once his mother's pride and joy, most of Rick's ginger hair had fallen out the first time he'd been arrested in Maitland. He swore it was the prison food, but Dace knew better. Rick worked in the prison kitchen and cooked most of his own food anyway.

"It's the drink," Rick's mother always said. Well, could be. Rick was always drinking some demon away. He'd been released on the manslaughter charge just last year—he hadn't got quite as much time as Dace — but had gotten into more trouble right away. Now he was doing more time for a heist gone bad.

For several minutes Rick tugged at his head, pulling it with both his strong, freckled hands. Dace stared gloomily at the sixteen cells across the way, their doors all askew, an open invitation to the prison at large.

"I think that we should leave the guards with Sandy," he finally said, feeling every inch a pompous ass.

Rick snorted. "Good one! You've seen Sandy. We can't let that stupid shit keep his dumb hostages. What do you think he'll do to them when he realizes Admin won't give in to his demands? He claims he was convicted with a bunch of lies. He told the Press he was forced to talk because somebody nailed his goddamn testicles to a chair. And now he wants a pardon, for Chrissakes."

"As if—"

Rick shook his head. "Well, he's not negotiating for better prison conditions for us, that's for sure. And now he's halfway up the hostages' asses. He'll whack them off one by one and have more fun than a fat brat shooting balls at the village fair. And where will that leave you and me, friend? Up shit creek without a paddle, that's where. I stopped by there and I'm telling you, he was drooling over Saksun. You know, the young 'un all the queens like."

"What? That fat—"

"I'm just saying there ain't nobody getting paroled if this bingo goes bad. That means you too, Dace."

"Let me get this right. You're asking me to take over for Sandy and babysit the most hated fucks in the Joint. Is that right? Fuck that. Do I look like I'm crazy? What do you think is gonna happen when the party's over? My guess is everybody will dummy up and we'll end up with a couple of shivs in our backs — if we're lucky!"

"Yeah, you're right. I'm a crazy man. Fuck, fuck, fuck!" Looking slightly surprised at his own daring, Rick grabbed Dace's green shirt front and shook him with each emphatic fuck.

"I'm losin' my cool! You see me running back and forth between the army outside and the hostages in here? Fuck, fuck, fuck," he repeated. "Where's it going to end?"

When Dace went limp, Rick backed up and smacked his own forehead with the heel of his hand.

"That's it for me," Dace said, straightening up and clapping his friend so hard on the back that he almost fell over. "I'm going back to my cell to get some shut-eye. Wake me up when the party's over."

Rick stared at him, looking surprisingly close to tears. "We're all going to die," he said with the deadly calm of a true believer, leaving the righteous implication that Dace was a deserter. Like you were on that day so long ago, his underlying tone implied. "They'll blow this fucking place sky high if anything happens to those guards. You know that. I need you to watch those hostages, Dace. You know I'd do the same for you. I'm the guy who stuck around to face the music when that stupid shit ass — what was his name again? Turpin?"

"Turbot," Dace said.

"Yeah, well when he died. Jesus Christ, clean out your ears and listen to Loony Tunes! Sandy's in a fucking fever and there's no telling what he'll do. I heard the shrink call him a megomaniac. That means — "

"It's megalomaniac, and I know what the fuck it means!"

"Well, he's recruiting every homicidal maniac in the Joint! They'll kill the hostages, man. You know that. Then they'll bring back the death penalty. We'll hang for killing coppers or we'll die in a hail of bullets." His eyes narrowed dangerously. "And your pretty little cousin will bawl her eyes out over a pauper's grave."

Dace stood up so fast Rick backed away. It was just like last time: a balls up, a fuck up, a big mess. Except this time he had no place to run. He shook his head, trying to clear his thoughts. Rick had bent his ear for so long he was starting to make sense. Dace glared at him, clenching and unclenching his fists as he thought. He could see Sandy — or Loony Tunes, as they had taken to calling him — was up to no good.

As if to underscore the dilemma, Sandy chose that moment to toot through his bullhorn, his voice loud and clear. "Get the hell out of your chicken shit cells!"

The hair on Dace's arms prickled. *What cells?* Everybody had already been liberated, except... Jesus, if Sandy was sniffing around the segregated men in the west wing, things were really bad.

Crashes replaced shouts. He'd never heard a porcelain toilet breaking before, but he recognized the sound now. He could almost visualize the water on the floor. Filthy water dumping from brown-stained porcelain. Where did the stupid fucks plan to piss if they wiped out the toilets? It wasn't like they could just go outside and spray the rhododendron bushes in the visitors' area.

Almost simultaneously, some of the segregated men started screaming—a sound he had heard before. Noise like this usually brought the screws running, like jackals to a fresh kill.

"They're trying to get the diddlers," Rick said, confirming their worst suspicions. His facial expression was a cross between I told you so and despair.

Dace leaned over the railing. "Shut the fuck up!" he shouted into the dome area.

"Easy, easy," Rick said, trying to ease Dace's quick temper.

The Joint was never quiet for long and the noise made Dace nuts. People had a habit of goading him: a raucous neighbour in the next refusing to do his own time, a power drunken guard bullying a new fish. He had kicked the noisy neighbour so bad he had even scared himself. Not that anybody minded. Even the guards had looked the other way.

"I'm okay, Rick," he said, the closest he could get to an apology. "But I don't want to start singing evangelistic hymns like Sandy just to drown out his crap. You could let him keep the hostages. He might be doing us a favour, you know. And maybe he's no worse than you or me. How does anybody know how they'll behave? It's a rare day goes by that I don't have a crazy desire to pick any three pigs in this shit-house and beat the living slime from their bodies."

"Yeah, but look at you. Strength always overrules insanity. Well, usually," Rick said when Dace scowled. "And I'm willing to bet that it would this time, too."

It was costing Dace though. He'd always enjoyed the strength his hatred gave him. Every time he subdued a violent impulse now, he felt a little disappointed. Like he'd left something important unfinished.

Rick kept on him. Man, the guy was persistent. "Listen, man, I know the pigs have tried to destroy us with every method they can conceive of, but those hostages are collateral and I don't know what else to do."

Christ, Rick was never going to shut up. "All right," Dace finally said, surprising even himself. "All right." Maybe, just maybe, he was thinking too much. He had always preferred to make decisions on the spur of the moment or not at all. *And look where that got me,* he thought. "Give me the fuckin' extra keys to the guard room, friend," he said sarcastically, not entirely convinced he was doing the right thing. "I'll watch the goddamn screws. And I'll keep watching your back while you're hobnobbing with the big shots. Just don't ask me for nothing more."

For a moment, Rick almost looked a rested, happy man. His sinewy body sagged, like somebody who had tapped into his final reserve of energy and could now afford to relax. "I won't ask for anything more," he promised.

"Yeah, I bet."

"And I'll take the rap when it's over," Rick assured him. "Like I tried to last time. You know I did. And you almost got away, didn't you? All the way to Timmins. At least you had a little fun," he said, almost wistfully.

Yeah, I almost got away, with a man dying on the floor and you stuck there, Dace thought. "Forget it," he said. "This is my trip."

For starters, he would move the hostages somewhere safe. It was no good down there on the first floor. Yeah. That should be easy. No problemo. Piece of cake. He rhymed off all the like-minded clichés he knew. If only he could have traded places with Rick, so he could be the emissary to the outside world, the person everybody wanted to hear from, the man who would save the cons and the fucking hapless hostages as well. But it was too late for that now. They wanted Dace's brawn, not his brains. Besides, he had as good as given his word and, well, he owed Rick. He really did. Christ, what a stupid little fuck he'd been.

"Hey, bring me back a beer and a cheeseburger," he yelled, watching Rick head off towards the enemy world.

Chapter Sixteen
Inglorious Babysitters

Maitland Penitentiary:
Trouble Doesn't Show—
On the outside, everything looks quiet.
Prisoners are no longer clanging on their cell
bars and they have stopped booing our troops.
There is no sign of surrender, though. It is
reported that inmates have homemade weapons
but no guns or knives. Although one guard has been
released, authorities are convinced the prisoners will
kill the hostages if necessary.
German Shepherd dogs arrived to stand guard
during the night.
—*Maitland Spectator*, September 7, 1971

Dace led his inmate police force downstairs and through a snarl of add-on halls, to get the hostages. Steve and Big Alf swaggered along after him, lords of what little remained. Broken furniture, sodden mattresses and garbage littered the Dome area, the pristine public place the Joint had always presented to the world.

Nobody else was around. Anybody with half a brain was fast asleep under a bed. On the second day of the riot only a couple of men—burglars mostly—had tunnelled through the ancient dropped ceiling in the Administration wing, looking for break and entry points into rooms below. The noise of them skittering and clunking was nerve-racking. What if some of the army guys got in there?

"So where the hell are they?" Steve demanded.

"Ah, Jesus, kid, can't you smell them?" Big Alf said, halting in front of a half door nobody had noticed before.

The door opened as if on command and Dace found himself face-to-face with inmates he didn't know. "Get the fuck out of here," he said.

"Yeah, assholes, we're taking over," Big Alf said, pushing in ahead.

From a distance Dace thought he could hear Sandy shouting. Without their leader around, Sandy's henchmen weren't putting up much of a fight. From the bored looks on their faces, Dace figured they'd guarded the hostages while Sandy partied all night.

Stooping down, Dace peered through the entrance, waiting for his eyes to adjust to the gloom. Part of him was afraid of what he might see. Eventually their outlines came into focus: six screws, face down on the floor, hands bound behind their backs. Dace entered the room and forced himself to take a good look around. None of the captives were moving, but that was probably because any sort of movement would have hurt, not because they were dead. The room was tight and hot. He doubted there was much air left, especially if Sandy's boys had kept the door shut all night.

It also stank. Urine accounted for part of that, as did sweat, but Dace could also smell fear. Somebody coughed and tried to move his bound arms. Christ, it looked like Murray. Too bad they'd gotten him. He was one of the few guards who had even attempted to be fair.

"Easy, guy," Dace said, bending down to loosen Murray's ropes. None of the hostages said anything. They were listless, their faces bovinely blank with despair.

"Hey asshole, it's for their own protection," one of Sandy's thugs said.

Dace sweated with the half-hearted help of Steve and Big Alf, who had followed him in. It took a long time to untie the captives in such a confined space. None of former guards had said anything when they came in, so it was a bit of a surprise when Murray spoke up.

"Thanks," he said.

"I'm not doing this for you," Dace said. The last thing he wanted was their thanks.

"When are we getting out of here?" the youngest hostage, Saksun, whined.

"Shut the fuck up," Big Alf said, waving his bit of steel in the general direction of the boy's head.

Cursing and grunting, they pulled their prizes into sitting positions. Dace felt sick. He couldn't look anybody in the face. He sent Steve for some cheese sandwiches instead. The sandwiches were sent in from outside, but all the hostages wanted was water.

"See? They're not even hungry," a Sandy clone observed.

"They ain't wanted for nothing," a second one said.

"They've got it way better than us. They always have." And so it went.

"This is the turd who gets his jollies using the strap," one of them said, kicking the rear of one unhappy man.

"Shut up and back off," Dace said, wishing to hell the job was just done.

With his arms folded across his chest and his head almost touching the ceiling, he waited, marvelling at his own patience. Jesus, if he didn't watch it, he was going to start feeling sorry for the screws. They were such sitting ducks! Then again, they all were. One little stink bomb and they could all end up dead. If this had occurred to anybody else, they didn't appear to care. Big Alf and Steve sat on the floor, a little apart from him and the hostages, arms wrapped around their knees. In the almost airless room, Big Alf's head lolled forward on his chest. The big man was so relaxed he'd actually fallen asleep.

Dace had to move them. "The bastards are going to suffocate in here," Dace tried explaining to Sandy's men. "Do you really want a freezer full of dead meat?"

"You gotta ask Sandy."

For a moment, Dace envied Sandy's hold on these men. He bided his time, though, knowing the fewer goons he had on his ass, the better it would be. Big Alf didn't think so. When he woke up, he listed the stuff he wanted to do to Sandy's henchmen. Ended up he didn't have to do anything, because after a while Sandy's men just left.

Dace followed them, stepping outside the heating duct and shouting at their retreating backs. "Is it something I said?"

The last man sauntered off without a word, perhaps in search of lunch. Who knew? Maybe there were still some sandwiches on the table they'd set up in the Dome. Dace's own belly had stopped rumbling hours ago, but he was surprised to notice he was beginning to miss the routines of the place. The smug, all-knowing clock outside the heating duct didn't help. It was almost noon. At this time yesterday they would have finished breakfast and lunch and still had dinner to go. Jesus Christ, had the highlight of his life really been three squares a day?

Better get everybody moving, he thought, but just as he turned back to the hostages' makeshift cell, he bumped into Sandy McAllister himself. They eyed each other, toe to toe.

Both Big Alf and Steve looked a little agitated. "Finders keepers," Steve said.

Jesus, Dace thought, recoiling from Sandy's alcohol saturated breath. He wanted to sock him, but he couldn't. He knew himself too well, and once he started he wouldn't be able to stop. What the hell did Sandy expect? He must have been gone for hours. Dace glared at Sandy, thinking about the sanctimonious pig and all the shit he'd started. Next thing he knew, he had Sandy in a neck hold while the guy made funny noises and pulled at his arm. Christ, it felt good.

"Dace," Steve said quietly, but he barely heard him. Dace wished he had killed Sandy a long time ago. If he had, they probably wouldn't be in this mess. Why the hell had he waited so long?

"Dace!" Steve repeated until Dace reluctantly released his hold.

Sandy went limp but straightened quickly. "Aw, Jeez. Aw, Jeez," he gasped, his eyes bulging. "Are you fucking crazy or what?" he demanded, spittle flying from his mouth. "Where's everybody? What's happened to my fucking so-called friends? Did the cunts all bail out?"

A big gob of saliva smacked Dace in the face and he fought the urge to jump Sandy again. Big Alf looked inclined to do the same, but Dace waved him back with one hand. He had almost lost it … again. Whatever happened, he had to keep his cool. Even if Sandy kept screaming "Give me my fucking hostages!" into Dace's face, over and over. His life, all their lives, depended on Dace's keeping control of his rage.

"Dace, allow me," Big Alf pleaded, licking his lips and rubbing his hands together with anticipation.

"No," he said. "It's okay. I think our friend is just leaving. Right, Sandy?"

Sandy stopped. He looked exhausted. He glared at them a moment, then turned and left.

It was the hostages' turn next. "We're not going anywhere," Murray said, evidently their spokesperson. "Some of those guys are worse than McAllister."

"You think?" Steve said.

Big Alf didn't wait for Dace's permission this time. "You ungrateful cunts," he said, seizing the man closest to him. Two or three minutes later, all the hostages had sailed through the door. Dace came out of the duct and assessed the men in their stained, ill-fitting inmate clothes. Five had landed on their feet. The sixth belly crawled along the floor.

Steve laughed. "Look!" he said. "What's the matter with him? It's Saksun, isn't it? Looks like a bitch in heat."

"Shut up. He's scared, stupid," Dace said, then yanked Saksun up by his collar and pushed him out where he could see him. He gave him a couple of boots, and the other hostages fell in behind, along with Big Alf and Steve.

Except for Saksun, the hostages were manageable. When they reached the Dome, Dace elbowed a couple of intruders in the gut and when one man persisted, he floored him. The look of gratitude on Saksun's face was almost comical. Men jumped out of hidden corners as they walked, and Dace wondered if they could smell the captives.

"Hey, Dace," one man shouted, delirious with freedom. "What are you herding bulls for? Can we come with you?"

"Look at us!" another one shrieked, leering in Saksun's terrified face. "We're free! We're free!"

From what Dace could see, several subgroups of prisoners controlled the living quarters in the cruciform. Those all appeared to be in a drug induced fool's paradise. The outside yard was No-Man's land. Fifty or so men were packed into the Dome in growling groups of four or five, like roving packs of dogs.

Although everybody figured the army was at the gates, their estimated entry time and choice of weaponry was still a matter of heated debate. Every time a shout went up, the rebels stampeded to the wall furthest from the broken gate, anticipating a tsunami of soldiers equipped with rubber hoses, truncheons or worse. Sometimes somebody shouted just for fun.

One end of the Dome, where the floor sloped down, was deep with filthy water, overflow from the broken toilets. When they reached this point, Saksun slipped and fell, his eyes rolling back in his head. An onlooker shouted, "Leave him, we'll take care of him!" but young Saksun didn't react. The other hostages took over and dragged him the rest of the way.

It concerned Dace that things were going relatively well. In his experience, when things got easy, it was time to watch out. Guards were wily. Their docility could be an act. On the other hand, the loss of their uniforms—a retributive tactic they themselves had employed many times before—could have contributed to their co-operation.

Had he been in one of their places, Dace would have been pondering his personal worth. Sure, it was in the inmates' own best interests to negotiate for these guards, but would they? Why negotiate for a guard who could easily be replaced when you could just throw him to the dogs? The public didn't want them hurt, but what if there were a greater good?

From the moment Dace had entered the heating duct, he'd known the captives were no longer prison guards, they were just scared people. But the thought was so uncomfortable he'd pushed it away. They got as far as Cellblock B before Murray, the oldest and heaviest of the hostages, saw the stairs. "Where the fuck are we going?" he asked, massaging his left arm.

Dace didn't hesitate. "Let's go," he shouted, taking the old guard's arm and ordering everybody else ahead. "Haul Saksun's ass upstairs." He matched his steps to Saksun's and Murray's, hoping the old guy wouldn't drop dead of a heart attack on the stairs. "It's okay, Gramps. We'll just take it easy," he said.

After they got everybody upstairs, Big Alf and Steve boarded up the pass at the top of the stairs with a heap of mattresses and some busted metal cots.

"Now what?" Steve asked. He looked a little green but still seemed to be raring to go.

"Easy," Dace said. "Our mission is to keep the hostages safe. How hard can that be?" he quipped. "Loony Tunes is our main threat. Sooner or later he's gonna want his hostages back. You saw him."

Big Alf didn't see a problem, but then he never did. "Aw, Sandy's crazy. He shouldn't even be here. He belongs in Penetang."

"He might be crazy, but he knows how valuable his hostages are," Dace said, then shrugged. "He'll definitely try to get them again. He assaulted a guard to get the key. That's worth at least five more years in jail. Those screws were the only leverage he had."

"Well, they're our babies now."

"You gotta take care of babies, though. Deliver these guys safely and we'll have something to bargain with. Get them killed and the whole prison population is done for. The army will come in and shoot half of us in the head, while the rest ... There's a lot of guys here with nothing to lose. You get a twenty-five year stretch, what's a few more?"

"Jesus," Steve said, "Not me! They were talking about paroling me in three months."

"Yeah, kid," Dace replied, scaling their makeshift barrier and staring down the narrow staircase. "Me, too."

Loony Tunes might come up with a couple of buddies at any moment, murder on their minds. A dark part of Dace almost wished he could be with them. "The stairs are too narrow. They'lll have to come up one at a time," he said, grinning at Big Alf and Steve. "I can't wait. One kick, that's all it'll take."

Little by little, the hostages settled in and everybody, Dace included, lost track of time. They were babysitters, inglorious babysitters, that's all. For a while the hostages even got a second wind, almost garrulous with relief that they were still alive.

"More food," they shouted.

"More smokes."

And "Jesus fuck, it's getting hot in here. What are you trying to do, roast us to death?"

"Ha, ha. Roast pig," Big Alf joked.

Periodically one of them even took it into his head to try and talk sense into his captors or plead his own case. Murray's heart was palpitating, or Saksun wanted to go home ...

"I'm getting to know more about these bastards than I want to know," Steve complained. "It's like they're regular people or something. I don't like it."

"Let me in there," Big Alf said, flexing a length of torn cloth between his two great hands. "I know what to do."

By the third day, every cell in Dace's body was screaming to shut down. He saw stars when he yawned, but when it was his turn he still couldn't sleep. Plenty of time for sleep later, he reminded himself, tightening a black bandana around his forehead to keep his eyes open.

Try as he might to convince himself that his job was as important as Rick had claimed, his euphoria was fading fast. He couldn't get past the notion that his inmate police force was a bit of a joke. 'Police force' implied members had competed for positions and undergone rigorous training, or at least pulled strings. 'Police force' also suggested members might be in uniform. Dace's team looked like they were auditioning for Moby Dick.

"Wake the fuck up," he hissed through clenched teeth. Big Alf's eyes were rolling back into his head. Christ, the guy looked stupid. All he had to do was watch the West stairs, one of three steel-edged staircases leading from different cellblocks.

It had been a mistake to take on a man over forty, but Alf had practically begged for the job. He was used to playing second fiddle in the banks he'd robbed and he didn't mind doing the same thing now. He liked life on the edge. And he was strong enough — when he was awake.

"I'm not asleep, I'm not asleep," he repeated, his bristly grey head bobbing up and down. He flicked his eyes towards Dace, then frowned. "Jesus, I was just checking for blood on the fucking stairs," he said.

"Okay, okay, man," Dace agreed.

Simmering down a little, Alf nodded at the cells. "It's awfully quiet in there," he said. "Do you think they're all right?"

"Look at them. They're just sitting at that little table playing cards. Kind like a bunch of old Greek guys in the park."

Alf smirked. "Probably all tuckered out."

At first the hostages had argued with each other, but they were playing euchre now and whispering too quietly for their captors to hear. Murray, who would have retired long ago if his youngest child weren't wasting time in the Music Department at Maitland University, occasionally stopped shuffling cards and yelled something like,

"What are you punks trying to accomplish? Rick Lowery and his goddamn Inmate Committee be damned! Do you really think Ottawa's going to cave in to your demands? What are your demands, anyway? Better food? You already eat better than most of us, that's why you keep coming back! C'mon, you jokers, you can't trust your buddies, you can't trust the authorities, you can't trust John Q. Public! Hell, most of you can't even trust your own mothers!"

At the mention of their mothers, two or three of the sentries bellowed back, "Shut the fuck up!" so he did for a while.

Dace had a bird's eye view of everything happening below if he leaned over the railing. Except, heights made him dizzy, something he'd found out when he got treed by some German Shepherds. Which is also how he found out that trouble can hatch in the most unlikely places. God help him, he really had learned something that boarding school.

As for here, it looked like things were going okay in the main cellblock. He couldn't help wondering what was going on in Segregation, though. He kept hearing awful sounds. And what about Outside? If only he could be in two or three places at once. He weighed the steel bar in his hand, tossing it into the air and catching it with one hand. At least he was armed.

The worse part of the job was keeping an eye on Big Alf and Steve. The more tired he got, the more irritated he felt about having to bribe, cajole and practically arm-wrestle the lazy buggers just to do their jobs. Not that he blamed them. They hated screws, they weren't supposed to be guarding them, and they were all going to pay for it once they were found out. In Dace's bleakest moments he suspected he was a patsy, a traitor, and that he was taking everybody else down with him. Everybody except Rick. Jeez, Rick had better get his ass back here.

Christ! What's that? He checked Steve's post again. Nah, it was nothing. Just his imagination. Nothing could get up those stairs. Just in case, they'd strung a thin wire across the bottom of the hostages' door. He prayed anyway, appealing to his dead mother, the Virgin Mary, and his cousin Liza that the whole goddamn mess would soon be over. Because if the hostages died, he'd die too, though he figured he was as good as dead anyway. Like he was trapped in a kind of European village infiltrated by informants and Nazi sympathizers, where men could be bought for almost nothing and often were.

Given half a chance, he'd trade a hostage for a cup of java and a fresh ham sandwich, even if the stupid bastards were starting to grow on him just a little. To say he was getting fond of them would be stretching the point, but he did feel sorry for them. That's all. Even feeling that much bothered him. Maybe that's what happened when you looked after someone, unless you were a Gestapo guard. Or maybe he was just too tired to think straight.

For the first time in his life, Dace wondered what the guards thought when they applied to work in a federal penitentiary. Had they wanted to protect the public at large? Did it make them feel morally superior to somebody else? Did they think having that kind of job justified treating men like scum? Had they really expected to earn a paycheck and go home to their families at night as if nothing bad ever happened? That they'd never have to pay for their sins? Well, maybe. A part of Dace still expected to go home when they got locked down at night. What am I doing here? Where and when am I going?

Enough of this. He rapped his steel bar on the iron railing. Several people looked up from the Dome and waved. He had to wake up, quit feeling sorry for the screws, with the possible exception of young Saksun. Careful, he cautioned himself again. It was much easier to think in black and white, like everybody else here did. Avoid the greys. Avoid the exceptions. Then again, as long as nobody found out what he was thinking, that was okay. As long as nobody learned he had supplied guards with his own cigarettes and blankets, and even asked young Steve to break into the canteen for extra chocolate bars, cigarettes, toothpaste and toothbrushes. How the hell would that look if anyone found out?

He was sick and tired of listening to Saksun blubber. If Rick still wanted to release him, a show of faith, Dace was game. The kid never shut the fuck up. Worse, after a while he started to look a bit like Dace's little sister, except Rosie was a helluva lot smarter and braver. Too brave, Dace reminded himself. She was always using her infant charm to wheedle out of trouble or wriggle out of Father Danby's hairy hands in that fucking school.

Said she couldn't remember any of that stuff now. Good for her. Not that he wanted to go down that memory lane.

He rapped the railing again, but nobody looked up this time. Probably because some stupid fuck was screaming bloody murder as they hauled him across the floor of the Dome. Saksun was almost making as much noise. He couldn't do much about the guy in the Dome, but ...

The last time he'd spoken to Rick, he'd promised on his mother's grave that nothing would happen to the screws. But he swore, if Rick didn't get his ass up here soon, he was going to put the boots to Saksun. So what if Saksun was the little bastard who'd let Sandy get the key, the guy who had set the whole goddamn bingo in motion? Let him go, please. Anything to stop the noise.

His head throbbed from the noise and lack of sleep. He rubbed it hard with his free hand and tried to reason with himself. Why hadn't he left the hostages in the duct? Because they were like a bunch of hens with a fox at the door. And maybe because Rick was his friend and he owed him—a fact which was getting harder and harder to remember the longer the riot went on.

Saksun was still crying. "Here, take this," Dace said, blatantly bribing him with the last Milky Way. The kid sniffled about seeing his new bride again as he licked the chocolate paper clean. Dace came real close to kicking him then. The rest of the hostages chimed in, claiming they were starving. Dace ignored them. They'd all had more than their fair share of food sent in from Outside.

Dace was also hungry, or would have been if he'd taken stock of his physical state instead of letting a little voice, still in touch with his old self, yap. Give 'em what they want. Let 'em out, let 'em out, let 'em out. That'll shut 'em all up. Dace smiled to himself, savouring the idea. One by one, right over the railing, plummeting to the cement floor four stories below. He wouldn't have to worry about them then. If they didn't croak on impact, some psycho would bop them off.

Tempted as he was, he headed back out and tested the mesh railing with his weight, although he was careful not to lean too far. At just under six feet, he was taller than most of the other cons. He figured they were all the stunted offspring of smokers who had suckled their children on bottled Coke if they fed them at all.

Jesus, what was taking Rick so long? He leaned over the rail again but couldn't make out anybody with a red bandanna like Rick's. Too much going on. The foyer entrance to the Joint was usually empty at this time of day, except for a janitorial prisoner dispiritedly dragging a stringy grey mop over the floor. The area was alive with rioters today, milling around like visitors at a country fair, most of them doped or punch drunk on the contraband substances they'd stashed or looted over the past few days.

At a distance of forty feet, equipped with nearly perfect vision, Dace could almost make out some of his fellow prisoners, although he was so tired some of their faces blurred. He relied more on the way people walked to identify them. A group of guys were acting like stagehands, setting up chairs around the huge radiator which dominated the foyer. Maybe they were arguing about the placement of the chairs, a dozen or more, but he didn't think so. He straightened up. Something about this didn't look good.

Jesus, he didn't have time for this, he thought, kicking the rail. He had two choices: stay and take care of the hostages or check out what was happening downstairs.

It was almost time to phone Rick again anyway. In addition to everything else, he had agreed to call him every hour to report on the hostages. That's how they were keeping the negotiating team informed. Too bad the closest black box was down a flight of stairs and around a corner. There were only a couple of wall phones in the penitentiary and the authorities had cut all but one of the lines. Fortunately they hadn't gotten to them before quick thinking Rick had notified a local radio station about what was going on. The radio announcer was young and radical and on their side, so he had spread the news. He had also reassured everyone that the hostages were fine, buying them a chunk of time, or they'd be dust by now.

Shit. He had to get his act together. He was starting to fall asleep on his feet. Everything was happening in slow motion. He didn't feel real. This was worse than the Hole, for God's sake. The next time he looked over the rail, only five minutes had passed, but the crowd had shifted, opening up centre space in the Dome.

"Holy Mother." He whistled through his teeth, noting the stage was set for something that looked eerily like Musical Chairs. He remembered that game from when they'd played it at school when it was somebody's birthday. The winner had merited the dubious pleasure of a walk in the bush with Father Danby. But that was long ago. Here today stood a dozen stacking chairs, their metal legs hobbled together with multi-coloured scarves, awaiting occupation by lottery. Who were the winners? Could he be one? For protecting the most hated group in prison: the guards?

The most hated. Well, not quite. Diddlers were more despised than the guards. Child molesters, stool pigeons. Dace was hard pressed to think of a prisoner who wasn't busting to bag one.

He remembered Liza writing about a short story called "The Lottery" and was momentarily ashamed about how happy he felt, imagining other victims in his place. But shame was a luxury at the best of times and one he could ill afford today, so he made eye contact with his sentries again.

One by one, each man's eyes assured him all's well. Well, almost each man. Alf, the stupid fuck, was snoring on the job. And Steve was just a kid. Seventeen. He'd had a rough time until Dace had taken him under his wing. One of the queens had wanted him, but Steve hadn't wanted the queen. Well, such was life. Steve had jumped three grades in the prison classroom and won a Rookie of the Year award just before they'd canned the athletics program. If he hadn't been raised in a string of foster homes, he would have made some mother proud. Dace caught his eye and winked.

Neither Steve, nor any of the other sentries could know what was happening below. They were too far from the action. Better not to say anything. They were too easily distracted as it was. He checked his Timex again. Christ, where had the time gone? He had to phone Rick.

Bam, bam, bam! The hostages were thumping their feet. "One, two, three, four, we want the fuck outta here," they chanted.

"Sure, guys." Steve snickered. "Nice rhyme."

He was oblivious to the extra set of hands which suddenly appeared behind his head.

"Look out!" Dace said.

Steve wasn't listening. He shrugged, rolling his eyes at the hostages. "They'll wear themselves out soon." Then his eyes bugged out when two hands wrapped around his neck.

"It's Bellissimo!" Alf shouted. "Little bastard snuck up the stairs."

Steve's homemade truncheon had rolled to the floor but somehow he kept his balance, perhaps because his assailant was twice his age and half his size. Dace, who had been diverted both by the vibrating door of the hostages' room and the scene developing in the Dome below, sprang forward just in time.

"Let go, Bellissimo," he whispered in the clinging little man's ear. Bellissimo wasn't strong, but he had the advantage of being crazy enough to stop at nothing that got in his way. Homemade toothbrush shanks were his speciality. He had

173

already killed two men in the communal shower; a seam-sized shank had been slipped between their ribs at an enemy's request and nobody had ever been the wiser.

"Whose side you guys on?" Bellissimo yipped, his hold relaxing slightly, although Steve was still coughing, his face turning purple. "I'm just gonna get me one of those mother fuckin' chicken-shit guards and have me a little fun."

"The same kind of fun they have with you, right?" Dace guessed, and as Bellissimo let go of Steve, both men nodded imperceptibly. "Well, see if you can get this, you dirty skinner. I haven't got all day to explain it to you. There's no teenyboppers here for you to ream," Dace said, staring into his opponent's eyes. "You got that? So keep your hands off our fucking hostages, okay? If you don't, we'll all be furniture dust before we know it."

Bellissimo ducked under Dace's right arm. In a reflex motion, Dace's arm shot out and the little assailant was suddenly flailing, his arms and legs reaching as he fell backwards down the stairs.

Staring down into the dark abyss, Dace shouted, "Are you okay?"

There was no response, so they kept squinting down, waiting. Gradually they made out Bellissimo, lying at the foot of the stairs. He was alive, just too ornery to answer.

"Fuck. Nothing's gonna kill that little snake," Steve swore as his assailant struggled to his feet.

By now there was so much noise coming from the Dome they almost couldn't hear Bellissimo. There was nothing wrong with the guy's voice box, though. "You broke something, Debo!" he screeched up at them, rubbing his jaw. "You're gonna pay for this, you and your little bum boy!"

Chapter Seventeen
Only Women Bleed
Maitland University, September 6-7, 1971

Who is the third who walks always beside you?
When I count, there are only you and I together
But when I look ahead, up the white road
There is always another one walking beside you,
Gliding wrapt in a brown mantle, hooded
I do not know whether a man or a woman
But who is that on the other side of you?
—Eliot, "The Waste Land"

Alternating between the penitentiary and the university, Liza reverted to the girl she had always been, one who'd lived on two continents in two different households, one who had always been torn between two lives. She even amazed herself, she had so much energy. Complete strangers were drawn to her, a girl with wild, unbraided hair who got by on four hours of sleep. She hardly even ate. She snacked on chocolate bars instead, and still she glowed. In her heart, she knew she had been born for this. Born to rescue somebody, born to get Dace out. But how?

The only person she'd confided in was Mel, but he really didn't have any idea either. And though he hadn't known her long enough to say so, he was plainly tired of the whole drama. She knew by the glazed look in his eyes that he wanted to pull back, to be the safe, small-town boy he had been before they'd met. For him, it was just one damn thing after another.

He couldn't though, just pull back. Because if he did, she might too, and he wanted her. Wanted her in the worst way. She knew that too. Before she'd come along, he'd had a couple of one night stands, just a couple of rolls in the hay. Liza had tried to diffuse some of his fascination with her by telling him everything about Tony in Dublin, but he didn't care. If anything, it made him want her more. He prepared for his Science classes during the day and although they were both too young to drink beer at the local pub in the evenings, she hung out with him in his MG late at night, listening to *Blood, Sweat and Tears*. It was the only place near the residence that was truly private.

"I'm not sure I care for your taste in music, girl," he said. They'd just been listening to "Some Sympathy for the Devil" for the third time.

"It suits my mood," she replied. "I'm so frustrated. I wish there was something I could do. It's driving me crazy, sitting here, waiting for some official to feed the reporters their stupid lines." The *Maitland Spectator* had interviewed all the family members of the hostages then reported that days might pass before anybody discovered the 'full extent of the horror' behind the penitentiary walls.

"Hmm. Maybe it's not such a good idea to keep carrying that placard. You don't want to draw too much heat."

"But I have to do something!"

"Well, you can't crawl inside the Pen," Mel reasoned. "Your cousin sounds like a tough dude. He can take care of himself. He'll be all right." The high-rise student residence loomed over them in loco parentis, doing a poor job. Many of its windows were still aglow at nearly 4:00 a.m.

Liza and Mel were sharing a joint. Neither of them had ever smoked pot before, but he was a small-town boy who had come well equipped to a big town university, mostly through his mother's efforts. He had enough quarters to wash eight months' worth of his jeans and underwear, and sufficient condoms to equip his entire dormitory floor. His mother, he'd told her, was determined that an early marriage would not snuff out a promising medical career, as it had for his older brother.

"You have to suck it into your lungs and hold it there," he advised, apparently pleased to be teaching her something she didn't already know. Maybe, he'd said, he could teach her how to drive a car, too.

"I feel shivery!"

"It's working," he promised. His arms wrapped around her in the front seat and he held the sweet smelling cigarette to her lips while his other hand slipped to her breast. "But you gotta relax."

"I can't," she said, staring out the window. They were less than two hundred yards from their student residence. A stream flowed to the left, lazy at this time of year, belying its reputation for claiming a young life every few years in the spring.

"Yes, you can," he insisted. His hand slipped lower and slid over her hip bone. These days Liza was thin almost to the point of emaciation. Her hip bones jutted from her sides and sharp angles planed her face. "You gotta eat," he kept saying.

After losing several pounds she could ill-afford to lose, she probably should have lost his interest, except he was inexplicably and thoroughly intrigued. He had never met anyone like her before, and her jailbird cousin, well, he was in prison! Of course she was concerned about him. She was a woman, or almost one, after all. His mother, who read Betty Friedan and was prone to saying, *Only women bleed*, wore her own heart on her sleeve. He was still a little hard-pressed to understand why Liza was even slightly interested in this convict, who was probably disfigured with tattoos and stupider than Curly, Larry and Moe combined. But that was a woman for you, and he liked her that way.

In the mood for some softer music, Mel yanked *Blood, Sweat and Tears* from his tape deck with his free hand. The car radio blared.

"One man is confirmed dead and another is close to dying after the worst riot in Maitland Penitentiary history," the announcer said, practically salivating. "The bodies of Robin Blake, 42, and Jake Jacko, 37, both convicted child-killers, were discovered early this morning. No details have been released, although there are unconfirmed reports that both men were tortured. The guard hostages, who many had feared dead, have all been released unharmed. All prison staff and inmates are now accounted for."

Liza sat up so abruptly that Mel's arms fell to his sides. He looked momentarily bereft.

"He's alive," she said, her voice soft with awe.

"Yeah, well, sure. I told you he'd be all right."

"But if he took the guards hostages ..."

"He's dead meat. Put yourself in their shoes."

Her face fell. A tear trickled from the corner of one eye. "But why would he take them? He was getting out in a couple of months! Anyway, the hostages are alive, aren't they?"

"But at least two guys are dead. Well, they're perverts, so I'm not sure how much that matters," Mel said hastily, taking a final draw on his stubby roach.

"Some comfort you are!"

"Well, c'mon. If this Dace guy hadn't been there in the first place ... What did he do anyway?" he asked again.

"I can't say. It's not my story to tell. Not to you, anyway. Oh, I'm sorry. I don't mean it like that. Dace, it's just, well, he's difficult to explain."

"Liza, what are you doing scrunched up over there and halfway out the door?"

"You don't know what he's like."

"Look, I'm sure your cousin is a swell guy, and it's really great that he's all right. Maybe when he gets out we can get together and have a beer or something."

"A beer?" Liza was laughing now as well as crying, although she didn't have the slightest clue why. The idea of Dace and Mel having a beer together was instantly hilarious, though.

She could almost picture it: Dace's reddish head, Mel's curly one, both bent over a little wooden pub table. What would they talk about? Not her! What did men talk about when they were out together, anyway? Sports? Politics? She had never seen Tony interact with other men, and her father rarely. He and she had both been loners and when she left home, her brothers had been too young for any real talking.

"That's very magnanimous of you," she allowed, then relaxed a bit as her relief that the riot was over slowly seeped through her veins.

"We start classes Monday. You've gotta start thinking about yourself, girl. My guess is they won't let outsiders into the Pen for a long time, anyway. You must've lost five pounds since I met you last week. Look how baggy your pants are." He tugged demonstratively on her jeans, looking at her through the dilated pupils of his hazel eyes.

"Oh, Mel, I'm sorry, but I can't stay," Liza murmured, starting to feel slightly nauseated even before the effects of the marijuana had worn off. Dace was alive, but something was wrong. She could feel it in her bones. And now the penitentiary was going to be shut tight. How many weeks until she heard from him again? How long before he confirmed the role he had played?

Great God in heaven, what was happening to him right now?

Chapter Eighteen
After Hell Broke Loose

> Riot Ends at Maitland Pen:
> 1 dead, 11 injured—
> One prisoner was found dead and 11
> others injured, apparently at the hands
> of their fellow inmates, as more than
> 500 inmates ended their rebellion at
> Maitland Penitentiary. The convicts
> capitulated after the federal government
> refused to bargain with them. All six
> hostages were released unharmed. A
> spokesman for the Solicitor-General said
> he didn't know the reason for the last
> minute violence, but some of the injured
> are believed to be informers and child
> molesters.
> —*Maitland Spectator*, Sep 10, 1971

"Get the fuck up," the voice said.

At first he thought it was the broken bell ringing, but it was just his ears. A plastic glass rolled into the black void under his cot, clipped the cinder block wall and stopped. He'd put the empty glass down on the floor when he'd first arrived, so thirsty he could have drunk toilet water. For some reason he was afraid to open his eyes, so when he did, it was just a crack. Fuck. What did they want with him anyway?

The sudden sense of déjà vu was almost too much to bear, not that these guys resembled Loony Tunes or his henchmen in the least. For one thing, they were dressed in full riot gear: black leather clothes and helmets with shiny visors. For another, they all had guns. Machine guns, in fact. Yep, this was a goon squad, the real McCoy.

What the hell? he thought, frowning with the irritability of the sleep-deprived. The riot was over and his, no the hostages were safe. People had shaken his hand. Was that before or after they had run the gauntlet? Forget it. No point in thinking about that now.

"Go away," he said, covering his face with a pillow. He had never been so tired, not even when he was a teenager and the heat was up his ass.

"Get the fuck up, Debrex," a helmet growled again, the overhead light bouncing off his visor. A second helmet booted the bottom of Dace's cot, happy to help. Groaning, Dace slid to his bare feet just as one leg of his bed collapsed.

"And if I don't want to?" he hedged, eyeing the open cell door as if they'd just let him go. There were six of them and one of him. He had no idea of the building's layout. He had been bussed here about ten hours earlier and had been sleeping ever since.

"Get moving," the lead guy said again, motioning everybody into the hall.

"At your service," Dace said, mentally adding *fucking space cadets* as he followed them to a staircase at the end of the corridor. Not that he had an option. Two guards brought up the rear, their black jacks aimed at his kidneys.

"You guys showing me the way to the breakfast room or what?" he inquired blandly.

"Or what," the spokesman snickered. When they reached the landing halfway down the staircase, a pair of grey mechanic's coveralls smacked him in the face. His eyes watered.

"Crybaby," the spokesman goaded him. "Not such a big man now, are you?"

Chicken shits. Mother fucking... He looked down, half-expecting all the obscenities in his head to spill onto the floor.

"You want me to put this on," he guessed. He stood on the landing of a staircase so new, he probably could have gotten high on the smell of fresh paint if he'd tried.

"You supposed to have a high IQ, ain't ya? I'll bet you think you're pretty smart, don'tcha?" the guy speculated. Dace doffed his pants and ripped the shirt over his head so fast that several brass buttons popped off and rolled downstairs.

A considerate bunch, they waited until he got the overalls halfway on before they started hammering him. The first blow to his head almost knocked him down. Blood dripped into his eyes as he crashed into the wall.

"It's just a head wound," one of them said helpfully. "Those suckers always bleed a lot."

And, "This is for our buddies," the rest of them grunted, until he was curled up on the landing with his arms raised to protect his face.

But when they hauled him up, dragged him downstairs to the next landing and started beating him again, he'd had enough. Jesus fucking Christ. He didn't go through a goddamn riot just to lie down and die. He got in several well-placed kicks before they'd even realized what was going on.

A wake-up bell clanged somewhere. One bull was doubled over, protecting his genitals when his buddies lost interest, yanked Dace by the straps of his overalls and tossed him like a bag of garbage through the first open door.

"We'll be back," they promised in unison, scattering like the cockroaches they were.

Dace examined his new surroundings. At first he couldn't see much, especially with both his eyes swelling shut. Judging from the pain, some ribs were cracked, but a careful inspection of his skull revealed that his brain was still intact. That was all that mattered. Saliva drooled from his busted mouth onto the clean cement floor, but he ignored it until a molar followed, square and almost perfect in the low light. He tried plugging it back into his mouth, but it didn't work.

This cell was like all the ones he'd occupied before, except there were no bars, just an electronically locked door with a slot big enough to accept a tray. There was also a sink and a concrete slab bed. It took a while to figure out where the toilet was until he noticed the hole in the floor.

The bed looked good. Craftily, he calculated how long it would take to crawl to the plywood mattress. His mind had slowed, so the calculation took a long time, but the crawling took longer still.

He also had trouble retrieving words. Sega ... ciga ... until the words segregation and disassociation came to mind. New names, old places. Also known as Solitary or the Hole. At first he startled at the slightest noise, then his eyes rolled back into his head, not caring anymore.

Late afternoon light filtered through the slot in the door where he would get his meals. If they fed him. And his mail. If they let him. His mail, his Liza letters. His... he drifted into dreams.

He lay on a bosomy, floral couch, its cushions warm and soft. A dark-haired girl pulled a down comforter over his chest, drawing it closer to his stubble-covered chin, but before it reached his face, his teeth exploded into his brain.

They shouldn't have. He was going to live forever. He was a young man. There was still time to make things right.

Chapter Nineteen
Cold Storage

Prisoners Turn on Their Own Kind—
Battered convicts told how hundreds of
prisoners screamed for blood as the last
night of the riot turned into a torture session.
The victims were fellow prisoners, stool
pigeons and sexual offenders. They were
tied in chairs around a radiator. Three teams
of five men took turns beating them for hours.
The beatings ended when the soldiers arrived,
but it was too late for one man. The dead man
was found under a mattress.
—*Maitland Spectator*, September 10, 1971

"He's dead," somebody was saying from the other side of the cell wall.

Dace lay where he'd fallen, on a concrete slab four inches off the floor. It was covered by a sheet of plywood and a three inch thick foam pad.

Dead. *Ha, ha. Fat chance*, he thought. He knew he was alive because some pig in the rifle tower shone a light into his cell twenty-four hours a day.

"Who, Dace?"

"No, one of the unwanted ones, you dumb cunt. His head was all busted up. Somebody pounded the shit out of him. He croaked in the army hospital today."

Maybe Steve's name was mentioned too, maybe not. He felt like he was in a coma, aware of what was going on, but not really there.

"Holy shit. I mean, who cares?"

Max, the prison trusty, a joint man, a stoolie, a rat, pushed food through a five inch square window in Dace's solid steel door. "Yeah, a second diddler died," he muttered. Dace learned more from tiny notes rolled and buried under his cold toast. Like the reefers he used to get.

"Rick's all right," Max added, then, "Watch the new Warden. He's been reviewing your file and has it in for you." The old Warden, so close to retirement, had left in a flood of post-riot criticism.

"Jesus!" Dace exploded.

"Ah, take it easy, man."

"Right. You got it right. I'm a man. Tell the Big Cheese that, too. You tell him everything else. At least I can live with myself when I wake up in the morning. Did he read the part where it says I never touched those fucking screws?"

Max didn't reply but shoved more items through the slot. He'd brought what Dace had requested based on the strength of Dace's promises: I'll protect you right or wrong when I'm in Gen Pop. Out in the regular population, a prison trusty needed all the help he could get. That's how Dace scored an almost full blue fountain pen and some unlined paper, water damaged but still usable. And that's how he got his books, mostly classics nobody else wanted to read, but also a coverless copy of *The Godfather*, a book he'd enjoyed several times before.

I'm fine, Dace lied, practice-sitting on his concrete cot with his cracked ribs. His journal, in the form of letters, he addressed to both Liza and himself. He wrote her almost every day. If she got his letters, she'd understand. She always had, even his conviction for manslaughter. He didn't like to think what that had cost her. He hated what he had put his family through, especially her. She was his future, his bright light, his ... *Aw, shit.* He was getting emotional again. He had to get a grip.

"Hey, guy," Max whispered through the slot in his door. "What are you doing in there?"

"Planning your demise. Yours and all the lying, cock-sucking ..."

"Duh-mize. Funny, man. Real funny. What's duh-mize?"

Although his parole was coming up, even taking into account the institutional charges and the "good time" he was likely to lose for this beef, he was considering serving all his time so he'd eventually be completely free and unsupervised when he did get out. He and Liza could go anywhere then. Anybody with half a brain could make a good living in this country. They'd find other people like themselves: people who liked to live and knew how to live good. "Good" as in really living, not necessarily as in living moral.

My cousin, myself, he wrote in every salutation. Sure, it was a little more maudlin than he liked, but that's what happened to a guy in the clinker, in the Hole. First you got cold, then your nerves went and the next thing you knew you were bawling like a girl. Her address—what the hell was her address? Oh, right, she was living in Maitland now, in the student rez. She'd visited him ... wait. Was it just last week? No, it couldn't be.

I don't want to leave you, her eyes had said when Savage led him away.

I feel so close to you, he added, rereading the last page. Christ, what a goof. He crossed out a line and tried again. There, that was better. He wanted to tell her everything. *Well, almost everything,* he thought, sifting through key events and the role he had so reluctantly played. The last thing she needed was to get all her facts from the press. Somebody should know what had really gone down. And who better than her, his repository, his alter ego, the only person in the world capable of relating to his point of view?

It was hard to explain about Rick, though. *He's my friend,* he wrote in the end, never mind if his loyalty hadn't helped him. He asked me to watch his back, that's all. Then we took control of the guards. If we hadn't... if anything had happened to the poor buggers we were all as good as dead.

The only thing he didn't tell her was how sorry he'd felt for the guards.

His decisions had made sense at the time, but they didn't now. If he'd had any brains, he would have crawled up into the ceiling and stayed there. Plenty of others had, men who valued their own skin.

Stabbing his pen into the tablet of writing paper, he crossed out another whole section and started again. After six weeks in solitary, he'd revealed more than he'd planned, his anger spilling out in a rush of words that were sure to worry Liza sick when the letter finally arrived.

What kind of man do you think survives this human pressure cooker for five or six years? That's easy. A strong, violent man. Some say that's me. A former Warden (a man I admire) used to call me a Dr. Jekyll and Mr. Hyde, but I haven't seen Hyde for a while.

Okay. So let's say a man understands this. He even realizes he'll have a difficult time surviving in society with the temperament he has. What then? What can he do to readjust himself so he fits the outside environment?

Nothing! Because to fit those surroundings would be to disgrace himself. Besides, a man isn't a robot, Liza. He doesn't change with a bolt here or a spring there. If he could change so easily, he wouldn't have survived all that time in prison, either mentally or physically. Also, he would find it totally impossible to understand why society would force him to be of such a violent disposition for such a long time, then abruptly force him into another entirely different personality.

Jesus, if he'd killed the guards, he wouldn't be in this mess. Okay, he'd be dead, but at least he wouldn't be listening to morons hassle the ex-biker next door, a big side beef of a man, with a tendency to mouth off just after 11:00 p.m.

> Six 'officers' just came and tear-gassed everybody. I have to lie down and cover my eyes for a while. They've been using it on cons for no reason. Just for something to do. Hard to believe, but it's true. I swear I'll spend money gallor(sic) to expose these people, individually, when I get out.

Usually the guards sprayed until their target fell and everybody else got coughing, too. Most men threw up. As an added bonus, the effects lasted longer than the usual fifteen minutes because there was so little fresh air intake in Segregation. On these occasions, no matter what he said—or didn't say—the guards kicked his door, grunting as they passed. "You wanna fight, punk?" But when he replied, "Okay, when?" they didn't follow through. "Whatsamatter? You just like rattling my cage?" he called, watching them saunter back to their own quarters with the man he always called that fat fuck Savage in the lead.

Just as well. Sure, Savage was a fat fuck, but Dace was in lousy shape now. He wouldn't want to meet any bad guys on the street. His busted ribs had slowed him down so much he hadn't started exercising again, even in his cell. Once he could have lifted three hundred pounds over his head with one clean jerk motion, but he'd be lucky if he could do two twenty now. Even though he'd always thought a workout was as good as a high, now he spent his days sleeping and his nights writing letters or rereading the paperbacks he extorted from the little delivery man.

One of the books was *From Here to Eternity*, but it was so draggy-assed in places that he had trouble finishing it.

Time helped. And cursing. Dace recited the same steady stream of expletives his father had once employed in the absence of his God-loving, Catholic wife. Motherfucker was the only word Liza might have recognized.

He also had trouble finishing his thoughts these days. He tried to sort them all out by writing to Liza, but it didn't always help. Days and nights ran into each; events bled and blurred. When had he taken custody of the pigs? Why? Was it really just to help Rick — and to help them — or had he just needed a starring role?

He's a hero, people were starting to say about Rick. What did that mean? Still, he hoped Rick was out in the regular Population somewhere, anywhere but here. So far he hadn't run into him during his infrequent visits to the Yard. No doubt they — the Authorities — had planned it that way.

If Liza couldn't keep track of all his ravings, his written record would be lost. For some reason he was getting most of her letters, but she wasn't getting his. He knew this from what she said. The new contact probably just needed a boot up the ass.

Tell me you're all right, she pleaded. She would go crazy if she didn't hear from him soon. Over and over she wrote, her bright light competing with the spotlight from the rifle tower.

Although he hadn't showered in two weeks or shaved in three — a true torture for anybody remotely fastidious — he no longer cared. A couple more weeks in solitary and he was so lonely he even understood why some of his fellow inmates had tamed rats. In the end the only thing that saved him was knowing how much he meant to Liza.

Dear Dace, she wrote, even in the apparent absence of a response from him. Is this love?

What are your feelings for me? he wrote back. Open up and tell me more.

You're so beautiful. I have a craving for the exciting and unusual. She continued on as if she'd heard him, her words thrilling him to the core.

But I've been jinxed and I have hurt the people I loved. I don't
want to hurt you too. Oh God, I'm afraid to tell you what I've done.

My God, what could a good little girl like her have done? He did what he could to reassure her.

There's nothing you could tell me that would scare me. You said you have a craving for the exciting and the unusual. I have, too. I always will, but now I understand it. Sweetheart, you can't crave or want to try anything I haven't already done, or thought of, or am waiting to do.
Put aside your fears. You can't hurt me because I see you in me and I see myself so clearly in you. There's nothing wrong with the way you think or feel. How the hell can you think there is? Stop being afraid.
You think you're a jinx because a past lover or a friend has failed you. They failed to accept you and your needs. They didn't understand you. Are we supposed to conform to 'everybody's' way of life? Like hell. I'm satisfied to know that you find me beautiful. And I'll prove to you that you are, too. Others will envy us because of what they failed to be. What they can't be. You'll see.

Sometimes he wanted to shake her. Everybody would envy them when he got the fuck out of here! Why couldn't she see that? He'd carry her through live minefields if he had to. God, she shone. And even if she were just trying to lure him back to safety by pretending to fall in love with him, it didn't matter.

Little Liza had always been a great pretender. Somebody had to dream. Besides, she was his cousin, no matter what. Family stuck together, or his did anyway. The Devereuxes were like the Corleones that way. Dad and Rosie had always hung tough for him, and Liza would too. All she needed was a sign that he was alive and well. God help her if the *Maitland Spectator* was all she had.

Ah, the *Maitland Spectator*. It was — what was one of Liza's favourite words? Omni … omniscient. His supper trays were lined with newsprint, as if he were a dumb animal. Somebody must have wanted him to see how positively ghoulish the *Spectator's* riot coverage had become. To get his goat. Sick bastards.

Where the hell did the *Spectator* get its news, anyway? Who was their source? Front page stories hinted at sexual sadism, torture and vampirism, although editorial pages attempted a more scholarly analysis of the facts, blaming everybody from society and the Solicitor-General to the overcrowded, nineteenth century jail and the warped inmates themselves.

The news about another little sit-down at the Joint was just a sidebar, but it made him crazy to read that most of the so-called ringleaders, his friends, were doing dead time, too. The day he found that out, he pounded the wall so hard with his right hand that he ended up writing the next two letters with his left. When he wrote Liza about the new Warden's decisions, secretly pleased to have a fresh target for his fury, she replied:

> I still haven't got a letter, but Joe says you're in
> the Hole now. Why do you think he knows so
> much? And what does being 'in the Hole' mean?

It means I'm in a cage twenty-three plus hours a day, little Liza, he almost snapped back.

Why was she talking to that dumb dick anyway? Not that he said that. No point in telling a smart little girl like that what to do.

He also didn't mention the absence of a toilet and the presence of a six inch drainage pipe at the head of his bed. Actually, the room was clean enough. No wonder. It was flushed every forty-eight hours by a large hose inserted through the slot in the door, the force of the water plastering him against the back wall, which he shared with an indoor ball court. If he waited long enough, the players on the other side tapped hello. He liked that. It was his way of keeping in touch with the world.

It was also part of his punishment. For being so full of himself, so full of shit. Just like Rick. For imagining he could redeem himself and make things right. A girl like Liza probably would have figured out something else to do and landed on her feet … although she goddamn well wouldn't have been in the Joint in the first place.

And she would have handled the press, who were flooding him with written requests for interviews. As if he had anything to say. Goddamn bottom feeders.

Although if you asked him, some of the movers and mooches inside the Joint were even worse. Jailhouse snitches liked to talk, something he figured out when he'd been bodybuilding.

"Christ, he's one tough mother fucker," they used to marvel. "I saw him lift half a ton."

"I heard he captured fourteen guards single handedly," they recalled.

"Yeah, I heard he wanted to cut off their fingers and their toes!"

"No," somebody else said. "Taking the guards hostage was just a snow job. You know Dace. He's wanted those mother fucking diddlers dead for years. Remember the sneer on his face when …"

They'd even started calling him the Master of Ceremonies, though not to his face. No fucking balls, the dirty stoolies. If he ever got a hold of the man who had coined that phrase, "Master of Ceremonies", he'd kill him. Of course the stoolies and joint men always dummied up when he was on the move, which wasn't too often. He was in Segregation, for Christ's sake. The bulls hauled him to the showers or the exercise yard once or twice a week, if they remembered to check the chart posted just outside his door.

To think that taking care of the guards had turned out to be the least of his problems. Stuck in solitary, all he could do now was listen to lies from sneaks and sleazes who had either hidden under their beds during the riot or — if they were feeling really cocky — moled through the heating ducts in search of contraband, as if the whole goddamn riot had been a super-sized frat party. They didn't have a clue about what had gone down, he wanted to write Liza, but man, they loved a good story about a sweet kid who was raped in his cell or the begging words uttered by some dying diddler.

She wouldn't know what he was talking about, though. She wasn't there. It made him sick telling her the whole story. A sweet little girl shouldn't know all about it. It didn't seem right. But he had to tell somebody the way he saw it, or at least the parts he'd seen, because he hadn't been everywhere. The letter took him several days.

> Well, Sweetheart, I'll try to be less secretive.
> I know I told you about my violent streak. What I didn't tell you was that I overcame it. During the riot, of all places.
> My guard post was on the fourth range, in clear view of the whole dome, which is a round area with stairs winding from the main floor to the fourth. So I could see if anyone tried to sneak up on my men or the hostages. People on three sides of the dome could see me too. Well, now people are saying I was directing the beatings of the diddlers downstairs. Sharp bunch of jerks, eh? They're saying a lot of things about a lot of people that are lies. And most of these so-called witnesses are going up for parole soon.

But like everybody else who had ever kept a journal, he also left stuff out. The human mind could only take so much. Although he'd seen men go insane, cut their throats, swallow razor blades and jump off fifty feet towers, he didn't like dead bodies. So he couldn't tell anyone, not even Liza, that he was haunted by what he had seen. In the end it didn't even matter if they were baby killers. Not even that one of them was guilty of having sexual intercourse with a girl not yet three.

"Close his eyes," he'd said to the convicts who'd wanted their handiwork admired. Although he didn't know how, the *Maitland Spectator* was spot on about this: the men had been hidden under a sodden mattress in a utility room, two victims, one dead and one dying. When Dace had entered the utility room, his friend Steve was just leaving.

Too late. There was nothing anybody could do, so he'd waited with his so-called co-conspirators for his name and number to be called and the chance to run a gauntlet. The rioters were stripped naked. The prison guards and army men waited outside on the lawn, a double row of cowboys and Indians with billy clubs instead of guns and arrows. Most of the prisoners could barely crawl when they got to the finish line, but Dace had footballed through the human corridor with just a couple of blows to his back. Looking back, he had no idea where he'd found the stamina, except he had run on adrenalin for so long.

At least the gauntlet wasn't personal. It was just mass punishment for the fright and loss of control the guards had suffered and for the implicit criticism they would face when their jobs and routines were reviewed. How did Sandy McAllister get hostages? In their place, Dace might have done worse. But it was a bit too personal, them coming to his cell.

Three weeks later he got out of Segregation just long enough for the croaker to tape his ribs and ply him with painkillers. He hadn't spoken to anybody except the little joint man for so long he was amazed when words came out of his mouth.

"A little late, but better late than never," he quipped as he got on the scales. He'd lost twenty pounds. He caught sight of himself in a little mirror over the examining table then. His long hair was falling out in clumps, but his beard was still thick and bushy.

The bespectacled little doctor with the black Brylcreemed hair tried to hold his breath as he taped his patient's ribs. He liked to talk, and for the most part Dace was the perfect listener: he didn't talk back. Dace kept quiet as the man opened up, sharing his thoughts.

He went home to a house on the lake where he was completely restored every evening. He'd never been married, but a silent woman came in to clean his house and cook his meals. She served no other purpose. He was past all that. He needed women even less than he needed men, although the latter provided entertainment in a job that left no time to read or reflect.

He'd taken this job in the penitentiary to avoid the pain habitually inflicted on innocents in everyday life. Everything here was black and white; people got what they deserved. There were no innocents, no children dying of leukaemia, no wild-eyed women screaming in labour, no old veterans dying of regret. He'd worked in prisons for twenty years now, stitching self-inflicted wounds and dealing with manipulative malingerers too stupid to bother researching the diseases they feigned. He supervised paddlings designed to inflict physical scarring and maximum pain. He had even attended the last hanging in Canada at the Don Jail in 1962.

He enjoyed it all and could still sleep at night, his stomach full of the fresh, non-penal meat and potatoes his Polish housekeeper cooked.

Adhesive caught in Dace's chest hair and the doctor's hand got caught in the tape, making him an inadvertent prisoner of his patient. He gave the tape a vicious tug before resorting to a pair of stainless steel Cross scissors he kept locked in a small desk drawer, just out of his patients' reach. Most of his patients were four time losers with a cunning born of desperation. D'Arcy

'Dace' James Devereux was no exception. Dace never even blinked through the ordeal, but the doctor saw him looking at the scissors. Perhaps he also saw him smile. He didn't seem to like that.

"So why haven't you taken the coward's way out and slit your wrists?"

"Nothing to slit them with, Doc," Dace replied. The little painkillers he'd downed without water were already creating a lovely sense of euphoria. "My teeth aren't sharp enough."

"A smart mouth, eh? Exactly what it says in your file—sorry, files. Some good, some bad. The last Warden described you as a real Jekyll and Hyde. He wasn't far off, was he? A murderer at seventeen, but a stand-up guy for all your friends."

"For the record, it was manslaughter."

"Killing's killing. Makes no difference to God what the courts call it. Makes no difference to me, either. And you're smart, too. Smart enough to weasel out of a jam with your high IQ. You know what that means, don't you? IQ? Luckily we've got people here smarter than you. All the riot instigators and hostage-takers are in solitary. Three have bled out."

"Who?" Dace asked too quickly. If he stayed quiet, the good doc might volunteer more. But Dace couldn't stop himself. The painkillers had loosened his tongue and he was craving human contact. "Just for the record, I didn't take those guards hostage."

"No, you were taking care of them," the doctor said. "So their friends came and beat the living crap out of you for no reason. No reason at all. So why don't you charge them? Set the record straight?"

"You want a little more drama around here, Doc?"

"Oh, you'll have drama, boy. They might not bother with the hostage-takers, but there's an ongoing investigation. Somewhere down the line they'll need somebody to take the fall for two counts of murder. Let's just say you fit the bill."

"Me murder ... who?" Dace stuttered. "I never touched a hair on their heads. Nobody did."

"Not the hostages, stupid. Those two cons who died. Remember? They were human beings too, you know."

Afloat on his bed that night, Dace almost forgot about wanting to get out, kill all the bad guards and run off with Liza. Free of pain for the first time in weeks, he worried about what the doctor had said, the possibility that he might be charged. That he might never get out long enough to do anything. To take Liza ... *Jesus fucking Christ, Jesus, Jesus,* he thought. *If I have to, I'll kill everybody here.*

Yeah, it made sense. Nothing had happened to the hostages, but the bulls had stomped him, so the warped bastards must have something up their sleeves.

Charge the guards with assault. His assault and maybe somebody else's. The goon squad was working overtime these days. There had been so much screaming at first he'd thought he was near the psych wing, but he knew better now. The guards were still collecting debts. Charge the guards with assault. The idea was a little pipe dream that kept him going for a while, occupying all that dead time when he had nothing else to do or read, when his pen ran out of ink, when nobody came, unless the disembodied hand shoving grub through the slot in his door counted.

He probably wasn't the only person thinking this way. Who knew how many men the good Doc had inspired to share their dreams with their friends? Maybe that's why the authorities had suddenly started talking about releasing him and quite a few other prisoners slightly ahead of schedule. The prisoners would never win, but there was no way the guards wanted to end up in court.

He slept better then. His dreams changed, too. He was no longer in prison. He lived with Liza, and his father and his sister lived nearby. Liza always wore a yellow dress. He didn't know if they ... well, none of that mattered. Because whatever she wanted, he wanted. In his dreams there were two motorcycles in his garage and always a party going on.

And the world was full of suckers. Dace was his own boss. He worked hard at something—he wasn't sure what—so they had lots of money. They lived on a mountain with only one way up, and D'Arcy Devereux was at the top, a young man still.

Months passed as he dreamed this way, in the Hole, on bullshit institutional charges.

Chapter Twenty
The Truth is Plain to See
Maitland University, January 4, 1972

People will talk. Even if a man has
been acquitted by a jury, people will
talk, and nod and wink — as far as the
world goes, a man might often as well
be guilty as not.
—Eliot, *Middlemarch*

L iza had just returned from Christmas vacation with her
mother in Toronto. Her mother was a happy woman now,
with no time left for grief — especially the grief young girls
were apt to bring. Liza had spent almost every moment
with her, catching up. Mostly they drank tea in the kitchen of her
mother's miniature flat. Night after night she had lived through
past lives, bringing the Magills up to date, her mother up to
middle age and herself up to age fourteen.

In the end she almost started seeing herself as her mother
saw her: a clever, moody young girl with a head full of dreams. A
girl who would do great things… without a man. She didn't need
a man. And Liza would go farther than the twins for the simple
reason that she had lucked out and inherited the family brains.

Thank God she doesn't know about Dublin or Dace, Liza thought glumly, though how her mother could have missed hearing her ex-nephew was a key player in a recent penitentiary riot, she didn't know. Maeve Magill rarely read the newspaper, though. She got most of her information through a network of family and friends. In some ways, the Magills had a lot in common with the Devereuxes. They didn't want to know terrible things. Even if they did, they really didn't like to say.

If only Liza could have been more like her mother, but she wasn't. Something told her it was better to face life head on, though that was difficult when it came to Dace. What had happened to him? Although only a couple of letters had arrived, he was probably writing every day. He must be! Good Lord, what else did he have to do?

By now she had figured out he was in Segregation. All the "ringleaders" were. Although there was no reason now to hope he'd make his parole, she still did. Prior to the riot, he had been just a couple of breaths away. The prison authorities, well, they moved in mysterious ways.

Once she was back in residence, Liza unlocked her room and almost stumbled over the pile of newspapers her roommate had stacked inside the door. Janice always meant to read the news but never found the time. Right now she was probably playing Bridge in the upstairs lounge. Several receptacles of butts and ashes testified she'd been there recently, if a jumble of clothes and loose-leaf notepaper wasn't enough. Liza sighed and waded into the room.

Janice had also been using her bed, presumably because she hadn't been able to locate her own under the mounds of dirty clothes. Although Lily of the Valley had been sprayed around in a touching, if ill-advised effort to mask the odour, the underlying stink was enough to make even a man retch.

Already upset because there hadn't been any mail on the hall table from Dace, Liza kick-boxed a pile of laundry out of her way. Dace's last letter, a note really, had been postmarked November 27. How long could they keep a man in Segregation, anyway? Then again, even if he'd been out in Gen Pop, the Pen was locked down so tightly nothing was going to get in or out except regular staff and supplies, and maybe some crystal meth run by a dirty guard.

Somebody was giggling in the hall. It sounded like her neighbour, a little doll-like girl. Liza quietly closed the door.

The papers caught her eye again, fresh and unread. Who knew? There might be something in them, a vital clue as to what was really going on. There had been nothing new in the Toronto papers. Stooping, she picked up a couple before she'd even taken off her coat. The headlines would probably be enough.

Too bad The *Maitland Spectator* didn't have a regular column called Pen News. She yanked off her knee-high leather boots and sat on the floor with her coat on. It was always cold in her residence room.

As the pile of half-read papers beside her mounted—in direct proportion to the innuendo and outright lies—she realized how blessed she had been to have grown up in Toronto instead of Maitland. Toronto was a big city, more anonymous than here. Even here, she had no family to keep her except Dace and Uncle Norm, and they were both fed up with Maitlanders glaring at Dace as if he was the de facto leader of an outlaw motorcycle pack, the devil incarnate, or worse.

She needed a Coke, but once she started reading the paper, she couldn't stop. On the other side of the wall her neighbour maxed the volume of Procol Harum. *And although my eyes were wide open, they might just as well have been closed.* Liza loved the song, but it was nerve-racking living in residence with so much extraneous noise. Especially when she had something else on her mind.

The song ended, but her dorm mate started it up again. Lord love her, was that the only single she had? Fortunately, catching up on Maitland news was relatively simple because the headlines were nearly all the same: Sit-downs … dissent … more calls to send in the army. *She said there is no reason and the truth is plain to see.* The prematurely opened Supermax was going to cause more problems than it solved, Liza thought, staring at a black and white photograph of the penitentiary and trying to figure out where Dace slept.

She had chosen Maitland University so she could get closer to him, but now he seemed so far away. The new prison complex, a monstrous squat of low brick buildings, was just outside the city limits. It was untarnished, but already rumbling with unrest. And Liza was in the wrong place as usual. Lovely little Maitland by the lake. *Swell*, she thought, burying her face in her arms. *Just swell.*

Liza, Janice and Mel settled back into residence and two girls left, one because she needed to marry her high school sweetheart and the other because she had a nervous breakdown.

The *Maitland Spectator* reported almost the same news throughout the rest of January and February 1972. A publication ban on the riot was rarely observed. The first prisoner was released on Valentine's Day on a previously agreed probation. He gave an interview to the CBC, speaking about prison conditions. Although Liza almost never watched television in the lobby of the residence, where the *Waltons* always seemed to be on, she caught the news that day.

The released prisoner was a small, nervous man with stringy, chin-length hair and pale eyes that lingered just a little too long on a group of pubescent school children in the television studio audience. Coached by his female interviewer, he reported some of the highlights of the riot. When she failed to look sufficiently wide-eyed, he embellished his stories.

It was crazy, but with The *Maitland Spectator* as Liza's only window into the prison, she found herself quickly becoming a slavish devotee to their post-riot coverage. She also saw more of investigative reporter Joe Armitage, because in January he'd replaced a tutorial assistant in her Journalism class. He was planning to finish his long-neglected Masters, he said, although at age twenty-seven he was old enough to have completed his PhD. After attracting several of Liza's nineteen-year-old classmates by hinting he would like to marry them, he zeroed in on her.

He fed both her obsession and her quest, and he knew it. No matter how fascinating her courses, all she really wanted to study was Dace. Once upon a time, reading had transported her to other worlds, but her small library of classics and childhood favourites was still unpacked. She hadn't borrowed any new books for fear her course work would suffer. Not to mention that the reading tastes of most of her dorm-mates ran to the likes of *Coffee, Tea or Me?*

With the campus in a deep freeze, the rest of the student body turned inward as well. Beer bashes still took place on the weekends and an all night film festival was held in the Great Hall. She attended it with Mel and Janice, and the three of them stayed up until dawn, watching *Wedding in White* and *Kamarouska.*

Mel hated both movies. He couldn't understand why Genevieve Bujold had immolated herself. Liza had found *Wedding in White* to be more disturbing, even if they were no longer living in the forties where a sixteen-year-old could be raped and forced into marriage with an old man.

Maitland was in a snow belt, but even so, there was an unusual amount of snow that year. The snow was like a drug to Liza. Her mind emptied when she looked at all the white. Physically, Mel had no trouble, ploughing through with his long, lean legs, but Liza and Janice could barely make it to class as the snow piled up outside the student residence complex. A snake of sidewalks transformed into icy, unsalted slides. The paperboy, a young man with a loud singing voice and a blaring transistor radio, didn't have any trouble either. If he had, Liza might have been able to ignore the rather suspicious inactivity in Maitland Penitentiary, and she might have felt less nervy, less unreal.

If anything else were happening—and there really wasn't much in the winter of 1972—the *Spectator* didn't care. Just as long as they could pander to their readers' tastes in a prison town. Most of Maitland's indigenous people were employed by the penitentiary system in some capacity, or their relatives were, so they shared similar opinions. If their opinions differed even slightly, nobody liked to say. Men got sent to jail for good reasons and when you considered how they lived for free in quite nice surroundings and decent folk struggled to make ends meet, well, it was goddamn galling.

Day passes were even more controversial. Citizens threw up their hands with consternation when some cons actually enrolled in courses at Maitland University — a totally lamentable situation. Why should the public pay for an inmate's education? Imagine sending your impressionable young daughter to school to take classes with a convicted felon! At least the riot had put a stop to that.

The seasonal occupants of the university and the semi-permanent residents of the military base shared a similar mindset, try as they might to be different. A handful of free thinkers sprouted in the enriched soil of the university, but these tended to be the more eccentric professors who had grown up in privileged homes and could afford to think differently from everybody else.

For this reason, Liza fanned a small flicker of hope when the *Spectator* interviewed a radical political science professor. Unbelievably, the professor criticized the Solicitor-General for refusing to release a conciliatory statement sent from the inmate committee during the height of the riot. Instead, they'd sent in the army.

Naturally the Solicitor-General responded in a general press release the next day. What would anyone else have done? Given in to madmen? he asked, adding — to Liza's horror — he had half a mind to charge the ringleaders of the riot as well. Sure, they'd tried to end the riot peacefully, he implied, but hadn't they started the whole damn thing in the first place?

Not to mention the stupid fucks killed two of their own men.

Really? people chattered. Is that what happened?

To their credit, the *Maitland Spectator* published one counter argument: a hostage's account appeared the same day as the Solicitor General's press release.

Liza read this account eagerly. From what she remembered about one of Dace's letters, their stories sounded the same. The moment Janice left the room Liza sat down to compare both accounts. The guard relayed how the ancient cruciform had been destroyed while drunk, deluded prisoners ran amuck, screaming, "We're free! We're free!" Then some of the inmates had grabbed the hostages, stuffed them into a huge heating duct and wired the grate shut until some more responsible men came along.

If only the guard had named the 'more responsible inmates', but of course the poor devil couldn't, not if he wanted to keep his job. On the second day some of the rebels had tried to restore order. They had even set up an inmate police force to protect the hostages, who were transferred from the heating duct to the fourth floor.

One member of the inmate police force had even promised to protect the hostages from 'the donkeys' downstairs. This reassurance was convincing enough that the hostages relaxed a bit, played some cards and dispensed unsolicited advice. One of those pieces of advice included instructions to break into a prison canteen for extra toothbrushes, toothpaste and tobacco to meet the needs of the unexpected guests.

He emphasized repeatedly that the hostages were threatened 'in no way, shape, or form'. But hope faded when Ottawa refused to concede anything to the rebels, not even when they released a nervous young hostage as a show of good faith. All the prisoners had wanted was to delay the move to the new Supermax and for the authorities to provide better prison conditions, the guard said. They hadn't even asked for amnesty, for God's sake.

Ha! Dace had noted at this point in his letter, for all the good it had done.

The guard said their food supply had started to dwindle about the same time they heard some agonizing shouts and screams. The riot ended on the fourth day almost as precipitously as it had begun. Their protectors came and told them, "It's all over, boys. We're quitting, and you're going home."

Possibly the interviewer was dissatisfied with the ex-hostage's answers, for he'd inquired: "But those screams. Why did they kill their own men? Do you think they killed them because they couldn't kill you?"

The ex-hostage diffused his question immediately. "The inmate police force was too busy looking after us to knock off anyone (expletive deleted)." Unfortunately, only a handful of readers would have gotten that far in reading his interview. They would be sidetracked by the criticism of the Solicitor-General's actions — apparently laudable actions if subsequent Letters to the Editor were any indication. None of the letters mentioned the guard's tale. In the end, his story was just filler to people like Joe and his fellow reporters so they could keep the riot alive.

Not that they had to work hard. True, the prison authorities were stingy with leaked information, but with any luck an anonymous source usually claimed first-hand knowledge of the damage as well as the atrocities committed during the four day riot.

At least the authorities were generous in their release of black and white photographs, so there was no doubt in anyone's mind about the amount of sheer destruction that had occurred. The old prison, including four chapels, had been destroyed. The bell that had measured out all their lives was cracked beyond repair.

In time there were titillating rumours of forced sex and bloody castrations, and a heated debate flourished regarding why several prisoners were tortured in the dying hours of the riot on the final day. The *Maitland Spectator* labelled the tortured men "The Unwanted." The castrations were later denied by both the incarcerated men and the outsiders, but it didn't matter. Two men — well, child molesters — were indisputably dead. That didn't seem to affect the general public all that much. It was the hostage-taking that really bothered people, not to mention the destruction of the prison and the fact that taxpayers would once again be forced to foot the bill. How much time would the bad guys get for that?

The coroner finally announced an investigation, although he voiced concerns about the feasibility of laying charges in a situation like this. For one thing, there had been six hundred inmates in the prison when the riot took place. It was going to be difficult to pin the murders on any one person or group of persons. Convicts weren't reliable witnesses at the best of times.

And he was right. Plus, the public wanted to believe every inmate was guilty. Otherwise the person wouldn't have been in jail in the first place. Logically speaking, some people had to be in the clear. After all, they couldn't all be murderers, Liza pointed out to Janice, Mel and anybody else who would listen, although most people just walked away when she started to talk about it. Some of the inmates had even been in the public eye on committees and had met the press. Dace's friend, Rick Lowery, for one.

"Look," Joe crowed when, in a moment of weakness, she agreed to coffee after class. They were in the new Social Sciences building, and he'd bought the coffee this time. He pulled a paper out of his pocket as they sat down at a table, and pointed to the headline: "There's A Hero Even In This Mess!"

Liza wriggled closer to him so she could read and he put his arm around her shoulders. He pretended to be hurt when she shrugged him off.

Rick Lowery was a high profile committee member, so he probably would have been lionized by the press even if his lawyer hadn't thrust him into the limelight. The lawyer claimed his client had saved six guards' lives, an action applauded by the political science professor, who was re-interviewed by the *Maitland Spectator* one slow news day.

"A hero, eh?" Liza said, jealous on Dace's account.

Yes, she thought, all Dace did was keep the wolves at bay and watch his friend's back. She examined Rick's picture. Dace always said Rick wasn't at all camera shy, but in this photograph he looked like a man in flight—a person always looking the other way.

Joe shrugged.

"So who's the villain?" she asked.

"You think this might be some kind of book? I was thinking the same thing."

"Well, it's a story all right," she replied vaguely, reminded of her embryonic novel.

"Okay. So Sandy McAllister should be the villain, I suppose. He hoisted the key and took six men hostage. But ..."

"But ...?"

"It's the headliner in tonight's news. His friends—Sandy McAllister's—have all dummied up."

"Well, of course."

"And none of the hostages could identify him in a line-up."

"Are you sure?"

"Maybe people think he's crazy and are too scared to talk. I dunno. He did an interview this morning. I couldn't stand the ass. Bit of a Bible thumper."

"Too bad I missed it. My dorm mates were watching The Price is Right. So he's not going to be charged with anything? Well, who then?"

"Don't worry," Joe assured her, trying to pat her hand. "I know somebody on the police force. They're expecting all sorts of charges to be laid. There's the riot itself, the hostage-taking and the fact that two men are dead. They'll lay charges soon and when the lawyers get in, the snitches will get out."

"Oh, c'mon! Surely people won't listen to them."

"Remember that sick little bastard on the CBC? You'll see. The authorities will cut some deals. Early probation, extra privileges for anybody who squeals. Hey, what's with you, Liza? Every time I talk to you, you turn a sickly shade of green."

"Oh, I'm okay. It's just this coffee, I think. It's swill." Her legs shook under her, but she stood up, hugging her books to her chest.

"Wait. Where are you going? If you come over to my place tonight, I might have something better. I never touch the stuff myself, but I probably could score some grass. You know, I have one of the few single rooms in rez. Unless you're waiting for your cousin to get out, of course," Joe said, evidently annoyed that she was still backing away. His eyes widened, but his mouth shrank. "That's it, isn't it?" he added when she stopped and stared at him. He shook his head with wonder. "Well, lucky you. You might not have to wait too long. That boy's hands are starting to look kind of clean. Not squeaky, but clean enough. Especially if he can pin a murder rap on somebody else."

Liza came over to him again, slammed her books down on the table and looked both ways before sliding back into her chair. Only a couple of other students were in the cafeteria and nobody within five feet.

"How do you know?" she whispered.

"I've got my sources, baby," he said. He rocked back in the chair, hands behind his head.

I bet, she thought, her face neutral. "So you think he'll get paroled?"

"Well, he's eligible, isn't he? I don't think they'll bother much about the hostage-taking. They'd like to, but they gotta pick their battles or they'll tie up the courts indefinitely. They can get a lot more mileage outta murder charges ... first degree for sure. There's a slew of men they can try on that charge. I don't know, maybe even some of the hostage-takers. There's a boy called Steve, who apparently went `round the bend ..."

"Steve is one of Dace's friends. Why would those guys be charged with murder?"

"I didn't say Dace would. A bit slow today, aren't you? But if they let him out and he testifies against Steve ..."

"If he snitches, you mean? Oh God. He wouldn't do that."

Joe looked puzzled. "Why not? Especially if he didn't do anything."

"He just won't, that's all."

Joe shrugged. "Well, no matter," he said, deftly highlighting his role in the upcoming events. The *Spectator* would be sending him. This was his big chance. This was a book for sure. "Baby, if you could just see the look on your face!"

Liza looked away.

"Ah, c'mon," he smiled triumphantly. "Are you sure you won't go out with me sometime? I dream about making you. You know, if you really knew me, you'd feel sorry for me. You feel sorry for your handsome cousin, don't you? You think he's a wronged soul? You're just like Dunia in *Crime and Punishment*. You want to save him, don't you?"

Liza stood up again. "What the hell do you mean?" she asked levelly, hating his smirking face.

"C'mon, you little bibliophile, you've read *Crime and Punishment*, haven't you? In fact, you've probably read it several times, considering ..."

"Once. I've read it once!" she snapped. Somewhere in the back of her mind she wondered why the only man she knew who could reference Dostoyevsky had to be this one.

"Don't you remember one of those nasty Russians — who the hell could keep all their names straight? It sure reminded me of you. Wait. Wait, I've got it marked right here," he said, pulling a paperback copy of *Crime and Punishment* out of his pocket. "Yeah, here it is: 'When a girl starts pitying — watch out, she's in danger. She starts wanting to 'save' you and bring you to reason; revive you and recall you to more decent goals; restore you to a new life and new work ...' "

"Stop it. You don't know me at all. Or him."

"I checked. There's no law — here in Ontario anyway — against having a relationship with your own cousin, but it's still not right."

"I'm not having a 'relationship' with my cousin, you dork. At least not in the way you mean. Besides, I've got a boyfriend."

"If you say so. Wait. Wait, don't go. There's more."

"No, there isn't. And shame on you, interested in a con lover like me," Liza hissed, embarrassed to be backing out of the college cafeteria with tears on her face.

It was eight o'clock. Janice was already snoring when Liza got back to residence. The girl lay on her back, her nasal passages dried out from the menthol cigarettes she had promised her Pentecostal mother she wouldn't smoke. Liza flicked on her desk lamp, aimed the sudden burst of light into the corner and dried her eyes with the bottom edge of her T-shirt. She had cried all the way back to the residence in the early winter dark, a five minute walk.

"What's the matter?" Janice muttered. She rolled over, her eyes still screwed shut.

"It's that Joe. He said Dace might get out."

"So why are you sniffling? Isn't that what you want?" Janice asked, blinking awake.

"I don't know. I mean, of course I do. I'm just worried," Liza said, grudgingly smiling at her roommate's optimism.

Chapter Twenty-One

Dreamtime
Devereux Farm, near Maitland, April 19, 1972

It was many and many a year ago
In a kingdom by the sea
That a maiden lived
Whom you may know
By the name of Annabel Lee

This maiden, she lived
With no other thought
Than to love and be loved by me
—Poe, Edgar Allen, "Annabelle Lee"

Spring came early that year. Liza had just finished her classes. She had even softened towards Joe Armitage because he had been right.

Hurry, hurry, everything in her prayed. Phone and tell me you're here to stay.

"April is the cruellest month, mixing memory with desire..." she recited, walking by the stream at Maitland residence, trying to keep calm. She was rereading T.S. Eliot for her English exam, but she was much too restless to stay inside. Trees were budding all around her, the scent of lilacs wafted on the night air, and the earth pulsed with life. Little silver fish, smelts, wriggled and twisted like flashes of light, spawning in the stream. Students, mostly boys, waded in the rushing water, catching fish with their bare hands. Liza wanted to study, though, to sink into books. Eliot's poetry was perfect: gloomy, but offering golden phrases she would remember her whole life.

"Liza!" Janice called, leaning out the hall window which overlooked the stream.

Liza started running. This could only mean one thing. Dace. Dace was home.

Ever since she'd heard his parole was really coming through, she had been nearly incandescent with joy, so energized she had practically flown through her exams. And everywhere she went she carried a letter of confirmation next to her heart, official proof via her Uncle Norm.

Yes, there was still talk in the *Maitland Spectator* about laying charges in the deaths of the two unfortunates who had died during the riot, but what did that have to do with Dace?

A taxi dropped her off at the end of the daffodil-lined lane. In memory of their meeting at the family homestead, butterfly clips held up snatches of her hair. It was too early for the real monarchs to have returned.

She spotted him first, walking from the garage to the house. He carried a can of stove oil in his hand, for the evenings were still cool. She was half an hour early, having left the student residence almost the minute she'd hung up the phone. She'd had to go to him, he couldn't come to her, not then. Hearing him say, *I want to stay home,* was poetry to her ears.

Less than twenty-four hours earlier he'd been paroled to the huge, veranda-swathed house his father had built on his three hundred acres just outside of Maitland, constructed in anticipation of the prodigal son's return. And just like he had in prison, Dace looked like he belonged there. As if she had spoken, his eyes shifted, finding her, focusing on her. Then he was moving with confidence, striding towards her with the lovely, easy grace of a Devereux man. A chameleon, she exulted, flying down the lane, almost stumbling over her own feet. It's all right.

He can fit in anyplace.

A Mennonite farmer drove by in a horse drawn cart and stared, for in spite of everything, Dace was a fine specimen of a man, dressed in blue jeans and a white open-necked dress shirt. He was somebody who could easily have tossed bales of hay. A scar carved a line over his left eye where the guards had beaten him last fall, but none of his other scars were visible. Nobody had cut his hair and, left unattended, it had grown out curly. A St. Christopher's medal hung in the opening of his shirt. Almost blinded by the sight of him, Liza tried, but failed to remember hair on his chest when he was eighteen.

They hesitated, meeting by the side door to the house and wondering what to say, where to start. She stooped awkwardly and placed a foil-wrapped pot of hyacinths on the closest lawn chair. Uncle Norm's dog, a border collie, barked a caution from inside the nearby shed.

"Little Liza," Dace said, placing the can at his feet. He held out his cleanest hand and looked straight into her eyes with a gaze so worldly wise, so tired, but then he probably hadn't slept for days. God knows she hadn't. He doesn't show it, but he's excited, she thought. Just like I am.

Accepting his outstretched hand, she walked into the arms of the man she had been waiting for all her life. *Home,* she thought, *home.* Circling his hands around her waist, he lifted her easily, a foot into the air, then gently deposited her on the ground, like somebody who didn't know his own strength.

"My hands are dirty and you're wearing a yellow dress," he groaned, wiping his hands on the back of his jeans.

"Dace," she whispered into his sweet smelling neck, almost robbed of speech. "You like yellow, don't you?"

"Enough of that," Uncle Norm said from the other side of the screened door before coming out to give Liza a quick hug. He couldn't seem to stop smiling either. "A hyacinth girl," he said, glancing at her offering, still wet from a recent watering. The strong scent of its tiny purple florets saturated the midday air. He did a double-take of Liza and patted her shoulder. "Ah, your cousin's a pretty girl, isn't she? Dace, bring her in and get her a drink. Mrs. O'Connor has left us some lunch."

Liza stayed with Dace all the first day, walking beside him on his father's farm. They carted beers around and he smoked continually, except when he was touching her. Like the old Devereux homestead, this property was also called 'The Farm', even though the barn was empty besides the dog. As of the third week of April, fifty acres of prime land were still unploughed.

"When Dad brought me home last night in his car, I was almost too scared to get out. Oh, you think that's funny, do you?" Dace confided. "But now I can't go back inside the house. I've been out here since dawn except when I spoke to you on the phone. The light, Liza. The light is so incredible I thought I was gonna go blind. I saw a gopher, six kinds of birds, squirrels … and the mayflowers are already out in the bush. It's too soon, isn't it? Come see," he said, pulling her hand so eagerly that she laughed. *He's like a kid, a great big kid*, she thought, almost swelling with maternal pride. "This is the first time I've been to the new house, but this farm is already more familiar to me than the streets in Maitland ever were."

"The alleys, you mean," she joked, pointing at some cardinals in the pine trees sheltering the patio by the house. She loved their song. "Have you forgotten your old buddies too?"

"Well, what do you think?" he asked, veering off the new grass into a budding maple copse. He tilted her face up towards his and kissed her so hard on the mouth that she gasped. "I probably shouldn't kiss a cousin like that, but …"

"I think you're a loyal person," she responded, her eyes sliding back to the brick house where Uncle Norm was retrieving burgers from the grill on his patio. Her hands remained planted on Dace's chest. "Too loyal, some might say. Is Rick Lowery out too?"

They were hidden by the trees now. "No," he said, his face dark until he kissed her eyelids then moved his lips to her neck. "My God. You smell so sweet. Are you wearing that stuff you put on your letters? Or is it your own special scent?"

"It's just me, I think. I showered and dressed so fast that I forgot. I was in the shower, three minutes tops. Dace, how do men in prison wait so long?" she whispered into his neck, unable to meet his eyes.

"For this, you mean?" he asked, almost crushing her against his chest. "Sweetheart, I'm surprised you waited so long to ask."

"It seemed a little prurient."

"Prurient? What's that? How do they wait? I don't know. I lived on dreams, I suppose. Most of us did. We thought about the future, you know. What we would do when we got out."

"And got into fights?"

Dace thrust her a little way from him then, seizing both her wrists and pushing her hard against the nearest tree. Her eyes widened, but she didn't protest. "Are you suggesting I substituted? My dear, I'm surprised at you. Next thing you'll be asking if I got it on with some guy."

"No... no, I wouldn't," she stuttered, but searched his face, almost sure he was joking.

"Why not?"

"Uh, because you just lifted my skirt."

"That's not all I'd like to do."

"Oh, Dace, I know you haven't in forever, but do you really think we should?" Nothing was ever simple. He needed her, needed her so much, and that was a powerful aphrodisiac for her.

"I know. We're cousins, for God's sake," he mimicked his father. "Please don't start that again. And while we're on the subject, I don't care about your past, the same way you don't care about mine. I'm home now. Everything is going to be all right," he promised. He took her arm and tugged her deeper into the bush where even Uncle Norm's collie would have trouble finding them.

"Where are we going?"

"Tut, tut. I've lost my way," he said, his arm resting on her shoulders, his eyes scanning the nearly naked trees.

He talked continuously, as if he couldn't stop once he'd

started. Maybe he didn't know his way around the farm, but he could still remember Christie Pits. He wanted to go back there soon. Everybody said Toronto was jumping. Yorkville was alive with action, and come summer there would be music at the Riverboat and in the streets. Sure, he'd heard about Yorkville when he was in the Joint. You didn't have to be a hippy, you know, although a long-haired little girl like her might pass. The Gas Works and Abbey Road would probably have lots of music, too. She didn't know where those clubs were? Well, they'd find them together. What a goddamn sin Janis Joplin died just last year. But Bruce Cockburn and Joni Mitchell would be playing and maybe even that sap Gordon Lightfoot Liza liked so much, although he was usually at Massey Hall. *Pussy willows, cat-tails, soft winds and roses...* Also, he was willing to bet, there would be lots of other good stuff because wherever musicians went ...

"Grass, you mean?" she asked, emboldened because she had smoked the stuff with Mel once or twice in his car.

"Maybe." He smiled down at the top of her head, his eyes shifting to the side.

"What about your parole officer?" she asked. Her hands slid underneath his shirt.

"I haven't met her yet," he said. His breath was coming quicker now and her heart pounded. His skin was soft on her fingertips, hard against her hands. "But I'll bet she's a busy lady, too busy for the likes of me."

"Really? But if you ..."

"Liza, little Liza, you worry too much. My Dad needs me, so I'll probably just stay with him until you're sprung. Don't you want to finish your degree?"

"Sure, but I've got two more years if I do a general B.A. It feels like a sentence after today."

A shadow crossed his face. "Baby, you have no idea what a sentence feels like. You'll never know, a girl like you. Now look here. Everything's going to be all right," he promised again. His hands pushed her white sweater down to her elbows and lifted her breasts from the halter of her dress. He kissed each one in turn, making her gasp. "Let me. I'll show you. I'll get a job when you go back to school this fall. And that will have the added bonus of keeping Miss Parole Officer off my back."

"D'Arcy! Liza!" Uncle Norm called.

"A bit of a pest, isn't he?" Liza said, no longer the least bit nervous. She was loathe to leave his hands.

Chapter Twenty-Two
I Want You
Near Maitland, May 1972

L ater she remembered the early Maitland summer, awash in green and gold. If she didn't remember the exact date they'd first made love, she never forgot the occasion. It was soon after he'd been released. He couldn't wait, she couldn't wait, and oh my God, she was so relieved to have him home, home for good. She remembered the golden showers of maple florets as they fell and stuck in their hair, so maybe it had still been May. His Harley lay on its side against a fallen elm trunk. It's all right, it's all right, she kept thinking, feeling his pull in spite of her own misgivings. By now her only real concern was that his lovemaking might fail to meet her wildest expectations, the ones she had never even admitted to herself.

In short, she was afraid he'd been in prison so long he might have forgotten how to make love. What happened to a man who spent so much time in jail? What if he got impotent or something? Like Popeye in Faulkner's *Sanctuary*, a criminal whose behaviour was never really explained. Or like Clyde Barrow in *Bonnie and Clyde*? Although that was just a movie. Maybe in real life he had been able to perform. But what if she had to …? She wasn't sure what to do.

Beyond that, she was afraid he might be reluctant to commit to her for the simple, bourgeois reason that he was her cousin. What he said and what he felt deep down inside might be two different things. Sometimes she was like that too, but right now she was past caring. She was almost twenty and ready this time. She had never wanted anybody so much.

Naturally she didn't mention any doubts about his prowess or his commitment. He'd come too far. In the bush at the farm, she'd decided he could have whatever he wanted, and how lucky, how wonderful if he wanted her. She had to say something though, so she blathered about their blood ties instead.

"Imagine the complications if we were brother and sister," Dace said, plucking a maple floret from her hair. "But we aren't." Winding her long hair around his hand, he pulled her head back and tripped her, his arms breaking her fall. She fell beneath him onto the sun-warmed ground, her eyes picking out bits of blue sky overhead. The trees were leafy, and as far as she could see, there wasn't a cloud in the lattice of their branches.

She closed her eyes, nervous, no matter how much she wanted him. It had been a long time for her, too. Almost three years. God help her, she was practically a virgin again. He was, too.

"I'm afraid," she confessed. What if it's not as good as I dreamed?

"You think too much," he whispered into the base of her throat. "Open up and let yourself go." She loved his urgency. She stopped trying to second guess herself, although having got this far, now she was afraid it might hurt. He was growing against her, so focused, so huge.

"Dace ..." she tried to say.

"Shut up," he said, covering her mouth with his hand. He was up her long jean skirt and inside her in less than sixty seconds. "Take all of me," he whispered, as if he had to tell her. Heat spread like lava, racing from her head to her toes. She wrapped her long legs around his waist, doing everything she could to help. *Take all of me*, she thought, arching her back.

Belatedly he started undressing her, then himself, absolving her of all responsibility. She liked it that way, so she lay back with her arms flung over her head and did what she was told. He moved slowly at first, now that he was in, but after a couple of minutes he plunged deeper, picking up speed.

"I can't," she thought she heard him say, his mouth full of one of her elongated nipples. There was a noise from the bush, the crack of a branch. She opened her eyes. A small animal, maybe. And water ran nearby in a thicket of flowering dogwood. Nobody was there, though. Really.

"Liza," he groaned, coming almost immediately, his mouth where she liked it, on her throat.

"Stay," she demanded, wrapping her arms around him. Now that her clothes had been removed, it was as if more than her body had been freed. She would do whatever he wanted, whatever he said. They had always been part of each other and now they were both part of the air, the sky. She ran her hands up and down his muscular torso, her fingers searching his smooth, tight skin for all his scars, those signs he'd been invincible and was invincible still, that he would always be here.

Her own unmarred body, usually unisex in a T-shirt and jeans, was large-breasted, small-waisted, and nearly perfect. It must have been, because when he rolled off her, he kissed every inch until his mouth settled on a small spot to which nobody had ever paid much attention before. Not Tony, anyway.

Not even her. Somehow it hadn't seemed right, and she had never been sure exactly what to do. Her eyes flew open at his touch and she tried to push him away, but he seized both her hands in one of his and held them firmly. He lifted his head from time to time to observe her reaction, wearing a cocky smile on his face.

She closed her eyes, letting him take her to a place she had never imagined before. What was happening? A flutter rose in her groin, sending a rush of warmth to her chest. Butterfly, she almost said, then the feeling spread down, igniting the walls of the place where he'd been so that they opened and closed, over and over, fast and hard. She clamped her mouth shut, still unsure about what was going on. All she knew was when she peeked, Dace was looking rather pleased with himself. Then … *Petals*, she thought as her body arched towards the sky and her toes curled into the ground. *It's me! I'm blooming.*

"My God," she said, when every petal in her had unfurled and the last spasm had subsided. "Can we do that again?"

"Probably," he said, then chuckled and stroked her trembling limbs.

Looking down, she saw he definitely could. His cock was standing straight up, ready to go. "Should we have … should we …?" she asked shyly, a blush still warming her cheeks. Determined to be prepared, she had gone to Student Services and was now on the Pill, but it had only been a week.

"I did, and I am," Dace said. "So shut up," he begged, crawling up from her lower body, sliding along her until he damn near got lost in her hair. He curled behind her, entering from the side, his large hands almost covering her breasts. "I wish you wouldn't talk," he said. "This one's for you too, beautiful," he promised, stroking slowly and shallowly with his penis, nudging up against her pubic bone until that feeling — that liquid, painless fire — spread from her clitoris to her throat again and she almost cried.

"I'm not the first," he said, sounding a little sad, after they'd come together at last.

"You're the first to make me feel …"

"Hmm, yes, but that's not exactly what I meant."

"I know," she said, ashamed. He was still holding her, though. She took a deep breath, languishing under the warm grip he still held on her breasts. "There was somebody in Ireland, when I was sixteen. The worst part is I didn't even love him, I don't think. Um, I don't know exactly how it happened. Well, I mean, I know how it happened, but he wouldn't … he didn't touch me there."

"On your clit, you mean?" Dace said bluntly, rolling her around to look at him.

She lowered her eyes, embarrassed to be blushing. "Well, okay, my clitoris. I guess it's a little hard to find."

"Trust me. It's not that hard. What did this Irish boy need, a road map?"

"Englishman."

"Whatever. Sounds like a goof to me. A man, eh? Somehow I doubt you knew a real man. What were you hanging out with him for anyway, a little girl like that?"

"Dace, you wrote me one letter. Then you didn't write for two years."

"Because I felt like shit. I was shit. So why didn't you mention him before, you bad girl?"

"But Dace, you always say the past is the past."

He sighed. "That's okay. Don't tell me more. You're not my first, either," he answered, ostensibly slapping several black flies dive bombing her posterior. "You have a great bum," he added, regarding the imprint of his hand.

"Well, you're older than me. Besides, there's the old double standard," she said, not even trying to escape. "Nobody expects you to be a virgin. How old were you the first time? Fifteen? Sixteen?"

"The first time I was with a girl? Baby, I was sixteen, just like you," he answered. One of his fingers traced the outline of her heart-shaped face.

"Really?"

He didn't answer, just gazed blankly at her face.

"Dace?" she said, unaccountably afraid.

Suddenly he was on his feet, slamming his fist against the nearest tree, a hapless poplar that swayed under his assault. He didn't look at Liza. "I was nine when somebody tried, but he didn't get too far."

Feeling almost sick to her stomach, she waited, watching him bend back down, rummage in his discarded jeans and light up a cigarette while he studied the late afternoon sky. Clouds were moving in.

"In that fucking school, there was a priest," he said in

monotone. "Father Danby. Nothing happened, I swear. You know--between him and me. But the old perv wanted me to touch him and he said *Rosie does,* so I socked him in the face with a Coke. He kept a case of warm Cokes in his desk. To bribe kids, I guess. Everybody at the school got real mad. At me. They said I was a liar and they charged me. But I had to hit the bastard, Liza. To stop him. And to keep him away from Rosie. Yeah, Rosie. He... did something to her. Something real bad. My Dad said don't talk to her about it, Dace. She'll forget, she's so young. But Dad went to court with me — after the priest's German Shepherds chased me up a tree-- and what do you think? The Priest's uncle was on the Bench. Silverton. I remember because he had silver hair. It was Silverton who convicted me of manslaughter too. I ..."

By now, Liza was on her feet, her arms wrapped around him, her face pressed into his strong back. His sex, she noticed, was nowhere in sight. "Dace, don't tell me if it hurts," she said. "I don't have to know."

"It's too late, baby. I can't stop now. That's what happens when I start talking. That's why I almost never do. It was really Rosie that Father Danby was after. She was such a little tomboy. You know what she was like. Still is. I went with him so he wouldn't, you know, touch her. Whatever those fucking creeps do." He closed his eyes and inhaled deeply. "Other than that the school wasn't all bad. I finally learned how to read."

"You should sue!"

He spun around to face her. "Do you think anybody would listen to me? Besides," he said, a little more quietly, "Rosie doesn't want to."

"Has she said?"

"She doesn't even remember the dirty old bugger who wanted to get into a four-year-old's pants."

"Is he still alive? Is he still here in Maitland?"

"I don't know. And it's really better if I don't."

"Dace, we've got to get out of here. I'll transfer, work part-time and we'll find something for you to do, too."

"Ah, Liza, little Liza! You can't do that. You've worked too hard to get here. Besides, I can't leave my father right now. All his business is here. And then there's the Wolfhounds. They're after me to join them. I'd like to ride with them for a while, have some fun."

"Ride with them?" She felt dizzy. So much had happened in the past few minutes, maybe she wasn't thinking straight. "A motorcycle gang? But Dace—"

"Ah, c'mon. They're all right. It's just bikes and stuff. And they throw a hell of a good party. Hey, where do you think you're going, Miss?"

"I don't know. I just want to walk," she said, pulling away. He caught her by one hand.

"Are you sure you want to go somewhere?" he asked, his other hand moving down her body to the place he had mapped between her legs. "Because you're not wearing any clothes."

"I don't know what I want."

"Yes, you do. You want me. Open up and let me in."

For as long as she lived, she treasured the interlude that followed.

Chapter Twenty-Three
Hold On Tight

And when we were children, staying at the archduke's,
My cousin's, he took me out on a sled,
And I was frightened. He said, Marie,
Marie, hold on tight. And down we went.
In the mountains, there you feel free.
—Eliot, "The Waste Land: Burial for the Dead"

Back in February she'd applied for a summer job as a counsellor at a day camp in Maitland. She accepted their offer the day after Dace came home. She didn't make much money, but thought maybe she could earn some extra cash typing term papers in the fall. To her great joy, she had also qualified for an English scholarship, so Granny Magill was off the hook.

For now she was staying in residence, where she paid summer rates and had almost the entire place to herself. Her mother had wanted her to come home, but she really didn't have the space in her flat. Mel was travelling in Europe, through Scandinavia. Janice was working on a tobacco farm not far from town. And Dace was staying with his Dad for now. He wouldn't be alone.

So things weren't perfect, but they were working out. She

got to see Dace whenever she wanted, no questions asked, and all she really wanted was to spend time with him.

"I'll get a job too," Dace promised when he saw her after work a couple of weeks later. They were eating onion rings at the local A&W. Onion rings hadn't been on the menu when he'd first gone to prison. The A&W hadn't even existed in Maitland.

"Well, you could work for your Dad, no questions asked."

"No, I can't," he said, his face expressionless.

By now Uncle Norm owned three automotive shops in Maitland. He would never belong to the Golf and Country Club, but he was an up and coming businessman in spite of Dace's less than illustrious profile. Sister Rosie, six years younger than Dace, was working in his west end shop. She'd started right out of high school and was doing so well she was engaged to a local boy named Ben, much to her father's relief. She had always been such a tomboy, he'd wondered. She was practically living at her boyfriend's now, but that was okay. Times had changed. Young girls did pretty much as they pleased.

"It's not that I mind hard work," Dace assured her. "And I've always liked fooling around with motors. They make more sense than a lot of other stuff does. I just don't see myself under the hood of a car every day. Maybe your hood, though," he said, flicking the green baseball cap with the day camp logo off her head and laughing at the startled expression on her face. "Or rear end," he added.

She caught the cap and tapped his cheek with the visor, more sharply than she'd intended. She still had to be careful around him. He was still on edge a lot of the time. His eyes narrowed and he captured both her hands in his.

"Careful," he warned.

"What about opening up a motorcycle shop?" she asked, looking out the A&W window at his carefully preserved Harley. His father had saved the bike for him, taking care of it after Dace was sent Inside. The chrome was so shiny she could practically see herself in it.

He shrugged. "If we stay here. I need to get some money

first."

Suddenly her onion rings didn't taste so good. She coaxed a strip of onion out of one ring and left the rest. He pulled her plate over and helped himself. "Hmm, these are good," he said.

Oh, no, she thought stubbornly, you're not changing the subject. "Uncle Norm would lend you money," she insisted. She'd already anticipated the obstacles he would have to overcome. It was so much more difficult talking to a real person than it was to write letters and revise. "It might be hard to get a job in Maitland and you can't go anywhere else," she added. "You're on probation and you haven't finished high school. What the hell happened to those courses you took in prison? Oh, right. A riot and a shutdown. Great excuses!"

He glanced at her then down at his plate. She watched the muscles in his forearms ripple as he finished eating the onion rings and she thought: What a waste.

"Ah, Liza," he said, finally looking up. He smiled, but he was slow to answer. "It's too soon to say much, but I've got plans. Sure, I can open up a motorcycle shop here or down in Toronto, or we could just get the fuck out of here. How about that? We'll go somewhere down in the States. I bet you could go to school anywhere, isn't that right? A little smarty pants like you?"

Liza frowned. She knew nothing about American schools, except from books. "Maybe. But how? You can't cross the border with a … a conviction."

Pushing the empty plate aside, he reached across the little table and took her hand again. "C'mon. You've heard of phony names. You can be Anastasia-Romanov-my-dark-eyed-beauty and I'll be Leopold…uh, something. Besides, I know some guys who can help me."

Bikers, she thought, smiling in spite of herself. But maybe they could run away. Life at university was starting to sound a little boring. "And Uncle Norm?"

"He can come, too. Rosie is all set."

"Ah, I don't know," she groaned, lacing her fingers through his. "He has his business."

"He'll come later then."

"But we'd have to leave before Thanksgiving. In early October, when the monarchs fly. Or earlier. The end of August would be best or I'll miss first term in a new place. That gives us three months at most," she blabbed on, excitement building.

"Whoa, now. Not so fast. I still have a couple of things to do here."

"Like what?" She frowned, waiting, but he just smiled. Her temper flared. "You don't want to tell me, do you? You think it's none of my business."

"Well, little darling, it's not," he said softly. "But I can tell you the stuff I've got to do won't take long."

Oh, no, she thought, her stomach turning over. Reason, she cautioned herself, she had to reason. "Is Rick Lowery involved too? And what about Steve? You told me he was only seventeen."

Dace jerked back his hand. "Christ, Liza. No, they aren't. They're both still in prison. Actually, I'm a little worried about Steve. Both him and Rick should be out by now. I don't know why they're not. There's no telling what those lying cock—Sorry, what the authorities will do. Rick has been moved to a medium security prison, though. When he gets out he'll probably shack up with some girl on the south side of town."

"A girl? Who?"

"Baby, forget about him. I know it would be easier if I worked for my old man, but I can't. I'm twenty-four years old now. It's high time I had something of my own. Aw Jesus, Liza. Stop looking so damn serious. I'll die before I go back Inside."

Well, that was true. He would. But what about purpose? Belonging? Everybody knew that's what an ex-con needed so they could live, not just survive. Especially her, with her half-Irish outsider's heart. But how was Dace supposed to get these things when he had to visit some parole officer? He couldn't just pick up, leave, start over. Oh God. Why had she been so greedy? If he'd served all his time, he wouldn't even be on parole.

He might be able to do something with motorcycles, though. He'd ridden his Harley-Davidson into Maitland today;

he rode it all over the place. What kind was it? Damn, she'd forgotten again. She didn't care what he did as long as he didn't go back to prison. Anybody could see how he loved that bike, his mastery over the machine, the heft of the leather seat between his thighs, the way the scenery blurred in his eyes when he went fast.

His bike was like another girl. "Your only competition, little Liza," he joked, laughing at her narrowed eyes.

As they'd walked into the A&W, he'd seen another motorcycle and stopped in his tracks, staring. Just the sound of one evoked a similar reaction. Bikes were everywhere in Maitland now that spring had come. Until now, she'd hardly noticed them.

It was like they'd come home with Dace: clusters of gleaming, silver-chromed Harleys with shiny black leather seats, bringing temporary life to a long dead town.

Chapter Twenty-four
Freedom

At last the *Spectator* had a fresh story. All that spring and summer, long, detailed articles appeared in the editorial section about outlaw bikers. They said that when the bikes roared down Main Street, Maitlanders shook with fear. But the real problem was the drugs, especially crystal meth: ice, jibs, shard, speed. The drugs were instantaneous, energizing, bad for the heart, but great for weight loss and perfect for people with stuff they wanted to forget. Outlaw motorcycle gangs might have been marginalized hives of deviant activities before, even if they had designated themselves One Percenters, but much more was at stake now that they had ties to organized crime.

The articles were unsigned but Liza suspected her nemesis, that frustrated investigative reporter Joe. It was his style. He was the first person to report the Wolfhounds moving into Maitland. He swore they were at war with the Hell's Angels, which was really scary if it were true. His article appeared on May 12, shortly after he saw Liza and her cousin together down by the lake. To her it felt like a personal attack.

"That's how I feel every time I read about myself in the paper," Dace said and shrugged.

They spent almost all their free time together now,

although she worked weekdays at the local YMCA camp, shepherding nine-year-old boys back and forth from the community pool. Caught between infancy and adolescence, her youthful charges knew no fear. They darted into traffic, teased stray dogs, contested each other on the slippery floors of the pungent changing room, and jumped into the deep end of the pool, though only a couple could actually swim. They frustrated her sometimes, until they flashed their adult teeth at her, large in their smooth little peach faces. Then she was lost.

They were nine years old, she reminded herself. The same age Dace had been.

She pushed the thought aside. The boys were still young enough to be co-operative if she asked them to be careful, but both the necessity for constant vigilance and the routine bored her to tears. After the first few weeks all she wanted to do was sleep.

Dace, on the other hand, never ran out of steam. He smiled when she yawned and acted as if he couldn't get enough of her face. "My little pussycat," he teased, his hands keeping her awake. And if he wondered what had happened to her need for excitement—because he couldn't get enough—he never asked.

At her request, he taught her to ride a motorbike. He sat shotgun behind her, his hands covering hers on the controls, his voice urging her to open her eyes and fly. Her hands were slippery with sweat on the handlebars, and she marvelled at how his stayed cool and dry. From what she'd always been told, she had been slow to walk, slow to skate, and slow to ride a bicycle, so she wasn't surprised when it took her a while to catch onto this new thing.

"I can't," she said, tears of frustration coming into her eyes. Her thighs shook as if she stood on the edge of a cliff.

"Yes, you can," he insisted, kissing the back of her neck. "And you will. You already know how to lean into turns."

"But I'm just following you," she objected, lips quivering. "Dace, I'm scared. You know I'm not coordinated."

"That's what you said the first time I asked you to dance.

Then after a couple of drinks … bingo!" he said, his fingers steadying her lips. "Jeez, Liza. What the hell have you been doing for the past five years? It looks like I learned more in the Joint than you did on the street. Look, darling, just ease off the clutch and give it a little gas," he repeated, until one day she was almost riding on her own, the wind whipping her hair into his face although they were only going a couple of miles an hour, driving across a flat, forgiving field on Uncle Norm's farm.

"Look at you," he said into her ear. He hopped off, encouraged by her recent success, and now jogged beside her. He let go of her waist, but the second he eased off she lost control. Looking back, she thought she might have given the engine a little too much gas. The bike popped a wheelie, flopped onto its side and she flew straight into the air. My head, she thought fleetingly, but somehow fell slowly enough that her helmet didn't even touch the soft ground.

"Liza!" he shouted, running to her side. He looked a little pale and when she followed his gaze she noticed the rock hidden in the grass, so close to her face. "You're a natural. You even know how to fall. Don't worry about the bike. It's just a little Honda and it was all scratched up anyway."

She stayed on her side, eyes tightly closed, too furious to speak. She desperately wanted to punish him. She'd felt all right up in the air, unafraid, but here on the cold earth she started to shake. My God. They would bury them both in the ground one day.

He ran his hand along her slender upper arm and thigh, checking for anything amiss. She wasn't even bruised.

"Right. Yes, the bike is fine," she finally said, although she still hadn't opened her eyes. "There's only one problem," she said, rolling over and shouting into his face. "You … you big dummy! You didn't teach me how to stop!"

Dace sat back on his heels, one hand on the ground. He looked angry for a moment—they were both quick to anger—then he laughed it off. "C'mon, what did I tell you? Your right hand controls the front brake, your right foot controls the back brake. You have to use both brakes at once if you really want to stop. Christ, a monkey could do that!" he said, getting back to his feet and holding out his hand.

She ignored his offering, smacking his hand away instead. Lips tight, she sprang up, elbowed him out of the way and righted the bike.

"Liza," he said, watching her warily. He shook his head. "Don't worry about it. You're just not a biker chick, that's all."

Lucky me, she seethed. She mounted the bike, checked the brakes and tried to remember what he'd just said. Then she started off by herself, going about five miles an hour, gradually picking up speed until she roared around the field and out into the lane.

"Go!" she heard Dace shouting. "Go!" Uncle Norm stood watching from the back door of his house, but she didn't dare take a hand off the handlebar to wave. I can do this, she kept telling herself. I'm on the edge of a precipice, but it's all right. He told her afterwards that she looked like she was riding a roller coaster at the Canadian National Exhibition. Ecstatic and afraid all at once.

"Marie, Marie, hold on tight," she recited to herself every time she got on the bike after that, with or without him. "And down we went. In the mountains, there you feel free."

When she pulled to a stop beside him, Dace was waiting, ready to fold her into his arms. "Good girl," he said proudly, and held a half full mickey up to her lips. In her excitement, she'd forgotten how furious she was at him. She drank at least an ounce and became more talkative at once. He drank the rest and they both laughed.

Drinking always smoothed things over. It made them both happy, though it seemed to affect him more than it did her. He drank whiskey with his father at the farm but beer almost everywhere else. The amount he consumed would have put most people to sleep, but he was a person who was energized by drink. Dace loved to party. He put away a prodigious amount of beer in the local bars before they closed at 1:00 a.m. Sometimes she did, too.

"Wonderful," she'd drawl, swallowing the cool golden liquid. "You're corrupting me, too." She knew by the third beer she wouldn't want to get up in the morning for work, but she always managed.

The white crystalline powder bothered her, though. More than once an envelope fell out of Dace's pocket when he was looking for spare change. Meth, she thought, but she didn't want to ask. Asking would have somehow made it more real. Even if he smoked meth when he was alone, it couldn't have been that often. He never acted high or intoxicated. He stopped talking, but this wouldn't have been very noticeable to her or to anybody else who was mesmerized by his face.

But drinking was different, wasn't it? Everybody drank. His father and his friends and everybody at school. Sure, some people drank too much, but he wasn't working yet, so she didn't care how much he drank. Sometimes she even thought it was a good idea. There had been thirty-six murders and fourteen suicides in Maitland Penitentiary during the time he'd been Inside. Best he forget the beatings, the knifings, the violence as summer stretched ahead, an endless chain of starlit evenings, a dream. He'd told her almost everything about himself in letters and he talked just enough now, his hands running through her hair, his eyes igniting as he pulled her into a dance at one of the few Maitland clubs.

For a while he got stronger and healthier, his upper arms rippling in the black T-shirts he favoured. If he sometimes said, "I used to be a bodybuilder," a little regretfully, she never understood why. His hair grew long enough to tie back with a leather thong. Her own unbraided hair shone with highlights from the summer sun and her skin turned a light golden brown. She was developing muscles in her arms and legs from running after her day camp charges all day.

Within two weeks Dace was so bored with the Maitland clubs they started sneaking off to Toronto in between his scheduled visits to his probation officer, an overworked young woman apparently bewitched by his deep-set eyes. They visited their old neighbourhood, watched a baseball game in Christie Pits and walked along Yonge Street, hiking from Bloor Street to the waterfront and back again, pursued by panhandlers and Hari Krishnas. Dace had little use for people who deviated from his dead mother's Catholic faith, but he gave most of his spare change to other beggars and Liza loved him all the more for it. Although he had borrowed enough money from his father to buy several custom-made suits during successive visits to a tailor, the only thing he convinced Liza to buy was a pair of black leather motorcycle boots with silver threads like his.

"Could I be charged as an accessory if they catch you?" she sometimes asked.

"After what fact, little darling?" he'd answer, reaching behind to hoist her onto his bike, his hands caressing her thighs.

"Oh, I don't know. Because you're violating the terms of your parole?" she'd say, then open her jacket and raise her shirt and bra until her bare breasts rested against his back.

But when they hit the Gas Works and Abbey Road or the Riverboat in the late evenings, she forgot her worries. Drinking really did help. And music. Dace had been right; there was music in the air. None of the clubs were air-conditioned, but a cool breeze blew up from the lake, easing the heat. Liza had started wearing a little more make-up so she at least looked her age, though if the bouncers got a good look at D'Arcy Devereux, they didn't card her.

Dace wasn't a talker, except with her. If he'd written long letters in prison, he didn't want to waste words now. Liza suspected prison life had fostered a natural taciturnity, an inherent disinclination to talk with strangers or share the minutiae of his daily life. He'd had to mind his own business for so long that even though he was a person with strong opinions, he didn't think anybody would be interested in what he had to say. Except her.

"It's okay," he said, hugging her. They sat beside each other, in front of a jug of beer at the Silver Dollar. "Nobody's going to find out I'm in Toronto. I'm going to make good, Liza," he swore, taking her hand and looking into her eyes so intently she almost cried. Nobody else would ever look at her like that again, she knew that with every fibre of her being. "I've promised both you and my father. Never mind. We'll stay here, at least until I'm off probation. I'll open up a little bike shop, right near Christie Pits in the fall. There's a garage for sale at the corner of Harbord and Ossington. Because it's summertime and the living is easy," he whispered in her ear, lifting up the great weight of her hair.

"Now that's an old song," she said. She didn't care, as long as this lovely interlude and their insularity lasted. As long as they stayed lovers forever, the way they were meant to be.

Chapter Twenty-Five
Something Wicked This Way Comes
Maitland, June 13, 1972

I fear for you,
I fear for me,
I fear of what
Will come to be.
—Densley, Matthew, "Fear"

Six weeks passed before they came for him. When Dace had been Inside, she had mentally catalogued all his letters and treasured everything he said. When he came out she could practically read his mind. Somehow she never figured he would let them get him, no matter what he said. Surely he could resist them. How hard could that be? But he went off with the bikers so fast it looked to her like falling.

"We're going to meet some friends," was all he'd said earlier in the evening when he picked her up at the residence. That should have tipped her off right away. He rarely said where they were going. They just went and she liked it that way. She was tired of making life-altering decisions. Please, she thought, just tell me what to do. Not that Dace had any idea where they were going either, usually.

The bikers were waiting with their big black machines on

the side of a dirt road just outside of Maitland, down by an old roadie bar. Judging by their disgruntled expressions, they'd been waiting a little too long. They got off their shiny, well-loved Harleys and sauntered over, their meaty hands hanging by their sides.

Dace stiffened when she sucked in her breath. "Be cool," he said, although his lips didn't move.

Common sense warned her to stay on the Harley, but when he turned off the ignition and nudged her with his hip, she swung her right leg back over the bike and slid to the ground. He got off the bike too, but he didn't take her hand. Because it's not cool, she thought crossly. Not cool if you're one of them: a biker, a real man. Seven bushy-haired, bearded bikers surrounded them. A relatively small club, she later learned. Liza wasn't about to challenge anybody. She lowered her eyes until all she could see were boots.

One man reached out and touched her arm. She automatically shied away, repulsed by his tattooed forearms.

"Meet Sal 'Dirt Beard' Perazzi," somebody said. "Eye-talian. One of our lady charmers."

Looks more like Dopey to me, she thought.

"What's the matter?" Dirt Beard challenged, his eyes measuring her protector's reaction. "Too good for me?"

Smiling nervously, she lifted her gaze to the bikers and held her ground, taking her cue from Dace. He said nothing to Dirt Beard. She almost died when he let it go.

At first glance the bikers looked as muscular as he was, but the older ones were also overweight, more like beer-bellied trolls than men. Three of the men, including Dirt Beard, were a bit taller and looked like they might be nearer Dace's age. The rest were in their late thirties and early forties. She was a little surprised by that, probably because she had always subscribed to the romantic notion that bikers were young men. Especially outlaw bikers.

The colourful insignia of three wolfhounds on their backs caught her attention. The men wore other insignia as well, but she didn't know what the symbols meant. She studied the wolfhounds and swallowed nervously. She had no great love of dogs, especially large ones. Granny Debo's dog had always tried to hump her leg. It had also liked to nip. If Granny hadn't been there she would have run. Oh, Dace, she thought, trying not to stare. That same impulse to run shoved at her. Some friends.

His friends were filthy, probably because they couldn't help perspiring in leather vests and knee high boots. Their hands looked as if they were permanently covered in motorcycle grease. The yeasty smell of beer oozed from their pores. Dace was always scrupulously clean. Obviously showers had been at a premium in prison because now he couldn't seem to get enough of them. He showered morning and night and sometimes in between. When the bikers met Dace and Liza, they were all smoking in an apparent attempt to ward off the black flies swarming in the swampy bulrushes by the road. She checked stealthily over her right shoulder but there wasn't another vehicle in sight, not even the Crown Vic that had tailed Dace off and on for the past six weeks. Where the hell had that cop gone?

Reluctant to take her eyes off the bikers for even a moment, she took another deep breath. She decided to pretend they were the seven dwarves. Dopey, Happy, Grumpy … what the hell were the rest of those names? Dace still hadn't said anything, but she wasn't going to be afraid because he wasn't. Besides, it was pretty clear from the moment they shook hands, thumbs up, forearms almost touching that they weren't strangers. They had all met before.

In the Pen? She hoped not. He wasn't supposed to fraternize, to mix. Maybe they'd met here in Maitland when she was working. Then it was her fault. She'd had to work, though. She sagged a little at the thought, but it didn't matter. A part of her was resigned, for he had warned her and somewhere in the back of her mind she had always known she wasn't the only person waiting for him to come home. If it hadn't been the bikers, it would have been somebody else, maybe somebody even worse, if that were possible. She watched, mesmerized, as a man wearing a blue checked bandanna around his head, sneezed, wiped his nose with his fingers and spat on the ground.

"Jeez, Boo-Boo," somebody said. "You keep doing that, Princess is gonna puke."

People need friends. Dace was no exception. If he had been, he would never have reached out to her in the first place. She had to accept these were simply that: his friends. Also, he'd probably been bored. For some reason he still wasn't working, and he needed something to do.

She must have missed a signal because suddenly the bikers got back on their bikes and she climbed back on Dace's, wrapping her arms around his waist. For a moment she was almost relieved. Then she realized they were supposed to follow. When nobody was looking, he cupped her hands.

Don't be scared, little darling, she heard him say, almost as if he had spoken aloud.

"Hey, Bro, is that your cuz?" the grey beard at the front of the pack inquired. His eyes raked Liza up and down, covering her damp T-shirt, her blue jeans and her black leather boots. At the same time, the man leaned off his bike and lifted her hand from Dace's thigh. He raised it to his own bearded lips and kissed the back. She smiled a little before she withdrew her hand. He looked as if he might pass for a banker if he were cleaned up and dressed in a suit. Or whatever. Doc, she decided, This one's Doc.

A cloud of black flies hovered over his head, though strangely, none of them seemed brave enough to land. What was he wearing, bear grease?

He must be the leader, she thought, surreptitiously wiping her hand on the back of her jeans.

Well, not the leader exactly, Dace explained later. That's Billy, the Road Captain. Tiger, the leader, he's in lockup downtown. He had some kind of beef with the law.

God, it was hot. She stretched up one slender arm to remove her silver helmet and her hair spilled down her back, flashing pinpoints of light like fireflies in the dark.

"What a mane!" Somebody whistled. "Let's get back to the

clubhouse, man, and we'll have a few."

"Any other ladies there?"

"You're not sharing? That's cool. Our old ladies are back there having a little party of their own."

Sharing? Liza straightened, trying to hide her disgust. *As if!* Who did they think she was? She wasn't sure what was happening, but she knew she didn't have much of a choice. Without meaning to, she had followed Dace, stepping over yet another invisible boundary.

Clutching him even tighter, she rode with him to a boarded up clapboard building five miles outside of town. Insignia flags flew in the dark windows where curtains should have been. They pulled up way too soon to Liza's way of thinking. Billy the Road Captain got off his bike, unlocked a metal gate topped with barbed wire, and ushered his gang inside the compound. A pack of wolfhounds growled greetings, but it was the floodlight that startled her. Dace was the only man who didn't laugh when she darted behind his back.

The building looked dark inside, but somebody whistled and a trapdoor opened up from the dirt ground. Inside she spotted stairs. She followed Dace as he took the stairs down into a dank cellar, then up to the rest of the house. The place was basically a few rooms with a cluttered table and several chairs, three or four filthy mattresses on the floor, fly-infested garbage in every corner, and some Nazi memorabilia interspersed with a dying Jesus on the north wall.

She also saw a rudimentary kitchen where she imagined they prepared the kinds of treats that kept them happy. A rusty, temperamental toilet teamed up with an outhouse in the back.

Liza's memory of that first evening in the Clubhouse was always fuzzy. She got drunk enough that after a while some of the bikers actually started to look appealing. When the club treasurer, Barry "Strangeman" Wilcox, an older man in his forties and the only one with glasses, asked, "What are you going to give me if I give you this, little lady?" she accepted the first Labatts with alacrity, desperate for the self-confidence only alcohol could bring.

Regardless of his moniker, Strangeman seemed all right, showing a glimmer of intelligence in his small, crinkle-cornered eyes. Or maybe he was just less high than the rest of them. This one's Happy, she thought. She drank the warm beer straight from the bottle, uncomfortably aware of the bikers staring at her lips. Across the room from her, the Road Captain swept everything off the chrome-legged table, dumping the mess onto the floor, then doled out a well-thumbed pack of cards decorated with busty mermaids.

The men started playing poker and Dace joined them, leaving her perched like a bright little pet parakeet on the edge of a mattress. By the time she'd downed a couple of beers, she felt more like a brainless sparrow. Her head swam and she wished she were back in her dorm, reading a book. Anywhere but here. God, she hated parties.

True to the Road Captain's word, several other girls were there, wearing skin tight jeans and teased, bouffant hair: deferential girls full of bravado. The place reeked of dampness and mouse droppings and urine; other women might have felt compelled to push a broom or do some simple tidying of the ramshackle Clubhouse. These women milled from room to room fetching drinks, stopping occasionally to drape their arms around their man's neck as he studied his cards, looking as serious as if he held the future in his hand.

The men appeared indifferent to their feminine charms and gruff with any responses, but each girl seemed more territorial than the last. They either ignored Liza or cast blatantly dirty looks her way. They had nothing to say to her, and she had no idea what to say to them. They were as blonde as the girls at school, although only one, Dagmar, was a natural. Her eyes were so blue she looked almost otherworldly. Three other girls had been named for objects: Crystal, Sherry and Tiffany. They were as young as Liza, except for a heavier-set one. She looked like she belonged to Billy the Road Captain and bore the more dated name of Doreen.

"Who's the long-haired bitch?" she heard Dagmar say when Liza finished her first beer and accepted a second one from Strangeman. Her English wasn't fluent. Probably his girl, Liza thought. Liza had no idea the smile of thanks she flashed Strangeman when he handed her a beer had lit up the room. If she hadn't been drinking, and if Dace hadn't been there, she probably would have feared for her life. She wondered if the bikers' ladies acted jealous because that was what passed for love in their world.

At least Dace was happy. He took little breaks from the card game, trying to pull Liza out of her shell and spinning all the girls around in time to Rolling Stones tunes on a transistor radio.

"It's okay, little darling," he murmured, bending down so only she could hear him. But he was inebriated enough to risk taking her face in his hands. "There's nothing bad going down here. These guys just wanna have some fun."

"Yeah, we just wanna have fun," one man agreed. A couple of guys snickered, but Liza melted anyway. She loved it when Dace touched her that way. If only he'd joined a more recreational bike club, she thought as the evening wore on. She grew more tired by the hour and tried not to drape herself over him, tempting as it was.

Crystal's man had taken her into a side room and they were going at it. "Don't stop! Don't stop!" they heard her shriek. Liza looked nervously around the room, noting a couple of the guys looked a little too interested in the cries, their glances flicking briefly on her. Please stay there, Liza thought primly, glancing at the rattling door. Drunk or not, group sex really didn't appeal to her.

She took a third beer from Billy the Road Captain, who was still eyeing her. Crystal had revved things up and the energy in the room had definitely taken on a lusty edge. Three beers was over Liza's limit and everything began to make a boozy kind of sense. She even smiled enough that Billy seemed to think he had a special rapport with her.

"Your cousin," he cajoled, "if that's what he really is, he's a real stand up guy. We've never had anybody like him in our place. He makes us all look good. And you, you could improve the place, too. Dace—Ironhorse—he'd do anything for his brothers. How about you?"

Well, what did she expect? Liza thought. She laughed and shrugged as diplomatically as she could. Dace had always been excessively loyal, something she could almost understand. At one point during the night he'd told her he knew some of the bikers from his teenage street life. He'd met the rest in prison. They were the brothers he'd never had.

Dace finally noticed the way both Strangeman and Billy were looking at her, slumped on the bed with her T-shirt hiked halfway up her torso, her smooth white skin glowing in the half dark.

"Like fresh meat," Dace muttered, coming over to the mattress and yanking down her shirt. Nobody else seemed to have noticed the two older bikers' interest, except maybe Dagmar. She stomped around the Clubhouse, waving her arms in the smoke-heavy air, yelling something about a stuck-up bitch and what she wanted to do to her.

"Why don't you go fuck yourself, you crazy broad?" Strangeman suggested, trying to pacify her. He looked pleased both with himself and with the cards in his hand. At least he was still in the game. To his right, Dirt Beard had passed out, a scatter of cards across his lap. Probably should have called him Sleepy, Liza thought. Meanwhile, two of the younger men, Boo Boo and Tank, were having a fist fight outside the back door. Something to do with the way his brother had looked at him, although nobody was exactly sure what had happened. As Liza was the only one who seemed even a little anxious, it must have been a common occurrence.

By now she was on her fourth beer. The floor was sloping up to meet her face, and although she still had a couple of dwarves' names left, the mental effort required to make any more matches was simply too great. Dace stopped dancing, took another slug of his beer, all of his attention finally on Liza. She looked away, almost daring him. The moment she scrambled to her feet and started dancing by herself, he came over, grabbed her by the shoulder and pushed her towards the back door. He gave her a smart slap on her rear and she laughed, too numbed with drink to feel a thing.

"Way to go, Ironhorse," Tank called, applauding. "Keep her in line."

She had a woozy concern Dace might follow up with more slaps, so she caught his hand to her mouth, kissed the palm, then sucked in his thumb for several seconds. He stopped dead in his tracks and stared at her, mouth partway open. He slung his left arm around her, pulling her closer.

"Liza," he said weakly. For the briefest of seconds he closed his eyes. The room went silent as the Clubhouse waited to see what Dace would do. Even Dirt Beard stopped snoring.

"You little ..." he whispered, extracting his digit from her mouth with a pop and almost carrying her out. "Not here. You can't do stuff like that in front of these guys or they'll —"

"What? What'll they do?" she asked as he deposited her none too gently onto the back of his bike.

"Nothing I'm not going to do to you when I get you home."

"Marie," she sang, the roar of the Harley ruining her performance. "Marie, Marie, hold on tight."

That was the first night, but they went back in the weeks to come. By then it was clear whose girl Liza was. None of the men would touch her. Dace was something else, though. In the clubhouse, the proprietorship of the bikers' girls applied only to themselves and their men.

He, Dace — their talisman, their prize — would always be fair game.

Chapter Twenty-Six
Waking Up

It's okay, she told herself, and it was, as long as they stayed mellow with beer and each other. As long as they made love. There was a faint undercurrent of unease whenever they discussed his growing involvement in the gang, but Dace wasn't really interested in what she had to say about it. By now she had done research — lots, in fact.

She could talk about butterflies or books or whatever the hell she wanted and he'd listen, but according to Dace, this was none of her business. "A prospect — a striker? Where do you get such crap? Have you been reading Joe's trash again? Those guys are my friends. We like to party, that's all. C'mon. Why don't you try it yourself? Loosen up and have some fun."

"But Dace, they have those emblems on their jackets!"

"Colours, Liza, colours," he said, grabbing her face and kissing her. "Give it a rest," he said when she went too far.

She knew she was trespassing. There was a protocol in any relationship, of what could and could not be said. Dace was an ex-con who not only needed, but demanded privacy. On their trips to Toronto, he knocked down the bold-faced drunks who verbally assaulted him in bars. She was well aware he would never have allowed anybody else to talk to him the way she did.

On the one trip they took with the bikers to see the Falls,

they stopped at a bar in St. Catharines and it was the same thing. So you think you're a tough guy, some loser had said. Biking was nobody's business but Dace's. As far as he was concerned, Liza was wasting time worrying about stupid stuff like one per centers and ex-cons, and he told her so.

When he was in a good mood, he might acknowledge her comments with implied agreement. "You're thinking that associating with such losers is a parole violation." Then he'd explode, demanding, "Do we have to talk about this shit again?"

Mostly he tried to distract her. Those times were the best. "You think too much," he would say, his hands sliding through her hair.

"I'm not thinking anything," Liza would murmur, trying not to force her smile.

This was her Dace, she reminded herself, wrapping her arms around him and pulling him down towards her student bed, and she loved him. She had always loved him. Even when she was trapped in Dublin and her goddamn life was going nowhere. She loved him here in Maitland, her legs wrapped around him, her fingers digging into his back and her mouth making sounds she hadn't known a girl could make.

His lifestyle wasn't going to destroy them. Nothing, absolutely nothing could do that. But what if his choices destroyed him? What if he got hurt? Bikers were dangerous and unpredictable. They even carried knives. She didn't think they had guns, but … This wasn't some suburban recreational biking club, that was for sure.

Somewhere in the intervals between their rare disagreements, she mourned the earlier summer. By midsummer, a drought had leached the grass until it was yellow. Already the maple trees looked tired, less green. Some of the birds and the bigger, smarter monarchs had flown south. Dace still hadn't started his bike shop. He was living off his father's handouts, he said, except there were also mysterious phone calls and assignations. Strange young men dropped by her university residence and asked for Dace, all the while checking her out: a slim, black-eyed girl in a white T-shirt and cut-off jeans. Janice would have had the good sense to send the strangers packing, but she was busy picking tobacco.

Most of the time none of this mattered. She was captivated and she always would be, as long as she was fertile, by him, by sex. She was happier than she'd ever been, even if Dace seemed happiest when he was riding with his gang. She had hoped the love and sex she gave him would have been enough, but knew they weren't. That was made painfully clear to her every time she had the misfortune of phoning his place and hearing Uncle Norm say, "Dace is out, dear."

Hearing this, she'd take the small motorbike her uncle had loaned her and track Dace down at a local bar. He never minded. His eyes lit up the minute she swept, wild-haired, into the room. Pulling her towards him by one hand, he'd whisper into her ear, *My darling, my life.* He was usually with a large group of people, including women who thrust their breasts forward as they laughed up into his face. Some she recognized from school.

"Your old lady is here," some joker would say.

Somebody else was bound to protest. "They're cousins, for God's sake!"

He would leave the bar, almost dragging her, the second he'd downed his draft. Because whatever else he was doing, he couldn't seem to get enough of Liza.

"Poor Dace," she'd tease him post-coitus when he was still astride her, down at the lake. "It must be so exhausting. Everybody wants to make love to you. All those silly little co-eds and sad-eyed biker girls." She didn't mention some of the boys would have been happy to love him too; she'd seen it in their eyes.

"And which are you? A little co-ed or a biker girl?" he'd ask, rubbing the tips of her nipples with his thumbs. She'd thought she was sated, but if he pushed it she'd go again and this time she knew it would be even better than the last.

"Well, not a biker girl," she'd reply, pleased to hear him laughing. No, she was definitely not a biker girl. Some of their men cleaned up okay, so it wasn't that. It was just that biker girls always did what they were told ... or else. The only time she liked a man to tell her what to do was in bed.

"Were you with the bikers before you went away?" she asked him once.

"No," he'd replied, sounding a little edgy. He hated talking about away and she knew it. She kept asking anyway. "But I always loved bikes and there was a biker in the next cell, Grumpy—"

"Jesus. Maybe you and those guys really are the seven dwarves."

"What?" he asked, lightly slapping her face. "Anyway, Grumpy told me stories about the parties and their life on the road."

Hmm, she thought, rearing up and nudging him onto his back so she could be on top. He hadn't liked her doing this at first, but he did now. She always came quickly that way and was ready for him again. Maybe he just wants to be number one somewhere, but that didn't bear thinking, never mind saying, so she pushed the thought away and rode him on a dark, humid carpet of night air.

He was too smart and too gorgeous to be some stupid biker. Please don't let him rise through the ranks of a motorcycle gang. She wasn't sure how motorcycle gangs worked, but this much was certain: she wasn't going to end up some gangster's moll. Not even for his love. He would have to change first.

Too bad his biking bros, those beer guzzling men with their tattooed limbs and wild hairstyles, wouldn't let him alone, but any fool could see why they didn't. From the first evening they'd spent with the bikers in their trash-strewn clubhouse, she'd realized his acceptance was a fait accompli. He was their ace to excitement and glamour; he was their rising star. Dace didn't have to do a damn thing to qualify. Striking, prospecting, associating—this job was his for the taking. His criminal record was the only assurance the Wolfhounds needed that he was a real wild one too. He'd spent time in the Big House. He'd earned their respect. That was all that mattered in their world.

Their limited world, she narrated for the unfinished novel she kept under her bed.

There came a time when Liza almost felt sorry for the Wolfhounds. Their lives had been curtailed by poverty and poor education. Like most men, they wanted to be stars in their own realms. And their women, they were like women everywhere. They wanted love. Maybe they weren't that bad after all. As long as they didn't do really bad stuff, like deal drugs or rape and murder ordinary people, maybe it was okay. So what if they liked wheeling around on their fat, cumbersome bikes, the wind blowing through their matted hair, the pavement threatening to splatter their bullish faces? Now they even had a uniform of sorts: they had taken to wearing T-shirts that said, *If you don't have a Harley, you ain't shit.*

Yes, they were ugly but from what she'd seen so far, a simple shower and shave would have helped most of them. Or even a change in venue, for they all worked intermittently at the local auto plant. By midsummer she could take some of them in small doses. Especially the family men who loved their children. Billy the Road Captain was one, the doting father of three girls in their early teens who had accompanied them on the trip to Niagara Falls.

Maybe it was just that biking was more of that male bonding stuff, she rationalized. And gang activity provided Dace with all the excitement he craved, hard on the heels of the sensory deprivation he'd endured during his incarceration.

He knew a price must be paid when a man died, no matter what the reason, but he'd missed so much during his adolescence. Not that he ever said, though. Like her, he almost never talked about his past. But it made sense. What could any reasonable person have expected? What had she expected and, more importantly, what did she expect now? That he stay out of prison. Was that too much to ask?

She was never afraid of the bikers, not then. She was Dace's cousin, a Viceroy butterfly, protected by her kinship and the bikers' assumption that whatever her irritating little peculiarities, she must be similar in nature to Dace. As long as she and Dace stuck together, she was good. There was a little review movie house in Dublin where she'd seen Marlon Brando in *The Wild Ones* at least six times. If only the police hadn't hassled those guys. Take Johnny, the wild one Brando had played. He'd had good stuff in him. He was handsome, too. Too bad he was set up. If he hadn't been, he might have married that young girl.

There was something else, too. Reluctant as she was to admit it, she had become almost as crazy about bikes as Dace was now. She loved the feel of a machine between her legs, whether she rode behind him on his Harley in a borrowed jacket and her black leather boots, or by herself on Uncle Norm's loaner. Free, she'd exult, her hair streaming behind her as she went downhill, the road rushing up into her face, the future stretching ahead.

By now her Uncle Norm, whose full head of hair had turned totally grey, would have made her an honorary daughter and a beneficiary in his will, as long as she kept Dace grounded and out of jail. And she would, she promised him. Rosie, his real daughter, was almost never there. She was expecting her first baby and must have hoped her family was all right.

"Don't worry," Liza always whispered in his ear when she said good-bye. "I'll keep an eye on him. I'll make him behave."

Back out on their bikes, the road opened up before them. Soon the rest of world would, too. Really, this biker stuff, surely it was just a phase. Dace was right. Everything was going to be all right. She would go back to school in the fall and the minute he got off probation they would head out of town.

Time evaporated. People worried about bikers in Maitland and got all pumped up about the Hell's Angels moving into southwestern Ontario, too. Sure, the Wolfhounds were on their own turf right now, but if they didn't merge there was going to be an all out war. Maybe it was all because of Joe's articles. Maybe just the sight of Harleys swarming the local bars, especially the roadhouses down by the lake, was enough to set people off.

So pathetic, Liza thought. She sat on a bus on the way to the YMCA camp, gingerly reading somebody else's discarded morning paper. What the hell were they trying to prove? They must have watched too many biker movies. The authorities were so antsy they had even put an Ontario Provincial Police Officer, Jon Anson, in charge of a special biker intelligence unit. That was the news all summer long, blown out of proportion, especially in the *Maitland Spectator*. That, and a lot of hype about drugs. Not pot, but crystal meth. Although some of the stoners, the ones who smoked several times a day when they were fifteen and woke up at fifty, probably didn't notice much of a difference.

Just a little media coverage. That's all it took in this redneck army town to make "biker" synonymous with "drug pusher". Liza, who hadn't trusted anything she'd read in the news for so long, might have been awed by the procreative powers of the local press, except she was a little worried. Those guys at the Clubhouse had to be up to something else at those Sunday meetings they didn't allow women to attend.

Then Dace started to change, although the changes were subtle at first, like the end of summer. And like so many lovers, she thought he must have a good reason. It was ages before she acknowledged that something was eating him alive. Maybe it had always been there waiting, like a genetic time bomb. He couldn't concentrate on anything she said and began to act peculiar, almost like he'd lost interest in her, although when he touched her she knew it wasn't so. He was always going to want her. He swore he loved her more than drink.

"More than those stupid Wolfhounds?" she asked, pressing her luck.

"Damn your eyes," he said, leaving a trail of kisses on her face and unhooking her bra. "They're my brothers, for Christ's sake. Would I do this with them?" he asked, dropping to his knees, lifting her dress, and cupping her behind.

"Smart girl," he said, coming up for air, "wearing a dress for once."

Uncle Norm left them alone in the house now and Dace

261

was almost insatiable. Now she worried too much sex was wearing him out. He looked as if he were losing weight; his already deep-set eyes had sunk farther into his bony face and his once well-kept hair escaped its leather tie.

It was only when he asked her for a favour that she realized how much he'd started to look like the rest of the gang. He wanted her to hide a small, irregular sized package behind a false plywood front under her residence bed. The moment he was out of the room she peeked inside the package and wasn't surprised to discover more white crystals. She didn't mind for herself; she loved him so much her sense of betrayal was almost immaterial. She had never said no to him before, and she didn't now. Not at first.

Another day he asked her to stow three thousand dollars in one hundred dollar denominations. Grasping the phrase *the lure of easy money*, she fanned the bills and gazed at him. He was sitting in her chair, his feet up on her desk, drinking a beer. He reached for her, rolling the cold bottle across the tops of her breasts, but he looked so agitated she knew she had to do something for him, and she had to do it fast.

Down, his eyes said. Dropping to her knees, she unzipped his pants, almost sick with excitement. It was the wrong excitement, though. She was scared. It must have been the money—that funny coloured paper stuff. She had never seen hundred dollar bills before. She raised her head, Where did you get this? she wanted to ask, but when she looked up, his eyes stopped her cold.

He relaxed a little once he came, but he was still staring at a poster of Marlon Brando on her wall, his fists clenched. My God, she thought, please let crime pay.

It was weeks before she found the courage to refuse taking the little packages for him, and doing it almost broke her heart. She wanted him to be happy and stay home with her, no matter what. He could look so damn explosive, although his usual tactic was to withdraw from arguments as well as implicit judgments about his lifestyle. Like his father, he rarely raised his voice. And she wasn't worried about him hitting her. He would never strike her, no matter what. Whatever happened, he wasn't the kind of man to displace his anger. Long ago, he had reserved his fury — all his fury — for something else.

"All you have to do is say no, little straight arrow," he said with disgust. "What am I, some bad guy? I don't need this song and dance." Then he bolted down the nine flights of stairs in her student residence, bypassing the elevators, fists balled at his sides.

And always there were rumours. People stopped her on campus. "Don't you know what he did to those poor buggers?" they'd ask.

If only she could make them understand Dace, she thought, trying to set his accusers straight. "He didn't do that stuff. He's not that way."

No matter what was in those packages he'd asked her to hide, she knew he'd been redeemed. He'd made one big mistake in his life, and he never would again.

Life was still so good when they went for long rides on his Harley, her legs wide open, her arms wrapped around him, her head on the back of his shoulders, her hands resting on his thighs. They flew up and down the empty concession roads around Maitland, avoiding full stops. They also got lost a lot because neither of them had any sense of direction. So they'd stop to make love and talk about their plans, because soon, somehow, they would get out of this place. They'd forget all about those stupid little packages then.

"Everything's going to be all right," he promised, his hands holding her face, his hard body sinking into her soft, compliant flesh. There were just a couple of hitches, though, things he had to do first. For the time being, even though the American border was less than fifty miles away, he planned to lay low.

In August they had to stop sneaking off to Toronto, where they'd been going to the Riverboat. It was getting ridiculous. The goddamn police wouldn't let him alone, even when she was right there. Her presence had protected him at first, but no more. She'd have her womb pressed up against the small of his back and everything would be fine until a red cherry whined and a Maitland police cruiser pulled them over.

"Who are you?" two close-cropped boys in blue would chime, as if they hadn't already met her and didn't know.

"I'm his cousin," she'd say. They'd smile and wink.

"What d'you do?" they'd ask.

"I'm a student," she'd say, and they'd smirk. So childish, she'd think, while Dace maintained his mask.

They rode less and less with the Wolfhounds on the open road, and she knew it was her fault. She didn't like the way people looked at them and more than once the gang had accused her of looking down her long nose at them. Well she did, sort of. At some of them anyway. And they couldn't understand her university English. They despised education and called her Teach to her face. They might have called her even more colourful names behind her back, but Dace would have killed them.

Still, none of this mattered during the long summer evenings she dreamed with Dace. Maitland would be history, he swore. And the bikers too, she hoped. It would all happen when things quieted down. They just had to figure how to keep in touch with Uncle Norm and Rosie and Liza's mother. They could take on new identities, head down to Mexico via the Rainbow Bridge in Niagara Falls rather than near Maitland so they could keep the authorities on their toes. Or maybe they'd head out to Vancouver, whichever was furthest away. Maybe she'd take some correspondence courses. They wouldn't even have to cross the border if they went to British Columbia, although B.C. wasn't Liza's first choice. She'd heard it rained all the time there. Besides, she longed to see the monarch butterflies' wintering grounds.

"Rainbow Bridge, by the Falls," she finally decided. "Okay? I like the name and they won't expect us to cross there."

"Sure," he said. "I like it too. "Somewhere over the rainbow..." Like her, he couldn't carry a tune, but he sang anyway. "No problem. I'll have to drive two hundred miles out of my way, but at least we'll have somewhere to jump if the cops are on our tails." In reality, he didn't care where they went, as long as it was away. She had been to Ireland; he'd never even left Ontario.

She had given up visiting the bikers' flea-infested Clubhouse, with its boarded windows some which looked like they had been shot up by rival gang members. Given up saying, "No thanks" when Dace's biking 'brothers' plied her with drugs, coming on to her just for sport. Lucky for her, she was a university student who dutifully returned to school. If she hadn't, one of Joe's creative headlines might easily have read: "University Co-ed Sucked Into Life of Crime."

One morning Uncle Norm called her at the residence. She picked up the phone and heard a grown man crying. "Liza," he said. "They got him. He's back in jail."

"No," she whispered, sliding down the wall and burying her head in her knees. "That's impossible. We went to the lake last night."

"It's true. They arrested him at a biker party. Then they came out here and wrecked his room. Tore up the shed, too. I had to put myself between them and the poor dog."

"Jesus! I told him all summer to stay away from those guys."

She didn't mention she had been to the Clubhouse, didn't tell him about the things she'd hidden for him. She felt sick to her stomach over the things she was keeping secret. God. She was only twenty years old and she already had so many stories she couldn't tell. Anybody could be listening on the phone. And Uncle Norm might blame her if he knew. Stupid, stupid! She had been responsible for keeping Dace safe. Maybe if she'd said no earlier, maybe if she'd taken him away... Just then, she heard a little hiss on the other end of the line: the sharp intake of Uncle Norm's breath.

"Sorry, what's that? Are you okay?"

"Oh, it's nothing. When they busted in here, one of the buggers twisted my wrist."

"You should go to the doctor, Uncle Norm. What are the charges? Is it a parole beef ?"

"No. Weapons. They said he had a knife, but that's a goddamn lie. It was a set-up. I don't know what's going on, but they want him back."

"It's okay! Don't tell me anymore. It'll be in the paper tonight."

"Lies, all lies. I have to go now. The lawyer says I can probably get him out if I post $50,000 bail. He'll have to stay here at the house, though, until the trial."

"Thank God. The locals are going to love that," Liza said wryly, and hung up.

She was relieved she and Janice had finally gotten a phone in their room. She collapsed on her bed, stuck her face into her pillow and screamed.

Chapter Twenty-Seven
Tough Choices
Devereux farm, near Maitland, August 27, 1972

He couldn't leave the farm, so the night before Dace was due back in court she met him there. She was so upset, she hadn't remembered to bring her purse, much less her pills and she had already forgotten to take two of them this week. Uncle Norm was in the woodshed, hammering together a five-tiered birdhouse: a Purple Martin house, he said. He was slack-faced with grief and looking old. What was he, forty-five? A cigarette hung from his mouth and a bottle of Johnny Walker waited on a three-legged stool by his feet, three quarters gone.

Dace was smoking too, balancing a metal ashtray full of reeking butts on his left hand. He wore a long-sleeved Levi shirt and soft blue jeans. On the outside he looked relatively calm. Like me, Liza thought, just before I'm about to scream.

Uncle Norm wiped his bottle off and offered it to her, but he had little to say. It was almost as if he thought if he didn't talk about Dace's court appearance, maybe it would just go away.

Liza took a small swig of Johnny Walker and welcomed its burning slide down her throat. "Uncle Norm, I'm s—"

"It's not your fault, little girl. It's nobody's fault. It's the police. They have it in for him."

"For the love of God, Dad," Dace said, kicking an old tire lying on the sawdust-covered floor. "Don't talk about me like I'm not here. It doesn't matter if they have it in for me. I'm my own man. C'mon, Liza, let's get out of here."

"We can't go anyplace," she protested, glancing at Uncle Norm. He shrugged and cursed when the hammer slipped, almost striking his thumb.

"Jesus Christ. I'm not in jail yet. We can go for a goddamn walk," Dace said, walking out the shed towards the back of the property. "Get over here. Take a look at the full moon."

"Dace," Liza ventured, running to catch up with him.

"Shut the fuck up," he said, putting his arm around her shoulders and squeezing her against his side. "I'm tired of everybody yapping at me."

"I'm not everybody," she snapped. She walked beside him into the tall uncut grass by the trees, until all they could see of the house Uncle Norm had built for him was the occasional twinkle of window light.

He tried to push her from him, but she grabbed his right arm and held on tight. He kissed her, going right for her mouth. "Liza," he broke off, pushing at the waist band of her pants. "I'm warning you, I'm not myself tonight. Get out of your jeans or I'll rip them off myself."

"Dace," she said between kisses, stripping almost as quickly as he did until jeans, shirts and underwear littered the damp ground. "What's the matter? Are you scared?"

He stopped kissing her then and held her out at arms' length. She looked at him warily, then closed her eyes, almost afraid of what was coming next. His eyes, his mouth and his nose had all narrowed; he had never looked so livid, at least not at her. He shook her for what seemed like a long time so that her head whipped back and forth and spittle flew from her mouth.

"Dace?" she tried to say, counting her blessings he wasn't a man to slap her, although she almost wished he were. Anything would be better than sensing his terrible fear. Twigs snapped underfoot when he finally stopped shaking her and took her in his arms. For a moment, her feet left the ground. She closed her eyes and held on tight until he dumped her back down.

"No," he said, thrusting a leg between her knees and burying his face in her neck, then in her hair. "Check between my legs. Does it feel like I'm scared? Goddamn, Liza. The only thing I'm afraid of is losing you. I've been to court for something much worse before. This is just a bullshit charge. To get me back in the can. The Crown Attorney visited me yesterday. Oh, yeah, that's right. Came all the way out here. Ate a half dozen of Mrs. O'Connor's muffins and drank some tea with a splash of whiskey on the side. Didn't Dad tell you? He's always yammering to you on the phone."

"Of course he didn't. He hasn't had time. The Crown — that's like the prosecuting attorney, right? What did he want?" she asked, taking his head between her hands and trying to focus on his eyes. He reeked of perspiration but she didn't care.

Dace ripped his face from her hands. She fell back, staggering a little, struggling to keep her balance on the uneven ground. He steadied her by reaching for her elbow, but he still wasn't ready to look at her or talk about what was really bothering him. Instead he stared at the sky. She stood alone, bereft, competing with the stars for his attention. "She. The attorney is a she. My God, a woman can do anything these days. Although I gotta tell you, she looks like she's one tough lady. Kind of like a Golda Meir."

Liza crossed her arms over her chest, barely suppressing a grin. "Meaning she was immune to your charms. So what did she say?"

"That they're charging a bunch of the guys with the murders of those diddlers last year."

"The riot victims?" she asked, raising her eyebrows.

"Yeah, those victims," he said, suddenly grabbing her hair with both hands and giving her head another little shake.

Tears sprang into her eyes, but she didn't care. At least he was touching her. "Okay, so it's about time."

He wiped the tears from her eyes with his thumbs. "Liza,

they're charging Alf and Steve with second degree murder," he whispered. His hands slid down her smooth cheeks and settled on her shoulders.

He still couldn't look at her, though. She rubbed her cheek against his right hand, trying to make him see her. "But weren't those the guys on your Inmate Police Force team? And Steve, isn't he the one who's seventeen?"

"Well, he might be eighteen now. But the point is, he didn't do anything like that. I swear on Granny Debo's grave that he was with me almost all the time."

"So you told them that," she whispered, wondering if it were just the moonlight that made him look so pale.

"Yes, but that's not what they wanted. They want me testify against Alf and Steve."

When her legs almost buckled, she lay down, trying to take him with her as she sank to the ground. "Oh baby, you can't. So that's that, right?"

He looked down at her and she knew he saw her as luminous, as she saw him. She was smiling and crying at the same time, beckoning him with her open palms. "Please," she begged, reaching for his stiffened penis, ready to take him in her mouth.

He slapped her hands aside. Some of their clothes had landed close by. Retrieving his discarded jeans, he lifted her hips and bunched them under her rear.

"Open," he said, placing his feet astride her and sinking between her spread thighs. He stayed on one elbow so he could keep one arm free. His sex bulged against her hip; they both knew he was good for a while. Her labia peeked from its nest of curly hair, blush pink, but he ignored it, caressing her erect nipples with his thick fingers instead. Nerve lines ran directly from her nipples to her clitoris, the beautiful place he had traced so many times before.

"So that's that," she repeated, taking a deep breath and trying to relax. "They'll leave you alone now."

"Maybe. I doubt it though. That's not the way it works. Uh

Liza, you aren't helping here, you've got to let me in," he said when he finally brushed her elevated sex. She was moist, but not quite enough. "And no more crying, for God's sake," he said, inserting two fingers inside her before seeking out her tiny bud again. "You gotta stop it."

"Okay," she gasped, grabbing his shoulders and arching both her neck and her back. "Sweet Jesus, that feels good. Don't stop, don't stop, don't stop. Yes, right there. Ooh. Maybe," she said, trying not to pant, "we should just run away. We could be at the Niagara Falls Peace Bridge before daylight and cross in the dark."

"It's too late now. They're watching us. They've been watching all summer. You know that."

"Wait. What's that noise?" She tried to lift her head and chest in the small clearing they had churned in the grass, but her hair looked like it had rooted to the ground. "I hear bikes. What the hell are bikes doing out here?"

"Shhh," he said, also lifting his head and listening to the noise only Harleys make. "Sounds like the guys."

"I thought they arrested all the bikers," she said, laying back down with him still between her legs.

"Not all of us. It's okay. They're probably just here to say goodbye, show the faith."

"But you're not going anywhere! You're going to beat this rap."

"Depends who's the judge."

"Can't you give him a little something?"

Almost deflating but not quite, he lowered his face until his forehead touched hers. He spoke slowly and distinctly through gritted teeth. "What, Liza? What should I give him? Some pot? Or maybe one of my bros, for Christ's sake? Or how about the title to the farm, my father's place? I can't just rat somebody out. What kind of life would I have after that ... if I could live with myself?"

"I wish you hadn't taken up with them."

"Baby, how many times do I have to tell you? It makes me see red when people tell me what to do. Even you. It always has.

I'm a man."

"You're a man," she agreed meekly, wrapping her legs around his hips. "You're not going to run off with your biking brothers tonight, are you?"

He lowered his face to her breasts, digging his hands into her rear. "No. Not as long as you're good. The way I feel right now, I don't want to party. Yeah, it's true. I've kind of gotten used to hanging out with my old man and waiting for you to call. Have a little faith, girl. Everything's going to be all right."

"I'd like to believe you," she said, sliding out from under him and rolling onto her stomach.

"You know it pisses me off when you doubt my word. Get the hell back here or I'll ..."

"Or you'll what?" she teased. "Wait. What's that?" She glanced back over her shoulder, into the woods. "Did you hear that? That snap, that crunch in the brush? Oh Dace, I think I see eyes! What if somebody's sneaking up on us?"

"It's just an animal," he said, stretching out and lightly touching her back. "A little fox like you. There now. You've scared him away."

"Darling, you're crying." She reached back a hand, looking at him through her hair.

He flicked her bottom several times with the back of his hand. "I'm not crying! Why the hell would a grown man cry? Enough of this," he said, grabbing her waist and positioning himself across her reddened backside. "You're being a really bad girl tonight. Open up and let me in," he insisted. "You're ready, aren't you?" He prodded two fingers inside, checking. "Ah, I thought so," he said, then rammed his penis between her quivering buttocks and into her vagina, full force.

She raised herself on her forearms, wishing her hair weren't in her face. "Wait. I don't like ..." she started to say, feeling a little too full, even though she had opened up almost all the way.

"But you will," he said, ripping the leather thong from his own hair and securing most of hers back in a ponytail. "Just wait."

Her eyes scanned the forest the moment she could see. The tips of her aching breasts brushed the ground. She squeezed them with her own hands. Who was there? Who was watching? What if somebody were behind them? Her rear was way up in the air. She had never felt so naked or exposed. Even so, she hoped he would keep slamming her hard.

"No, I ... I don't want things to end. I mean, I don't want to come yet. I ..."

"Yes, you do," he said, reaching around and stroking her clitoris with a finger at the same time as he plunged. She looked back over her shoulder, just once. He was wide-eyed, upright on his knees, all the protection she had against whatever hid in the trees. "Everything, my darling. Everything's going to be all right," he repeated, thrusting into her as if he wanted to go deeper than he'd ever gone before. The walls of her vagina clamped down over and over, determined to hold him in. Her hands and knees shook, but she didn't want him to stop, no matter what she said.

"No," she cried, overwhelmed. "No!" even as they both came.

Much later he wrapped her in his soft blue shirt and held her the rest of the night, although neither one of them really slept. Liza watched the night eyes in the forest and made wishes on falling stars. Dace was the air around her, his warm breath a breeze on her neck. He couldn't make love again, although she wanted to, wanted to see his face above her once more. She wasn't worried, though, not then. They were safe as long as all they had to worry about was the night. In the dark they were safer than they had ever been in the light.

It was a trumped up charge, but it might do. Dace had been there, that was all, but the *Maitland Spectator* called him a full-patch member. The reporters were so thrilled they might as well have gotten high. D'Arcy Devereux was about as bad as a Maitland boy got. Hell, the *Spectator* had called him worse over the years, Dace confessed to her during the final hours of his freedom. Come court time, his attitude didn't sit too well with long-time resident Judge Silverton. This desperado, this infamous defendant, was a probationary member of society, and a man well known to the police.

"He's a vicious thug now and he was a vicious punk then," Judge Silverton took the liberty of volunteering off the record later. He hadn't said a word in court. *No sirree*, Liza thought. Silverton was much too smart. Probably figured he could do more good sitting on the Bench than sitting in some dusty office working on an appeal that he had brought on himself by speaking too loosely. Like maybe he could keep Maitland streets clean. Juvenile records were supposed to be sealed anyway, and he liked to keep law and order, though he didn't necessarily agree in this particular case.

Later he was happy to tell anyone who would listen that men like D'Arcy Devereux always got too many chances, but in 1972 there had been no telling what he might do or say. Why, some ex-con from Maitland Penitentiary had recently published a book which had said plenty about nasty foster parents, police brutality and the whole goddamn legal system.

Judge Silverton rolled off the phrase 'a man well known to police' several times more, hoping the press might be clever enough to remember D'Arcy Devereux had gone bad long before he was put away in 1966, but they weren't.

They also weren't clever enough to figure out that Dace knew the Judge. A lot of things might be forgotten, but a first time experience hardly ever is. Dace would never forget this man. The grey-haired man on the bench had helped seal Dace's juvenile fate.

It wasn't just the name he'd recognized though, he told Liza a little later. It was the shape of his mouth. Judge Silverton had the same thin lips as his nephew Father Danby. Just my luck, other people might have thought, but Dace didn't think that way. Only fools believed in luck. Besides, professional people were nearly always related. Especially if they had lived in the same small towns.

"If you aren't going to listen," Judge Silverton shook his mane of grey hair, affecting rock bottom sorrow. Dace observed that his lips were the grim lines of a man who had hoped to mitigate the testimony of a ten-year-old child. And while the child wasn't exactly believed, he had still been instrumental in the disgrace and expulsion of Silverton's beloved nephew to a northern residential school.

Liza could only guess what Silverton was thinking. In the courtroom, for one brief moment, she saw Dace through his cold blue eyes. Jesus, the man had been Outside for less than six months and by violating his parole and associating with losers, he had risked re-incarceration and ended up right back here. Why had he abdicated so much control? What had they talked about all summer? How many times had she pleaded with him to stay away from the Clubhouse? How many times had she waited until he was gentle with love?

Too many times, because they had been observed by Jon Anson, the OPP specialist from the Biking Unit on numerous occasions. Anson had gone undercover, passing for a biker most of the time, and had been partially successful in infiltrating a rival biking club, although he couldn't be a full-patched member unless he was linked to a crime.

The court relied on him to corroborate the evidence against Dace. Anson was only too happy to inform the court that D'Arcy Devereux was a loose cannon. He said his fellow bikers feared for their women's reputations when he was around. Even the men were afraid of Dace, mindful that he had tortured to death two of his own men in the Maitland Penitentiary Riot the year before.

Dace's expression never betrayed his feelings, but Liza's did. This biker wannabe, Jon Anson, was a twisted, pathological liar, even if that bit about the women was true. Fortunately, nobody was looking at her. D'Arcy Devereux was the man of the hour; they were waiting for his reaction.

"Strike that last bit," Judge Silverton hastily interjected before Dace's defence could object. "He hasn't been convicted of those murders."

Or even charged, Liza mouthed.

Then Jon Anson said something about the accused having a sexual relationship with his own cousin, a university co-ed with no record. He made the word 'co-ed' sound especially salacious, but nobody was listening this time except Uncle Norm who already knew, and Joe Armitage who turned around, winked at her and mewed.

Maybe if he co-operated and fed the redneck judge some tidbits about gang behaviour. Maybe if he lied, Liza prayed. She sat on the hard, wooden bench in the Maitland courthouse, a supposedly educated person, the only person who had chosen to know her cousin inside and out.

On the third day, Dace turned around and looked at her from his fixed position at his lawyer's side. She sat on the bench just behind him, in enemy territory, on the right side of the law.

Stand by me, he telegraphed. *You know I had no choice.*

Yes, you did, she thought sadly. *Why do you care about those people when there's you and me? For God's sake, give Silverton something. Anything. Anybody. A name.*

Dace tried smiling. Reassuring her that in spite of his crippling dependency on trouble and excitement, he would make good and be normal someday. Whatever the hell normal was. That was all dependent, of course, on if he ever found his way.

So what if there were other women, so what if the informant was right? she raged. She was the only one he loved. She didn't give a fuck about the other women. She could almost understand why Dace had to have them, to prove over and over to himself that he was valued and loved and to fill his immense craving. It wasn't that they meant anything to him. Sure, his promiscuity might be a problem someday, but not now. She was so worried about Dace going back to jail she just didn't care.

Judge Silverton caught Dace's smile and graciously returned it. Liza had been unable to stomach a spoonful of her Campbell's Vegetable Soup in the courthouse cafeteria, whereas the old man had come back after a lunch of steak and kidney pie looking positively gleeful. A couple of Scotches in his office had probably helped. Silverton rambled on in his closing remarks until he finally appeared to recall the reason he was there. In sober tones, he announced he was putting several bikers, D'Arcy Devereux included, back behind bars. Especially considering the weapons charges.

The local press went crazy, but he ignored them. He ignored Dace, too, when he stood up and shouted, "That knife wasn't mine. That's a goddamn lie!"

Liza stood up, one hand clamped over her mouth, careless of the picture she presented to the press. An illegal camera snapped. *No,* she thought, as he was led away. *No.* This wasn't supposed to be happening. He wasn't supposed to go back after all the money Uncle Norm had spent on the fancy lawyer and his pending appeals. He wasn't supposed to go back to prison after all the love she had given him.

He wasn't supposed to, but he was.

Further to Judge Silverton's decision, the Wolfhounds folded. The menace was gone and the town was saved. The road out of Maitland emptied to nowhere.

Chapter Twenty-Eight
Déjà Vu

Where are they gone, and do you know,
If they come back at fall o' dew
The little ghosts of long ago,
That long ago were you?
—Jones, Thomas S., "The Little Ghosts"

Then Dace was nowhere too, caught in the limbo where every prisoner lives, somewhere between the living and the dead.

I refuse to be tied to the past. But my past molded me. It will take many years to undo, he wrote before she got around to visiting him again. Apparently he thought she was too busy for him now. She was in her second year at university, a different person, a girl Mel's family would love.

I doubt it, she thought, crushing his letter. Jesus — Mel's family. Sure she wanted a family, but that didn't mean she wanted Mel's! Their censure — what was she supposed to tell them, anyway? She couldn't live a lie. She wanted people to know all about her and love her despite it all.

Once, she'd imagined everything would work out. Now she saw trouble everywhere. She should have known better, an educated girl like her. She should have known things would work out this way instead. That he would, well, go back.

He was allowed a few mistakes, her wild gorgeous cousin, but so far he hadn't met anybody's expectations except maybe his own. Had old Judge Silverton been right? What if Dace was hell-bent on the self-destructive path of a career criminal? He was that compulsive. Why, what gene, or what event had caused him to lose his way? She didn't care to speculate, although surely trouble such as this wasn't entirely manmade.

Had his criminal acts really escalated? She thought constantly about his association with the bikers, because that's where, at least on this occasion, everything had gone wrong. So what if he'd run with the bikers and gotten a little wild when he drank? So had his own father, like hers in their long ago youth. Dace was an extraordinary person. In his letters and in his loving, she had always seen glimmers. She saw them still. He would make good someday. Of course he would.

I want you, Dace, she thought. *I don't want to be reasonable. I'm not giving up. I'm not going to do the 'right' thing again.*

At least time's still on his side, she thought, smoothing out and shoving his latest missive into *Dante's Inferno* before speed walking to class. In addition to her course load of classics, Liza had started reading everything she could find on crime in the sociology section of the university library. According to statistics, Dace might be straight by the time he was forty. Oh God, why hadn't she studied biology instead? she sometimes wondered, thinking about the girl she'd once been.

If he weren't dead by then. It was different for her. She didn't have as much time. She'd be thirty-six when he was forty. *Many years to undo*. What on earth was he thinking? Maybe it was just a phrase written in a terrible moment of despair, but—oh God. She didn't have that many years.

Thirty-six was awfully old to start making babies, and she was almost a woman now. And Liza wanted babies, somebody to treasure, to call her own. Maybe it wasn't fair, because children were people in their own right, but Liza craved somebody to fill her body and bring her joy. Like he had.

The cold wind blowing through her was intolerable. And in Dace's place came reams of letters with their tamped down rage, prison room visits and their smouldering sexuality. She'd had him. For weeks. For months. Letters would no longer do. She was way too old to settle for second best.

You've got to stop. I can't take anymore, she scribbled in her notebook as she sat in the lecture hall for English 201. She glanced around at the other students, feeling ... she wasn't sure what. Except she would never fit in here, because she looked like one of them now. A prison groupie. A haggard old crow not yet twenty-one. How could she just wait? She had waited for him ever since she was fourteen, waiting as if he were the only one. But what if he weren't? What if she could love somebody else? Was it worth a try?

She couldn't just abandon him, though. Not like the biker girls they said he'd slept with in the Clubhouse, who were petrified of their old men but not afraid enough to resist him. She couldn't just leave him. She'd loved him for too long. So she kept visiting him at the new Maitland Pen, fuming at first but just sad in the end. He was angrier than she was, angry with the system and with her, close-mouthed and contemptuous, although that didn't stop him from taking cigarettes from her. He had no choice.

"Darling," he said at Thanksgiving. She'd brought him a third carton of cigarettes then quipped about bringing him poison. He looked her in the eyes for the first time in weeks. "I don't care if this stuff kills me. I'm just trying to kill time."

"Well," she couldn't resist saying, "you're good at that."

Dace ignored her comment. "Whatever happened to that college kid?" he asked instead. "Why don't you bring him here sometime?"

"He was in Europe this summer. That's what his family does after school. And he studies a lot," she said, playing along, relieved he was no longer acting like he was mad at her. She knew he only behaved that way because he was ashamed.

"Liza, listen to me. You can't keep coming here. It's no life for a girl like you. Books, babies, butterflies, that's all you want."

"And bikes. I love riding that bike." *And making love with you.*

"So keep the Honda. Dad will give it to you. You know he wants to do something for you. And sex isn't everything, is it?" he said, raising an eyebrow. He knew what she had left unsaid.

"No," she lied, forcing a reluctant smile.

"Besides, from what you've said, it sounds like what's- his- face, Mel, loves you."

She stared at him, stunned, saying nothing for what felt like forever. She felt sick, then angry. "Jesus, Dace, what are you saying? I'm not a ... whatever, a doll, a trophy. You can't just give me away!"

"Liza, look at me. It's like I keep telling you. I'm in no position to rescue damsels in distress, and I'm pulling you down."

She shook her head. "It's you. You're destroying yourself. And you know what? I can't take anymore," she blurted into the prison phone.

"I know, Liza," he said, so irritatingly soothing. If there hadn't been glass between them, she would have jumped through and pummelled him to the ground. "But you can still have a life." He shrugged, giving her a wry smile. "A boring life, granted, a life lived in your head, but you can have it. And you know what? I think it'll be good for you."

"Thanks a lot! Jesus. What kind of life are you having here?"

"I'm not a lifer. Someday I'll get out for good."

Yes, she thought. "Of course you will," she said loyally. *When I'm old.*

"But you don't want what I want."

Trouble and excitement. Life on a limb. And vindication, yes, some of that, too. No, Dace. The only trouble I ever wanted was you.

"I'm not in love with him," she protested. Forbidden tears burned behind her eyes. He hated when she cried. He needed her to be strong.

Dace looked down the counter rather than at her, but he was implacable. For a moment, she almost saw him as his criminal associates might see him: a strong, silent, violent man. And she was afraid.

"You're not trying hard enough," he insisted. "You can love anybody if you try. It's not that I don't love you, darling girl, you know I do. But you need somebody to take care of you and there's no way I can. Aw, c'mon, I'm walking out of here if you're going to start that. Liza baby, have a heart."

"I can't." Tears and mucus streamed down her face, but she didn't move.

"Hey, guard, get over here and make yourself useful."

Mel had never seen him in prison, so perhaps it didn't matter. It was all new to him. God, she hated hearing Dace chatter about his friends to Mel, his fucking criminal associates, although he never once violated the inmate code by volunteering any names. Oh no, not him.

A criminologist would explain his relapse like this, she thought coldly, leaning back on a stool beside Mel and studying Dace's suddenly too handsome face. He was conditioned, no matter what he said. She knew this now because she had read so much, though she wasn't sure how much good that had done. Dace had spent his youth in prison. Here he had friends to visit, games to play, work to pursue, authorities to aggravate.

Except his identification with the inmate subculture, which was so important if he were going to survive the jungle Inside, had stopped him from becoming an individual, from ever growing up. And without individuality and independence, rehabilitation was an almost impossible goal.

Sure, he had a cruel, restricted life, where order and security were jeopardized and insurrection and revolt threatened. But it was a life just the same.

What if he didn't need anything else but this? What if he didn't need her?

Mel liked Dace, but Liza suspected he was also glad to see

him back in prison. So glad, in fact, that he didn't even mind when she seethed after every visit.

"Did you see the way that guard Savage looked at him?" she said. "He's got to get out of there."

"Liza, it's out of your hands. You're grieving, aren't you?" he replied, trying to hug her again, but she was a mannequin, her arms hanging by her sides.

"You're such a good person. I don't want to hurt you."

"You're not hurting me, you're hurting yourself," he swore, his hands moving lower and stroking her body until she finally gave in, just after Halloween, although she would have been just as happy to sleep in his arms. "I'm not a teddy bear," he'd insisted.

And it was all right, even good, after she showed him what to do. Jesus, she told herself. Maybe Dace was right. All she had to do was try.

"It's tragic, what's happened to your cousin, the choices he's made," Mel coaxed. "But you're young. You'll move on and you'll get over it." He was a born optimist, but he was lying when he said Dace would be okay. Optimistic or not, she knew Mel expected Dace to fetch up dead.

Dace was one of those handsome, charismatic men who drew women to him just by looking at them. He was the same with his male friends. He had almost drawn Mel, the first time he'd visited Maitland Penitentiary and had seen Liza in his eyes. Dace and Liza looked even more alike these days, now that she had shorn her hair to her skull. She was both a younger and an older version of herself, her dark eyes huge in a white, bony face.

"What the hell did you do to your hair?" both men demanded on separate occasions. "You look like Liza Minnelli, for God's sake."

"It was too much trouble," she said and shrugged, her thin shoulder blades poking out like wings. She cut it even closer when the *Maitland Spectator* finally announced that D'Arcy Devereux was one of thirteen prisoners charged with the murders of two inmates who had died during the riot in

September 1971. Their trial would begin in November 1972.

Dace was sent back to solitary, to cold storage in a concrete vault. All visitation stopped. *It isn't supposed to be like this,* she'd fumed as chunks of her hair fell into a porcelain sink. She wielded the largest pair of scissors she could find and hacked without a plan.

Things weren't supposed to keep getting worse, but they did. Dace wasn't just in the Hole, he was back up a goddamn tree.

Not for the first time, she wondered: surely this wasn't all because of some fucking priest, was it? She shuddered, recalling what he'd said about his school. They'd talked about such things from time to time, especially if he'd had a few beers. He'd always sworn that nothing had ever happened to him anyway, that he'd gotten away. But what if something had happened? What then?

After enough time she wasn't angry with him anymore, though only a fool would stop feeling afraid. A fool, or some girl who hadn't fallen in love with D'Arcy Devereux when she was fourteen.

Chapter Twenty-Nine
Bird on a Wire
Maitland Courthouse, November 1972

The murder trial of thirteen federal inmates began after a long delay. On a damp, dismal day, the prisoners shuffled off the Maitland Penitentiary bus, the former army vehicle that had hauled them into town. Somehow they figured out how to move in unison, then filed silently through a narrow limestone underpass. The passage, straight ahead under a dripping, arched stone roof, was lined with crowds of strangers jostling for a better view. At the end of the tunnel was a set of stairs which led into Courtroom B.

The prisoners had winter pale faces and downcast eyes, but what most people noticed were the chains and handcuffs. A little excessive perhaps, considering they were also accompanied by armed guards who knew how to follow rules. Many of the viewers were struck by the youth still visible in the lines of the prisoners' faces, but only relatives felt any sympathy. And much of what they felt was a convoluted mixture of sorrow and exasperation. When the hell was he going to learn?

"I'm not superstitious, but ..." more than one spectator was overheard saying. It was hard not to be a little superstitious about thirteen prisoners. One for each man who had suffered at the hands of his fellows during the final hours of the Maitland Penitentiary Riot, although only two had died.

In addition to the murders, several charges had been laid relating to the kidnapping of the guards, and the Crown was holding out for more. After investigations at both the federal and the institutional level, they were confident these men were not only the ringleaders in the largest riot in Canadian penal history, but apparently so depraved that they had overstepped their own fluid and shifting moral boundaries, allowing them to murder their own kind.

The Crown also thought they knew who had directed the beatings that left two men for dead. They spent several weeks assembling the facts on a storyboard that even a jury could understand.

"How's about a little smile for the cameras, boys?" one of the swarming reporters joked, prompting Steve to say, "I can't. They smashed my teeth."

"Who's they? Who's they?" the reporters asked as the shackled boy with a missing front tooth was pulled up short by Dace.

It looked bad, but maybe they wouldn't be railroaded. Their cases had attracted thirteen of the best criminal defence attorneys in the country, a situation previously only enjoyed by Dace, blessed as he was with a solvent father. But what if they never found out exactly what had happened on the final day of the riot? A couple of months ago people thought they knew, but now they weren't so sure. There were so many different versions, as if everybody had watched multiple televisions in a department store but nobody saw the same show. How could that be?

Maybe the truth will still come out, the men said, shrugging whenever they congregated in the prison cafeteria, the exercise yard or the showers. Whatever the truth was, anyway. By now the story had been told so many times it had almost been reduced to a fable.

Police and prison guards accompanied the prisoners. If they were lucky, friends and family waited inside too. Not everybody would come back again, but this was the first day. Fathers rested their eyes, reflecting on the day's pay they could il afford to lose. Mothers — and there were more of them — clutched Kleenex inside their purses and prayed to God they wouldn't live long enough to make fools of themselves and hear someone say: "Get her out of here. She's too unstable."

It's hard to hold your head up when your son's been charged with murder, they told their best friends, and even harder not to be able to help him. Whatever they told anybody else, they blamed themselves, knowing in their hearts there must be something they could have done. Maybe they could have lured men who would have been better role models for their sons. Maybe they should have driven off their kids' delinquent friends and made the family go to church more often. Perhaps they could even have found their boy the love of a good girl.

They were also grieving, for the men on trial were strangers. Most of the mothers had lost their real sons long before and could barely remember the troublesome children they had been. They dreamed of little things instead: an infant's foot, a gap-toothed smile, their own Dennis the Menace playing hockey in the street.

Showtime, Dace thought. Whatever happened, at least he wasn't in his cell. Better still, the spectacle was about to begin. Things were off to a fitful but predictable start. The uninitiated appeared slightly disappointed to discover court wasn't more like the *Perry Mason* dramas they loved at home. Maybe it would be more like *Front Page Challenge,* though. They sat back, waiting for the 'truth' to be revealed.

Strangers swelled the ranks of family and friends: court appointed lawyers for the Crown and the Defence, courtroom junkies and a lone stenographer off to the side, recording the spoken word. There were no videotaped recordings of the whispered consultations between lawyers and their clients, no clips of the sleep-deprived accused or the eager eyes of the spectators as they leaned forward to catch a lawyer's conversation or interpret a prisoner's expression.

It was unprecedented to have so many accused people in the prisoner's box. It would have been impossible if the structure hadn't been enlarged. A list of the prisoners' names, ages, hometowns and most recent crimes had been published in the newspapers. In the absence of more knowledge, those had been reiterated every day. Except for Big Alf, Dace and his fellow accused were under thirty and had grown up in jails. At the end of the first day, news reporters tried to add a couple more colourful details about the prisoners, but most of their descriptions ran to their stock phrase: *the accused showed no emotion.*

The trial witnesses: murderers, convicted thieves and confidence men who'd had previous disagreements with some of the accused and were understandably concerned about reprisals, were offstage in anterooms, eating bologna sandwiches and waiting for their cues. This was their opportunity to step into the limelight. Their only tangible compensation was the free cigarettes the Crown attorneys doled out like Valium. Relax. Have a Menthol.

Understandably anxious, the lawyers spent most of their time either pacing or talking. Their witnesses would have to wait for days like ill-prepared understudies, their agitation and erratic behaviour escalating as their dreams of stardom died.

After less than an hour, some of the spectators grew impatient waiting for the courtroom drama to begin. They left as quickly as they'd come, careless of banging the double doors behind them. The more committed — or perhaps just the courtroom junkies with more time on their hands — breathed sighs of relief and spread out in the gleaming oak pews. They swivelled their heads, contemplating paintings on the walls depicting the colonization of Upper Canada, of Indians meeting the White Man for the first time.

Liza rushed into the courtroom just in time to see Dace straightening the red tie his father had bought him. Her face was so expressionless he knew she must be holding her breath. She didn't know her feelings still showed in her eyes as she paused in the entrance to Courtroom B. She scanned for the most advantageous seat: a bench she deemed close enough to watch him, but not close enough for her to be scrutinized by the Prosecution or the press, both of them out for blood. Preferably his blood, although hers might do.

Dace's attorney Hubert Gold spotted her at the same time. Gold already had a small dossier on her, put together by his research assistant after they'd noticed Liza coming to the preliminary trial, held in voir dire late last month. She had been hard to miss: a taut young girl with anxious eyes who looked like she wished she didn't know so much. Her presence had also been duly noted last week when the jury had been chosen. He'd talk to her, he told Dace. A pretty, clean-cut schoolgirl could help jurors visualize him in a different light.

A rising young criminal defence lawyer, a decade older than Dace, Hubert Gold had offered to take Dace on pro bono, although if his father wanted to pay him, that was just fine. 'Huey' as his friends preferred to call him, was a small, lithe man, known to enjoy sparring with legal minds. Sparring was also his social style. Dark and Jewish, he preferred to augment his looks by keeping a svelte blonde girl by his side—a shiksa, the kind of girl he would never marry.

To his credit, Gold had visited Dace several times in prison, more than most of the other defence lawyers had. He had argued for his release from Segregation so he could help his client, although he'd been less successful in talking to the other inmates. His passion for his work was so contagious that Dace had sat up and started eating again. With the trial of thirteen convicts sure to garner publicity, Huey Gold wasted no time in letting everyone know that he had given up his fledgling practice in downtown Toronto and was living in a hotel in Maitland during the preliminary hearing and trial. He had also lined up over sixty witnesses by mail.

Meanwhile the Crown attorneys gossiped about the spectators, close enough for Dace to hear every word they said. "Ah, that's number three's cousin. The college kid, washing her life down the drain. And right behind her is number eight's old lady. One of Maitland's finest: a third generation welfare recipient. And that's number four, no, number five. Number four grew up in foster homes, surprise, surprise. The little pervert ain't got no friends."

The Crown and the press shifted their collective focus back to the infamous thirteen, an unused chain gang idling in the rebuilt prisoners' box, an insult to everybody who worked for a living.

"It's a holiday for them. The bastards should be put to work," muttered one of the Crown attorneys.

"A baker's sad and sorry dozen," somebody else commented. "And I'm willing to bet there's not one innocent man among them."

A defence lawyer spoke almost simultaneously. "Thirteen of us stepping on each other's toes just to keep these animals out a few more years. Shouldn't they be looking more scared?"

"Too disoriented. I don't know how my client's holding up. He's not too stable as it is. He's already tried to hang himself once. The poor saps have been in solitary for so long this is just like a little outing for them. They don't know what the hell's going on."

"'Poor saps', my ass. Take a look at number three. What's his name? Oh yeah. D'Arcy Devereux."

"The sharply suited one with the foreign-looking eyes?" somebody said with a snicker, pretending to scan some documents on the table in front of him. "He's some cool customer. Didn't even blink when his cousin showed up for him."

"Wait. Did you see that? Davo ...Devereux ... How do you say his name? He just signalled the girl with his eyes. There she goes. She's sitting down in the third row, close enough to smell him and count hair follicles on his clean-shaven neck. Christ, if that were my daughter, I'd wring her neck. What do girls like that see in guys like him?"

"A big dick going to waste."

"Well, he is one hell of a good-looking kid. Doesn't exactly look the part."

"Oh, sure he does. Not looking the part, that's just part of his con."

"What's Devereux' story, anyway? We've gotta know a little bit about all of them, don't we? Has anyone done homework on someone other than his own client?"

"You'd better kick some ass. Didn't your new cutie-pie brief you?"

"She was too busy briefing someone else."

"I can't keep track of all their sob stories. I'm here for my client and that's it."

"C'mon, fellas, this judge is a fucking dinosaur and he's hungry for meat."

"D'Arcy

'Dace' Devereux, he's my boy," Hubert Gold volunteered affably. "Phenomenal IQ, but so far he's never used his brains for anything except crime. He might have had some learning problems when he was a kid. You know, that Einstein disease, dyslexia. But he either got over it or he was misdiagnosed. Otherwise a normal childhood, our psychs are claiming. Until he was eight or nine, anyway. Then he went away to school."

"Priest run?" somebody inquired sharply.

"Yeah, sure, most of those places are priest run, aren't they?"

"Well, I've been hearing those priests got caught up in some lurid deeds."

"As a matter of fact, I think both D'Arcy and his kid sister were abused at this particular school. There's a lot of stories coming out. A class action suit, but that's decades in the making."

"Oh, horse shit," a female lawyer interrupted. "Those kids were no angels, but I'm the Crown. I did a little extra homework on everybody. This is strictly off the record, because he was a juvenile, but D'Arcy Devereux was charged with assault at ten. "

"Wait a minute. Why was he sent to this school? Was it a training school?"

"Mom keeled over from the Big C. Dad couldn't take charge of his kids, you know the story. How was the poor bugger supposed to look after two brats and work, too? The parish priest probably recommended the place."

"Well, apparently you're superwoman, with your three kids and a law degree. Who's raising your kids? Your Mom or the Filipino nanny?"

"Stick to the facts, guys. At least I'm having kids before my eggs are totally dated. Where's your spawn?"

"Look, I'm running out of time. I don't feel like reading a book on this Devereux character or the rest of the stupid fucks, for that matter. After he graduates from the Little Shoppe of Horrors, what then?"

"He never graduates from anywhere. He skips school and the next thing he knows he's plugged somebody with a bullet, except this time he's over sweet sixteen and the judge decides he's ready for the Big House."

"So he's a killer then?"

"Well, he got away with manslaughter, though he's been nothing but trouble Inside. The kid's got a big mouth."

"And during the riot he gets a big bullhorn ..."

"And directs the murders in the Dome below ..."

"And has good reason to feel he's doing society a favour."

"Well, I've spoken to him a few times," Hubert Gold interrupted. "Very articulate. And he's not really a murderer. Strange as it may seem, he didn't intend to kill anybody the first time. It was an accident. May I remind my esteemed colleagues, that's what manslaughter is under our British penal code. He wanted to protect his friend. Similar situation this time. He was protecting the hostages three floors away."

"Except he had a clear view."

"What do you mean, protecting the hostages? Is that what you call tying up officers and letting them starve? What are we doing here, rewriting the past?"

"Oh, shit, I don't know. Let's just get this farce over. You know what's going down here. Thirteen beating victims, thirteen men, thirteen defence attorneys. Each con's lawyer doing his best to get his guy off. Careers are going to be made here, boys and girls. What about the rest of the psychos? The ones who aren't here today. What role did they play? We can't get everyone on murder and we know from interviewing witnesses there's about forty more men who should have been charged."

By now, Dace had stopped listening. If he heard another word he'd go berserk. More people slammed in and out through the doors. A court officer told Liza not to drape her coat over the back of the bench, adding for good measure, "And mind you don't take notes, either. You don't look like no court reporter to me."

Dace smiled. It was either that or go for the guy's throat.

Liza stood up and rearranged her coat, almost stepping in front of the prisoners' box. Don't smile, she telegraphed him. Remember not to smile.

At last the Jury filed in, no doubt unhappy about it. They were fine, upstanding citizens who hadn't been able to avoid conscription. Several looked confused about where they should sit. Only the thirty-eight-year-old high school teacher chosen as foreman looked vaguely excited. Perhaps he viewed this as both an opportunity to learn the workings of a criminal trial and a chance to perform a public duty, although he probably would have found it difficult to support his family on ten dollars per diem if the Board hadn't been augmenting his salary.

The jurors were followed by Judge Walter Silverton, standing head and shoulders above most of the boys in the prisoner's box. He looked regal in his dark, flowing robes, and he knew it. He dwarfed the huddled lawyers, too.

Aw Christ, Dace thought. *Silverton. I should have known.*

The entire courtroom breathed again. The trial was about to begin. Knowing Silverton liked formalities, both the Crown and the defence attorneys stumbled over themselves, genuflecting, referring to the judge as Your Worship, motioning behind their backs to their audience: All rise.

The spectators rose clumsily as Silverton sat in his leather maroon chair behind the Bench. Many were uncertain about courtroom etiquette, although the court officers, retired army men from the local base, were happy to advise.

It was almost a relief when Judge Silverton shuffled some papers and cleared his throat. "This trial is a huge waste of the taxpayer's money," he intoned, after dispensing with a few legal formalities. "Since we are obliged, however, let's proceed."

Court officially began with the Crown counsel offering his version of the events of the riot, comparing the events to a kaleidoscope that no two people would have viewed the same way. It took the better part of the morning for the Crown to relay what had happened.

Liza left her seat at noon recess, reaching Dace just before he was marched off to enjoy a lunch of Kraft cheese slices on white Wonderbread. One of the courtroom guards tried to stop her, but several spectators were in the way.

"Go back to school, Liza," Dace whispered out the side of his mouth the minute she reached the prisoner's box. "This is none of your business."

"The press is here, Dace. The CBC is televising."

"I don't want you listening to this bullshit." Although he was staring straight ahead, he knew her eyes had filled with tears. "Oh baby," he mumbled, "Stay away." He was quiet, reluctant to share their conversation with the two cellmates between which he was leg-chained, so maybe she didn't hear him. She reached for him.

Suddenly the guard was there. "You stay away from the prisoners, Miss, or I'll have to ask you to vacate the courtroom," he barked as Hubert Gold approached.

"You're Mr. Devereux' ...?"

"Cousin," Liza confirmed stiffly, reluctantly taking her eyes off Dace.

"Ah, I thought so. Like you, he likes to hold his cards close."

Dace couldn't help himself. He shook his head.

"But whatever he says, he needs you here," Gold said. He brought out his left hand from beneath his black robe, clutching manila folders to his chest with his right. "I guess you know I'm his lawyer, Dace's defence. And your name is?" he asked, although Dace suspected from the look in his eyes that he remembered her name and more.

Seeming flustered, she accepted his smallish hand, but she must have held on a little too long because he let go first. "Elizabeth Devereux. Liza," she said, then dove straight to the heart of the matter. "Dace did his best during the riot but he was caught up. Is he going to be all right?"

"Well, to be honest, I was just transferred to his case in time for the preliminary," Gold said, apparently unwilling to lay all his cards on the table.

"He didn't do it," she said, laughing nervously. She shot a quick glance at Dace, who was careful to reveal nothing. "I guess you've heard that one before."

"I'm afraid the jury might find out he had a reason."

"To do what?" she demanded, then grabbed the side of the bench when her legs buckled slightly.

"Are you all right, Miss? Don't get the vapours on me now, please. I mean he had a reason to kill two men like that. Two men who were pedophiles."

Liza closed her eyes. "His sister ..."

"And Dace, too."

"You're not saying he was sexually abused, are you?" she whispered with a frantic glance at Dace. He stared straight ahead, showing nothing in his dark eyes.

"I'm sorry. It's an all too common story these days, but there are a lot of stories coming out of the school where he stayed."

"Still. He didn't do it. I have a letter, written right after the riot."

"I'd like to see the letter. Even so, there's still a lot of witnesses who say he did."

"What kind of witnesses?"

"Other prisoners."

"Have they been granted immunity, by any chance? Are they murderers, thieves and robbers?"

Good girl, Dace thought.

"Well, that's the kind of people you're cousin chose to live with, my dear." For a moment, Hubert Gold looked genuinely regretful that his client had evidently made such bad decisions. "Look, I'm going to go back to the office to catch up on his case, but for the record I think he's innocent this time. Liza — may I call you that?"

"Yes, of course. I—" Liza answered warily.

Gold touched her shoulder with his right hand. "A little discreet crying is okay, a hankie dabbing your eyes, but anybody can tell by looking at you that you're wound pretty tight, so you'll have to be careful."

She blinked at him, calculating. "You want everyone to think he comes from a good family, don't you?"

"I also don't want our boy upset. His co-defendants are going stir crazy. Sure, they look pretty calm now, but these boys aren't too stable. Given the conditions they're living under, there's bound to be several outbursts. Some of them have just got out of solitary. D'Arcy has been in and out."

"I know, I couldn't—"

"The reporters are just waiting."

She nodded. "And salivating."

Gold permitted her a small smile. "And Judge Silverton is very formal. He'll have them gagged or put out of the courtroom. I've seen him do it."

"I've seen Judge Silverton in action before too. At the Wolfhounds' trial. Isn't it some kind of conflict of interest that he's on this bench, too?"

Hubert Gold smiled condescendingly and shrugged. "Really? I suppose I should have known that. I'll have a word with my assistant later today," he said. "As for you, you're a smart, devoted college girl, his cousin, and that's all the jury needs to know." He gave a little queen-like wave and tried to back out a side door, hidden in the wall panelling.

Dace had to go too. One jerk on the lead chain at the front and they were all gone. Liza probably had a hundred questions to ask, but she hadn't gathered her wits about her fast enough, so Hubert Gold had been saved. He must have known she would never follow him into the secret recesses of the courthouse.

From a back room window, Dace saw her pacing around the courthouse, a small, solitary figure in a fitted grey maxi-coat with her thin arms wrapped around herself. She wanted to stay as close to him as possible. She stopped in her tracks and looked up, straight towards him, but he knew she didn't see him. He doubted she saw much. She looked like she had fled someplace where she couldn't be touched.

It was November, so cold that every last leaf had fallen from the elm trees around the courthouse. The morning rain was developing into a light snow. She was humming, he could tell. In his mind, he heard her singing: *All the leaves are brown and the sky is grey … I've been for a walk and on a winter's day … if I didn't tell him, I could leave today …*

She was so afraid he would be convicted of murder. She wouldn't leave, he knew. His father hadn't come. Norm kept saying he had too much work but maybe that wasn't the real reason. Maybe he just couldn't face his boy getting more time … perhaps a lot more time.

Christ, he wished to fuck Liza would go back to school. She could earn a degree or whatever the hell you did in the Ivory Tower. What was she doing here in court? he fumed. But he knew. She was here on his account. It was all too humiliating for him. For her. And where the hell was her straight shooter boyfriend anyway? Mel, the stand up guy.

The back room was a makeshift lunchroom for the prisoners and their custodians. It was dominated by a large, boardroom style table and a stack of grey plastic chairs. Dace and his co-accused sat around the table, still chained to each other. A cardboard box full of cheese sandwiches and coffee had been brought in. It was only 12:45 p.m., but they had been up since 5:00 a.m. A long day for anybody.

"Why's your cousin looking so sick?" Steve, who was seated to his right, asked. "It's not like she's on trial."

"I don't know," Dace mumbled into a paper coffee cup. The cardboard smelled less like coffee and more like stale peanuts. "Smart girl, but she needs somebody to look after her."

"You gotta take care of yourself, man. Where the fuck are our lawyers? Alf's was just here, that big stupid-looking guy who's always grinning like he's at a party."

"Sure," Dace said. "I'll be noble and give her up. I already tried that. She keeps coming back."

"A lot of men try to hang onto women who deserve more than they can give," Steve observed sagely.

"Where did you read that? Ann Landers?" Dace asked.

Steve was right, he knew, but Liza had something to say about this too. She hadn't let go, had she? There was nothing, nothing she could do for him. A girl like that … She would go crazy. She would end up hating him for what he had done – for what he had done to her. What had happened during the riot couldn't be helped, but what had happened before …

Too many mistakes. How had it come to this? He'd thought it was hard to pull out of trouble before, but it was much harder now.

"Well, I'd go out for a drink if I were her. Lots of drinks."

"Sure," Dace agreed, anything to blunt the reason they were all there. He and Steve had both noticed a little English-style pub on the southwest corner when they'd been bussed in from the Joint. Liza was underage, though. She might push her luck closer to campus, but she wouldn't try drinking around here, especially not in a bar with black wooden shutters where police and lawyers hung out. All those wheeler dealers, plotting and conniving.

"Goddamn inbreeds," he muttered to no one in particular, hoping Huey Gold was just as inbred as the rest of them.

When Steve's lawyer finally came to visit, Dace tried to sit straighter on his wooden chair, but the prisoner to his left was slumped over the Formica table, tearing bits of his Wonderbread into little pills. As a result, Dace had no choice but to slump, too. His right shoulder was killing him.

"What am I?" he yelled at his startled neighbour. "A fucking Siamese twin?"

They were all getting on his nerves. Every time the two young guys at the end of the line poked each other they yanked the whole chain. Dace picked up his half-eaten sandwich and crammed it into his mouth in an effort to fuel his body. He was so angry his hands shook, and he almost choked on the dry bread. He was going to crown somebody if he didn't get a grip soon.

"Stop it, you stupid farts," he growled. Both the guards and a couple of prisoners tried to intervene as Dace's fists opened and closed, as if they were saying, Let me at 'em. Steve's lawyer left, all the violence in the air evidently putting him off, and in walked Gold. Jesus, he wished Gold hadn't talked to Liza. The stuff he'd said to her ... Lawyers were always coaching family members to project a certain image. Like they were casting directors ... or God.

"Watch your smile," was all Gold said, keeping a wary eye on the two boys at the end of the table. They were busy pretending to fall off their chairs. Taking Dace's nod for a yes, he backed out of the impromptu lunchroom almost as quickly as he had come.

A guard booted the door shut, but he must have heard Alf. "You're the one who went back and hit him one more time, Steve. If you hadn't, we wouldn't be in this fucking mess. The goddamn bingo was over. We were almost home-free."

"Don't you know what that bastard did to his own children?" Steve demanded.

"I don't fucking care! What about the rest of us?"

"You bloody rat fink! If you hadn't squealed we'd all be playing poker."

"The hell we would! We've been vacuum sealed in our drums like tuna fish for months on end. It was a fucking tactical error to take hostages in the first place, goddamn that Sandy McAllister. Then you had to go and have some fun."

There was a loud crash, followed by a chorus of: Shut up! Bugger off! and What the fuck?

Almost instantly, several armed guards burst into the lunchroom, pistols drawn, billy clubs raised. They looked like they were aching to club the prisoners, but they had their orders and they were in a court of law, so they smashed the Formica table instead. Several cracks cut through the mottled pattern, but they went unnoticed until the next day. Somebody's fingers got in the way of one of the billy clubs—the boy who was making bread pills—and he screamed so loud everything else stopped. Somehow he was separated from the chain and within an hour he'd been hauled back to the penitentiary, along with the two pugilists. None of them came back for three days.

Almost envious, Dace watched them go. Maybe he should pick a fight, too. Even with three men in lockup, there were too many defendants and too many stories to tell. From the books Liza and the prison librarian had encouraged him to read, Dace had learned you couldn't tell a story from too many points of view or people would lose interest. Experience had also taught him Judge Silverton wasn't a patient man. The lawyers knew this too. Nobody was that stupid, were they? How long before they decided they'd all had enough publicity, thank you, and everyone danced to the tune of the truth be damned?

Gold said he had fifty good witnesses to tell his side of the story, and Dace knew the men. Well, sure. The sheer weight of evidence might work and he might come out smelling like a one-of-a-kind rose, an exception to his so-called co-conspirators. But what about the rest of the attention-loving, bloodsucking lawyers? His friends' lawyers? What if everybody decided to call fifty witnesses? Could he possibly be the only person streetwise enough to do some simple math? My God, he hadn't even finished high school and most of the people here had been in school for what—sixteen years? He almost despaired at the thought, but letting go was even scarier, so he asked for another cheese sandwich instead. Please, sir, may I have another? Naturally the guard, who'd already eaten three, refused. He did it because it was within his power to do.

Dace tried to convince himself he had a real good lawyer. Huey Gold had been his Dad's choice, so it was probably better than any decision he could have made. At least on this occasion he was an innocent man.

An innocent man, he repeated. It might be a long and painful fight, but he had to trust in the fact that the truth was on his side.

Chapter Thirty

The Unwanted

Maitland Courthouse, December 1972

The trial limped into an even darker December, with only nine holdouts in the prisoners' box on any given day. One man was in Segregation because his co-accused had turned on him, two more had been transferred to Maitland Psychiatric Hospital for undisclosed reasons, and a fourth was too ill to leave the Penitentiary. A fifth man had tried to hang himself, but he was allowed back into court wearing a turtleneck.

Green and red lights decorated the main street of Maitland, twinkling with the merriment of the season. Greeting cards flooded mailboxes, Santa lured children and their doting parents in for photos at the local Stedman's. Housewives had scouted out the plumpest Butterball turkeys and, though it was easier to buy cannabis than aromatic spices such as cinnamon and nutmeg, their eastern aromas infused the crisp winter air. Most people had finished their Christmas shopping. Odyssey and UNO were all sold out, although a local call-in show revealed a fair number of people were still having trouble finding the Christmas spirit. The usual crap, Liza thought sourly, listening to Janice's little transistor radio in their student residence.

Several callers mentioned they were troubled by the murder trial. The defendants were convicted felons, weren't they? And the men who had died, who had been murdered so viciously, well, who the hell cared? For the love of Mike, why didn't they just lock 'em up and let them take care of their own? Natural order, natural selection, whatever the hell it was called. If the stupid arses wanted a trial, it should only have been about the guards.

Stuck in a motel on the outskirts of town, the closeted jurors and the out-of-town lawyers dreamed of hand decorated balsam and spruce trees, candlelight services and Waterford glasses of spiked eggnog. Some of the accused even remembered the penitentiary usually served damn fine farm turkeys with all the trimmings on Christmas Day.

At last the Crown counsel finished presenting their cases. Over several successive days the defence attorneys began their cross-examinations. Personalities emerged and little courtroom dramas promised to unfold. Liza was rapidly losing track of the individual defences of men she had never met. The jury members looked as if they, too, were suffering from information overload.

She was constantly sweating in the overheated courtroom. When the lawyers conferred with each other and nothing else was happening, she could barely stay awake. She did, though. One of the jurors, a woman in her fifties, didn't even bother trying. She barely stirred when the crime scene photos were passed around.

"I just want to smack her," one of the lady lawyers said.

The man who had tried to hang himself was also a sleeper, but he had an excuse: he was heavily tranquillized. Liza wasn't sure what the juror was on. She wore a shiny gold corsage that followed her breathing pattern. Liza was mesmerized; her mother had always bought a similar corsage at Christmastime.

But perhaps the lady juror didn't need to look at photos of burned books and furniture floating in brackish water or at black and white eight by tens of the men who had been bound and tortured. How much did she really need to know? What was there to decide? She had already read the papers and even if the accused men weren't guilty of the murder of two pedophiles, they were no doubt guilty of other undisclosed and equally heinous crimes.

The Crown was convincing. For two days they talked about the jungle atmosphere inside the penitentiary and how it had led to the deaths of the two unfortunate men. In the end everybody in the prisoner box looked guilty of something. Even Liza started to believe that everybody must be guilty, at least everybody except Dace, and that was because she knew his side. But the rest of the courtroom had no such inside information. What if he hadn't written to her so soon after the riot? Would the Crown have convinced her of his guilt too?

The Crown focused on Dace almost exclusively. Surely they didn't think he was solely responsible for both the riot and the outcome? Christ, it was unbelievable.

The *Maitland Spectator* had another field day with the Devereux name. Life was so much more interesting when a home boy got in trouble. *Why I remember when he was a boy and he had a slingshot. He called that teacher bad names.* What was it that made a boy bad? It hardly seemed possible that such a miscreant had come from a decent little place like Maitland. Although the Devereuxes weren't really from Maitland, come to think of it. They were from Toronto, big T.O. That figured. A lot of bad stuff happened there.

Liza didn't believe it for one moment, but D'Arcy 'Dace' Devereux was alleged to have said, Let's smash some pumpkins while he was on a leisurely stroll from his guard post on the fourth floor to locate potential victims. Under the circumstances, it sounded like any suckers might have been fine, but the pre-existence of the segregated pedophiles was definitely a plus. The jurors looked at D'Arcy Devereux when they heard this: the strong, handsome man, third from the left, with the murderous rage in his dark eyes. Well, maybe he'd had a couple of buddies with him, thugs just like himself, but the witness swore Dace had led the hunt for the sexual offenders, those they called 'The Unwanted.'

Liza had barely dragged herself into the courtroom that day. By now everybody recognized her as a permanent fixture. She was occasionally accompanied by an older man who looked a little like D'Arcy Devereux, but who always rushed out, visibly distraught.

She never saw the pictures the lawyers passed around the jury, but a newsreel of the riot played continually in her mind, a backdrop to her everyday life. She might be climbing stairs in one of the faculty buildings, but wild-eyed rioters raced at her side and surprised her out of closets with machetes in their hands. Sometimes they found her asleep in her residence bed. She wanted to shut her eyes like the dozy lady juror when the Crown went after Dace, but she was on show, too. She didn't dare risk the headline: "Devereux Cousin Doesn't Care."

She raised her hand to her lips and bit her knuckles when Hubert Gold finally began his cross-examination; she hoped nobody noticed. She had to control herself, but it was an effort. Gold ignored the first witness for the Crown. He was a soft-spoken man called Bellissimo who used a lot of malapropisms, difficult for even the most discerning ear. The little man said Dace had broken his arm and the jurors looked as if they believed him. Why would he lie when he was still doing time? Bellissimo would have to go back to the Joint and face both the well-muscled Dace and his almost equally muscular friends. The fact that the little man had been segregated from the rest of the prison population was lost on the jurors.

Gold focused on the second witness instead, a man who had served time on fraud charges and was now living in Texas under an assumed name. Judge Silverton was plainly unhappy when this got out in court. He glared at Gold as if he were the adversary. He stopped Gold and instructed the courtroom reporters to ignore what they had just heard.

As if the witness' tan wouldn't have given him away. Obviously he had been somewhere warm; even his nose was peeling. His right hand twitched as he pocketed his sunglasses at the judge's request. He could hardly look Hubert Gold in the eyes and never once looked at any of the defendants.

As for Gold, he was obviously pleased to finally have the floor. He paced in front of the witness for a moment, smoothing his hair back and straightening his tie. Watching his preparations, everybody in the courtroom sat up a little straighter.

"Mr. X," he said, "you were telling us you witnessed certain events that took place in the dome in the early hours of Sunday, isn't that right?"

The witness paused a moment, perhaps trying to figure out what Dace's defence lawyer meant. "Yes, sir," he finally said.

"Now when you were watching these events, you were standing on a tier? A sort of balcony that encircled the whole dome? And this was the second of four tiers?"

The witness' brows creased. "Uh, yes," he replied.

"And it was between three and four in the morning?"

"Yes, sir," the man reported, sounding more confident this time.

Gold faced the courtroom then spoke over his shoulder at the witness, as if he really didn't care about the answer. "So it would be dark outside. And there were two or three lights broken in the dome, weren't there?"

"Yes, sir, there were," the witness agreed. "Well, it was never well lit anyway," he elaborated, ignoring Judge Silverton's frown.

"And the army was outside?"

"Yes, sir."

"And the floodlights were on and German Shepherds were patrolling?"

The witness nodded, smiling. "You got the picture. I mean, yeah. Yes, sir."

Gold pulled a piece of paper out of his pocket and checked it, as if he had forgotten some vital item necessary to set the scene. "And there was talk about gas?"

"There was talk about everything," the witness said with a shrug, appearing perplexed.

"Were you a bit nervous when you knew the army was outside?"

For the first time, the witness looked straight at Gold. You got it, his eyes said. "Yes, sir, I was scared," he admitted. "We were all scared."

"So when you were hauled out of bed and told to watch the events in the dome, you disapproved of them?"

"I guess. I mean yes, sir." He lowered his eyes until he stared at the floor.

Gold rubbed his chin and he also looked down. "Yet you heard screams and you saw twelve or thirteen men blindfolded and tied to the radiator in the dome. And you didn't do anything to stop the beatings," he observed.

"No, sir, I ..." the witness squirmed in his seat, his eyes appealing to everyone in the courtroom. What could I have done?

Gold softened a little. "You were afraid of the army coming in and shooting gas?"

The witness looked relieved. "Yes, sir," he said.

"And weren't you also afraid to join those unfortunate men? Afraid you might be put in the circle and tied to the radiator along with them?"

"Yes, sir." The witness grew even more confident at this point, sitting bolt upright in his leather chair as he caressed the lapels of his new brown suit.

There was another longish pause as Gold checked the paper in his hand again. "Did anyone give you orders during the riot?"

"No, sir."

"Who told you to come and watch?" he asked.

The witness narrowed his eyes. "I don't remember right offhand."

"So how did you know it was time to come out?" Gold asked, sounding pleasant enough.

"Somebody had a bullhorn," the witness said sullenly.

"How long did you watch?"

The witness shrugged. "Maybe an hour."

"So you thought it would be best to keep watching the beatings," Gold speculated.

The witness got a little excited. "Yeah, until they started busting heads! And cutting. I could see them smacking somebody around, but not like that. Brutal, they were, brutal. That's why people got killed."

"Objection!" shouted the Crown, as the witness looked meaningfully in the direction of the jury. Several members unintentionally nodded back. We understand.

"I think you told my learned friend, Mr. X, that you saw one of the beating victims being brought out? One of the child abusers? Let's call him Mr. Smith?"

"Okay. I mean, yes, sir."

"And you said it was Mr. Devereux, for whom I act, who brought him out?"

"What ..." He frowned. "Mr. Devereux? Do you mean what did Dace do? I don't understand the question," the witness stammered.

"I was asking," Gold repeated slowly, "if my client, Mr. Dace Devereux, brought one of the beating victims out to the circle."

"No, sir. He's the one who started smashing heads," the witness replied.

"But didn't you say during the preliminary trial that Dace Devereux was on the fourth range?"

"He was on the fourth range most of the time, but he came down to the first range to smash some heads," the witness insisted, his head pushed forward, his eyes searching the jury box.

"All right. I have a letter addressed to my firm which I would like to present to the court."

There was a sudden rustle from the Judge's chair. "Probably better have the jury step out," Judge Silverton advised with an audible sigh. Almost before he had finished his sentence, the jury members had left.

Hubert Gold approached the bench. "Your Worship, when I attempted to see the Crown witnesses in the penitentiary, I was denied the privilege of talking to them for reasons unknown to me. So I wrote everybody, put forth my client's defence and asked, 'Do you know anything?' Mr. Smith himself wrote me back and said, 'Devereux never harmed me in any way. He was up on the fourth range all the time.'"

The two Crown attorneys had followed Gold to the bench. "Well, surely my learned colleague is not suggesting this kind of letter is evidence," the female Crown attorney interjected. "Surely the evidence must come from Mr. Smith himself."

"At the time when this witness says Devereux was in the dome beating up Smith, Smith says he wasn't there at all. The jury is entitled to know the witness is a fraud. By the time Smith testifies, the damage of this witness will be done," Gold insisted, although from the way Silverton was shaking his head, he could tell the Judge didn't see it that way.

"Well, it's a dilemma," Judge Silverton said, although from the look on his face the whole matter seemed straightforward to him. "But I don't think I can allow you to introduce a letter this way.'

"I have several letters, Your Worship," Gold said eagerly.

The Judge closed his eyes. "No doubt you do."

"Just wait, Your Worship. I haven't finished my cross-examination."

"No letters," Judge Silverton repeated. "May I bring the jury back now?" he asked with exaggerated politeness.

Once the Jury was back in the courtroom, Hugh Gold had evidently decided to try a different tack. "Tell me," he said. "You say my client, Mr. Devereux, broke Mr. Smith's head."

"Yes. Then he killed the other one."

The Judge could have admonished the witness at this moment but he didn't, so Gold rapped the edge of the witness box. "Just answer the question, please. Mr. Smith himself advises me he did no such thing. He says Mr. Devereux stayed on the fourth range."

"I will have to contradict that," the witness said smugly, perhaps having surmised that at least one person in the courtroom was on his side.

Gold practically shoved his face into the witness box. "You are contradicting the victim?"

"Yes, sir," the witness answered, although he sounded a little less confident this time.

"All right. Who else did Mr. Devereux strike besides Mr. Smith?" Gold asked, as if he were playing along.

"Postiuk, Tait and two or three others I didn't know."

Gold shook his head incredulously. "Don't you know who all the thirteen inmates tied to the radiator were?"

"No," the witness admitted, reverting to sullenness.

Gold tapped his fingers on the witness box for a moment, as if thinking. "How many people were there in the dome doing the attacking?"

"Maybe twenty-five. They aren't all on trial."

"Hmm," Gold said, walking away from him. "Could you identify all the attackers?"

"No, sir."

"You watched for an hour, but you can't identify everyone?"

"Well, it's been a year since the riot."

"I suppose it's plausible that you might forget," Gold admitted. "But you still remember seeing Mr. Devereux coming down to the dome from the fourth tier."

Too late, the witness realized his mistake. "Bellissimo said that. I didn't," he amended. "I didn't see him come down. He was just there all of a sudden. Maybe he had to phone Rick Lowery. There was a phone on each tier and he was keeping touch with Rick cause he was on the Inmate Committee."

"Did you hear him say anything?"

"Yeah. He said let's break some heads."

The Jury was hanging on every word, but Gold looked sceptical. "You were up on the tier and you heard him say that? Wasn't there a lot of noise? And screaming? Did he have a bullhorn?"

"No, he didn't have no bullhorn."

"But you could still hear him."

"He has a loud voice." A couple of people in the gallery tittered when he said this, but the Judge rapped his gavel and they stopped.

"Did he have a weapon in his hand?" Gold continued.

"I don't believe he did, sir. But he's a bodybuilder, see. He didn't need one. He had his fists."

"Well, surely you were taking notes at the time so you could go to the authorities," Gold suggested.

"No, sir, not until they started bashing in heads and there was so much blood. I never seen such blood. Then they sliced—"

In response to the jurors' horrified expressions, Gold's face remained impassive. "Please just answer the question," he said. "That's when you decided?"

"Yes, after they started hitting those guys with bars. Poor Mr. Smith couldn't recognize Devereux because he had a sheet over his head by then."

"So now Mr. Devereux had a weapon? And there was a sheet over his head? Are you sure you want to change your evidence at this point? How did you recognize him?" Gold looked like he was about to fire off several more questions, but the witness interrupted.

"I'm not changing my evidence, you are! Mr. Smith was the one with the sheet over his head." When several of the jurors laughed, the witness became more confident. He settled back in his chair and glared at his opponent. "You just keep repeating questions, trying to get me mixed up."

Gold glared back. "Are you sure?" he asked. "Did you or did you not say to someone in the penitentiary: I know Devereux had nothing to do with the beatings, but he will when I get through with him."

"Why would I do that?" the witness asked. His voice sounded innocent enough, but he was clearly trying to suppress a smirk.

"Because you like to hurt people."

Judge Silverton slammed his papers together, almost causing one to fly to the floor. "Ask a proper question!" he roared.

Not to be deterred, Gold went on. "You were promised an early release, weren't you?"

Instantly, the witness' demeanour changed. He stood up, clearly furious at this commentary on his character. "That's a goddamn lie!" he swore. "I was innocent, so —"

More nervous laughter from the jury followed his indignant reply. In vain, Judge Silverton tried to restore order, then one of the thirteen inmates on trial for the penitentiary murders must have decided he'd had enough. It was the boy who never took his eyes off Dace. Several guards tried to push him back into his seat as he shouted at the judge.

"He's sick! He's a bloody liar! He's lying for his own fucking benefit!"

Dace tried to pull the boy back down onto his wooden chair, but there were so many people milling about in the courtroom that Liza couldn't see what else was happening. By the time the crowd cleared, it was too late. They were all gone. She stood motionless for a moment, willing Dace back. Then she left too.

"I thought this trial would be over by Christmas," a spectator was saying as she squeezed through the right side of the double doors. "But the jurors will be lucky if they're home for Easter. Did you know they only get paid ten dollars a day? How are they going to feed their families if they don't go on Welfare?"

"Haven't you been reading the editorials? Everybody, including the judge, thinks the trial is a waste of time. Mark my words, those jurors will be home for Christmas," her friend assured her.

Liza pushed past the women with only one thought in mind. Where was the washroom? She spotted it to her left and rushed inside, but the women followed her.

"I suppose you're right. I doubt those mucky-muck lawyers are going to want to spend their holidays here in Maitland. I just hope they don't decide to let those bastards off scot-free," the second one added just as the cubicle door swung shut behind Liza. She stared at the open toilet and waited for her lunch to spew from her burning throat.

"Don't worry. Your hair's okay," the first woman said, clearly having gone no farther than the sinks and mirrors.

"I'd rather use my own toilet at home. Lord knows what kind of germs they have here. Did you see that bag lady — a street person — sitting on a bench pretty as you please?"

Liza's stomach waited until the outside door had closed before it exploded for the second time that day. She vomited until she had nothing left to give except possibly the lining in her stomach. Then she flushed the toilet and went out to the sinks. She was still alone.

The thought of lying down on the filthy tiled floor and dying seemed quite appealing all of a sudden, but she rinsed her acid coated teeth with cold water instead. A whey faced girl stared back at her when she looked into the water-spotted mirror and she shook her head with disgust. Much good she was doing Dace, coming to court looking like death warmed over. What the hell must he think? No wonder he scowled and mouthed, Go back to school, whenever he got the chance.

After washing her face and hands, she still felt so nauseated she could barely stand the smell of the yellow, Castile soap. She checked for an empty paper bag in her purse in case she got sick on the bus again.

She had to force her way back into the hallway. She could barely put one foot in front of the other, but her only other option was to crawl back to residence and pray the women were right — about a quick end to the trial, at least.

Chapter Thirty-One
Limbo
Maitland University, December 1972

Janice came over to the bed and plied her with sweet tea. An illegal electric kettle bubbled under the bookshelves on her desk. Neither one of them was on the residence Meal Plan this year, either.

"Do you want to go to Student Health Services? You've been sick for so long."

Realizing she was going to have to try harder to fool her friend, Liza got up and carried the steaming mug over to the window between their desks. It had snowed again, a light dusting on a treacherous underlay.

"No, I'm okay. Anyway, the only way we could get out of here is in a sleigh." The sidewalk outside was so icy they would have to take tiny, mincing steps everywhere they went and even then she would probably end up falling flat on her face. Besides, no student doctor could help with what ailed her. Her grandmother Magill's nurse friend, maybe.

"I hope it's not the stomach flu," Janice fussed, one hand resting on her own flat stomach as she watched her patient sipping the honey-sweetened tea. All weekend Liza had kept to the residence, unable to rest or work. Now that she had an opportunity to wash her hair, she lacked the energy.

I don't give a goddamn how I look, she thought every time she threw up. In between visits to a toilet, she rested on her bed and prayed for oblivion. Her nausea, the same kind her mother must have suffered, was so pervasive every cell in her body felt invaded. She counted backwards to her last period in August, although she already knew the answer. Nobody was this sick with the flu for so long. How on earth had she functioned over the past five weeks? By living off hope, she thought. At least Mel was back home visiting his Mom and Dad. The way she looked, even he might have noticed.

She was almost miserable enough to reveal what she had so far been afraid to believe, but some innate sense of privacy stopped her. That and the fact she didn't want to overwhelm Janice with too many of her problems, each one inviting censure. So far her roommate had tactfully refrained from mentioning the newspaper accounts of Dace's most recent court appearance, but she was bound to be influenced by what she read. She was only human after all.

Even knowing the allegations were false, Liza wondered if she could go back to court after what had happened, knowing she was a highly visible but silent witness to a losing battle. In her present condition, that man with the alias had been the last straw. And Dace, her Dace, well, he didn't want her there anyway.

They hadn't spoken to each other since the first day, and she knew how closely watched they were. Why would a girl like that …? people whispered. Lately everything about the courtroom bothered her: the overheated air, the guard who snored in the corner, and one spectator in particular. She was a regular Madame Defarge, always knitting booties and eating up the drama with hungry eyes. The knitter, and a lot of people she represented, wanted D'Arcy Devereux and his co-accused to be found guilty of murder, torture and worse. Like the "witches" who drowned when they were put to the test, it seemed the fact that the defendants were getting thinner by the day, wasting away before her eyes was evidence enough of their sins.

It was only two weeks before her last midterm, and Liza was reluctant to face her classmates. Her reaction shamed her though. She knew Dace wasn't some kind of sick, sadistic monster. No matter what people said. Devereux Smashes Man's Skull, the Saturday edition of the *Spectator* had said.

She had to go back to school and make everybody understand. But would she be able to finish the school year? Even Janice thought she was going to drop out. She could tell by the look of pity on the girl's face every time they discussed living arrangements for next term.

Liza picked up a list of assignments from her desk, mentally calculating the number of days left in the term. Counting, that's all she seemed to do these days. Where was her mind? She had to concentrate. She could do her assignments, all right. Especially — she suddenly panicked — if the trial ended and they kept Dace in jail. She stood up quickly in her agitation and her mug sloshed over, spilling a little tea on the rug. She stared at the spill but felt too sick to bend over. Janice came over and sopped it up with a wad of tissue.

"You're as pale as a ghost, but you're sweating. Is there anything I can do?" she pleaded, her blue eyes swimming with tears.

"It's Dace," Liza confessed. "I'm so afraid for him."

Sitting back down on her messy bed, Janice lit a Rothmans and examined her penny loafers. They were a little retro, but she liked classic clothes. "Liza," she said, between staccato puffs, "I hate to say this, but maybe he belongs in jail. Two men died, and somebody has to pay."

"Those men ... you know what they were."

"You're thinking just like him and the rest of the men on trial. Somebody killed—"

"Please don't believe what you read in the newspaper. About Dace, I mean."

"But if he gets out again, he'll still be on probation, won't he? And what will you do? You'll run off with him, won't you? Across the border, straight into the waiting arms of the police.

How are you going to finish school in an American jail? My God, Liza, you could end up dead! What if there's some kind of shootout?" Janice stood up and started pacing around the little room.

"Oh, for crying out loud. Sit down. Dace doesn't even have a gun. And dammit, of course we'll leave. That's what we should have done last time. It's our only chance."

"Just listen to yourself! Okay. Supposing you get across the border. Where will you go? What'll you do? Oh, c'mon, you can tell me. I've seen you studying that book: *How to Be Anybody: Change Your Identity and Live the Good Life!*" She shook her head, incredulous. "I can't believe the books they have in the public library."

A brief smile crossed Liza's face. "Me either. I was thinking about Mexico. The monarchs ..."

"Monarchs? What's Mexico got to do with monarchs? No, don't tell me. I haven't got time for a botany lesson. So it's Mexico then. Love in the Mayan ruins. Very romantic. Hey, maybe you could just hop a plane to Brazil and live in the jungle. I've heard the Cayman Islands are nice, too. No taxes. Or is that the Bahamas?" She inhaled her cigarette deeply and blew the smoke straight out in front of her, long and slow. "But how would you support yourselves? Have you thought about that?"

"Well, not with crime, if that's what you're thinking. As long as he stays away from the Wolfhounds, he'll be all right."

"God, Liza, I still can't believe he was with them. He doesn't look like a biker. He just doesn't. Not in the *Spectator*, not in that suit."

"A lot of them don't. They're just regular guys."

"Hmm. That's not what you said when I came back to rez in the fall. Anyway, if you leave Canada, you won't have any papers, no health insurance, nothing!"

"We'll go to California then. And do whatever the great underbelly of the States does, all those illegal immigrants. We can work under the table, in a store or a restaurant. I'll clean house. Dace can work too, and Uncle Norm will help. I know he will."

"Are you sure about all this?"

"Yes," Liza answered, her nausea abating slightly now that she was on firmer ground. She needed a plan, that was all. "The Devereux can't take any more chances. I can tell from Uncle Norm's face that he'd rather lose Dace than bring him back here where all his trouble began."

Janice groaned elaborately. "I can't believe I'm saying this, but maybe you're right. His old friends would draw him in and the rival motorcycle gangs would target him. He needs a fresh start and I don't see that happening here. I have a bad feeling — oh, don't look at me like that — you do too! You never sleep. If I weren't such a sound sleeper, I'd probably hear you screaming half the night. Listen, I'm going home tonight for the holidays so my mother can give me the third degree. But promise me this: whatever happens, you'll take care of yourself. You've been trying to take care of Dace for far too long. He's the only one who can help himself. You know that, don't you?"

Chapter Thirty-Two
Secret Deals

"You have a visitor," the joint man said, fiddling with the belt buckle on his pants.

"A visitor? In the Hole?" Dace joked, totally prepared for a guard-assassin to bust through the steel door. "I'm not dressed." He was, though, in a grey jumpsuit.

"It's me, D'Arcy. I called in a favour," Hubert Gold said, coming from behind the joint man's back and bravely, from the look on his face, allowing himself to be locked in. For several weeks, the lawyers had tried to get all thirteen clients out of Segregation. They really had tried, but they had lost.

"Sorry the place is such a mess," Dace said, shifting slightly closer to the sink to make space in his eleven by seven concrete vault. He stroked his chin. "If I'd known you were coming, I probably would have shaved. Maybe even had this leaky pipe repaired. Or ordered some coffee or tea with some ladyfingers on the side." He shut up then, looked more closely at Gold. "What the hell are you doing here? You talked my ear off at the courthouse on Friday night." He shook his head slowly. "Tell me that they didn't take the fucking plea bargains."

"Take it easy, buddy. It's all right."

Dace's body went rigid. "All right? All this shit for nothing?"

Gold held his ground. "Well, I don't know about shit," he said, "but it's a fait accompli now. Or will be as soon as we have your co-operation. You're the single hold out. I just got back from lunch with Judge Silverton and some other people you don't know, but who have your best interests at heart."

"That son of a bitch!" Dace knew if his mouth weren't so dry he'd be frothing at the mouth. "A month and he's ready to give in. You'd think he was the one who'd spent the last four weeks going to court in shackles. How long did he think it would take to try so many men?"

Gold pursed his lips, looking as if he were so tired of having to explain everything. "He's tired, D'Arcy. Everybody's tired. The Judge, the jurors, the families. Your father's aged twenty years. Would you like to talk to him? I might be able to arrange it. And Liza's so pale. Is that her natural colour? I'm sure she just wants it to stop."

"Leave Liza out of this. She wants what I want. She always does."

"And what's that?"

"Justice and truth."

"Very dramatic," Gold said smoothly, tapping Dace's forearm with his knuckles. "You know, lots of the men I spoke to in here say you're a real stand up guy. That you'd do anything for your friends. Now all you have to do is sacrifice a little—"

"—of the truth," Dace said coldly, jerking his arm back. "Nobody even heard the rest of the cases! Don't some of my buddies deserve a chance?"

"They're taking their lawyers' advice, D'Arcy, and pleading guilty to manslaughter. They'll get an additional ten to fifteen each."

"Ten to fifteen! Oh, that's rich. Fucking, fucking, fucking rich! Get this. I'm not, I repeat, I am not pleading guilty to something I didn't do. I made one mistake, not two. And I already paid for that mistake, I think."

"Assault, D'Arcy. A simple assault. It's a good deal."

"Assault? On who?"

"Bellissimo."

"Are you nuts? That asshole tried to attack the hostages."

"I know, I know," Gold soothed.

"Jesus, people will think I got away with murder if I do this. I don't give a fuck about the time, it's that—"

"Look, it's all or nothing. You guys are a package deal. It's always been that way. If you don't agree to your charges, your friends might end up doing twenty-five for second degree murder. Alf will die in prison. He's forty-six now."

Later she regretted missing court on Monday morning, although there was nothing she could have done. Everything was over before the lawyers and their defendants got to court. So much took place behind closed doors. That was the only time she missed.

The next day she got up so late she almost fell over her copy of the *Maitland Spectator*, delivered to the door of her room earlier that morning. She had run into the delivery boy a couple of times during one of her nocturnal trips to the bathroom. An underpaid and underfed high school dropout, he took malicious delight in whacking newspapers into the doors of the privileged co-eds as hard as he could. He also liked to sing during his early morning deliveries, usually a rousing rendition of "Ninety-Nine Bottles of Beer on the Wall." The thwack of the paper had probably awoken her, but she was also hypersensitive to the slightest disturbance in her environment, the result of growing up in a house with paper thin walls and a mercurial man.

It was December 8 and Janice had left early for Christmas, leaving most of her assignments undone. Reluctant as she had been to abandon Liza in her present state, she had also left an unmade bed and an unwholesome clutter of lined Hilroy paper, wizened apple cores and cigarette butts on her desk.

Liza's throat tightened just looking at the mess. She grabbed a slice of whole wheat bread from a bag on her desk and started cramming it, piece by piece, into her mouth. Although it defied reason, she felt better when her stomach was full.

Her Smith Corona was buried under papers somewhere so if she wanted to finish typing her English essay she would have to tidy up, whether she felt like it or not. The maids weren't due until Friday and they wouldn't touch Janice's clutter anyway. She had to do something about the overflowing ashtray, too. Just the sight of it was enough to make her retch, which was a loud noise in the sepulchral atmosphere of the student residence, eerily quiet this late in the year.

"I'll get a doctor's note," Janice had said blithely, tossing her belongings into some Glad garbage bags, although Liza knew she wasn't nearly as sanguine as she sounded. "And maybe you should too. That trial has just about killed you, although why you went every day—"

"Well, I didn't go yesterday, but nothing happened."

"You should have loosened up a little and partied with me. Christ, Liza, what do you weigh? I can see the bones in your back even when you're dressing in the closet like that." Janice said, struggling to pull a thin, stretched sweater over her head.

Janice had spent most of her allocated student loan on beer and cigarettes and was in no position to ask her struggling parents for more. They still occupied the family homestead in Luther Township where the Hughes had lived for generations, ever since arriving from Cornwall, England in the 1840s. Liza had met Janice's parents, who worked the family farm. She had also met the brilliant older brother, Wesley, whom they couldn't afford to send to medical school.

Janice probably would have had no choice except to succeed under such circumstances, but all she wanted was to fit in at Maitland University. She would have loved to join a sorority in their first year. She had even dragged Liza to ritualistic rushes in candlelit sorority houses, although neither girl could have afforded the initiation fees, let alone the European vacations the sisterhood enjoyed. Instead Janice had held illicit parties in their room during Liza's extended absences and was now facing several residence imposed fines she couldn't pay.

Liza sighed. If she had been here more, instead of making herself sick at the courthouse or stewing in Mel's car, Janice mightn't have gotten so lonely. She was still a virgin though, her parents would no doubt be happy to know. That was all that mattered in some families if you were a girl. Her virginity was due more to the fact that she was a late bloomer rather than to her self-control, but Janice had also mentioned on numerous occasions that she had no intention of being like her mother, a trained nurse whose pregnancy had forced her out of her job back in the fifties.

Fear of failure. It was so easy to diagnose other people's problems, Liza thought. She stepped out of the communal bathroom and took a breath of non-chlorinated air as she unfurled the newspaper. She was procrastinating, she knew, sitting on the edge of her bed and shaking the paper out. She had to get back to court today, but it was a thin paper and would be even thinner if she ignored the ads for Christmas shopping, so it shouldn't take long.

And it wouldn't have, except …

The front page headline exploded in her face. *Secret Deal Ends Trial.* She had to be imagining things. Holding her breath, she read the headline twice more before she aimed the paper at Janice's wastepaper basket and missed. She tried to breathe, knowing she had to get a grip. This rush of anger could be toxic in her present condition.

But she had to know. Goddamn Dace's bleeding heart lawyer, she thought, retrieving the paper. So far all Gold had done was yap about the big city bucks he had lost on this case. Common decency suggested he might have given her some warning, but he was probably too busy digging up somebody else's dirt when he wasn't playing chess. With Dace. With her. With everybody.

The morning passed with her trying to read and reason. It was a process that had eluded her for several days, leaving her in a maze of dead ends whichever way she turned. Well, maybe it would still be all right. Maybe Gold had gotten Dace a good deal. He was such a well-respected lawyer, after all.

Sitting cross-legged in her tangled sheets, her gorge rising in her throat, she read through three lengthy articles in the *Maitland Spectator*, practically the only news in the paper. "Secret Deal Ends Trial," "Judge Washes His Hands" and "The Reasons For The Bargain." She read each article at least three times, but it didn't help. She began to wonder if she really were going insane. Nothing—nothing made any sense.

The defence lawyers had made their decisions over a Christmas lunch in a suburban motel, in cahoots with both the Crown attorneys and the Judge, although Silverton claimed he couldn't remember why the defence lawyers had wanted to see him. Couldn't remember? Wasn't the lawyers' seasonal invitation only a few days old? The whole deal had almost been quashed by the Attorney-General who couldn't—or wouldn't—promise not to appeal the sentences.

Several of the accused prisoners were unhappy with their plea bargains, possibly because their own stories hadn't even been told. Only two of thirteen cases had been heard and unfortunately D'Arcy Devereux' had been one of them. Two unidentified prisoners had also held out for trial by jury before succumbing to pressure from their fellow accused and their own attorneys. Let's go home, everybody'd said.

No opinion was expressed about how the jurors felt about seeing their virtually unpaid labor for the past few months get flushed down the proverbial toilet, somewhere between the overcooked luncheon turkey, the canned cranberry sauce and two or three twenty-sixers of Johnny Walker. But even if they hadn't concurred with Judge Silverton when he doubted their ability to untangle the mess, they were undoubtedly relieved to be packing their bags and going home, as were the thirteen defence lawyers and two Crown attorneys who had already checked out of Maitland's finest motel.

Long before Liza was through, the newspaper was strewn all around the room. If she had allowed it, a low keening would have risen from her throat, try as she did to convince herself this was the best of all possible outcomes. Dragging herself over to the window, she leaned her elbows on the sill and stared at the grey sky outside. The facts were these: Huey Gold was a good lawyer. Her cousin had pulled the lightest sentence: two years to be served concurrent. Concurrent. If she'd been related to one of the victims instead of to Dace, she would probably have asked what the point was of doing that.

She picked up her phone and dialed Hubert Gold long distance. She'd gotten his Toronto number from Directory Assistance. It was the first time she had ever called him. She was surprised when he answered his own phone.

"What happened? Why?" was all she said.

"I'm sorry," he replied. "I should have called you myself. It's been so hectic, you know. I just got back to Toronto. It's a normally a three hour drive, but it took me four."

"Dace ..." she said, gripping the phone and closing her eyes.

"I know, I know. You must think it's ironic that your cousin was actually convicted of assaulting Bellissimo, a man who hadn't even been in the victims' circle. He had a sprained wrist, a bruised jaw and no sense of self-preservation. One of D'Arcy's friends will probably kill him before the year's out."

"Great. So justice will be served. And Dace? My Dace? How's he? Is he still in Segregation? Or couldn't you even get him out of the Hole?"

"Look, Miss Devereux, Liza, I did my best. I don't want you think badly of me. In the end I think the court grasped the situation, that the presence of the sex offenders produced an undesirable effect, especially among the accused. We were just talking about this at lunch. And the army, well, let's just say that in retrospect, they probably shouldn't have brought the army in on the last day. Negotiations were going well and I'm telling you this from the authorities' point of view. Anyway, we know that some of the inmates went a little crazy when they saw the soldiers in the yard. D'Arcy's friend Steve wasn't actually in on the beatings, but we think he offed one of the victims later, when he was drunk or high."

"But not Dace. He didn't. And he protected those hostages, you know he did."

"I know, I know. We've been over this before. But that's the way the game's played, and he knows it. Courtroom outcome isn't predictable. It's a game, not some *Perry Mason* drama with a neat and tidy outcome. Luckily I know how to play it. You know he got the lightest sentence, Liza, in spite of the fact Silverton really wanted his throat."

"Uh, huh. And why's that?"

"Well, Judge Silverton, you know, he really should have excused himself from this trial, considering his prior connection to Dace. I checked and his nephew is still working in some northern school."

Hurting more children, she thought. "So Dace is jubilant, I suppose?" she said aloud, furious there was nothing she could do without exposing both Dace and Rosie.

"Your sarcasm—I can see it's a family trait. Well, he's a little under the weather, I admit, but that'll pass. He's tough. It's not the first time something like this has happened to him. My dear, he's only twenty-four and he's already spent almost six years in jail. After we got the verdict—it only took the jurors a couple of hours yesterday—he stopped speaking to me. We wondered what had happened to you. You'd never missed before. In retrospect, I'm glad you weren't there. And I believe D'Arcy was glad, too. He looked … ashen, although of course he never said a word. He didn't make a sound."

"My God. I wasn't there!"

"Liza, there was nothing you could have done."

"But I've got to do something! Please, Mr. Gold. I've got to see him. Is there no way?"

"Oh Liza, I'm so sorry. It's not in my power, young lady."

"It's Judge Silverton, isn't it? He couldn't get him on a murder rap because you had something on him," she reluctantly conceded. "But he's still calling the shots."

"Maybe," Gold demurred. "He's a powerful man, at least in Maitland."

"Oh, c'mon. Several people heard him in the lunchroom at the courthouse talking off the cuff. He said Dace was a vicious punk then, and he's a vicious punk now. What does "then" mean? Was he talking about that school?"

"I don't know, Liza, but there's another problem. Those prison guards carry more weight than we realized."

"So he's screwed Inside or Out?"

"Now, now, I wouldn't say that. He'll be fine as long as he doesn't do something, uh, rash, like attack one of the guards or try to escape."

"Escape?" she echoed doubtfully. "Yeah, maybe he could go after Silverton."

"That would be very foolish indeed."

"My God, do you really think Dace is a cold-blooded killer? That he would execute that creep?"

"My dear girl, of course not. I ... sorry, that's my other phone ringing. I've got to go."

"Well, go then," she said dully.

"Listen, Liza, all he has to do is watch his back, keep a cool head and he'll be all right. He'll do that, won't he? As long as you're there for him? I'll get him to write you a letter when he's feeling better. You mustn't worry. The moment he comes around we'll launch our appeal."

"Great," she said, reaching over and double-locking her door in case she started yelling. She didn't want anyone coming in to find out what was going on. "Another letter," she added listlessly. "Well, put it in the mail."

After Gold said good-bye she left the phone off the hook, pinned a brown wool blanket over her window and went to bed. The phone stopped buzzing after a couple of minutes. Thank God Janice was away. She felt like a Victorian lady with an opiate addiction, but nothing induced her to move, not even when somebody came to say Joe was on the hall phone or Mel was calling long distance. She thought about taking the train to see

Mel in Trenton, but in the end she didn't dare. No way she could face Mel now.

She had no way of knowing if Uncle Norm and Rosie were at home or out celebrating at a local pub as Dace lay on a cot, rigid with shame because he had sold himself out. But she guessed.

Dace must have seen this one coming, but he hadn't been able to steer clear. Stupid. It made him sound almost hapless, everything he was not. But in the end it was just like he'd predicted. Unless he wrote a book or went on radio talk shows — or she did — people were always going to think he got away with murder, weren't they? For the rest of his life. Or longer.

His name would always be linked to the beating and torture of the two men who had died during the Maitland Penitentiary Riot.

Chapter Thirty-Three
Wanting and Wanted

Even though she knew they wouldn't let her see Dace, Liza petitioned the prison. She also wrote or called everybody she knew with even the most remote connection to his case, but it was no use. She briefly considered confessing that she was pregnant, wondering if that would help, then decided against it.

Hubert Gold was also unsuccessful. Based on his experience, he said Dace and his so-called fellow conspirators would probably remain in Segregation for at least a year. Nobody was in a hurry to let them out. Of course that meant no visitors. *A year!* Liza sobbed, then raged. By now, all she wanted was some assurance he was all right, that he wasn't going to stick himself or maybe several guards with a knife. And to be with him one more time. Oh how she longed for that: his eyes, his arms, his hands, his lips ... It had been so long since she'd touched him. *And I used to want so much else*, she thought. *Babies, books, bikes, a great love affair and a chance to write.*

She wrote him several letters — *I'm not going anywhere until I know you're all right* — and every night when she went to sleep, the same dream came.

The door, a metal weave with dime-sized holes, opened and closed behind her with a bang. A furtive little man let her in.

Strange, he didn't look like a guard. "Twenty minutes," he said, bouncing up and down on the balls of his feet like a squirrel. "I'm not really one of them. That's all I can risk."

Dace stood by a space saver sink, the smallest one she'd ever seen. Its chief virtue was that it was almost new, though the pipe underneath leaked.

"Liza?" he said, his face almost lost in his hair and beard. "Are you really here? Or is it my imagination? How did you get in? What did you have to do? I must be seeing things. This whole place is just one big mind fuck."

She crossed the floor in two strides, pushing herself into his chest until he had no choice but to hold her in his arms. "Don't ask," she whispered, her mouth brushing against the skin under his unbuttoned shirt. "What's this? This cut on your chest? It looks like it's getting infected, it's all —"

"Savage. It was Savage. He has a little pen knife he likes to play with. One time he almost cut off ... My God, you must be real. You're crying again and you shouldn't. Do you know what that does to me?"

"I'll stop," she promised, "if you…"

"If I what? Good God, girl, I haven't showered in two weeks. You smell like a flower and your hair is growing out like a weed. It's going to be halfway down to your bum again by June."

If you only knew, she thought guiltily. Even her pubic hair was growing, exceeding all expectations, curling down between her legs. *It's the baby,* she almost blurted. "I don't care. How are you going to… What are you going to do?"

"What do you think? Everything I can," he said, sinking with her until they sat on the floor, her legs wrapped around his waist. "I know how to play their games. Don't ask for anything. Watch my mouth. Answer in monosyllables if I answer at all. Don't worry. I'll wait this out and stay calm."

"But the guards are striking for overtime, none of the prisoners have gone back to school or work and you're stuck in here because not one of the bastards you protected came to your defence. And now the *Spectator* is talking about another riot. Dace? Dace, you're shivering. Why the hell is it so cold in here?"

"Some people hope there's going to be another riot here and the guards are doing their level best to provoke one, but I'll kill the bastards rather than go through that again," he vowed, burying his face in her hair.

"But you just said you were going to stay calm!"

"Yeah, yeah, and what are you going to do, Liza?"

"I don't know," she said miserably.

"Yes, you do. You can write a book. Better still, we'll write a book together if I ever get out. A kind of family affair."

After a couple more phone calls, a letter finally arrived on December 21, courtesy of Hubert Gold. It was one page long. Although Dace was only allowed out of his cell one hour a day, he had joined another inmate committee to keep from going crazy. Well, people's committee, he amended. Following the riot, the use of the word inmate was deemed a pejorative term. Nothing else had changed except there was a big master plan in the making. Not to worry though. Because even if the pigs were trying to destroy them, he would make out just fine.

> It's snowing. The wind whistles and the temperature is 9 degrees. The night is black and I am surrounded by the enemy. But my mind is quick. My muscles are hard. My knife is sharp and my heart is full for you, my darling. Don't worry about me. I'll make out just fine. I pledge my undying loyalty. Liza, I love you so.

Brief joy and utter despair. Life, love. Her life, his love. *Love,* she thought. *It's not enough anymore. It's you, just you, I want, no matter what.* But love alone couldn't help him, so she wrote back:

Darling, you're not just fine! You're a dead man if you don't get out of there soon. You with all your muscles. Please keep writing me. In fact, you can do better than that. Do what we talked about all the time, but take real good care. You can keep sending mail to this address because I'm not going home for Christmas, although I might visit a friend. Not Janice, though. Too much work to do and too many decisions to make.

Chapter Thirty-Four

Christmas Day

"What did you talk about all the time?" Hubert Gold demanded when he finally got through to her on Christmas Day. It was nearly 5:00 p.m. and the almost dark had socked her in. She sat at her desk, methodically working through a box of Whitman's chocolates and flipping through a calendar for the New Year. The baby was due the first day of summer in June 1973.

"What?"

"What stupid bonehead thing did you urge him to do?" Gold spat.

Liza closed her eyes, took the phone off her ear and pressed it against her neck. Gold must be calling from a party. She could hear background noises over the faint, suspicious buzzing on her line: music, the tinkle of glasses, the explosive guffaws of men, the high pitched sound of women's laughter. They sound like birds, she thought. For a moment she almost wished she were there. Anywhere but here.

"Miss Devereux — Liza — are you still there?" he pressed.

"What are you talking about? What do you mean?"

"The Pen phoned me. He's escaped, you little idiot!"

Liza's heart almost stopped. She got up from her chair so fast that she backed into her waste paper basket, toppling it over.

So he had, he had! My God, he was fast. But no, not necessarily. He had been planning this for ages.

"Wh-when?"

"An hour ago. Held up the prison doctor for his uniform, locked him in a closet, put on his clothes, walked out the door, then just hopped into the man's car, pretty as you please."

Liza had always believed she would be overjoyed to finally get such news. But what she felt now was sheer terror. She put her hand over her heart, wanting to make sure it still beat. Maybe he'd been safer in prison. At least then she had known where he was, and now...

Maybe he had a shiv, though. *My knife is sharp for you, my darling.* Cute. She'd thought he meant something else, but maybe ... Oh God, where was he?

"Why was he seeing the doctor?" she asked, stalling, trying to think. "And where was his guard?" As if that mattered, now that Dace was outside somewhere, running down a track where he could be hurt, where somebody might try to stop him, where he might end up dead.

"How the hell do I know? No, wait now. They said that he had an infected cut."

Of course, she thought, remembering her dream. It was Savage, she almost said, fear overcoming rage.

"He needed a penicillin shot. They've already had one unfortunate incident where an inmate died from a small cut on his finger. Oh, well, never mind that. There was some kind of Christmas party going on and all the guards are working to rule right now."

"So this happened—this afternoon?" she asked. A quick glance outside the window to her left revealed no cop cars in the parking lot, though they could have been hiding out back, near the garbage dumpsters. She wouldn't put it past them. There was only one thing to do. She had to get out of there fast.

"As if you don't know, you little ..." Gold stopped and took a deep breath, sounding as if he were unable to go on until he was back in control, the way he should have been, the way he would have been, in a court of law. "The police are waiting for him in Toronto. Scared the shit out of your mother. Probably figured you'd be home for Christmas, but then the Warden read me your letter over the phone. I'm surprised they haven't contacted you yet. Too busy securing the border and the roads, I suppose. But they'll be there any moment. My advice is that you be more co-operative with them than you are with me, Missy. The cops won't fool around with you, not when there's an armed and dangerous man on the loose."

"Well, I was going to visit Uncle Norm today, but I was too … uh … sick," she huffed, holding the phone out from her ear with her left hand and reaching far enough with her right to retrieve a soft, zippered bag from under her bed. She had left some folded laundry on her desk, which she tipped into the bag. She had only five bucks to her name, though. She felt it with her fingers, folded in the back pocket of her jeans.

Mel, she thought frantically. *I'll hitchhike to Trenton if I have to. He'll keep me, and it won't be the first place the police look. No, they'll come here. They've already checked Toronto and when they find my room empty, they'll go to Uncle Norm's, if they haven't already.* Should she drop by the farm? No, Dace would never risk going there.

Jesus, Gold was still talking. The man went on and on, talking about responsibility, asking her why she hadn't taken up some more worthwhile cause. The Vietnam War, the seal hunt, even Women's Lib. What the hell was wrong with young women these days? In the sixties, they'd … If she'd been his daughter, he'd …

She couldn't answer. Say something, she ordered herself. "I had the phone off the hook until just now," she managed. "I was going to call my mother."

Gold hooted with disgust. "You took your phone off the hook on Christmas Day?" he asked sceptically.

Yes, she thought, because nobody I wanted to hear from was supposed to call. "Oh God. You don't think Dace tried to call me, do you?"

"Look, Missy, I really don't appreciate you dissembling with me."

Not that she could blame him for this attitude, but she was getting pretty tired of it. "So where did they think I was hiding him?" she demanded. "At my mother's place? Maybe under the diving tower at Christie Pits?" She looked wildly around the room for her shoulder purse. Ah, there it was, right on the floor by her feet.

"Huey," somebody coaxed in the background, "come back to the party!"

"Where is he, Miss Devereux?" he hissed, all patience spent.

"I haven't a clue," she said, pondering how much more she could say. She wanted desperately to confide in someone, but Gold had become a liability. She stuffed her arms into her maxi-coat after letting the phone drop for a moment so she could dart into her closet. He'd turn his client in, post-haste, for the sake of his reputation and all that.

What had Dace done? Ditched the doctor's car in the lake and gotten a ride in a truck? There were so many trucks on the 401. When they'd been on their bikes they'd weaved in and out, reckless and stupid, but oh, so fucking brave. The only way to live, they'd said. Christ, she wished she were on a bike right now. If he were headed for the Falls, he'd probably follow the highway past Trenton and Toronto ...

"Well, that's funny, considering you can practically read his mind," Gold said sarcastically. "Or so he's always said. You know, I can't help him if I don't know where he is. And if the police get to him first there's no telling what they'll do. Last week they shot an unarmed fifteen-year-old who was driving a stolen car."

He'd fled at 4:00 and now it was 5:00. There was no way he could have gotten to Toronto yet. So where the hell was he? Freezing his ass off in some farmer's barn? God, she hoped not.

And where did he think she was? Would he risk going to Mel's? Maybe. He knew Mel lived in Trenton. A slight detour. How difficult could it be to track down a doctor's son?

Liza, I love you so.

Surely he would try to leave her a note. Surely he wouldn't just go, a man like him.

"You're trying to scare me, Mr. Gold," she said, snapping off her desk lamp and staring out at the empty parking lot. Jesus, a car was coming down the hill. A long, dark car. A Crown Vic. Even from the ninth floor window she could see there were at least two adults inside — males, she bet.

"You're damn right I'm trying to scare you."

"He was as good as dead in prison. The guards would have killed him," she whispered, glancing frantically from the window to her locked door. Good God, what was that noise? Was somebody already in the hall? Everybody except the janitor and maybe a few international students had gone home. Stupid. If she had visited with one of the Asian students today, like a good girl, she might have been able to hide in their room.

"There are some Christmas carollers at my door. I gotta go," she said, dropping the phone. She hitched both bags over her shoulder with one hand and gathered a fold of her long coat with the other so she wouldn't fall flat on her face.

"Listen, Liza," Gold shouted, his voice so loud she could hear him even though she was almost halfway out her door by then, heading for the back stairs. "If he comes to you, and you know he will, do the right thing. Turn him in. That's all you can —"

Her legs felt so stiff. Run, she told herself, run! Down nine flights of stairs, out behind the garbage cans, then follow the stream to the other side of town. Careful, careful, watch your step. The baby …

By herself, she had walked along the stream many times, dreaming, so she knew how to get to the highway from there. It might take a while, but there was no other way.

Luckily the only person she encountered in the stairwell was a lonely, drunken foreign student on the fifth floor landing who looked like she'd have trouble describing her own kin, let alone a white girl on the run. A fugitive. My God, she and Dace were now fugitives from the law. What if there was a shootout? Don't be stupid, she told herself. It would never come to that. This wasn't television or the movies. It was just her life, her crazy life.

Run, just run. Don't stop. Watch your footing, you fool.

It was a long way down, but she made it to the bottom of the stairs and slipped out the back door. She heard somebody whistling and saw a plainclothes policeman approach the rear of the student residence from the opposite side. He missed her by inches in the dark. She crouched behind the closest dumpster, watching him. If he glanced in her direction, he would see her eyes glowing like a feral cat's in the dark. Her hamstrings started to ache. At the entrance to the residence, the policeman looked both ways then slipped a credit card into the lock.

Joe Armitage would probably phone later on, looking for the scoop, but by then she was on her way to Trenton in a National Grocer truck, clutching her scarf around her throat, listening to the driver complain about his wife. The burly, black-haired man was about forty with sideburns and a moustache, and he thoughtfully shared the sandwiches his wife had packed, white turkey on rye with lots of mayo. He even offered her a beer from a six pack under his seat.

He told her she looked a little peaked. An old fashioned word, she thought, glancing at him with surprise. A pretty girl shouldn't study so much, ha, ha. Shouldn't hitchhike either. Where was her boyfriend on Christmas Night? She had one, didn't she? He knew what little co-eds were like. Long hair, hot pants, like to dance …

Yeah sure, Liza said, playing along. By now she was too paralyzed with anxiety to even think up an excuse for her flight. Please God, she thought, trying to look past the man's lewd idea of jokes. Please be all talk and no action.

At her pace, it took almost an hour to hike along the river to the highway. The ride to Trenton should have only taken another hour or so, but an accident near Belleville held her and her rescuer hostage, taking too much time.

Time she didn't have.

Chapter Thirty-five
Shelter

Sleep, my darling, sleep;
The pity of it all
Is all we compass if,
We watch disaster fall.
Put off your twenty-odd
Encumbered years and creep
Into the only heaven,
The robbers' cave of sleep.
—Macneice, Louis, "Cradle Song"

D ace stepped out of the shadows when she arrived at Mel's late that night, just like that. *Thank God, thank God, thank God!* He'd been waiting for hours, though he'd occasionally snuck into the basement of the house to get warm. Well, why the hell not?

He was there!

Breathless, wild-eyed, her bell-bottom jeans sodden with snow, she stood frozen for a moment, staring, slightly shocked to see him standing next to a blue fir, dead centre on the lawn. Behind him the windows of the Melvilles' red brick split level house glowed, competing with the multicolored Christmas lights outlining every door frame, every eave. Besides being cold, he had a three-inch-long cut on his chest. He had lots of penicillin so it would be all right, he assured her. He opened both his cotton doctor's shirt and his thin jacket to show her. He was coatless. High spots of red blazed on his cheeks.

She'd only had to walk a block from where the truck driver dropped her off, but she'd forgotten her boots and her running shoes were soaked. Her nose was dripping. She found a crumpled tissue in her pocket and blew into it, still staring at his face. He looked much older, but so dear, so ...

She lunged forward, trying to hug him without pressing too hard against his hurt chest. She could barely stop herself from sinking her fingers into the lank hair curling at the back of his neck. Much as she had hoped to find him here in Trenton, she hadn't really expected him. What a risk he had taken, just to see her!

"The basement door was unlocked, wasn't it?" She took his face in her hands. It was slick with sweat, although his teeth were chattering. My God, it had been months since she'd touched him, except in her dreams. But he still smelled the same and oh, he would taste so good. She fell on him, kissing him over and over, wanting to swallow him whole. He held onto her like he would never let go.

When her bag slipped from her shoulder to the ground, she stopped kissing him long enough to kick it under the fir tree with one foot. "Mel said it's always unlocked. Nothing bad ever happens to them."

Glancing in both directions, she grabbed his arm and tugged him, wanting to take him somewhere—anywhere but out here in the open where all the neighbours could see. "Let's get inside. You look like a bum even in the doctor's clothes."

"Thanks, lady."

She stepped back a little and took another look at him. "Why are you sweating? And your hair—what have you done to your hair?" she asked, her voice rising. "It's all slicked back, kind of Mohawk style. Looks almost black."

"Shhh. It's Doc's Brylcreem. A little dab will do ya ...," he sang off-key. "I took that and his scissors, too," he said, stopping to kiss her again. "God, I've been wanting to kiss you for so long—all through that frigging trial while you sat there looking like you were at a public hanging and I was next."

"Great. So that's what Gold meant when he said you were armed. Are they big scissors?" she asked, steering him through a rose arbour to the yard behind the house. He stopped her just before they collided with a bird feeder on a pole. "Oh, yeah, well, they're pretty big. Put them away for now," she ordered, then gasped, startled by a fake deer. The swimming pool must be covered. She couldn't see it in the dark under the snow.

Ah, good. There was the basement door. She felt a bit like Dorothy trying to escape the tornado in *The Wizard of Oz*. "Hurry, Dace. If anybody sees us, they'll think it's Mel's father, that he's having some kind of romantic assignation! His grandmother—oh, there'll be hell to pay. Oh my God, I just heard somebody come out on the front porch."

"Shh, it's just some neighbours. They'll be gone in moment," he said, his arm around her shoulders, his dead weight almost drilling her into the frozen ground. "Big shebang here tonight, a drop-in affair. Everybody's half-corked, but it works for me. If anybody saw me, and I don't think they did, they probably thought I was with somebody else. There are lots of strangers in town, people with out-of-town guests. Stop pulling me, Liza. I can't hang around here much longer, skulking in shadows. Even the cops aren't that stupid. If they don't find you in rez, they might think about coming here next."

"All the more reason to get into the basement. Quick. This way," she said, bending to lift the storm cellar door off the lawn. The latch slipped in her cold hands, but he came forward and grabbed it.

"I know, I know. Jesus, I've been alternately boiling and freezing my ass off for the last two hours, running in and out. I've got chills, I guess. Where the hell have you been? I spent half an hour in payphone at a gas station, calling collect."

"My God. How many people saw you?"

"I dunno. Not too many people; the gas station was closed. Merry Christmas, I kept saying, like I was making a bunch of Christmas calls. There was no answer at the rez. I couldn't even raise the switchboard, so I called our parents. They were all wrecks, although I don't think your mother even realized who I was. Your father—fuck, I'm sorry, darling, but is that redneck really related to you and me? 'I won't accept the charges,' he said. Then I called Mel's. 'Guess who?' I said and some lady goes, 'Oh, don't try to fool me, Howard. Patty said you'd be calling for directions.' And then she told me how to get here! Good people, the salt of the earth. Little darling, you could do much worse." He stopped, his teeth chattering again.

Liza looked at him in amazement. He had never talked so much. "Slow down, Dace, slow down. It's okay."

"I probably could have waltzed right in the front door, but then I wouldn't have been able to watch for you. Mel's with a hot little number in a blue velvet dress, but she doesn't hold a candle to you. Have you slept with him yet?"

"What did you say?" she asked. She didn't move quickly enough to avoid a smack on her rear.

"You heard me," he said with some difficulty. His voice, with each little exertion he made, had begun to come in short gasps.

"No, of course I haven't. I'm like you. I don't like doing what I'm told," she lied, edging down the wooden steps as quietly as she could. He closed the heavy door stealthily over their heads, and she felt as if he were sealing them in a tomb. "There's another exit from down here. A side door. This house is on a corner lot so it goes out onto a different street."

"I..." he tried to say, going down a few more stairs.

"Dace, for God's sake, stop trying to talk. You've been practically babbling! It's hard to understand you when your teeth keep making that noise. And it's annoying besides. Are you all right? You should have been at the border by now! It's almost a four hour drive to Niagara Falls, even from here. The Peace Bridge ..."

"Baby, I know that's what we talked about, but I can't go that way."

"What do you mean? You can't cross at Thousand Islands. It's much too close."

He paused for a moment at the bottom of the stairs, resting his hot face against a cool cinder block wall and breathing hard. "It won't work," he managed. "The trucker who gave me a ride had a CB radio. They had a description, but fortunately it didn't match mine. Still, they say I'm armed and dangerous. All major checkpoints are closed. The moment they sober up and get the right picture, I'm screwed."

She reached out a hand towards his shoulder but there were obstacles in the dark. She'd only been in the place once before. "Oops. I forgot how much junk there is down here," she whispered, bending down to nurse a bruised shin. "The Melvilles don't throw anything away. It foils intruders, I suppose. I can't see—did you find a flashlight?—oh, good. Be careful, don't flash it around like that."

"Would you stop telling me what to do?"

"There's a bomb shelter in here someplace. Mel showed me. They almost never use it. Behind some tools on a fake wall."

"I already found it," he said, pointing proudly. "There was a razor there, so I had a shave in the laundry tub or you might not have recognized me. Cut a bit of my hair, too."

"You didn't!" Liza dashed over and stared in horror at the deep tub on the right, thickly coated with his reddish dark hair. "My God," she scolded, scooping large clumps up and stuffing them in her pockets before turning on both taps to rinse the rest of the evidence away. "You left hair in the sink!"

"I even had a little nap, waiting for the penicillin to kick in. Stop splashing around in that water and get over here. Look," he said, taking her arm when she reached him.

He opened a metal door to a room about the size of his former cell and they both went inside. He shone the flashlight onto a sleeping bag on the tiled floor and clicked it off. Liza maneuvered the wall back into position and closed the heavy door behind them, bolting it from the inside. Unwinding a six foot woollen scarf from her neck, she rearranged it at the bottom of the door to block any light. A candle burned in the corner, illuminating steel walls. The light wouldn't be visible from the tool side of the wall.

"Hmm, real cosy. Any food?"

"Canned stuff, but they forgot to pack an opener. So if a bomb doesn't get them they'll starve. I opened up some sardines, though, with the little key. Don't worry, I also ate a whole package of mints. There's some money here, too. An emergency fund, I guess. And there's a first aid kit with some antibiotics, a bottle of Scotch and a stash of grass."

"Oh God, I hope Mel doesn't decide he wants to smoke up tonight. Take everything, Dace, take everything. I'll get some cash out of the bank after Boxing Day and pay them back."

"Liza, you don't have two hundred bucks to spare," he said, watching her eyes glow in the candlelight.

"Yes, I do. Second semester's tuition will just be a little late. And who knows? Maybe I should just forget about school."

"Don't you dare. My father will pay you back. Liza, he'll help you with whatever you need, do you hear me? Go to him. He'll never refuse you and he'll know how to get money to me, too, whenever I ask. He's done it before. C'mere. You're shaking like a leaf." He laughed. "Looks like it's not enough that I've made you totally wanton, you're a little crook now, too," he said, pulling her to him by the lapels of her coat. He laid her down on the sleeping bag and covered her body with the length of his. For several minutes, they just lay there. Then he started to relax a little, his breathing coming easier.

"Baby," he whispered, wrapping a large hand around her throat and kneading. "I'm so sorry. Everything's going to be all right. Open up and let me in."

For the first time, she refused him. "Shh, Dace. Don't," she said, pushing her hands against his shoulders and freeing her throat. "We can't. What if somebody hears? Besides the police are probably on their way."

"Darling, you give them too much credit. I was worried when we were outside, center stage, but it's safe enough in here. Listen to that music. Some kind of classical stuff."

"Yeah, sounds like a dirge. Very lugubrious."

"Nice word. I can almost see what it means, but talk English next time, smarty pants. The party's upstairs. Nobody will come down here tonight. Quit squirming, I want my Christmas present. It's almost Boxing Day. What do I have to do, tie you up?" he asked, pinning her wrists together above her head with one hand and grabbing her hair with the other, forcing her to look into his eyes.

I wish you would, she thought, surprised to feel a familiar little thrill in her groin, although most of her was wet, cold and spent. I wish I could get on all fours and present myself to you again. When had that seemed like fun?

"Stop it, Dace, stop it!" she said, much against her will. "Right now. You're shivering. You're sick. It'll be at least twenty-four hours before that penicillin really kicks in. How are you going to get across?"

"At Akwesasne."

"Aqua what?"

"Akwesasne. I'll have to backtrack, but it'll throw them off the scent. Yeah, Akwesasne. It's a Mohawk reservation near Cornwall. Straddles the Quebec and the American borders just like I'm straddling you. Lots of smuggling going on. Mostly cheap cigarettes, but it's pretty easy to get across."

"Smuggling? Oh so, the Wolfhounds …"

"Yeah, they're getting in on some of the action. Dirt Beard's cousin will pick me up in a car when I double back. I phoned him collect, too. The stupid bugger nearly hung up on me."

"I guess the police won't be expecting you to do that. The Wolfhounds are history as far they're concerned," she replied, no longer struggling, now that she knew he had a plan. A network of bikers would lead him down through the States. His father would finance him, and …   "That's what they think, but while I've been Inside, they've been growing, regen —"

"Regenerating."

"And you—you never thought my bros were going to do me much good, did you?"

"I'm coming, too," she said, ignoring his last comment. "And you know what? I bet we both have native blood. I used to hear stories. Granny Debo … our eyes …"

"No." His voice was gentle.

"No what?"

"No, you're not coming, Little Liza. I had to see you one more time. Aw Jeez, stop hitting me. You'll be happier here, finishing school, hanging out with Mel. Look at you. You're almost getting fat, you're so relaxed. I used to be able to feel your bones. You can do anything you want, but I liked you like that, soft and bony all at once."

"Relaxed! Oh God, I want to get out of here too. Or at least I used to. Before I went to Ireland that's all I ever wanted to do."

"You can't come. Absolutely not. Too risky. If they find me, they'll shoot to kill. Besides you're not a biker's girl, remember? That's what you always said."

"But Dace, the Life, that's what got you back in jail, so they could—"

"And we both know that I might not be able to change quickly. I thought I could, but— Anyway, I'll do what I have to do. Maybe with the bikers, maybe not. It's high time I made my own way. We'll see."

"Give them up, Dace. For me."

"Aw Liza, c'mon. It's never that easy. And you'll do what you have to do too. Remember all you wanted? All you wanted to be?" he said, almost burying her body with his. "Neither of us can do anything if we're not free."

"Dace, I can't breathe," she said, struggling to free her face from his chest and cocking her ears towards the door. "What's that? I think somebody's coming downstairs!"

He half-rolled off her, hoisting his upper body on his forearms. They hadn't got all of him yet. He was still strong, she could see. Maybe he would be all right.

"Shhh, I heard it too," he said, gripping her mouth so hard with his right hand he would leave a bruise. He kept it there through the next exchange. "Probably Mel wants his stash."

"Melo!" a woman's voice called then, much to their mutual relief, although they were still trying to ease behind a couple of boxes in the corner. Dace had already pinched out the candle with his free hand. "What are you doing, honey?"

"Aw Ma, can't you leave me alone for five minutes?" Mel said just before he kicked the fake door.

Please, Liza prayed through Dace's fingers. *Go away, Mel.*

"But, Mellie, we have guests! You have a responsibility! And this is your party. Have you spoken to the little Dyson girl yet?"

"Little! Look, I don't mind the fact that she weighs about four hundred pounds, but I do mind that she simpers. Wants to marry a doctor, I think."

"Well, what's wrong with that? Lovely family, Mel, she has a lovely family, unlike that sly, sharp-faced little Liza Devereux. Oh, I don't know what you see in her. She's not even pretty. You could do so much better."

Too late, Dace took his hand from Liza's mouth and plugged his forefingers into her ears.

"Mother!"

"Mel, I'm going to get your Dad." Her voice dropped slightly as she apparently turned away. "That's okay, Mrs. Stewart, just put those little cocktail sausages on the counter." Then her focus was back on her son. "If I told you once, I've told you a hundred times, you're going to get us all in trouble, smoking that—that funny stuff, grass, whatever it is. The Mayor's family is here tonight and … Oh, Mel, why do you have to… Where do you get this rebellious streak?"

Feeling Dace's mouth move against her face in a smile, Liza almost dissolved in giggles before she started praying again: Go Mel, go.

"I was just checking the furnace, for God's sake," he answered, his voice retreating a little on the other side. "It's colder than a witch's tit down here. Did somebody leave the storm cellar door open? There's snow on the back stairs. Footprints."

"Mel!"

"Okay, I'm coming, I'm coming, but I swear to God that come summer I'm getting my own place," the reluctant host said, his feet pounding upstairs to his mother's kitchen.

"Whew," Liza said. "That was close."

"Are you sure you don't want to?" Dace said, stretching out on her again, although neither of them dared take off either their clothes or their shoes.

Later, when she still hadn't said another word for fear she might confess the one thing that would keep him and put him back in harm's way, he spoke again. "Go now. It's almost four and I want to leave in the dark. Get your bag from under the tree and let Mel know you're here. He'll be over the moon. His bedroom window's unlocked. I already checked it out for you. At least it looked like his room. There were chemistry books all over the floor."

"Dace," she said, not moving, her eyes tracking dust motes on the floor. "Do you really want me to?"

He went silent, rummaging through a small cupboard of spare clothes.

"Dace?" she tried again, raising herself on one elbow, her bangs veiling her eyes.

"It doesn't matter what I want, Liza. It's what's right for you. Never mind that the thought of you with that baby-faced boy makes me want to beat your ass. As for him, well, don't ever leave me alone with him, that's all I ask. Now drop it. Just drop it," he said, pulling a sweater over his head. "This is good. A hand knit pullover with reindeer and an Arctic parka. Very Canadian. Look at the hood. I can close it right over my face!" he said, then demonstrated, pulling the material so close she could barely even see his eyes. *You look like an anteater,* she thought.

She wanted to cry, but something in her was hardening up for the time ahead. She watched him for a while instead, suiting up for the worst. He pulled back the hood of the jacket temporarily. He was paler now; the fever must have broken.

"Maybe you should leave first," she finally said, lying limply back on the sleeping bag.

"All right," he said, kneeling beside her and looking straight into her eyes. "For God's sake, why are looking at me like that?" He took her face in his hands. Like I'm abandoning you? she thought he said, although his lips didn't move.

Her lips quivered and tears spilled over. She couldn't say anything. *Because you are*, she thought. *You don't want to, but you are.*

"What aren't you telling me?"

"For God's sake," she said, sniffing and wiping her face with her sleeve. "Hurry. Go. Just go!" she said, half sitting up, taking his hand and kissing the open palm. "I've given you my body, my love and my loyalty. What more can you want?"

Dace stood up. He looked down at her. Somehow—it looked a massive effort—he shook his head. "Darling, you've given me everything I knew enough to want, but that doesn't mean you haven't held something back."

"And what are you holding back?"

"Nothing. You know all my secrets now, good or bad, everything I'd hoped to hide."

And I still want you, she thought, rolling over and burying her face in the sleeping bag so she wouldn't have to watch him go.

All I ever wanted was you.

Chapter Thirty-Six

Homecoming
Melville residence, Trenton, January 2, 1973

Surfacing from a deep sleep, she squinted at a small leather folding alarm clock in Mel's parents' guest room. For the first time in three weeks she felt almost rested. Dace was safe. He was listed as one of Canada's Ten Most Wanted Men, according to the *Star*, but safer than he'd ever been in prison, where Savage or one of his henchmen would have gotten him for sure.

Dace's last message, courtesy of a very cold biker passing through Trenton, was in her purse by the bed. *Monarch butterflies make a perilous journey*, was all it said. When nobody was looking, she took the paper out of her purse and touched it with her lips, thankful she still had some of his hair in her pockets so that when she closed her eyes and touched it, she could pretend he was there.

Everything was beige in the Melville guest room except a single-sized corduroy bedspread in a deep, chocolate brown. The clock sat on top of a three tiered metal bookcase crammed with literary erotica Mel's parents must have been too enlightened to purge: *Fanny Hill, Harriet Marwood, Lady Chatterley's Lover, Lolita, My Life and Loves, The Pearl, Tropic of Cancer, Story of O*. The room had belonged to Mel's older brother George, who was now a high school librarian in Toronto.

It was nearly 11:30 a.m. on January 2 and they were leaving Trenton to go back to school, though Mel's mother worried about the snow. His father was already back in the Outpatient Department at Memorial Hospital. Classes were starting tomorrow and Mel couldn't miss Chemistry, not if he expected to get into Med School in two years.

Surprised to have anything on her mind besides Dace and her pregnancy, Liza found she was still mildly curious about her marks. Somehow she'd met all her deadlines with just a couple of extensions, performing on remote control. The phrase 'personal problems' had done the trick. People had their own problems. They didn't need to know anything more. The Sociology professor was the only one who had said he was sorry about her cousin. He'd even suggested another lawyer who could launch an appeal. Dace had been fed up with appealing, though.

"Give him time," Uncle Norm had counselled, but that wasn't what he was really saying. Where is he, Liza? He had begged so often that she was almost afraid to call again. He was reckless in love, just like his son, but they had to be careful; his phone might be tapped.

Stretching her arms and legs, she flexed her toes beneath the comforting weight of wool blankets that smelled of mothballs. Mel had come to visit her during the night. Oh God, how could she say no again when he'd been so kind? But she had so much on her mind.

She pulled the blankets up to her chin and although it was becoming more difficult, she lay on her back and listened to the voices in the next room. Mel's grandmother had been hanging around her son's house all New Year's Day, picking over the carcass of a second seasonal turkey. Why was she back in the kitchen talking to his mother? At almost eighty, Liza expected the old woman to be tucked up under a hand crocheted afghan, watching *All My Children* after all the visiting back and forth the day before.

Mel's mother looked like a middle-aged woman badly in need of a rest from her mother-in-law and assorted relatives, not to mention her unexpected houseguest, Liza Devereux, who had been there a week. "Thank God they're all gone," she had muttered when the last guest had departed at just after 11:30 p.m. last night.

"She's getting a belly. She didn't look like that when we saw her at Halloween," Granny announced now, probably louder than she intended because she had lost most of the hearing in her left ear.

Liza held her breath and waited. There was nothing wrong with her hearing. Mel's parents lived in a five bedroom split level house with a swimming pool in the backyard, even though they were quite close to Lake Ontario. The guest room was only separated from the kitchen by a narrow hallway and a breakfast nook at the back of the house. Grandma had probably entered the kitchen through the rear door from her own yard, which happened to be next door. The Melvilles were always fussing about the possibility of her falling into the pool.

Mel's mother's voice was a little harder to catch. "Oh, I wouldn't say that. She's so thin. Too thin, if you ask me. I could stand to lose a few pounds, but if that girl swallows a cookie, it shows." She was talking louder and more emphatically than usual. Liza could almost imagine the poor woman's thoughts: *The police came here on Boxing Day looking for an escaped convict and now this?*

"Well, somebody has to say something. Didn't you see her picking her way down the steps when we went to the Wagner house for a drink? She walks like a pregnant woman."

Mel, or somebody, came into the kitchen then, because the two women stopped talking. The next thing Liza knew, he had burst into her room and was kneeling by the bed. She might have felt a little frightened then, except he was wearing his Levis and nothing else and he looked so earnest and sweet that she just wanted to take him in her arms.

"When were you going to tell me?" he asked, tugging the blankets out of her hands and down to her waist. Although his face was usually easy to read, she had no idea what he was thinking now.

"After the trial. I don't know. Then it was after Christmas. When I was sure it was real," she whispered, placing her hand on her heart. It felt as if it had almost stopped beating, though she could see Mel's kicking in his naked chest. His uncombed hair was wild around his head and he looked like he hadn't shaved for days, probably the result of several New Year's celebrations with his old high school friends rather than anything he'd heard in the kitchen. Her own shoulder-length hair was a knotted mess due to his nocturnal visit.

"I should have known. Your tits are so big," he said, moving his hands up under her flannel pajama top, capturing both breasts and crushing them gently together. The nipples were browner and nearly as large as the tips of his thumbs. When a familiar surge of desire betrayed her, she crossed her legs.

"Oh, how would you know, Mel? We didn't sleep together until well into the fall." And only once, she thought.

"Right. And during the trial you were so burnt out, we didn't make love at all. Actually, I was real surprised when you showed up Christmas night, looking like God knows what...although I guess with Dace on the lam you got scared." He sighed. "Some doctor I'd make." He tugged her pajama bottoms down and stared hard at the slightly softer belly beneath her navel, although she doubted he could see the slightest bulge, not when she was lying almost flat on her back. If he measured her fundus, though, her uterus was bound to feel enlarged.

"Look at me, Liza," he said. She shivered as he ran his hands over her torso then stopped and squeezed her breasts tighter this time, rolling the tender nipples between his forefingers and his thumbs. She made a small noise, somewhere between a sob and a moan.

"Shh," he whispered, covering her mouth with his. "They'll hear." She quieted down immediately. The idea of Mel's mother or grandmother knocking on the door or bursting into the room was just too much to bear. "We have options," he told her, and she saw tears in his eyes. "Every problem has a solution."

She was still crying soundlessly, but the word 'we' thrilled her immeasurably. Maybe there was a solution. Maybe she didn't have to do this alone. She sat up a little, wrapped her arms around his long, lean body, put her head on his shoulder and sighed.

But she also heard what he hadn't said. "I know abortion is an option," she confessed. "Especially now that it's legal in Ontario. But it's too late."

"Too late? Already? But didn't you have any clues? Missed periods? Nausea? You were sick through that farce of a trial, but I thought—"

"I thought the trial was making me sick. The way those men died … I didn't want to think." *And Dace*, she thought, *I was so scared. And probably would be now, if my hormones weren't tricking me into this beatific baby calm.*

"Jesus, Liza, how could you be so careless with your health? But I suppose it's as much my fault as yours. Maybe the condom leaked at Halloween. We were both kind of out of it." He stroked her hair. "Have you been to the Student Health Services? Do you know how many weeks?"

She looked away. "About eighteen," she blurted.

Mel was quick, too quick at math, quicker than she ever would be. "Not mine," he confirmed immediately, burying his wet face in her neck.

"Not yours," she agreed.

Still, he got up off the floor and lay beside her on his brother's narrow bed. His tears had stopped hers cold, but she also felt something akin to peace. Even relief. They stared at the ceiling, side by side, until he went through the night table drawer and came up with a pack of Marlboros. Liza was surprised to see him smoking tobacco, but she didn't say anything.

The front door to the house slammed. His mother and his grandmother must have gone out to give them some privacy. Finally.

"When you were away in Europe," she started to say.

"I don't need to know everything, Liza. I don't own you now and I didn't then. No wonder you wouldn't sleep with me last year. He's the one who's away, though. A jailbird — or at least he will be when they catch up with him in a few days."

"No."

"And sure, he'll get a little more time. And be out in two or three years. Or less. That's how it goes, isn't it? And what will you do then? What can you do? He's your family as well as your ..."

Liza took a deep breath. "I'll do what I should have done in the first place," she admitted. "And it's not because of the riot, although I know, deep down in my heart, he's innocent of murder. Even his lawyer thinks so. He was quoted as saying as much in the *Spectator* just last week."

"Yeah, yeah, I saw that. So why then?"

"Because he's a recidivist!" She clenched her fingers in her hair with frustration. "God, I hate that word!"

"A what? Oh, you mean you're scared he'll re-offend."

"Well, that's what he's done so far," she whispered, a small sob caught in her throat. "And I still don't know why. I tried to give him up the last time he went to jail, but I couldn't. I had to be there for him during the trial. He had no one else."

"Goddamn it, Liza, he had his father! Maybe he couldn't tolerate the inside of the courtroom as well as you could, but from what you tell me, the man has spent a fortune on him over the years."

Mel smoked two more cigarettes, staring into space. When he spoke again, his voice was soft but decisive. "I'll marry you then. Like you said, you have no choice. You have to give up on him. Your only crime is that you've waited so long to do what's right. But that doesn't mean I have to give up on you. And as for my family, well, it's been done before. We'll put my name on the baby's birth certificate."

"You can't!" she cried, but when she raised herself over his chest and looked into his eyes, she saw that he could. A well-loved boy like Mel, almost twenty-one, probably did have the inner resources to grow up in a blink.

"But what about school?"

He shrugged. "We'll figure something out. Do you think my parents are going to toss my education out the window because of you? Oh, my father might bluster, but they can afford it and they'll pave the way. I'm their baby, their last hope. If we get married right away and move into the Married Students Residence, you can probably finish your year, too. That's what you want, isn't it? You really should. The baby's due in what, June? You can finish your year and maybe take some part-time courses next year. A cakewalk for an ambitious girl like you."

He took a deep draw on his cigarette, letting the smoke circle over their heads, then shook his head gently. "Christ, you were so full of hope when I met you. The way you talked … And you love all that English twaddle, those big fat tomes of books, the stuff nobody else reads, the stories that I don't have time for and don't pretend to understand. And you were going to write. That's what you said. Before … I'm sorry. I was going to say before you met him, but he was always there, wasn't he? Your one."

"But I'm pregnant!" Liza almost choked on the words.

"My parents will want us to put the kid up for adoption," Mel said flatly, flicking the ashes off his cigarette into her water glass. He wasn't looking at her now. "Even if they think it's mine. It's just too soon. We're too young."

"Oh, Mel." She reached for her belly and laid her hands flat on it. The swell was larger for sure, and unbelievably taut. She knew exactly when it had happened: the last night, at Uncle Norm's house. In the grass. True, she had got her pills a little mixed up that week, but it had happened because she had willed it. She must have been crazy—crazy with grief and what she feared about Dace—that he wouldn't, or couldn't, change. That he'd be in and out of jail all their lives.

But she was exactly the same as he was. She couldn't change either. Couldn't change who she loved. Maybe nobody could change who they already were. She was just a girl who had wanted a great passion, babies, and a chance to write books. And she had blithely, foolishly, insanely hoped to somehow have it all at once.

Still, I'm a woman now, she thought, liking the sound of that phrase. She could almost think clearly, now that she had passed the three month mark and was no longer sick. Even if it were just that false hormonal calm, the sacrifice of a girl-woman ensuring the future of the human race. It really didn't matter. For although she had been anxious and would be anxious again, she knew she could do this. She could keep going to school and get a job, maybe even live with her mother for a couple of months after the baby was born. Somebody had to look after the baby. Summertime in the city. It wasn't a perfect solution, but it was the only one she had come up with so far, in between exams and letters of appeal. Because in her experience, mothers and grandmothers came through in the end, even if their only solution was poison.

Poison. Well, she had briefly considered that. But it had never really been a possibility. She had known all along she wanted Dace's baby if she couldn't have him. It might be an unreasonable choice, a crazy choice, but it was the right thing for her.

Still. How wonderful if she could have wanted Mel too, a boy so loving and so breathlessly uncomplicated. Sometimes she felt like she had come home. Especially now that he wanted her, even when he knew. But, clamoured a practical little voice, belatedly born of necessity, *how long will that last?*

"Something tells me you don't want to do that."

"Not this, no. I mean, no, although if you asked me when I was so sick ..."

"So we'll keep the kid. We'll both be old enough. What the hell's wrong now?"

She hesitated. "It's just ... stepfathers. You know."

"What do you think I am, Liza? A lion?" Mel looked so indignant she nearly laughed. "Do you think I'm going to eat Dace's kid?"

"Some do."

"Look, anyone can see you and Dace were connected. Did you think I was blind? The thing about him was anyone who knew him was attracted to him. Even men. That's both his weakness and his strength. I don't know why. It was just him. And I don't know why he can't stay out of trouble. Do you?"

"No. Well, I have some idea, but it all amounts to the same thing. He didn't really have any choice. Maybe he was programmed. Maybe it was something innate."

"Aw, Jesus Christ. Everybody has choices."

"Not always good ones."

"Well, tell me again. If he showed up right now, would you go with him?"

But he did and I didn't, she thought. If it hadn't been for the baby, she would never have been able to let go, to let him go alone. She wouldn't have had the strength. Jesus. Did she get pregnant just so she would be trapped?

"Of course not!" she said out loud. "It's not an option. Even if it were, I've got the baby to think about now. If he gets sent back to prison, my baby's daddy will be in jail."

"He will."

"Well," she said and sighed. "It's not like he's been trained for anything else. But I will not take my kid, even if it is his kid, into a prison visiting room. Some people might think they were doing the child a favour, letting him get to know his Dad, but I don't. Dace wouldn't either."

"You haven't told him?"

"No. What's the point? He'd go nuts. Worse, he might have stayed."

"Are you sure?" Mel asked slowly. Then his eyes widened. "Wait a minute. What do you mean he might have stayed? Did you talk to him before he left? Did you lie to the police?" He sat up, grabbing her by the shoulders and giving her a little shake.

"No, of course not," she lied. "Let go of me!"

"They'll get him. Extradite him if he's gone down to the States."

Liza shrugged. Maybe not, she thought, unless he commits another crime. And he won't, now that he's away. It's only at home he wasn't safe — where he should have been safe, where all his troubles began. "Besides, Dace and I, we've had our chances. Now it's all about the baby once he's born."

"'He'. So you think it's a boy. Right. Makes sense. Dace would have a boy for sure."

She lay on the bed, thinking. She was going to need help. She had always known that. Even if she got a job, she couldn't work and look after the baby, too. And Mel was so dear... But she couldn't. He didn't deserve...

But there was somebody else who might not mind. Why hadn't she thought of this before? All along she had wanted to help her Uncle Norm, to protect him ...

"Liza?" Mel asked. He'd turned his head on the pillow and now he eyed her suspiciously. "What's happening?"

"Um, I've just thought of something. And you're the reason," she said, running her fingers down his chest, her eyes briefly alight. "If you're willing to help me, and you're a man ..."

He flicked one eyebrow. "A mere man."

"Oh, don't look at me like that, you know what I mean. The thing is, I bet Uncle Norm would help me."

"Dace's father? Are you nuts? What's he going to do with a baby? Jesus, don't you think the poor bastard might need a rest?"

"But it's his grandchild, Mel. He was never able to help Dace, which is a terrible torture for any parent. You heard me talking to him yesterday. He's heartsick about Dace."

"His guilt is hardly your concern. I bet he regrets leaving him at that school, though."

"I could probably finish school while I lived at his place. It's only twenty miles outside of Maitland. If he loaned me a car ..."

"And the baby? What are you going to do, lug him to class?"

"They have those carrier things now, although I'm sure my uncle would pay his housekeeper a little extra to watch the baby while I went to school." Dace said Uncle Norm would help me, told me to go to him for anything, she almost added.

"But if you and I got married, Liza, you wouldn't have to rely on anyone. How about next week? We'll go to City Hall in Maitland and tell everybody later. Face the music. Maybe we can have a little party on Valentine's Day."

"I'd still be relying on you," Liza said. She tried to hug him, but he was board stiff on his back, both hands locked behind his head. She sat up and really looked at him. Oh God. This wasn't right.

"Sweet boy, I can't get married and live like this," she muttered, her eyes filling with tears she tried to hide by fumbling on the floor for her clothes. "I want to. I want to, so much. I want a normal life and I'm scared, but…" She pulled a paisley granny dress over her head, a garment she now wore most of the time. She'd been able to secure the zipper of her jeans with a safety pin just last week, but after several days of three square Melville meals, she couldn't anymore.

"Like this? What's wrong with this?"

"It's too … I don't know," she said weakly. "It's too not me."

For the first time, Mel looked slightly angry. "You mean it's too easy here, I suppose," he replied, removing one hand from behind his head. He reached towards her, looking like he couldn't believe she would be stupid enough to let go of the lifeline he was tossing her way. "Do you think you'll be riding a motorcycle when you have a kid?"

She shook her head. "Oh, I don't think it would be easy living here. Not for me. What do you think would happen if your people found out more about Dace?" she asked. She came back and took his hand, holding it like a prayer book between hers.

"Well, we'd never let on it was Dace's kid."

"Still ..."

"Okay, so you're related to a convict. Who the fuck cares? They'll get over it. Everybody has a few bad apples on their family tree."

"But he's not a bad apple, he's not! Oh, I don't know. People don't know anything about him. Not really. Except that he got away with murder, or so they think," she said softly, turning away and poking through her purse on the desk.

Mel sat up and swung his legs over the edge of the bed, his eyes intent. "It doesn't matter what they think. I could help you, Liza. And you, you would love me in the end."

"Probably," she agreed, securing her growing hair with an elastic band. "And I'd love to have your help, but it wouldn't be fair. Besides, your family hates me. They didn't like me in the first place and they liked me even less after the police came," she reminded him, tossing the rest of her clothes into the small duffel bag at the foot of the bed. She headed for her coat and boots in the front hall. "Your grandmother—"

Mel followed her, pulling a T-shirt over his head in case his mother came back. "—will probably be dead in a couple of years," he said ruthlessly. "Liza, if you walk out now ..." His expression hardened. "You're going to find him, aren't you? Jesus Christ, you really are a reckless girl. Reckless, reckless, just like him." He stopped, jamming the heels of his fists into his eyes and watching her unlock his front door. "Liza," he warned, "you can't go anywhere in this storm. There's already a foot of snow on the ground. And I'm not driving you. Jesus fucking Christ. You're not planning to hitchhike again, are you? You were half dead last week when you showed up here like some stray cat."

He was never going to stop asking her. Do you still love him, Liza? Do you still love him more than you love me?

"No. Please believe me. I'm not going back to him. How the hell could I? I'm a liability to him. Jesus, I don't even know where he is." *Not to mention he doesn't want me*, she thought, feeling a great tear rip inside her chest.

Mel folded his arms across his chest, staring down at the Oriental runner in the hall, dark and intricate, on the shiny oak floor. "But you'll find out. You've romanticized your relationship with him because of the drama. That's what you've done all along."

"You're right. It's probably all because of those books I've read," she said, awkwardly manoeuvring herself and her bag out the front door and onto the snow-dusted porch.

She paused to take a deep breath, bracing herself for the terrible journey ahead. God, it was so beautiful in the open air: the bulky, cloudy sky, the fresh snow on the trees, even the dry, brown wisps of a climbing rose on the arbour at the side. Why had she stayed inside so long? Everything would bloom again, given time. Like Eliot's lilacs out of a dead land.

And the monarchs would come back too. Because somehow they knew where they belonged. Lucky them, they didn't care with whom. She would have to hurry, though. A door opened and closed across the street. Mel's mother was on her way back.

"C'mon, Liza. You're pregnant. You can't do this by yourself," Mel said, shoving his bare feet into boots.

"I know. I'll stay at Uncle Norm's for a couple of months, even a year if he lets me, and I think he will. When Dace shows up, if he shows up, I'll be gone. Long gone. Me and the baby." She shook her head. "No, Mel, really, it's okay. Please don't put your jacket on. I promise not to hitchhike. Really. The bus station's just down the street. I'll wait there until the storm is over," she said, pushing her hands against his chest.

Suddenly she was glowing with so much vitality, she thought her eyes must look feverish. She distinctly felt two bright red spots burning on her cheeks. For weeks she hadn't been cold, with the baby growing inside her, millimetres every day. All his organs were developed now, she exulted. He weighed half a pound and he could cry. Her baby. Dace, Dace's son. Their Devereux boy.

"Maybe I should call my father," Mel said coolly. "Get something to calm you down."

He thinks I'm insane. Well, maybe she was. If she didn't leave right now they would sit around all day, arguing until they were both weak and broken down—a tedious argument of insidious intent. His parents and his grandmother would get in on the act, too. How ironic that Dace, the escaped convict, had been spared all this. For a moment she felt a pang of envy so sharp for her renegade cousin that she almost stayed.

But in the end she couldn't. She was busting to get out of this place. Looping her purse around her neck, she lifted both her bag and her coat and glided down the porch steps. She made it down the Melvilles' recently shovelled front walk to the road, although she could tell by the look on Mel's face that he didn't think she would. Maybe he even hoped she would fall. He watched her go, his high forehead pressed against the frame of the open door. But when she looked back over her shoulder and smiled, he closed his eyes. The snow, big, wet flakes, had temporarily stopped, and his mother, still across the street, hung back, her expression palpably relieved.

Yes, I'll wait again. And Dace's baby and me, we'll both have a life. Without you, she thought, following tire tracks in the snow down the street to the bus station.

And oh my God, without Dace.

AKNOWLEDGEMENTS

Many thanks to my husband (my other half) John R. Allen who helped me pull *From the Chrysalis* out of the dark. He was my first reader and he has always given me the love, support and encouragement I needed (except when I was writing late at night!). Thanks also to my beautiful children whose lives both inspired me and provided numerous distractions, and to the rest of my family who rooted me and rooted for me. It is no accident that my characters Dace and Liza Devereux are first introduced at a family reunion: the birthplace of every story is the family.

ABOUT THE AUTHOR

Karen E. *Black lives* mostly in Toronto, Canada surrounded by her family. Black's coming-of-age novel *From the Chrysalis* about Devereux cousins Dace and Liza begged for a sequel, so she wrote *Feeling for the Air*. This second novel focused on Dace's escape from a corrupt penitentiary system and his and Liza's dual mission to clear his name and find out where the Canadian monarch butterflies really made their winter home.

Take to the Sky, the final novel in this trilogy, is not only a sweeping saga of the life that Dace and Liza dared to dream for their large family, but of the monarch butterflies in Toronto, Canada and Michoacán, Mexico so many people have fought to save.

In January 2016, Black finally traveled to Michoacán, Mexico to see the monarchs' wintering grounds. At the El Rosario colony, high up in the rugged forested mountains, millions of monarchs coloured the oyamel trees orange and bowed their branches with their collective weight. Black's timing seemed perfect. She could still get on a horse. Better still, the monarchs, long threatened by illegal logging, the use of pesticides and the eradication of milkweed, had made a big comeback. Six weeks later, at least 1.5 million monarch butterflies were hit with a deadly freeze during an unusual ice and wind storm. The storm hit the colony just as the spring migration to Canada was beginning. Luckily, many butterflies had exited the mountains before the unexpected freeze.

Black did her Master's in Library Science at the University of Toronto and completed several certificates at the Institute for Genealogical Studies, but her undergrad years were spent at the University of Western Ontario. Though Black's first loves are English literature and family history, she values the insights she gained into social problems, human social relationships and institutions when she studied sociology.

Please feel free to contact her at:
- karen.black@sympatico.ca
- http://karenblackauthor.com/

From the bestselling author of *From the Chrysalis* comes the sequel, a twisted tale of forbidden love, monarch butterflies, and living on the lam:

By the author of *From The Chrysalis*

Feeling
FOR THE
AIR

KAREN E. BLACK

In this final moving, lyrical novel in the Devereux Cousins trilogy, it's the nineties in Toronto, Canada. Liza has almost everything she's ever wanted. Like the monarch butterflies that they both long to see again, Liza and Dace Devereux are in the summer of their lives. But life's complicated. Sometimes ghosts come back to haunt you.

By the author of *From The Chrysalis*

Take TO THE SKY

KAREN E. BLACK

www.ingramcontent.com/pod-product-compliance
Lightning Source LLC
Chambersburg PA
CBHW020323180626
46812CB00001B/20